S0-AID-705

PRAISE FOR
THE HOUSE OF LINCOLN

"What a gift Nancy Horan has for conjuring the past and bringing it vividly to life! Here, she turns her considerable talents to Lincoln's strange road to the White House and the turbulence of his presidency, illuminating lesser-known perspectives and details that resonate eerily with our contemporary times. This is top-quality literary time-travel, and the trip is well worth taking."

—**Therese Anne Fowler**, *New York Times* bestselling author of *A Well-Behaved Woman*

"Nancy Horan's nuanced portrait of Abraham Lincoln as his thoughts on emancipation evolve and her deft, revelatory use of narrators from marginalized communities enhance this compelling, beautifully crafted novel. *The House of Lincoln* evokes the past to illuminate the present as only the very best historical fiction can."

—**Jennifer Chiaverini**, *New York Times* bestselling author of *Mrs. Lincoln's Sisters*

"Brimming with a rich and unforgettable array of imagined and real historical figures who helped to shape Springfield, Illinois, and the nation beyond during the turbulent time of slavery and the Civil War, *The House of Lincoln* is storytelling at its best."

—**Gail Tsukiyama**, author of *The Color of Air*, *The Samurai's Garden*, and *Women of the Silk*

"The gifted Nancy Horan once again brings readers into a story—inspired by real events—that will forever change the way they perceive famous historical figures and their times. In the captivating and important *The House of Lincoln*, the young Portuguese immigrant Ana is hired to help in the Springfield, Illinois, home of Abraham Lincoln as the Great Emancipator is on the rise. Through Ana's relationship with Lincoln's wife, Mary, and her close friendship with Cal, a free Black girl, the novel explores a lesser-known aspect of a crucial historical period."

—**Marie Benedict**, *New York Times* bestselling author of *The Only Woman in the Room*

"Here, happily, is Nancy Horan doing once again what Nancy Horan does best—telling us the part of the story we don't yet know. Strong on fine detail yet cognizant of the expansive historical context, Horan's newest is wonderfully immersive, memorable, important, and pertinent. An ambitious and accomplished work."

—**Karen Joy Fowler**, *New York Times* bestselling author of *Booth* and *We Are All Completely Beside Ourselves*

THE
HOUSE *of*
LINCOLN

a novel

NANCY HORAN

sourcebooks
landmark

For Kevin

Copyright © 2023, 2024 by Nancy Horan
Cover and internal design © 2023 by Sourcebooks
Cover design by Heather VenHuizen/Sourcebooks
Cover images © Mandel Ngan/AFP via Getty Images, Gustavo Ramirez/Getty Images
Internal design by Tara Jaggers/Sourcebooks

Sourcebooks and the colophon are registered trademarks of Sourcebooks.

All rights reserved. No part of this book may be reproduced in any form or by any electronic or mechanical means including information storage and retrieval systems—except in the case of brief quotations embodied in critical articles or reviews—without permission in writing from its publisher, Sourcebooks.

The characters and events portrayed in this book are fictitious or are used fictitiously. Apart from known historical figures, any similarity to real persons, living or dead, is purely coincidental and not intended by the author.

Published by Sourcebooks Landmark, an imprint of Sourcebooks
P.O. Box 4410, Naperville, Illinois 60567-4410
(630) 961-3900
sourcebooks.com

The Library of Congress has cataloged the hardcover edition as follows:

Names: Horan, Nancy, author.
Title: The house of Lincoln : a novel / Nancy Horan.
Description: Naperville, Illinois : Sourcebooks Landmark, 2023.
Identifiers: LCCN 2022050991 (print) | LCCN 2022050992 (ebook) | (hardcover) | (epub)
Subjects: LCSH: Lincoln, Abraham, 1809-1865--Fiction. | Springfield (Ill.)--History--19th century--Fiction. | LCGFT: Historical fiction.
Classification: LCC PS3608.O725 H68 2023 (print) | LCC PS3608.O725 (ebook) | DDC 813/.6--dc23/eng/20221031
LC record available at https://lccn.loc.gov/2022050991
LC ebook record available at https://lccn.loc.gov/2022050992

Printed and bound in the United States of America.
LSC 10 9 8 7 6 5 4 3 2 1

"To this place, and the kindness of these people, I owe everything."

—Abraham Lincoln

PART ONE

CHAPTER ONE

FEBRUARY 1909

B ELOW, THE MEN ARE EATING TURTLE SOUP.

Seated in the gallery above, Ana follows the courses outlined on a menu tucked into the souvenir program. Happily, she thought to bring her opera glasses. Never has the Arsenal looked so festive, with swooping buntings and American flags suspended in pairs like giant butterflies over the long banquet tables. She recognizes many faces above the boiled shirts: judges, bankers, lawyers, doctors, land developers, politicians— more than seven hundred of Springfield's "quality." On the main dais, two foreign ambassadors sit admiring the immense French and English flags floating for their benefit among the Stars and Stripes. How festive, she thinks. And how utterly different from the way the building looked six months ago.

From the gallery she can see tension melt into camaraderie among the men as the waiters circulate, bottles in hand. Amusing that only the priest and one other fellow have turned their glasses over. The others drink champagne as they study the menus, remarking on the crabs, the guinea squabs, the tenderloins yet to come. A tittering glee sweeps through the auditorium as oysters arrive.

"Five barrels of them," comments a young woman seated to her right. "And more than a ton of ice cream for dessert. My husband helped haul it in."

Unlike the other women in the balcony, Ana does not have a husband or brother who is a member, nor has she paid the twenty-five-dollar ticket fare to be here. She knows why she has been invited to the birthday bash: she's meant to be a decorative relic from times past, and that is all right. She has dressed the part by wrapping her throat in a piece of her mother's lace, stuck through by an ancient brooch.

At the podium, the first speaker is throwing his voice. "Picture for a moment Lincoln's arrival in Springfield, a poorly dressed young man riding into town alone, bent on making a name for himself..."

Her stomach lets out a gastric rumble and she thinks of the uneaten lamb stew in her icebox. It will be a long evening. If Robert Lincoln shows up, though, it will be worth near starvation. She shifts in her seat, closes her eyes, and prepares to endure the affair to its end.

"Arrival," she hears the speaker say again. And as if she's sipped the Log Cabin punch the men are now enjoying, she feels light-headed and almost swoons from the sudden, vivid memory of her own arrival in Springfield in 1849, some sixty years ago.

"The exiles are here!" someone had shouted that day as she tumbled off the train into the chilling November morning.

Clusters of men and women stood waiting for them. A man wearing a minister's collar shouted out names—Vasconcelles, Ferreira, DeFrates—while a big blond woman in a fur hat sorted Ana's family and the others into shivering groups. Ana hunched beneath a thin wool cape the Presbyterian ladies in New York had given her.

Family groups were directed to spare bedrooms or a few empty houses the church people had found for the ragged band of religious exiles. One hundred thirty Portuguese immigrants were in their group, and not one of them fully understood the words puffing like clouds from the mouths of the welcomers.

Ana was nine years old at the time, but the image in her mind of that day was precise as an engraving. She'd stood with her hand in her father's grip and stared out at a river of mud that was said to be the main street. Pigs with feet sunk in the oozing mess nosed around the half-buried wheels of a driverless carriage. Just beyond it, a spread of abandoned boots—perhaps twenty-five or thirty of them in all sizes—poked up from the porridge-thick earth. This was the first of many mysteries she encountered in her first months in Springfield. It was likely the children had been lifted out of their little boots by their parents—she could imagine that—but what about the grownups who left behind their large leather footwear? Who lifted *them* out of the muck? Her mother would say such a feat was the work of God, as she often said about odd things difficult to explain. Ana had pictured a whole collection of shoeless citizens being sucked up into heaven in one grand resurrection.

She'd not bothered her mother with any questions that day, for Genoveva Ferreira had nearly collapsed in a fit of weeping. Ana understood now that she was heartsick with longing, standing there remembering the lovely cobblestone streets of her hometown in Madeira. But Ana's father was beaming. He had looked around at the foraging animals in the mud and uttered one of the few English expressions he knew: *Good morning!*

"The Great Emancipator," comes a voice from the podium. Ana shakes off the gauzy reverie and scans the crowd on the main level.

"You knew the Lincoln family," says the young woman next to her.

"Long ago." Ana now regrets mentioning it earlier.

"He would have been pleased by such an event in his honor," the woman adds in a hushed voice.

"Mr. Lincoln?" Ana presses a finger to her lips but the words come out anyway. "Oh, my dear, he would have leaped out the nearest window."

CHAPTER TWO

July 1851

The limestone paving heated her thighs through her dress as she watched the shoppers across the street on Chicken Row. From her perch on the top step of the huge stone Capitol, she could see men hauling gunnysacks of flour and tubs of grease to canvas-hooded wagons with chairs lashed to their sides. Yoked oxen were bellowing in the street. Beside one wagon, a woman with a bolt of cloth in her arms argued with her husband. It was 9:00 a.m. and every pole around the square had a horse tied to it. Weaving through the human and animal legs in the street, a black-and-white hog went about his business.

"*Pocilga*," her mother said of Springfield. A pigsty. The remark pained Ana. She loved this town. When they came at dawn to set up their stand, she liked nothing better than to feel the morning unfold around the square as awnings lowered, newspapers opened on benches, wooden sandwich boards took their places in front of stores. Today, yes, she could see garbage all over the place. Food scraps, chunks of broken bricks and wood, rags, and fat piles of horse droppings that made women lift their skirts. Filth like this, her mother was quick to point out, would never be permitted in Funchal, her hometown in Madeira. A merchant would be fined if he failed to sweep the section of road in front of his shop.

Ana glanced from time to time toward the spot where her mother had positioned her stand, right at the corner where Chicken Row met the street market around the corner on Sixth. From the Capitol's steps, she could see Genoveva Ferreira hold up a plucked bird for a shopper's look. Ana watched to see if her free hand would beckon her to come translate. Her feet itched to run on the grass. She was thin and long-legged and could outrun her brother, but she stayed still on the step. Of the five of them in the family, Ana was the one who spoke English best. It was a mark of pride, but it kept her tethered to her mother, who spoke only Portuguese.

Sitting nearby, her friend Cal traced with a finger the small shell shapes in the steps. She turned to Ana, lifting her face, freckled as the chicken eggs her own mother was selling at the street market. "You hungry yet?"

Ana nodded.

"What you got?"

Ana sighed and laid out what was in her sack. An apple and a hard chunk of sausage. The stray dog called Jasper who ate rocks all day came over to have a look and turned tail.

"Even he don't want my lunch."

Cal waited until Jasper had scampered a distance off, then

produced a surprise out of a square of newspaper—a thick biscuit slathered with applesauce. She pulled it apart and gave Ana half. In the sunlight, Cal's hair was an explosion of curly red tendrils jittering around her head.

They had been friends since the first day Ana's mother joined the other vendors at the market. Cal was the same age, eleven, and had the same job, watching over her younger brother, Paul, while her mother worked.

Ana had a second job, running errands for people in her neighborhood. Cal often went with her through the downtown area, delivering notes to the druggist or buying some item at the general store for an elderly *senhora*. It was a new privilege and a streak of freedom for both girls to go out together into the busy streets on their own. Ana had been lonely and awkward two years ago when they first arrived. She thought only in Portuguese. Every sentence she ventured back then felt like a wobble across a rope bridge. Not anymore. She had ripped a blank page out of the back of her father's Bible and made a small map of the businesses surrounding the square, labeling each store with the names of the merchants in tiny print. Now she thought in English part of the time. She knew more people in the shops, knew more about the merchandise and shopkeepers than most people in her neighborhood.

She and Cal took little notice of the men in tailed coats who moved in and out of the Capitol carrying carpetbags bulging with papers. Other people interested them more: the butcher, his belly wrapped in a clean white apron every morning, whistling different bird sounds as he swept his section of the walk. The afflicted young man who sat on his haunches on an old church pew outside the saddle store, spewing ugly words. And there were always people passing through, heading to California or Oregon. Across the street was one of them, that woman holding a roll of fabric who looked just now as if she might cry.

"What does she say to him, you think?" Ana said. It was a watching game they had.

"Who? That lady over there? I know what *he's* saying. 'You're gonna wish you had food instead of cloth if we get stuck in snow. It tastes better.'"

"Ugh." Ana put down her biscuit. "Why you bring that up?"

Everybody in town, even Ana, knew the tale of the families who had set out from Springfield with a wagon train for California seven years ago. Trapped in the mountains by blizzards, they ended up eating the bodies of the dead to survive.

From the corner of her eye, Ana spotted her mother's hand go up. She jumped to her feet and raced over to the stand, where a short, dark-haired woman was examining the chicken pies spread out on her mother's crate. She had a boy with her who looked to be about eight, her brother Joao's age.

"Ma'am?"

"How much for three?"

"*Quanto custa para três?*" Ana asked her mother.

"*Vinte centavos cada.*"

Twenty cents each did not please the woman, whose mouth puckered like a coin purse. "It should be less if I buy all of them." Her son turned away, embarrassed.

"*E possível pagar cinquenta centavos para os três?*" Ana asked. Her mother's face spoke her dismay. She smoothed her apron, looked down. Ana knew she was weighing whether to hold out for full price. She nodded finally.

"Maybe fifty cents," Ana said.

The woman savored her triumph with a grin as she filled a sack with the pies and walked away with her boy.

"*Raios te partam,*" her mother sniped as the woman departed. *May thunderbolts cleave you.*

"Joao! Food!" Ana spotted him chasing a ball and waved the apple in the air. Her brother ignored her. "Joao!" she hollered again, just to irk him. He wanted to be called Joe, but their mother wouldn't hear of it.

"He wants an American name," her father had argued in Joao's defense.

"Joao is a strong name," her mother argued back.

Emmanuel Ferreira dismissed the remark with a philosophical shrug. "It doesn't matter."

"It does."

"You are too proud," their father always said.

Ana knew what he really meant. Genoveva Ferreira still clung to the high position her family held in the old country. Emmanuel, who came from humbler people, was more practical. *Adaptar*, he told her. *You will feel better.*

Ana went back over to the market where her mother stood a stone's throw from some Irish vendors who called out to people in an accent the girl found musical. Her mother was wary of these people. "Catholics," she had warned her children. It was the Catholics in Madeira, after all, who had terrorized the Presbyterian converts and chased them out of the island. But their father had already become an American. "Here, they are the despised ones," he would say. "Don't be afraid of them. They are running from their own troubles."

Ana could see with her own eyes that some of them were as tattered as her family had been when they came to this town. The vendors were a jumble of immigrants, mainly Irish and German. Some were longtime Americans but new arrivals in town—from Missouri and Kentucky mostly. Friction snapped among them, but they kept their tempers in check, lest the market master throw them out.

Cruel remarks made in English by customers flew right past her mother's ears, but they reached Ana's, who sometimes felt as if she were a spy in the land of Illinois. Locals didn't expect her to know what they were saying.

"Those are no good," one woman remarked to another as they paused in front of the stand.

"*O que ela diz?*" her mother asked.

"Good pies, Mama."

Today Ana had two errands: medicine from Birchall and Owen, and new heels from the cobbler for her father's boots that swung heavy in her burlap bag. She did her business at the drugstore first, presenting a note to Caleb Birchall with a drug name she'd copied down from a *senhora*'s medicine bottle.

"Another liver problem over in Little Madeira, Ana?" Mr. Birchall said, shaking his head.

"He is the same liver, sir. Of Mrs. Santos."

Mr. Birchall laughed and Ana shrank back, her ears and cheeks burning.

"You said it fine," Cal whispered. "Don't be ascared of him."

While the man noted down the purchase in his record book, they studied the patent medicines lining the shelves. The tins and bottles and paper boxes were an ongoing wonder to both of them. Cal read out a name on a blue bottle that captivated her. "H. G. Farrell's Celebrated Arabian Liniment. Says you can use it on men or beasts." They stared at the label picturing a desert oasis with camels, a tent, and palm trees.

"You ever seen a camel where you come from?"

"Yes."

Cal eyed her in awe. "You ride one?"

Ana smiled. "No, I never see one," she said, caught out. "But I see these." She pointed to the palm trees. "In Trinidad."

In the shoe shop, the cobbler looked over the battered boots, deciding whether they were worth saving. "Come back tomorrow afternoon," he said and gave them each a horehound drop. Together, they walked east on Jefferson toward Cal's house, and then Ana split off to head up Ninth. She continued north four blocks to the neighborhood the townspeople called Little Madeira, where Portuguese was the language spoken under the roofs and on the porch stoops of the two- and three-room cottages lining the streets.

There were three rooms in this rented house—the kitchen, her parents' bedroom in back, and a middle room with two makeshift sleeping areas outlined by blankets on clotheslines. Beatriz and Ana had one section; Joao had the other. Ana

walked into the kitchen picturing in her mind how the evening would be, as it always was on hot summer days.

Her older sister, Beatriz, was home from her cleaning job.
She'd already had her way with the latest newspapers Ana
brought home, having cut out pictures of hairstyles and dresses
she liked. Beatriz stood cooking at the stove, while her father
scrubbed his face and hands in a bucket. Her mother was in bed
with the door closed. In a few hours, after dinner, the grown-
ups would drift out of the other houses into the street. A man
people called Six Bits would deal out cards to his friends in a
game of *bisca*. He had acquired this name because he sawed
trees for a living and went down the streets offering to cut up
cords of wood, calling out, "Six bits, no split!"

Another man, a brickmaker who wore a blue *carapuça* cap,
with its high skinny tail pointing up like the spout of an oilcan,
would continue teaching Joao how to play the *cavaquinho*. Ana
wondered how it was possible that little guitar as well as the hat
had both made it unbroken from the old country to this town.
The man always sang sad songs about a lost love.

Ana would kick a can with the others on her block, then sit
on the stoop and listen to the women tell stories. In the dark,
they'd remember walking as children to white houses tucked
into the green hills of Madeira. Their talk would be of birdlike
orange flowers shooting up out of the earth, of creamy white
flowers drooping like soft bells from trees, and mountains soaring into the clouds.

That evening played out as she imagined. Fireflies winked
as conversation turned to their fearful passage across the ocean
from their green homeland to the muggy fields of Trinidad.

"I carried the Lord's Prayer under my dress all the way from Funchal," an old woman reminded everyone. She went inside her house and emerged with a faded piece of parchment paper, its gold lettering nearly erased by its long journey plastered against her chest, as she traveled from the island of Madeira to the island of Trinidad to this landlocked island called Springfield in the middle of America.

CHAPTER THREE

WHILE HER MOTHER TALKED CONTINUALLY OF OLD times, Ana's father seemed to arrive home each day from his construction job with a new excitement. Recently, he'd made a barter exchange with a fellow carpenter. For building some cabinets in the man's house, Emmanuel Ferreira received a set of wood combs and rollers for painting. The fellow explained that these were tools for making patterns. You could make cheap wood molding look like walnut or oak or mahogany by combing grain patterns into the wet paint with the tools. The man showed Emmanuel what he knew.

Her father brought leftover paint from a work site and experimented on the wood trim. Something lit on fire inside Emmanuel Ferreira that summer night he finished the parlor baseboard. To his daughter's list of errands, he added a stiff skunk-hair paintbrush.

It was nearly noon on Wednesday by the time Ana got to Cal's house four blocks away to collect her. Usually Ana found her on the porch, ready to go, but today Cal invited her to come in and eat lunch with her mother, brother, and an aunt who lived with them.

"Callie Patterson, bring her that chair," Cal's mother said. "Sit down, child." She went over to an iron pot sitting on its legs in the fireplace ashes, lifted the lid, and scooped out a ladle full of stew. "Eat now."

Ana spooned up the stew, thick with rabbit and carrots and potatoes. She liked the browned corn cakes, all the food coming out of that fireplace. The stew tasted so much better than what her sister made. She smiled to hear "Callie" across the table. The Patterson family members were the only ones allowed to call her that. Cal preferred Cal.

With her family and Ana, Cal was a great mimic. She could imitate the walk of a policeman or the body of an angry child throwing a fit, and she did a fair imitation of several accents, though she never mimicked Ana's. Today she playacted the weeping woman holding the fabric as her auntie, a big-boned, serious woman, allowed a smile. Ana stared at the men's boots the woman was wearing. Cal had once said her aunt liked to hunt and trap.

After eating, the girls went to a couple of stores looking for the paintbrush. The owner at Barton's Dry Goods stood at the front door working a wad of tobacco into his cheek. He was short and thick. When they stepped to enter, the man stuck out his leg to block the door without uttering a word. Ana was confused and then hurt. She felt as if she'd been slapped. Cal spun on her heels and kept walking. "Don't look back," she said.

The second store's clerk knew both girls and said he could order the paintbrush, and they were laughing again as they walked over to Fourth Street to collect her father's boots. Arriving at Coleman and Donnegan's, they paused to examine a poster in the window featuring a man's boot.

"French and American calf, sheepskins. Oak bark leather soles." Ana mouthed each word as she read.

Inside, the air was heavy with the stink of tannin, probably coming from a four-foot-high pile of leather hides stacked in a back corner across the room. The owners of the shop, both in leather aprons, were sitting at their cobbler benches behind the front counter.

"Almost done," Mr. Donnegan called out. The girls walked over to a shelf where shoe samples were displayed. These were not for touching, but Cal was a neighbor to the Donnegan family and felt comfortable stroking the kid leather of a lady's slipper.

Ana heard the door open behind them and a new smell entered the place, a sweaty horse smell. She turned to see three men, one of whom carried a handbill in his fist. All of them were wearing guns, and one had handcuffs looped over his belt. Lawmen, she thought.

The oldest man, whose hair hung like pale corn tassels from under his hat, held up the picture of a man with a description of some kind written below it. "Any of you seen him?"

Ana looked at it and shook her head, as did Cal and Mr. Coleman, who appeared terrified.

Mr. Donnegan did not rise to have a look but continued away at his work.

"Which one is Donnegan?" The man turned his gaze toward Coleman first.

"I am." Mr. Donnegan stopped sewing and stared back at the rude man.

"Heard you might know his whereabouts," the lead man said. "Show it to him." He shoved the picture toward Cal, who reluctantly took it, ducked under the pass-through section of the counter, and handed it to the cobbler.

Mr. Donnegan glanced at the poster. "Never saw him."

Ana stood frozen, holding her breath. The other two men beside her muttered to each other as the second yellow-haired man, probably the son of the lead man, lifted the counter gate and walked over to where Cal and Mr. Donnegan were. He reached for something in his shirt, and Ana felt her knees wobble. She steadied when she saw that the thing he pulled out was not a gun or knife but a pouch. He opened the drawstring and dumped a pile of gold and silver coins into the cobbler's apron.

"Seven hundred dollars," he said. His mouth was a menacing smirk. "I'll be back when you've had time to think on that."

William Donnegan sat staring at his lap, as if cow dung had just landed there.

The men left the shop cursing. The last man out slammed the door furiously, causing the whole room to shake. Just then, Ana noticed the stack of stiff cowhide pelts in the corner begin to slide. In a split second, fingers reached out from the bottom of the stack and stopped it from cascading further, then disappeared back under the pile. Startled, Ana looked to Cal, who refused to look back at her.

Mr. Coleman leapt to his feet then, took Emmanuel Ferreira's boots from his partner's worktable, and handed them over to Ana. "No charge today," he said. He offered the hard candy to them and saw them to the door.

"Did you see the hand?" Ana blurted when they were outside.

Cal grabbed hold of her friend's elbow, sucked her lips inward, and shook her head.

The men were out of sight now. Ana longed desperately to be under her mother's arm, and they walked quickly toward the market.

"Who are they?"

Cal was straining to hold back tears. "Slave catchers." She turned to Ana. "If you tell, they won't let us out of their sight." She was talking about their mothers, and she was right. "It's a secret." Cal searched her eyes. "Are you going to tell?"

Ana hesitated. "No."

"Do you promise?"

Goose bumps rose on Ana's arms. The terror she'd felt inside the shop returned to make her knees shake. She hugged her chest to stop her body's quivering.

"All right."

CHAPTER FOUR

———

S PENCER DONNEGAN WALKED INTO HIS BROTHER'S SHOP TO find him sitting at his bench with a pile of money in his lap.

"Lock that door, Spence," William said softly. He made a funnel with his apron and dumped the money into a bucket near his table.

Landon Coleman, William's partner, stared at the bucket. "This can't keep up."

William stepped over to the window and peered through the square panes. "They're out there showing people that ridiculous drawing." He glanced at his brother. "It's official," he said. "This town's a hunting ground."

"You all right?" Spencer asked.

"Whew," William said, tipping his head in the direction of the stack of leather hides. "Got a visitor." He walked over to that part of the room and spoke calmly. "Just hold on for a while longer and we'll get you out of there."

"What are you going to do?"

"Wait until tonight to move him."

Lord, the chances William takes. Spencer was no stranger to his brother's work; there had always been tension. But the cat and mouse of moving runaways had changed since last year's Fugitive Slave Act replaced the old one with harsher punishments for those who assisted runaway slaves, including stiffer fines and jail terms. Some people on the street, folks he knew, were afraid. If they saw a colored person they suspected was on the run, they were now obliged to tell the authorities.

Thank God a lot of people paid no attention to the damned bloodhound law. Springfield had its fair share of antislavery advocates, but there were plenty of Southern sympathizers in town. And new immigrants too, who were trying to lie low themselves. They didn't want trouble. They'd made it this far, and they planned to stay.

"I saw Cal and another girl leaving before I came in," Spencer said. "Did they see anything?"

William shrugged. "Cal knows not to talk. But her friend? I don't know... I hardly noticed her before. Portuguese. The two of them travel around town together. She carries a map. First time she came in here, she wrote down my name so she would remember it." William shook his head and laughed. "I got my own map."

Spencer knew what he meant. William was the conductor in the family, but inevitably the rest of them got drawn into his work. He had acquainted Spencer with the secret safe places in town: the shed behind the Globe Tavern, where up to three runaways could be stashed, the coach house on South Eighth Street that had a horse ready to go on the spur of the moment, a root cellar on Madison. William's mental map contained fields beyond town where corn cribs were daylight hiding places. It had trees marked up high with white paint and back roads that offered different ways to get to Spring Creek.

Spencer had been in Springfield nearly a decade now and knew these and its other parts pretty well. He also knew a couple of additional people in town who moved freedom seekers north. Old Erastus Wright, a white abolitionist, had been hiding fugitives in his basement for years. As for colored conductors in town, Reverend Henry Brown came to mind. He was a friend and an AME preacher, as Spencer was. And Jameson Jenkins was a drayman who could get somebody out of town in his cart under a layer of hay. William tended not to work closely with other conductors. He knew from experience that in the middle of the country, in the middle of the night, he preferred his own instincts to save him and his passengers. "Conductors rarely even exchanged names," he once told Spencer. To know a name was to risk having it beaten or burned or cut out of you.

William had brought the escapee to their mother Leanna's house, where he also lived. She had fed the man and put him up in the garret. She kept a supply of clothes there, and she fit him out with boots left for repair by some prospector who had moved on without them. When dawn came, William brought him to the shoe shop, thinking to move him when it turned dark. Now, with slave hunters about, he said, he would have to wait until after midnight.

"Unlock the damn door or you're going to raise suspicion," Landon groused. He took up a piece of leather and began cutting.

"I'll just stay, if you don't mind," Spencer said.

"No need. I have this under control."

Such a stubborn cuss. "If it's just the same, I will be here when they come back. I don't have any appointments this afternoon." Spencer sat down and opened a newspaper.

"The eternal big brother," William sighed.

The afternoon dragged on. Around four o'clock, the shop door blasted open, and the three men clomped in.

William walked to the counter and pointed at the bucket full of coins he'd placed on the floor next to the pass-through. "No sign of your man."

The head slave hunter's eyes bored into his. "I'm told you got quite a business in this town, hiring out other people's property."

William stared back and said nothing.

The man hissed his disgust. He remained upright, unwilling to stoop for the money. One of his henchmen stepped forward and poured the bucket's coins into his pouch. The three stormed out of the shop then, trailing threats.

"Jesus." Landon was shaking. "I'm going home."

William swept up, cleaned the counter and bench, and said again, loudly, "Hold on." He locked up the shop and pulled down shades over the front window. He went then to the stack of hides and lifted them one at a time off the top until a curled-up man appeared. He unbent with difficulty and rose slowly to his feet.

"Thought I was found." The man's face was dripping with sweat, maybe tears.

William walked over to a wooden box and pulled out rolled-up trousers for the fellow. "You must be starving."

The man turned to look at Spencer.

"My brother," William explained. "You're safe."

From where Spencer sat, the man appeared to be in his forties, with knots between his brows where his terror had bunched up and a scar that ran from his drooping left eyelid down to his jaw. From the look of his abused coat—one ripped sleeve had been sewn up with animal gut by a clumsy hand—he had been traveling for a long time. He was struck that the man had made it this far, apparently alone.

"You sure don't look like their picture. Where'd you start from?" William asked.

"Jacksonville."

"No, I mean, where you from?"

"Kentucky."

William handed him a chunk of bread and a cup of water. "So are we." He showed the man two buckets, one full of water for washing up, one for using as a toilet. "I'll bring you food in a couple of hours. Get back under that pile for a while. We'll move you after midnight."

When Spencer and William got to the house, they found their mother in front of a bubbling iron pot. Leanna Donnegan Knox stood with a long-handled spoon, stirring in a cloud of steam, a blank look on her face as if her mind were located elsewhere. When she looked up, Spencer noticed her eyes looked droopy. The only sign of real strength in her fifty-seven-year-old body was the sinew of her arms. Those ropey muscles were hard-earned. She was the daughter of a white woman and a black man. Because her mother was white, Leanna was considered freeborn.

She had raised her eight children with her husband until he died back in 1839. She kept working, taking in laundry. Somehow she set by enough money to move a couple of mountains.

She'd been a strict mother, and her children were known to behave in their Hopkinsville settlement. You couldn't allow wildness in your children. You could lose them in a heartbeat that way. But she had understood that they were all different, and she made allowances for their varied natures as she could. William had an adventurous streak that made him climb high in trees, jump off rocks into the river, take risks. He didn't like to be penned in. As for Spencer, his mother had once called him the gatherer. He loved wandering the woods and returning with its wonders—mushrooms, feathers, arrowheads, weird mosses, the black tail of some creature otherwise disappeared. She had given him his own corner shelf in the cabin to store his treasures.

Before she came north, Leanna had managed to buy both a plot of land in Kentucky and her second husband, Joe Knox. On paper, she was a slave owner. It was what you did to keep your family whole.

Spencer and Wiley, his brother, had come up with their wives to Springfield first, back in '43. They had started the AME church, gotten to know folks, then gone back to Kentucky to bring the rest of the family up in '45. Leanna sold her land and came to Springfield by wagon with Joe and her grown children. She obtained a certificate of freedom for her husband as well as the others, even though her children were born free because she was. She then registered those free papers in Illinois so that if their papers were stolen or lost or if, God forbid, any one of them were kidnapped, a record of their freedom existed with the state.

Despite the state's Black Laws, which were intended to keep free colored people from moving into Illinois, they felt safer here than in Kentucky. She bought a lot in town, built this house, and planted beans and greens.

"I'll be needing some of that to take," William said.

"I know." His mother didn't ask the full story. She appeared to be ready for whatever came through the door.

"I'm going to bed," he said, "after I eat."

"Why's it got to be you doing this?" Leanna shook her head, unable to hold back. "You've done your share of it. You have a business…things to lose now…"

Spencer could see that she didn't understand, and William couldn't put it into words. Spencer suspected his brother did it to come up against himself. To see what was inside him. Certainly it wasn't for glory. When William risked his life, no one held up his hand like a victor's. Once after a long night, he said to Spencer, "Sometimes I feel nothing but fear out there. Other times there is a jolt of excitement that lasts for days."

Spencer thought William would be done with it by now. He had been conducting runaways north for four years. Dozens of them had been up in his garret, and it wasn't getting any safer. Some conductors had thousand-dollar bounties on their heads. Others, the dead ones, got their names added to a list that nobody wanted to be on.

All Leanna's children were grateful to be freeborn, but as a young man, Spencer felt it was not entirely a grace and blessing. To be a free person among enslaved brother men was also to be encumbered. In a far lesser way, to be sure, but it rested on all their shoulders. Every one of them in the family felt they must *do* something.

William said he wanted to stop, but the runaways just kept coming. They came from as far away as Mississippi. Sometimes a couple with a baby, occasionally whole families. Once there were five, hiding in the back of a wagon under a pile of hay topped by a layer of infant cradles.

More often, they came alone or in pairs, which was easier. They had hidden their scents from bloodhounds by rubbing garlic over their shoes. One man told of roasting horned toads in the fireplace, then covering his footprints with the ashes to throw off the dogs on his trail. They had taken cover in barns, attics, root cellars, high grasses, trees. At night, they came out from their stopping places and looked at the sky for the drinking gourd—if it was visible. They knew what they'd been told. If on a dark night you lose your way, feel for moss on the trees. North is the side where the moss grows. Walk against a current in a river. Most rivers flow south. It wasn't much advice to go on.

Yet here they were, against all odds, on William's back porch. Many came from Kentucky and Missouri. They dared not come up to Springfield from Cairo, which might as well be New Orleans. Located at the bottom of Illinois, Cairo's heart belonged to the South. Runners stood a better chance coming from Missouri across the Mississippi into Quincy and then over to Springfield. Some fugitives came on their own without the help of conductors, walking north. They were known to hide in the woods in the southwest area near town and dig holes in the hills to conceal themselves until it was safe to move on.

They arrived by wagon and were sometimes dropped by a man William called "Blue." Blue came over from Jacksonville— far away enough that his horses were lathered up from the journey. He was a man who wore an old blue shirt, one of a number of white men in central Illinois William had met who risked their hides to conduct escapees north.

William usually moved them on the next night. By day was far more dangerous. You could clothe a man in a woman's dress and a veiled hat, you could hang a sign around his neck that said "deaf and dumb," and the ruse might work, but in the light of day, often hot behind him, was an angry man with a blood-hound looking for his property.

"I need sleep," William said.

After they ate, Spencer and William went to the back of the house to a dark bedroom. William stood at the window and wondered aloud if the catchers were out in the dog fennel, hunkered down, waiting for him to make a move. He crouched below the windowsill, silently cracked the window open, and sniffed for tobacco smoke. "Nothing," he said.

Spencer stood in the dark, looking out the window. Clouds blocked the moon; a drizzle had begun. It was a lucky night. If they were out there, the catchers would be soaked and tired by midnight. Spencer felt close to his brother, close enough he could guess what he was thinking about—Spring Creek and where to cross it so he could get the runner to Gardner's house in Farmington. In a couple of hours, William would go back to the shop, double up with the passenger, ride to the edge of town, then take turns on the horse, one riding, one walking fast along country roads, covering the eight miles to Farmington without tiring his animal. He would rest for a few hours out there and be back to Springfield by late morning.

Spencer embraced his brother and took his leave. When William woke from his nap, their mother would have a pail of food ready for him to take. And she would send him off as she had done since they were children. She would feel his shirtfront for the pouch with his free papers in it. Her hand would rest on his chest, but only for a moment.

CHAPTER FIVE

LYING IN BED THAT NIGHT, STILL SHAKEN, ANA LISTENED to the rain and wondered what Cal was thinking and feeling. Before today, she had not given much thought to the fact that Cal was called a Negro girl. She could not pinpoint when she became aware of that fact. Cal's mother and auntie had brown skin, though Cal and her brother were paler and freckled. Cal did not talk of her father, who lived in Tennessee. She must have gotten her looks from him.

It made no difference to Ana or the other young people they knew. They played at each other's houses. They ate each other's food. Any pecking order among them had to do with their size, not the color of their skin. They were all shades of poor. If it made a difference in their dealings with the white merchants in town, it seemed a small difference. In her errand rounds, Ana was accustomed to sometimes being treated as too young for grown-up business. That was the extent of it. Or was it? They had been turned away from Barton's dry goods store today, and Ana had gone in there alone once before without trouble. Perhaps it was not just that they were considered children but that one of them was a colored girl.

That was it. She stared at the ceiling. Of course it was.

It was also the reason, she had come to understand, that she and Cal did not attend the same school. There was a school for whites and one for colored children. Ana attended a different school, the one at the First Portuguese Presbyterian Church that had been set up for the Madeiran exiles who spoke little English.

Since the two girls met two years ago, their friendship had grown mostly on the steps of the Capitol. At first it was finding strange bugs, making up stories, and playing store that amused them. She smiled to think of it. Cal was always the merchant in those days and Ana the customer. She had learned English words from Cal in that way or in exploring around the town square. There had been a couple of visits to each other's houses. They had traveled out into the country last fall to ride bareback on old horses and pick apples. That had been the most wonderful outing—just one old man from Ana's church driving a wagon full of youngsters. Cal had shown herself to be an experienced rider, unlike her friend, who could not still her horse when she tried to reach up and pick. In fact, the horse kept wandering off, taking Ana on his own route, rubbing his side against trees in an effort to throw her off. Ana had clung helplessly to his mane until Cal came to her rescue. In the end, they had eaten bitter little apples until their bellies hurt, then sung the whole way home with the others.

With her newfound freedom this year, she discovered that Cal had already enjoyed some independence on her own and knew the town in a different way from Ana's map of stores. If they needed a toilet in the middle of the day, she could lead Ana to the outhouse of a family friend. Or, in an emergency, she knew of a particular bush in a weedy grove not far from the square. Cal loved walking the alleys and bringing home discarded books or broken things she could fix. She knew people who worked downtown, like the porter at the American Hotel who attended her church. He always greeted her warmly and once let them look into the lobby.

Cal knew quiet places too. She had led Ana to a spot in the woods near a stream, timing their hike so as to see a cottonwood tree letting go its May snow onto a field and leaving drifts of white along the water's edge. It was a windless day, as still as a picture, and they were in it. The only movement was the faint breeze from a passing bee that caused the weightless flakes to flutter into the air. Sometimes Ana could think of that day, the low hum of that bee, and drowse off to a deep sleep. But not tonight.

Had Cal lied today? Had she really seen the hand? Ana thought it was not her nature to lie. But she was private. Ana knew that she did not care to speak much about her family, though it was clear Cal adored her mother. Ana, for her part, did not hesitate to tell Cal about her family's struggles in Madeira, how the people of their faith were jailed and had to go into hiding. How they had to worship in secret. How her mother was unhappy in America. Cal listened, seemingly absorbed by the Ferreiras' troubles. But in all their talking, she offered up very little of her own family's story.

Once, on a hot day last August, Ana spotted Cal with her

mother and brother and a group of others, all dressed up, walking along Fifth Street in a procession with banners and music. Cal was wearing the prettiest bonnet with a blue ribbon at the back. Ana knew the hat; she had watched Cal crochet it. Walking with her was another girl about her size, wearing her own best clothes. Later, she explained they'd gone to a picnic in a grove to celebrate the rebellion that ended slavery in the West Indies. It was not a picnic that white people went to, but it looked like such fun Ana had longed to slip into the crowd and join them. She had felt a stab of jealousy to see Cal with another girl, laughing and talking, a person Ana did not know.

Cal was her best friend, but she did not know if the reverse was true. Cal kept some of her feelings private.

What happened in the shoe shop today made Ana queasy again in her stomach. She would keep the secret, even if they never spoke of it again.

CHAPTER SIX

FROM THE BEGINNING OF HER SCHOOLING IN SPRINGFIELD two years ago, the words that failed to stick on the tongues of the others in her church school came fast to Ana. Pronouncing them was a trouble until she learned the rules, and arranging them was more trouble until whole sentences came leaping out of her mouth and she found herself ahead of the other students, many of whom could read English but not speak it. She was managing to do both, though she couldn't spell to save her life. When she began writing down the questions and requests of her Madeira neighbors and carrying notes to the grocer or doctor or dry goods man, she waited to see if they would laugh in her face. It turned out the town was full of bad spellers.

Springfield was a newspaper town, and in her daily rounds, she found discarded papers wherever she went—lying on benches, flying in the wind, waiting in barrels to be burned. She rescued all she could haul home with two arms. The wonder to her was that a morning paper, so precious to people on one day, was of little interest a week later. Front page stories gripped her. A huge flood destroyed the town of Des Moines, Iowa. Seventeen-year locusts in Washington, DC, were being eaten up by birds and hogs. At home in Springfield, there were noted thieves caught in the act of stealing chickens and fist-fighting men bloodying each other's noses on the square. Sometimes there were letters to the paper from former townspeople who had traveled west and written back to warn of dangerous routes.

She liked the obituaries. She skipped over the old people and focused on the young. Babies died stillborn. Older children, and there seemed to be a lot of them, died from the illnesses they caught—summer complaint, flux, measles, smallpox. And then there were the odd ones, such as a three-year-old named Matilda who was "shot by her brothers." More than one brother would shoot a little child? A three-year-old?

She plowed on through columns of ads for things her family lacked, for looking glasses, clocks, mattresses, and other goods meant to suit all fancies. These things, along with bloody fights and unanswered mysteries, went into the basket in her brain.

"*Esperta*," the teacher said to Genoveva Ferreira of her youngest daughter during a school meeting. Clever.

Ana watched her mother's face brighten at the remark. "I have told Ana this myself," she said in Portuguese. She had also let Ana know, in little ways, that she would not have great beauty like her sister's to count on.

At first when Ana began bringing the old newspapers into the house, her mother had cast a wary eye at the piles stacked on the kitchen floor. But her attitude changed when the first snow came and the newspapers, folded just so, could be placed inside shoes to cover holes in their soles.

Now she was pleased when her girl read the stories and translated for her. Ana interpreted the advertisements, and they began to understand what a normal price was for a store bonnet or a pair of shoes. When they looked at pictures of furniture, though, her mother's mood shifted. Genoveva Ferreira had lived for twenty years in a big pink house where her grandmother—a Lisbon girl who had married an island man—marked every table, chair, bowl, bedstead, and silver pitcher she had acquired over the years with the name of a grandchild for whom the object was intended someday. A favorite of her grandmother, Genoveva found her name on a number of treasures as she grew up—in particular some silver bowls and a wonderful desk. The memory of the desk in particular made her grieve when she recalled the magical fish with perfectly carved scales swimming along its apron. Her grandmother was bedridden but still alive when Genoveva escaped with Emmanuel and the children. Lost were her beloved *avó*, her brothers and sisters, her parents, her promised treasures. "*Todos perdidos*," she had sighed, still in disbelief.

Ana had little memory of Madeira. She hadn't been born yet when a Scottish doctor named Kalley stopped off in Madeira on his mission to China and decided to stay. He opened a free clinic where his wife read the Bible to the people while they waited to see the doctor. He started a day school for children and night school for grown-ups, and over time, he converted thousands of Catholics to the Presbyterian faith. Sometime after Ana's birth in 1840, her parents joined the Bible readers.

She had a fuzzy memory of attending Sabbath school when she was five years old. There she learned to read some English words out of a storybook about Jesus.

She had heard many times about angry popish people beating and jailing the newly converted Presbyterians on the island. Some converts were tortured and a couple of them died. She learned these details over years of talking with her parents around one small table or another. Just a few days ago, her mother had repeated the stories.

"My own mother, my brothers and sisters turned against me," her mother had said.

"The bishop became jealous of Dr. Kalley's success. Suddenly, the Bible readers were jailed. We were afraid," her father said. "Our families were told by the priests to excommunicate their own relatives."

Ana knew the rest. A mob, helped by soldiers, tore through her parents' house, smashed the tables and chairs. Her family ran and hid with others in a cave in the hills. An English ship took her family out of Madeira. It turned out the ship's master was recruiting workers for sugar plantations far away.

"What did we know? We couldn't keep living in a cave. We made our way at night to a beach where we boarded a ship bound for Trinidad. We heard there was religious freedom there." Her mother pressed her fingertips into graying black hair, rubbed her temples. "*Um desastre!* They worked us without mercy."

Her Portuguese spilled out of her furiously, and Ana, wiping plates in the kitchen, listened for something, anything new.

"The English had freed their slaves and the growers needed new workers."

Her mother had seen women collapse in the marshy fields, sick with a tropical fever that would soon kill them. Her fingers that had once embroidered delicate whitework were cut and calloused from harvesting cane. Her back was nearly broken in that hot, humid place.

Of all the troubles they had lived through, her mother was saddest about her family back in Madeira. She had written so many letters and not one was answered. "They just let me go." Her mother's voice still filled with wonder that it turned out this way. Her eyes filled too. It was the part of the story that pierced Ana and made her wish it would not be told again.

She found it hard to picture her parents first noticing each other, her mother sitting on a balcony and her father below, gazing longingly and tipping his hat. Or as young lovers walking hand in hand to hear Dr. Kalley preach. She found it hard to picture Madeira at all, but Ana remembered Trinidad well enough. When she heard the stories repeated from the pulpit at the First Presbyterian Portuguese Church of Springfield, she closed her eyes and saw her mother's back moving among sky-high sugar plants, where a child could get lost in a heartbeat. She and Beatriz watched from the edge of the cane field until her red apron disappeared.

Had her mother painted into Ana's brain the picture of the cane fields, the blistering sun, the cane rats darting across her feet? She didn't think so. She remembered wading into the fields with her mother a few times—how her legs ached, her dry throat longed for water. How the sharp-edged cane leaves cut her skin. Just now she could hear the swish and thud of machetes hitting the stalks. She could smell the sickening sweet odor coming from the boiling house vats.

Their luck changed when their pastor from Madeira sent out pleas for help, telling of the poverty and sicknesses of the workers, how the children slept on rags and were nearly naked. A Protestant society in New York helped them get to America, where a hemp company located between Springfield and Jacksonville promised the exiles jobs, houses, and land if they came to Illinois to work. But by the time they arrived in New York, the offer was withdrawn. Undaunted, the good people of Springfield and Jacksonville, two small towns in the middle of the state, had said, "Send them to us anyway. We will take them all."

The happy ending was the part of the story folks in Springfield mostly knew about. But Ana could not fail to see how sad her mother was. How she couldn't seem to settle in to Springfield. How she had lost interest in doing the things she loved most. It was a worry Ana forgot at school or when she walked around downtown with her map, but it seeped into her when she went through her front door, as if a cloud of sadness filled the inside of the house.

CHAPTER SEVEN

AUGUST 1852

WALKING TO WORK ONE MORNING, SPENCER PASSED A clutch of white men on the square talking about a Colonization Society meeting they'd attended the night before. Wander by any open church door, almost any door downtown, and you'd find some kind of meeting going on. The people of Springfield were a bunch of meeters, and their favorite causes were schools, liquor, and lately, colonization. Temperance wasn't a big draw for the town's colored citizens, but education drew a crowd. It infuriated Spencer that the state taxed his people for public schools that did not allow their children to enter them. The subject of colonization was equally maddening. It was all the talk in the local newspapers, which would have you believe that Negroes were dancing with glee about the idea of moving to Africa. White anti-slavery people talked mostly of gradual emancipation, along with colonizing the masses to Liberia or someplace else far away. Even some abolitionists, who demanded an immediate end to slavery, went along with the idea of removing ex-slaves from American soil.

A local man from the Baptist church, Sam Ball, had actually gone on a mission to Liberia a few years ago to look at the place as a location for asylum. He was a smart man and he had come back a believer, arguing that their people would be better off elsewhere. There were a few other colored people in town who were believers, but most everybody Spencer knew was opposed. They had been born in America. There was no "going back home" to Africa.

William was not one to sit hours on end in a stuffy room arguing, but Spencer didn't mind it, and when business was quiet at his barbershop, he liked to drop in at William's, where Landon Coleman could usually be found talking politics. Landon kept abreast of national and local news. From the outside, he looked to be a quiet type, a rule follower—but Spencer knew that inside his skin, he was on fire.

Landon stayed on top of what was being done in other states about starting schools for their own children, about abolition, about the status of Illinois's Black Laws, which had the most severe restrictions of any other Northern state's race laws in the country. Landon would chew on the various arguments and talk them out with the brothers. Recently he'd read about Indiana's state colored convention and he'd gotten himself into a fit. "Other states have been holding conventions for years. What's the matter with us? It can be done in Illinois," he argued. "Easily."

Landon knew where every politician in the state stood on

the antislavery issue. He knew the firebrands, the wire-pullers, the resolution drafters, the doughfaces, the wafflers, the cowards.

William always claimed he didn't need to attend meetings as his brothers did. He had Landon Coleman.

This humid August morning, when Spencer visited his brother's shop, he found Landon's nose buried in Frederick Douglass's newspaper.

"What's he onto?" Spencer asked as he wiped sweat off his forehead.

"'Colonization. Listen to this." Landon stood with an old back copy of the paper and paced as he read, his voice full of drama as he became, for a moment, an orator. "'It may seem ungrateful, but there are some of us who are resolved that you shall not get rid of your colored relations.'"

"Who's he talking to?"

"It's a speech he gave last year…"

"Just read it, Landon," William said. "This ain't the senate floor."

"'For two hundred and thirty years and more we have had a foothold on this continent. We have grown up with you; we have watered your soil with our tears; nourished it with our blood, tilled it with our hard hands. Why should we not stay here? We were the pioneers of civilization on this continent. We leveled your forests; our hands removed the stumps from your fields, and raised the first crops and brought the first produce to your tables.'"

Landon's voice went quivery, and he paused before resuming. "'We have been with you, are still with you…'"

"…and we damn well plan to stay," William said.

Landon put down the paper, sank into his seat. "Why would any intelligent man want to be sent to Africa? We were born here! We deserve the same rights as anybody else born in this country. Who cannot see the logic in that?"

William stared out the window, nodded at passersby. "A lot of those people out there."

That was how it went with the two of them: Landon throwing hope into the tannin-thick air, William batting it out the door, Landon coming back at him, insulting his new waistcoat and watch chain as a "gambling costume."

Spencer found the discussions enlightening. He looked over at Landon, who never tripped on a word when the talk poured from his heart. Twenty-three years old—ten years younger than Spencer—and mentally planning out an Illinois state convention.

His brother and Landon had come together because of shoemaking. Both were freeborn, both had followed shoemaking as a trade, instead of barbering or blacksmithing or carting. Kentucky was a state full of colored shoemakers, and William had begun training at sixteen under one of the best. When he'd come to Springfield, there was room for another shoe shop. Back then, the town was five years into being the new state capital. Businesses and houses were popping up all over. There were plenty of new feet to shoe.

Illinois had called itself a free state from its beginnings and their mother's words—"Buy land...put down roots"—had seemed like a real plan. But Spencer and William learned that as early as 1819, the state legislators made sure that freedmen were only half free when they created the Illinois Black Laws. And now? There was talk of tightening them further.

Lately Spencer felt as if the map of his world was shrinking, burning up around the edges. It was more and more dangerous to leave the center of town where he was known. Anything could be waiting outside the bounds. He was never without his free papers, but there were cutthroats who could grab you, toss your papers, kill you or sell you down the river before anybody knew you were gone. He knew his brother felt the same.

Landon's approach to fighting back made William say aloud, "I can't follow that road." He was born impatient. His body was too restless. And there was the thrill of moving people north. To help one fugitive was to feel, for a moment, a dose of manhood.

The bell on the door jangled, and a woman came in to collect a pair of shoes she'd had repaired. Mrs. Lincoln was short and round—quite a contrast to the man she'd married. "He's away," she said of her husband when William asked. Otherwise, she made little conversation, paying quickly and hurrying out.

"He's somebody in the legislature to watch," Landon said.

"Man's got the biggest feet I ever fit," William said.

"Six foot four if he's an inch. She's probably what? Five foot one or two? How him and her…"

William laughed hard. "Easy now…"

"He's a fierce Whig," Spencer said. "I've shaved him and listened to the man talk. And I have heard a fair number of stories from his friend Fleurville. Have you heard the one about when the Democrats controlled the legislature, maybe twelve years ago, there was a big issue over the state bank, which the Whigs supported? The Democrats needed a quorum to call a vote to adjourn. That way, the issue would simply die. Other

Whigs had left the building, but Lincoln was their floor leader and still present when the doors were locked. So what did he do? Jumped out a window so they wouldn't have their quorum."

"Clever," William laughed, "but not very dignified."

"He's on our side," Landon said. "You know of Reverend Billious Pond out in Farmington?"

"Mm-huh."

"Well, Lincoln defended his son Marvin a few years back when he was tried for harboring a woman runaway. Jury came in with not guilty." Landon's face brightened. "Say, his law partner Herndon is speaking tonight at the abolition church if you want to go."

"Not tonight," William said.

Spencer knew his brother had a plan he was not mentioning. He had talked about the girl who lived next door to their mother and her husband, Joe. William had noticed the girl named Charlotte coming and going lately and had told Spencer he liked how she carried herself. He'd gone over to the Baptist church so he could "bump into her" somewhere other than her front stoop, where her mother could be found often enough, snooping. The girl was a beauty, gentle as a fawn, bright and curious, William had told Spencer, the kind of girl he imagined when he pictured a someday wife. "She agreed to see me this evening." William was beaming.

Spencer rose to go to his own shop and slapped Landon on the back. "I'll see you at the meeting tonight."

CHAPTER EIGHT

OCTOBER 1853

THEY WERE NERVOUS. TWO COLORED MEN TRAVELING together was probably already violating some damned code. They carried their free papers, but nothing was assured as they moved north by stagecoach.

Changes in Illinois's Black Laws had been the last straw for Spencer.

"It's all the old code in the constitution plus the vicious new exclusion laws designed to keep our people out of the state," he told William.

"No *free* Negro from a different state dare rest his feet in Illinois for longer than ten days or he'll be jailed. And if he can't come up with the fifty-dollar fine? The sheriff will auction him off to the highest bidder who'll pay the costs and then work the poor devil for the fewest days. How merciful! And if that man or woman doesn't leave the state, well, the whole thing starts over, with the fine increasing by fifty dollars each round. It's essentially slavery, don't you see?" Spencer had stood, pacing his barbershop. "The convention is a three-day meeting, plus getting there and back. I've talked it through with Eliza, and she thinks I should go."

They both understood what going meant—agreeing to be a delegate to the Illinois Colored Citizens Convention in Chicago, leaving their families and losing work days.

"Landon can't go," William said. "His wife is sick."

"I know, I know." Spencer stared at him, waited. He was bigger, beefier than William. He took a step closer, put his hands on his hips, and eyed his brother. "Well?"

"Don't be looking over here."

"So I take that ride alone."

"Aw, sweet Jesus. All right. I'll ride up with you. I'll have a look at Chicago, but that's all."

It was the beginning of October when they set out. Bumping along in a mail coach on the Springfield stage road to Ottawa, mud holes repeatedly swallowed the wheels, and the whip man up top had the brothers push the wagon out of the mire. The only other rider with them was a young white man made so sick by the motion of the stage that he hung his head out the window throwing up until he got to his destination.

Free to talk quietly, William pointed out the towns where safe houses were said to stand. He had been sending fugitives up this direction for years but he had no picture of the land until now.

Spencer found the landscape much like the farmland out-side Springfield, dotted with bundled stalks of corn standing like tepees across the acres. But the trees this year struck him as brighter than any other autumn he could recall. Blazing yellows and oranges and reds lit the woodlands like a celebration, and he remembered the pleasure he'd felt as a boy kicking through the deep fall of leaves in Kentucky.

In Ottawa, they boarded the Chicago and Rock Island Railroad train and breathed a little easier. Another passenger in the colored car invited them to share biscuits and popskull whiskey out of his bottle.

Spencer's legs were jelly when they finally reached Chicago. It was almost dark. As they emerged from the train depot into the street, he spotted a few brown and black faces in the passing crowd. How freely they moved along, talking and laughing. He and William melded into the crowd, and a man said, "Evening," as if they belonged.

They found their way to the Dearborn Street house of another delegate, a heavy man named John Jones who wore muttonchops that wrapped around his big head like shrubbery. Spencer had little information on him except that he was a tailor. A wealthy tailor, it appeared. The house was a fine one, full of carved wood and heavy curtains. Jones's wife, Mary, escorted them to the parlor where her husband and another man were discussing how to word a resolution. Jones greeted them and soon enough they all adjourned to a table laid out with a beef stew dinner. There were cigars thereafter and more talk until it was time to turn in.

Jones showed them a basement room fitted out with four cots and said, "It has gotten a lot of use this year."

"My garret has been full as well," William said.

Jones studied his eyes and smiled. "It's an honor to have you, sir. You won't be bedding down here. You and your brother will stay upstairs." He escorted them to their room. "Sleep now. We'll go over to the hall early."

"I'm not a delegate," William pointed out. "I thought I'd have a walk around town tomorrow."

"This is history, my man. Frederick Douglass is coming. You can leave when you choose but you should at least look in. You'll regret it if you don't."

In the morning, fortified with bacon and eggs, Spencer, William, and Jones went to Warner's Hall, where a few other delegates were already gathered. By ten o'clock, there were some forty people in the room. Spencer had already made the rounds and found that there was a preponderance of barbers and ministers as representatives. They fretted that the great leader, Frederick Douglass, had not shown up yet. Some of them had come simply to be in the same room with him.

They started with a prayer and went to hell from there as far as William was concerned, talking about minutes, motions, pro tems, amendments. "All this makes my skin itch," he told Spencer during a break. "I'm going out for a walk."

Spencer took his seat again at a long table with the other delegates. Within minutes, John Jones was voted president of the whole shooting match. He was a tailor, but he bore himself like a judge. When he spoke, Spencer caught phrases relating to his agenda. "The education of our children...repeal of the Black Laws...temperance..." There was no doubt what the man really wanted to talk about. Jones had located his outrage right in the middle of his oratorical sandwich, and as he discussed the subject of the codes, he pounded the table in fury.

Spencer was a confident writer and got himself onto the committee to put together the formal address to the people of Illinois that would express their demands.

When Frederick Douglass finally arrived, a quiet descended on the crowd. He was over six feet tall and wore a black frock coat that made him look even taller. Beneath it, a silk printed vest and an elegant high-neck shirt with a striped silk bow tie peeked out. His facial features looked chiseled as a statue's, just as John Jones had described them.

Douglass began with jokes that drew laughs, and the whole audience seemed to lean in closer. His voice was calm as he laid out his case against the mass removal of Negroes to Africa, then it began to rise. His own pain was palpable as he spoke of such a betrayal.

"For more than two hundred years, the colored man has toiled over the soil of America, under a burning sun and a driver's lash—plowing, planting, reaping, that white men might roll in ease, their hands unhardened by labor. And now that the moral sense of mankind is beginning to revolt at this system of foul treachery and cruel wrong and is demanding its overthrow? The mean and cowardly oppressor is meditating plans to expel the colored man entirely from the country."

Douglass's voice roared. "*Shame* upon the guilty wretches that dare make such a proposition!"

The men rose from their chairs and clapped each time Douglass paused in his speech until he sat down.

That night, while his guests sat around his table, John Jones worried out loud that the meeting had been thrown off course. "Douglass shifted everybody's attention away from the Illinois laws. I understand. I admire him. But tomorrow belongs to us."

The men returned stirred up the next day, and Jones laid out the insults of the new Black Laws. He spoke without notes, his outrage forceful enough that the seams of his coat appeared near to bursting.

Jones pulled from his pocket a folded piece of paper that everyone recognized. "My certificate of freedom says right here that I am a 'free person of color entitled to be respected accordingly, in person and property, at all times and places, in the due prosecution of his lawful concerns.'

"Sounds good, does it not? But from the beginning, we couldn't vote or testify in court against a white person. From the beginning, if we assembled in a group, we could be punished. Now the legislature has added new codes to peel away what freedoms we have left."

Jones paused to survey the faces in front of him.

"When our state legislators wrote up their dandy new constitution, they violated a previous constitution that was made by Jefferson, Franklin, and Adams. There is nothing to show that color is a bar in *that* agreement. A man is a man, whether his skin be black or white."

Resolutions were created and voted on throughout the convention. On the second day, Spencer and William listened as the group formally thanked Harriet Beecher Stowe for *Uncle Tom's Cabin* and objected to the taxes they paid for public schools their children could not attend.

"Who are you talking to with all these resolutions?" William asked.

"To the people of Illinois. To the powers that be. And to each other," Spencer said. "We have to be unified if we are to be reckoned with."

It all appeared far too mild-mannered to William. Spencer watched him pick up the piece of stationery where he had noted down the points his committee had made for the formal written address.

"What's this?" William read aloud the wording of one part of the address. "'In a spirit of meekness and patriotic good will.' And this one about the prejudice against the colored people of the United States. Here," he said, his finger on the paper. "'The prejudice is not against color, but *condition*, and that we must change that condition, by using economy, amassing riches, educating our children, and being temperate.'"

William looked up. "Let me understand this. Do you really believe that's what it will take to change our situation? When four million meek, educated, rich, teetotaling Negroes persuade legislators of our virtues? You think that will do the trick? I don't share so sunny a view, Spence." William leaned back in his chair and put his hands behind his head. "Though I'm all for amassing riches. You have some power over your life when you have money. John Jones understands that."

Behind all the convention resolutions, Spencer saw Frederick Douglass at work. The man traveled constantly from state to state, and his many speeches were proof that English rhetoric did not belong only to Yankee preachers. The words coming from Douglass were pearls, finer than he'd heard from any other mouth.

"Aren't you tired of words?" William asked him late on the second afternoon. "Let's cut out for an hour or two."

They went into the street, and Spencer's thoughts turned to Eliza. Their house was still full of the things he'd given her when he wooed her—a fancy carved mirror, painted boxes that fit one inside the other; a small gold ring with a blue stone. He was just twenty-one and she seventeen when they married back in Kentucky. He had loved her so much he thought his heart might bust through his ribs and fall into her lap. In receiving his gifts, Eliza lit up with delight, as if each object was rare and much too fine. When she told him she was carrying his child and lost her waist, she only grew more beautiful to him in her full dresses.

How he wished she could see this town. Somebody had said there were over thirty-eight thousand people in Chicago now, some four hundred of them colored, and that number was said to be growing fast. The word in Springfield was that once escapees made it to Chicago, they were safe. It seemed a good place to put down roots. And Eliza would have an opinion. Twelve years into their marriage, with four children filling the house, she was as lovely as the day he married her. More forceful now, though. She would not be keen on leaving her relatives downstate.

As they wandered south of the business district, Spencer observed pockets of his people going about their lives. Most dressed better than they did back home, and he noticed in particular a handsome woman in a fine straw hat. She took no offense when he approached her, and she cordially gave him instructions to find the milliner a couple of blocks away.

The shop owner seemed unruffled by two men coming in

the door. What size, she asked him. He had no idea. He guessed and bought a straw summer hat decorated with silk flowers. William bought a similar one for their mother. They returned then to the meeting, sheepishly carrying two large hatboxes.

For three days, Spencer and two other men had been working on the official address of the convention to the people of Illinois. Its polite tone was still there by the third and last day, but angrier words had been added, listing the outrages of the new Black Laws. He felt the anger, though his knees quivered when he was called on to read the address.

"Spencer Donnegan, founder and pastor of Springfield's AME Church…"

How many sermons had he delivered in the past decade? Yet here was his stomach in knots for having to follow "the colored man eloquent," as somebody at the convention had called Douglass.

Spencer began calmly, stating that as a group, they were asking for no special privileges or favors, only even-handed justice. When he enumerated the obstructions that past legislators had seen fit to heap upon them, though, his face grew hot.

By the time he got to Patrick Henry's "Give me liberty or give me death" quote, he felt his face burning with anger. "Is it possible that men, women, and children are to be doomed to lifelong slavery for the simple act of coming into the State of Illinois to gain an honest living? Is liberty to the colored man about to languish and die? Think for a moment of the death struggles of a people; for there are no death struggles like those of expiring liberty."

The applause at the end washed over him; he felt buttressed.

He sensed in that moment that together they formed a real force.

As the convention drew to a close, the crowds started chanting for Frederick Douglass. He rose, spoke, and brought the house down. A church choir followed up with a rousing, joyous hymn.

Let waiting throngs now lift their voices,
As Freedom's glorious day draws near…

Glancing sideways, Spencer saw a man weeping, and then another. His own eyes were dry. He doubted freedom's day was anywhere near. Still, he was struck by how few moments in a colored man's life he was able to be proud, to have three days free of some kind of humiliation.

On the long ride home, carrying the cumbersome hatboxes, he pondered how his life would be different if he moved up to Chicago. He and William talked about the possibility of making such a change. They had both tasted greater freedom there. The Chicago city council had actually passed a resolution condemning the Fugitive Slave Act and instructed their police department not to enforce it. It would be a much safer place to live.

As the miles passed, though, they persuaded themselves that as Springfield was the state capital, it would grow and offer more opportunities in the long run. And after all, the whole family was there.

CHAPTER NINE

November 1853

HE WAS CUTTING THE LAWYER'S HAIR WHEN THE QUES-tions started.

"How do you like these boots your brother made for me?"

"They're handsome."

"And they actually fit. He tells me they are the largest boots he's ever made."

"William doesn't lie."

"Never had a sense what size my shoe was until I came to this town. I rode in here in pot metal boots. They cost me eight cents out in New Salem. Felt like I was wearin' a pair of buckets on my feet."

"I suspect those on your feet cost you more."

"They did. Worth every penny."

Spencer studied the lawyer's hair. His old partner, Billy Fleurville, usually cut Lincoln's locks, but he was not yet back from a trip. It was clear Billy hadn't touched the man's hair for a while. It stuck up and out like a nest just vacated by a crazy bird.

Lincoln's shirt cuffs were smudged with newspaper ink, and his coat was worn near through at the elbows. Looking him in the eyes, Spencer noticed that his left one would roll upward from time to time, then down again to look straight ahead. How did Lincoln see right? How did he read his legal books?

The lawyer was just one of the shop's clientele, but he was memorable for his friendliness and his political talk while he was in the chair. He and Fleurville had known each other for many years and had helped out the other on numerous occasions. Billy had once nursed Lincoln through a worrisome illness. There was a tenderness between the two men.

Spencer planted a comb in the coarse mess of cowlicks, but it wouldn't move in any direction. He might as well be trying to comb twigs. He took in hand a brush and worked through the stiff hair until he had flattened it, then divided it into sections with the comb and began cutting.

"I understand you went to the convention in Chicago last month."

"I did. I was a delegate."

Lincoln shifted in his seat. "And what was the talk of?"

"The Black Codes. Taxation for schools, colonization."

"Of course. Was there a consensus?"

"About…?"

"Colonization."

"Fully against."

Lincoln blinked. He tucked his chin into his chest. "Fully against," he said. "You too, then?"

"Against."

A silence fell. Spencer moved on to shaving the man, maneuvering his razor carefully on Lincoln's upper lip, around a large wart and some moles on his cheeks, then down near his large Adam's apple. "Eyebrows?" he asked.

"Always," said Lincoln.

Spencer caught sight through the window of Billy Fleurville bending to pet Lincoln's dog, which the lawyer sometimes tied up outside, before he came in.

"Mr. de Fleurville," the lawyer said, using Billy's proper birth name.

"Monsieur Lincoln," Billy said. "Just went fishing."

"Let me hear it," said Lincoln.

Spencer knew Billy had traveled to see a relative and his trip did not involve fish. Fishing was a code he shared with Lincoln that a joke was forthcoming. A round of puns and country humor followed, then talk of wives and children and a property sale the lawyer was managing for Billy, who bought new lots as his business thrived. Spencer had heard Fleurville tell the story many times of how the two men met back in 1831. Billy was a Haitian who immigrated first to Baltimore with his godmother. As a young man, he set out to see the country and seek his fortune. Coming up the Mississippi from New Orleans, he found himself in Illinois, where he bumped into a twenty-two-year-old nobody named Abraham Lincoln in New Salem. Lincoln set him up cutting hair in a boarding house for a day so he could earn enough to travel on to Springfield to get a job. He eventually opened a shop, advertising himself in his droll style as "the Emperor and Autocrat" of all local barbers and his place as a "Tonsorial Palace."

Billy was educated. He played a number of instruments and had kept a violin in the shop. When Lincoln came in, Billy sometimes played a couple of tunes, and each time magic seemed to happen. They all paused to savor the music and their talk would turn nostalgic. Lincoln and Fleurville would spill stories.

Back in '47, when a nearby building caught fire, it took down the barbershop. The violin had miraculously survived. And then it disappeared from the wreckage. Billy put an advertisement in the paper asking for its return, but nothing came of it. Spencer missed that piece of his barbering life, the violin part.

Standing together talking after Spencer had brushed off his jacket, Lincoln and Fleurville made an odd picture. Billy was a small and compact man, a fashionable dresser who groomed himself meticulously each morning. His cheeks were fragrant with aftershave, his hair close cut, his coat spotless. Lincoln must be six foot four, Spencer thought, slender to the point of hungry-looking, with wrist bones hanging below his coat sleeves—a white man who resembled a giant marionette, encumbered by parts that didn't quite operate in concert, but with kind eyes. Spencer liked Lincoln.

In Springfield, the barbershop was one of the few places where black and white men mingled in the same room. It was a close, familiar thing for a white man to have his face shaved by a black man. Some customers did not open themselves to talk. Or one might talk to the man in the next chair as if the man wielding the straight razor was not present. Billy kept with the going custom of accommodating only white clients.

"Have you noticed that eye rolling around?" Spencer said when Lincoln had departed.

"Got kicked by a horse when he was a boy."

"He wanted to know my mind for some reason."

"He's got his ear to the ground. Wouldn't be surprised if he goes back into politics."

"Is that a prediction?"

"I know him better than any other man in town, I think. Certainly known him longer." Billy smiled. "Yes, that's a prediction."

CHAPTER TEN

WHEN ANA WOKE, THE WATER IN HER WASHING BOWL was frozen, and when she looked outside, the whole world was blanketed in snow. A party of fat robins decorated a naked tree, taking turns to swoop down and eat berries on a nearby bush. In the next yard over, the neighbor's clothesline was hung with stiff long underwear, like a row of visiting ghosts. Her father was up and already hammering together a crude sled from pieces of a broken-down ash hopper while her mother cooked porridge and told stories about Madeira.

"We used sleds in all kinds of weather," she said. "We'd climb up the road to the cathedral on Sunday, then glide down the cobblestones on the way home." Her mother shook her head as she bundled her children in wool. "You'll be lucky to find even a little bump around here."

As it turned out, they found a perfect mound where her father and brother and Cal, who joined them, took turns sliding and squealing among a pack of Germans who had already found the hill. After her father and Joao left, the girls stayed on until their toes felt frozen. They walked back on a street that Ana thought she knew. As they continued farther, though, the houses looked unfamiliar. A pack of three boys raced across the street all at once and blocked the path. Ana held the rope of the sled tight as the tallest boy demanded it.

She looked down at the sled. "No," she said. "It's ours."

When she looked up, the boy closest to Cal pushed her. Cal swung at him, hitting his chin as she fell backward onto the snow. The tall boy yanked the rope from Ana's hand. She began to pummel the boy's belly as she hollered. He knocked her over, then pushed her face into the snow.

"Francis! George!" a female voice was shouting. A woman flew down the steps of a house across the street and was quickly in their midst. Her dislodged hair switch was swinging like a horse's tail as she hauled the tall boy by his collar and another by his sleeve toward the street. "You get your thieving selves home this minute. And you, Albert Meyer, you little snot. Your mother will beat your hiney when she hears."

Ana and Cal walked back to the house, hobbled but laughing.

"What happened?" Genoveva Ferreira gasped when they walked in the door. She ran to fetch a wet towel and wipe the blood from Cal's lip and Ana's forehead.

"Too crowded over there. We bumped into another sled."

Joao stood by the kitchen stove. "What did the other sledders look like?"

"About as bad as us," she said, aware that Cal was keeping her mouth shut.

"I should have stayed there with you, Bean," her father said when he came into the room. He was looking into Ana's face, perhaps suspecting she was lying. She had considered telling the truth, but her brother would have gone after the boys with his neighborhood pals. Or her mother would have squelched future trips to the park. It would have worked against them somehow. Instead, cocoa was heating on the stove. They hung their wet stockings in front of it.

Cal shot a conspiratorial glance at Ana. In all their adventures together, they had never had to fight. They had run, hidden, played hard, but never hit other boys or girls before, except their own blood. Obviously, combat with their brothers had taught them a thing or two. They had not humiliated themselves this afternoon. They had defended each other with their fists.

They sat on the floor next to the stove. Cal was looking up at the corn Genoveva had hung to dry from the kitchen ceiling last summer, same as her mother had done in their house. She was smiling between sips of the cocoa. When her gaze fell on the painted woodwork and table, though, she was puzzled.

"Why'd you make it like that?" she asked Ana's father.

"People want pretty things." He pulled out a board he had painted. It was covered in blue and yellow flowers and stars that looked just like the painted tiles in Madeira.

Cal stared at the picture for a long time. She seemed undone by it, her expression shifting from wonder to dismay.

"Did Cal not like the painting?" Ana's father asked after she left.

"I don't know."

Ana had sensed a subtle shift in Cal's mood before she went home. They had walked to Ana's house, both of them giddy, as if they were a team of two who had just won a battle. Now, she suspected, the sight of the lovely painting suddenly tipped the balance between them. Both their homes were humble, but Cal had no paintings where she lived. What she did have in her house were lots of visitors and no corner of her own. The painting of azulejos had touched her, because Cal was drawn to pretty things. How many hours had they stood in front of store windows, fascinated by the delicate teacups and flowered hats and fine dresses?

That night, Emmanuel Ferreira talked about art over dinner. In the past year, he'd made a leap from carpentry to decorative painting. Recently he'd found a wealthy customer who let him cover the walls of one of her rooms with the pretend Portuguese tiles. The woman had said they looked real.

"There are opportunities in this town for the painter," her father mused. "For the artist."

Genoveva snorted. "There aren't *that* many wealthy people here. What will you do when you run out of pine woodwork to disguise as oak? What will you do when that fashion changes?"

"I will paint portraits."

"Emmanuel, you are a grainer, not a portrait artist."

"Not yet. But I could learn and someday master it. Anything is possible here."

Ana knew this line of reasoning held little influence with her mother. She found central Illinois devoid of promise. Who would be inspired to greatness in this utterly flat place? It lacked beautiful mountains to uplift and remind one of higher things.

"Don't you see the changes, woman? The new train tracks? A state capital only gets bigger. A man can make his fortune here."

Emmanuel Ferreira, Ana realized, was born happy. He was a man who rose every morning, looked out the window at any time of the year, and said, "Another perfect day." It was his nature to cheerfully accept things that the world presented to him. Dressed in his work clothes and a knitted fisherman's hat that flopped over to one side of his head, her father was the first to leave. Whistling, of course.

Ana believed her father's claims about the town. She had seen the signs herself. On the north side of the square, some of the old buildings were coming down. The squat, unkempt stores across from the Capitol, lined up like a row of roosting hens, were being replaced with solid brick buildings that rose two or three stories, and some city father had already proposed a more dignified name for Chicken Row.

"*Commercial* Row," her mother said sarcastically, her accent imbuing the sterile business strip on the north side of the square with banana trees and blue jacarandas.

Running her errands, Ana had sensed the townsfolk's blooming optimism. A strip of plank sidewalk had appeared on Fourth Street, and there was talk of laying more like it all around the town. Even without any sidewalks, there was more bustle on the streets, a sense of busyness that was expanding block by block beyond the throbbing town square and into the neighborhoods where frame houses were popping up like mushrooms.

Their own family's life was improving. Her mother had left

behind her market stand when she returned to doing embroidery work, and her father's painting business was growing.
Emmanuel Ferreira said it often: he had escaped a certain fate
by departing from Madeira. Here he would not have to till
another man's soil until he dropped over. There were a lot of
men in town who had come from somewhere else, intent on
escaping similar fates.

Even at the makeshift school Ana attended in an old house
near hers, the children of the lowest junk man expected to get
forward. That was what you did in America. You started at low
wages toiling for somebody else, but with hard work, in a year
or two, you could have employees working for you.

There were folks in Springfield who had piles of money.
Her father worked for one of them, Mrs. Alsop. And there were
other people who were comfortable but still looking to move
up. He worked for those people too, the ones who could afford
a little bit of his faux designs. He was painting doors for one
such woman now, Mrs. Lincoln, over on Eighth.

"I told her about you, about our family," her father said later
that evening when he pulled Ana aside. "She asked to meet you,
Bean. Do you like that?"

Ana had nodded. She liked it when he called her Bean,
even if it *was* for her skinny shape.

"She needs a Saturday girl to clean and help with her little
boys." He patted her head. "You will be too busy for fistfights,
my child. Be clean and nice when we go."

CHAPTER ELEVEN

March 1854

They walked to the Lincoln house on a rainy March morning. The wet grass soaked Ana's socks and made her feet squish in her shoes. On South Eighth Street, they found a long row of mostly neat houses fronted by wooden sidewalks. Her father slowed as they came to a corner and stopped in front of a story-and-a-half house with green shutters. On the front door, a black plaque with silver letters announced the owner's name: A. Lincoln. They climbed the steps and her father knocked on the door. Ana looked at her soaked shoes and exhaled a nervous sigh.

Mrs. Lincoln answered the door herself. She was round-faced and smiling, dressed in a cape. She greeted Ana and her father breathlessly and welcomed them into the front hallway.

"I have to run out, but our house girl Catherine will show you around. She'll be here any minute. Come with me, back to the kitchen. I want you to meet Mariah."

Ana's father excused himself, and shortly after he left, Mary Lincoln abandoned Ana to a woman who seemed unhappy about her presence.

"You sure are little." Mariah Vance, the Lincolns' commanding laundress, looked Ana over top to bottom. She stood at a stove over a copper boiling pot and stirred the clothes with an enormous wooden tool. "How old are you, child?"

"Almost fourteen."

"You don't look it." The woman was unsmiling. She wiped the sweat off her forehead with her sleeve and turned to stir the pot.

At that moment, a young woman came through the front door.

"Late as usual!" Mariah let out from the kitchen.

Ana walked out to the parlor to meet her.

"The old hagfish," the girl whispered as she tied an apron around her dress. She looked to be about seventeen or eighteen, with wind-chapped cheeks and red hair. "Yer the new Saturday girl." She shut her door gently. "What's yer name?"

"Ana Ferreira."

"Spanish?"

"No…"

"Portagee?"

Ana nodded.

"Catherine Kelly. I'm to show you the ropes. The missus has gone to her sister's, who's sick. She's wantin' everything perfect when she gets home."

"And Mr. Lincoln?"

"Gone 'til next week. You came at a good time."

Catherine led her to the kitchen, where Mariah eyed them

suspiciously. The girl cut two slices of bread, buttered and jammed them lavishly, then poured herself a cup of coffee. They sat at the dining room table.

"Take the plates back to the kitchen," Catherine said when they'd finished eating. "That's yer first job." She was steering clear of Mariah.

When Ana returned, Catherine had a broom in her hand. She bent down, pulled out a straw, and commenced cleaning her teeth with it. "On Saturdays, you get the dust out from under the beds. Don't wake the two little ones or you'll be sorry. They are wild." They went upstairs to the hallway where she handed her a wet rag. "That's the bedroom of the mister and missus. Start there. Put this over the end of the broom and get all under the bed. She checks."

Ana followed orders, pausing to study photographs of the Lincoln children on a shelf.

Catherine put her head in the door to check on her. She came into the room and pointed to the picture of a child of perhaps two years. "Eddie. Dead." Her finger went to the next photograph. "See how big this one's head is? He's called Tad 'cause he looked like a tadpole when he was born. Still does. This is Willie; he's everybody's favorite. And that's Robert when he was a baby. He's eleven now."

"Oh. Where is he?"

"At his cousin's house. You got an easy day today."

After cleaning the bedroom and sitting room downstairs, Ana was taught how to wait on certain visitors. The sisters of Mrs. Lincoln got the best English tea, and when men showed up, a cigar stand was put out. Mrs. Hufnagel, a neighbor, always wanted a glass of water when she was served food. "She's a gagger," Catherine explained.

The Lincolns' neighborhood was an assortment of wood frame houses, some of them handsome two-story places and others small cottages. The neighbors, Catherine had told her, were all kinds: Germans, English, Negroes, Swedes. Even a couple of Portuguese families lived nearby. Walking down the block to work, Ana could hear two or three accents when people passed by.

She liked the feel of the area right away. People visited each other's houses, and in time, she figured she would be doing the same—borrowing sugar or returning a playmate who had spent the day with Tad and Willie.

On her third Saturday of employment, Ana went out to the backyard, which was more a wood lot than grassy. She'd been told that Mr. Lincoln chopped wood for exercise, and the high piles of split logs were proof. She found the boys' yellow-coated pup lodged between palings in the picket fence, and he was putting up a howl. As she got on her knees and tried to remove the dog, a tall man came walking up the back path. From her kneeling position, he looked like a giant. He took off his hat and coat, rolled up his shirtsleeves, bent over, got his fingers astride Fido, and pulled him out.

"The grass musta looked greener," he mused, then turned to Ana. "Hello there, young lady. What might your name be?"

"Ana. Ana Ferreira."

"Are you from Madeira, Ana? I think I hear a bit of it in your voice."

"Yes, sir."

"Well, welcome, Ana," he said, then ambled into the house. "I am supposed to be the master of this circus, but don't believe it."

It was her first close view of Mr. Lincoln. Taken separately, his features were not handsome at all. He had lines like cracks in a rock on either side of a large nose. A big wart on his right cheek. But such eyes—gray eyes that crinkled with fun.

Not a day went by that Ana didn't have a story to bring back to Little Madeira. The children were wild when Mr. Lincoln was home, and the walls echoed with the boys' screams. He laid himself down in the sitting room while they climbed his body like a hill, then he flipped them topsy-turvy to their screeching delight. He carried them on his shoulders, wrestled with them. If Fido or a cat was involved, all the better for Mr. Lincoln.

"Father! Stop that!" Mrs. Lincoln would call out.

Mr. Lincoln's voice would come back, "Yes, Mother." But the chaos continued.

Sometimes, when it was all too much, Mary muttered bitterly to herself, "Oh God"—a curse that was forbidden in the Ferreira house—and began hollering at whoever was in her path.

One afternoon, while Ana was peeling potatoes over the sink, it was obvious some disagreement was brewing between mister and missus. From the parlor, Mary Lincoln's words grew louder. Ana heard fragments of her shouts. "You're never here…"

She entered the kitchen in a red fury. Straightaway, Mr. Lincoln loped past her, carrying his carpetbag full of papers. Without a word, he left through the back door. Mrs. Lincoln grabbed a potato out of the bowl; her aim was poor, but her arm was strong enough that Mr. Lincoln clutched the rim of his hat as the potato whizzed by.

Beatriz and Joao laughed at the story, told in Portuguese for the sake of their mother, and Ana savored her siblings' amusement.

"I have heard worse," Ana's mother said. "I heard she hit her husband with a log one time. On the nose. The poor man went around with a plaster on it for days."

Ana was doubtful. "I don't believe she'd do that."

Genoveva nodded her head knowingly. "Do you remember the lady who came to my stand and always wanted to bargain? That was Mrs. Lincoln. She's a tough one. The women in my sewing group who knew her before her boy died say she changed after that."

"And how is *he* to you?" Ana's father asked.

"Mr. Lincoln? He seems happy to see me, if he notices I'm there." Ana considered thoughtfully. "But so sad sometimes."

Mr. Lincoln's workplace at home was in the parlor. In the morning, he might load the stove with wood, eat breakfast, then sit in his favorite chair with his lap desk on his knees. The only sound in the room was the crackling of the fire and the scratch of his quill pen on paper. He had told her she might clean around him, and she tiptoed at these times.

One such day, when the shelf needed dusting, she found him deep in concentration. He was wearing slippers, and his hair was messy. He appeared completely absorbed in his work but he noticed her.

"Ana, did you hear a dog bit the postman?"

"No! How terrible."

"Yes," he said. "Poor dog was trying to get the taste of a lawyer out of his mouth."

He let out a high-pitched "heee" at his own joke.

The joke was the first of many, and sometimes Ana felt as if he was trying them out on her; if she laughed, then he could get a laugh out of anyone. He didn't seem to be teasing her. He appeared to want to engage with her. When he asked about her family's journey from Madeira, his whole attention was on her. That, she thought later, marked the beginning of warmth between them.

There were other times, though, when he seemed completely unaware she was in the room. He might flick his head as if a mosquito were buzzing him. Occasionally, in an abstracted state, he muttered to himself. Other times, he would get up, unfolding to his towering height, then leave the room.

There were shelves of books and a couple of stacks on the floor. Once, after he had departed for his office, she found a volume of poems by Lord Byron sitting on a table. A page was marked where the poem "To Inez" appeared. Ana read it through, hoping it was a love poem, but it held no romance. It was a sad poem, and one verse in particular struck her.

What Exile from himself can flee?
To zones, though more and more remote,
Still, still pursues, where'er I be,
The blight of life—the demon Thought.

She caught her breath. That's him! Was it terrible thoughts

that occupied him so? She didn't know, but she understood. Her mother was afflicted in the same way and just as powerless to banish whatever filled her head.

CHAPTER TWELVE

———

JUNE 1854

THERE IS ANOTHER WOMAN WHO WANTS TO MEET YOU, Bean. Mrs. Carrie Nell Alsop. She's the one I painted the tiles for."

Ana eyed her father suspiciously. "*Another* job?"

"She has a maid who does the work. What she needs sometimes is a companion. She can help you with your English and your studies; she was a teacher before she married. She's a widow lady now. Goes to the Presbyterian church. No children."

Soon enough, Ana found herself in an after-school routine with the woman in a big house on Second Street. Mrs. Alsop was, as her father had said, an old woman who was lonely. She had a British accent like the planters in Trinidad who made each sentence she spoke sound a little condescending. But she talked to Ana as if she were an adult, and for that she was grateful.

Three afternoons a week, Ana left the one-room

schoolhouse she had been attending for the past year, walked to the Alsop house, and clanked the horse head knocker. Greeted by the maid, she counted the shiny brass rods pressed into the carpet where the steps rose to the second floor and entered an open door to the library on the left where Mrs. Alsop waited.

During the mathematics lesson that followed, Ana was mostly attentive to the ticking of the big clock in the hall. But she loved reading aloud the stories that were part of every afternoon, even if Mrs. Alsop interrupted repeatedly to correct her pronunciations. At the end, there would be tea, proper eating manners, and a conversation in which the "ain't" she had picked up would be shamed out of repeating itself.

"I think highly of the Portuguese people. Decent, hard workers. And right thinking."

Ana knew by now that "right thinking" equaled "Presbyterian" in Mrs. Alsop's mind. She attended the Second Presbyterian Church, a denomination, she explained, that was formed when members of the First Presbyterian Church split off over the issue of slavery. Carrie Nell Alsop was proud of her part in the split and prouder that the Second Presbyterian Church was known as the abolitionist church.

"It's a dirty word—abolitionist—to a lot of people. They think we are unpatriotic and weird and dangerous because we want change now." She laughed. "Unpatriotic? The opposite, truly. Eccentric? Well, I suppose Erastus Wright fits that bill. For a time he had an elk that he used to pull his cart into town for errands. But dangerous? Not nearly enough.

"We are nothing new here, dear. This area was settled early on by New England abolitionists. But it was also settled by

Kentucky corn crackers and other uplanders from down South. We may live side by side in this town, but we don't always understand each other."

Ana supposed Mrs. Alsop was considered a bit strange. She wore her thin hair in stiff curls pressed around her face, as though she'd applied wallpaper paste to each swirl. Her dresses were girlish, in particular this one dress she wore, a bright green gown with coquettish flounces around her wrinkled bosom. It was a frock Beatriz would have died for.

When Ana departed, she often came away with another borrowed book and a chest full of guilt. How could she describe to her sister the luxurious vases and fabrics she saw in the Alsop house? Or to Joao the fact that a sandwich and a dish of spice drops were placed within her reach the minute she arrived in case she was feeling "peckish"? As far as they knew, she was simply getting after-school lessons.

Her father didn't speak of her privileges either. He did tell Ana, though, that Mrs. Alsop believed she had promise as a student and would be happy to pay for better schooling for her.

In late August, as they walked to the Alsop residence, Ana's father warned her mother, "It's a big fancy place."

"I have been in fine houses before. I grew up in one," her mother had replied. But standing in front of the Alsop house, Genoveva Ferreira appeared tiny and stunned.

"Aristocracy Hill, they call this neighborhood." Her father motioned to the mansions up and down the street. Even the smaller houses had grand porches with wicker chairs and trees in pots.

Directed into the drawing room by the maid, they found Mrs. Alsop waiting. Tea arrived as introductions were made, with Ana translating for her parents.

"Sangamon Female Academy," Mrs. Alsop announced. "It's where the *quality* send their children." The old woman held a paper close to her face. "Abel Estabrook is the principal. He teaches mental and moral philosophy over there. He's a good abolitionist, a good Presbyterian, and a good teacher. Listen to some of the accomplishments you will take over the time you are there. Natural sciences, mathematics, modern languages, rhetoric and literature, and drawing." She seemed almost giddy. "Oh, to be fourteen again."

Ana's brain spun as she translated the course names.

"I think French is best for a modern language, and you will need Latin too," Mrs. Alsop said. "You can get that over at Ursuline Academy after your regular classes. There is an Irish nun there who teaches Latin."

Her parents listened intently as Ana explained that Mrs. Alsop thought she could get her into the fall session at the academy starting in September and would pay for her education at both schools. Sitting on the divan beneath a chandelier, her parents were wide-eyed. Mrs. Alsop's thin, high voice warbled like the old instrument it was, making it hard for Ana to take in all she was saying.

Her father sighed. "It is very good," he said in English, then switched to Portuguese.

"He says you are very generous and kind, but he does not like me to have the Irish nun."

"Oh, I understand," Mrs. Alsop said. "You may fill your postal and police jobs with bogtrotters from Tipperary, but you don't want them to teach your children. Tell him not to be afraid. I don't know how the Irish nuns are for other subjects, but they're the best Latin teachers in town."

"It is not that," Ana translated. "We have suffered from the Catholics. He don't...he does not want one teaching me."

"Well, I wouldn't recommend it if you were going to be indoctrinated. I know of the nun through the governor. He's a Protestant and sends his daughter there. She sits out the religion classes. I'm sure we can make clear to the head nun, Mother Joseph, that we want no conversions."

Ana translated and was surprised when her mother sat up straight and spoke.

"Mother says she does not object that it's a nun," Ana said. "She was sent by her parents to a school run by nuns back in Funchal. They taught her reading and numbers and embroidery. She wants me to be educated."

"How admirable." The old lady tipped her head to Genoveva Ferreira. "I would like to tutor Ana after school to keep helping her along. She will need it at first."

Then she swept out of the room to allow the parents to confer. Ana saw the last exchange sink in for her mother and knew immediately how the proposal had been received. When Mrs. Alsop returned, she told her yes, she could attend Sangamon Female Academy. Thank you, madame. Thank you.

Out on the sidewalk, Genoveva looked back at the house. "*Que pena*," she said, putting her arm across her daughter's shoulders. *How pitiful.*

Ana knew the rest of her thoughts. *Childless and alone in that big house.*

CHAPTER THIRTEEN

MAY 1855

EMMANUEL FERREIRA HIRED A WAGON TO TAKE THE WHOLE family over to Jacksonville for a reunion. There would be people Ana had only heard about, friends who'd made the journey from Madeira to Illinois at the same time as they had. Packed into the wagon, the whole family buzzed with excitement as they rumbled past stretches of prairie alternating with woods cut through by rushing streams. Blossoms dotted the trees along the ravines. The ocean of waving grasses running out to the edge of the blue sky caused everyone in the wagon to fall silent.

As they approached Jacksonville, new farms rose up. Split-rail fences, zigzagging like earthworms, surrounded a few homesteads. The countryside took on a look of prosperity.

Sitting next to Beatriz, bumping along in the sun with the wind yanking strands of hair from her braids, Ana felt warmth flow into her arms and legs. None of them had enjoyed any periods of leisure since they'd arrived in Illinois six years ago. There were no cross words today.

They toured Jacksonville, which had its own Madeira neighborhood and a "Portuguese Hill" to boot, but they were eager to get to the farm where the gathering was being held. They had no sooner climbed down from the wagon than a crowd of laughing, weeping women were embracing them and pulling them toward a group of tables under the trees. Nearby, men were cooking pork over a brazier. Laid out on the tables were cheeses, fried maize flecked with green, *caldo verde*, and a catfish and onion stew. As they ate, Portuguese flowed among the adults, English among the children.

Almost immediately after she'd finished her dinner, Beatriz was swept off by a young farmer, the owner's son, to tour the house and barns. The fellow had been talking her ear off since she sat down at the table.

"We broke up sixty acres—two dollars a day, hired out," he said. "Harvested twenty dollars per acre of wheat clear of all expenses such as plowing, which is a dollar an acre, seventy-five cents per acre for sowing and harrowing. You got to trench plow for sweet potatoes in April."

"You grow sweet potatoes? I love sweet potatoes!" Beatriz purred. She threw back the curls framing her face—curls she'd suffered into her hair by sleeping with knotted socks all over her head. Why was she gazing at this oafish, boring boy and feigning interest?

Ana glanced at her mother and noticed her brows go up. "These Portuguese over here are getting rich," she whispered when Beatriz was gone.

Two nights in a row, they sang and danced under the stars. Her mother knew all the dances, all the steps. She threw her arms in the air, snapped her fingers, hopped, and swirled her skirt around from one partner to the next. An accordionist, a drummer, and a guitarist played one tune after another as her father and the rest of the crowd sang Portuguese songs at the top of their lungs.

The picnic lasted three days. Some slept outside, while the Ferreiras and others were put up by Madeirans in the town. At the farm, Ana ran with the young gang of children in and out of barns, hiding and seeking on the second day until her legs began to ache. In the afternoon, she found her parents at one of the tables and lay down on the bench near them. She felt oddly tired, her hips aching. Lying on the bench, she watched the young ones running around in the bright sunlight. Waves of wind gushed through the lacework trees, sending leaf shadows skittering across the lawn, dappling the children's heads with light, now on, now off. The day seemed dreamy. A silly French lyric she learned at school kept eddying around in her head. *Cadet Rousselle has three houses. They have not beams or rafters.*

Ana shook her head to throw it off, closed her eyes, and listened to the grown-up talk around the table. A man from a nearby county had come to the gathering to visit friends. He was one of them, a Portuguese, he said, and was in a terrible predicament. His name was William Dungey. From what she could gather, he had moved from Tennessee with his parents a few years earlier and had married a local girl after he arrived in Illinois. About four years after the marriage, his wife's brother took a disliking to him.

"New Year's Day, he went through town calling me 'Black Bill' and telling folks I'm one-fourth Negro. Do you know what that means?" the man was saying. "I could lose everything."

Ana lifted her head to look at Dungey. His skin was dark brown, the color of a chestnut. He looked to be in his twenties.

"I was set to buy a farm before all the Black Bill business. But the seller backed off." The man shook his head. "If I can't buy property, what am I to do? How can I farm?"

There was a murmur around the table. "To be colored is dangerous," someone muttered.

The minister from the Portuguese church in Jacksonville broke in. "I read of a free colored man who got kidnapped by slave catchers and taken to Paducah, where they sold him." The group fell silent.

"I am working with a lawyer," Dungey said. "It will cost, but I have no choice. He's pressing a case of slander against my wife's brother."

"What is the lawyer's name?" someone asked.

"Abraham Lincoln."

Ana was surprised when she heard the name. And then she felt alarm. Her father's skin was already darkened by the spring sun. By August, he would not be much lighter than William Dungey.

On the way back to Springfield, her parents discussed what Dungey had told the gathering and then they spoke about slave catchers.

"I couldn't pick out one on the street," her mother said.

"I saw some once." Ana bit her lip as soon as she'd uttered the words.

"Where were you? How did you know they were slave catchers?"

Ana held her breath now, horrified at what she'd just blurted out. "On the street, near the square. I was with Cal. It was a long time ago…"

At home that night, unplaiting Ana's hair, her mother spoke softly but firmly. "We do not want you to spend time with Cal anymore."

"Why? She's my friend!"

"There are other girls…at your school."

Ana stopped her mother's hands and turned to face her. "Cal is my best friend."

"For now, you must stay away." Her mother's voice was stern. "Do they teach you the laws at your school?"

Ana began to weep. "Her skin is whiter than mine. Some of us are brown. Doesn't that make us colored?"

"We are not Negro."

"Listen to me, Ana," her father said, stepping in. "We have been through too much already. I *like* Cal. But she could be rounded up by some slave owner looking for his property—and you with her. She's mulatto."

Ana knew the word *mulatto*. She was surprised at her father, who ordinarily did not worry.

"Cal has a paper that proves she is free." Ana knew her friend wore it in a little cloth envelope on a ribbon around her neck that she kept tucked under her dress. It had printing on it and a gold seal.

"Slave catchers can toss those papers in the river."

"Were we property in Trinidad?" she asked after a silence.

"No," her mother replied.

"Were we considered white or colored in Trinidad?"

Her father emitted a little laugh. "*Nem carne nem peixe.*"
Neither meat nor fish.

"We were white," her mother said.

"Well, Portuguese people are considered white," her father
corrected. "And we were Europeans like the landowners and
planters, but we were laborers like the African and Chinese
and Indian workers. Some of us managed to move up from the
fields and become shopkeepers or servants or gardeners. But
no, we were not really considered entirely 'white' since we had
almost no money. We were powerless. Still, we were treated
better than some."

An old memory flashed in Ana's mind. She was in a market
in Trinidad and had wandered away from her mother. A dark-
skinned woman held her hand and comforted her until she was
found. The woman's forehead was marked with a single red dot.
Her wrist was heavy with bracelets.

"The descendants of the original African people who had
been brought to Trinidad, they were not happy to have immigrants like us coming in to compete for jobs. They never saw us as
a class above them," her father added. "Many felt superior to us."

"Did we have to get special papers when we moved here?"
Ana said.

"No, no."

The bleeding began that week. She had been warned of it by
her mother. *You are becoming a woman.* But it brought upon her
a terrible sense of shame. It felt like a punishment.

How had Beatriz kept the wretched secret to herself all this time? Ana thought then of the wooden box each of them had been given long ago by their father for storing school supplies and such. Beatriz was often furtive in opening and closing her box.

Lately, Beatriz had become even more secretive. During the reunion, Ana had come upon her and the young farmer kissing in a dark corner of the barn. It dawned on her she hardly knew who her sister really was. Could Beatriz at seventeen already be picturing herself as a farmer's wife? She was only two years older than Ana, who could not imagine wanting for herself a life of feeding hungry farm hands or the cold loneliness of a farmhouse in winter. From the day Ana had arrived in town, she had loved the daily bustle of Springfield. Until this week, she could not picture where else she'd rather be. Now, though, she wished she were a million miles away so she would not have to tell Cal she couldn't see her anymore.

At night in bed, steeped in regret over blurting out her remark about slave catchers, she tried to talk to Beatriz but got no response. She suspected her sister was only pretending sleep. She prayed furiously instead. *I will read the Bible. I will be nicer to Joao. I will work harder at home.*

The next few days as she walked to school, she feared running into Cal. She could not think what she could say.

CHAPTER FOURTEEN

JUNE 1855

I GOT NEW SHOES." CAL PUT OUT HER FOOT AND MODELED FOR Ana. They were standing on the southeast corner of the square. Ana had not seen her in almost two weeks.

"They're nice." Ana was glad to have a reason to avert her gaze from Cal's smiling face. The boots were ordinary, brown lace-ups, but they were new, not hand-me-downs.

"Nothing special." Cal shrugged. "Mr. Donnegan made them."

Ana looked up. "Cal, I need to talk to you about something. My father got an idea we could be stolen off the streets by slave catchers. My mother...she says I can't...can't be with you."

Cal flinched. "You told, didn't you?" Her eyes penetrated Ana's.

"Not everything. It was an accident."

Cal stared at Ana as if she were stupid. "I'm *free*. I have a certificate."

"I know! I explained that, but…"

"I thought I could trust you." Cal's voice was shot through with disgust. She made a waving motion with her hand to say, "It doesn't matter." But her mouth, tight-lipped now, was quivering. She brushed past Ana and walked away.

An ache expanded in Ana's throat. She wanted to curl into a ball in her bed, but there was no going home. Mrs. Alsop, or "Alsop" as Beatriz called her, was waiting for her to show up for the weekly dinner they shared. She walked on, fighting to keep the tears in.

Alsop was pouring port in the pantry when Ana arrived and had questions prepared. "What did your teacher say about your paper on Walter Scott?"

Ana answered as briefly as she dared. She'd begun to feel that she was the subject of an experiment. Can a peasant girl be made into a scholar, a person of significance? The question brought on more weeping. Alsop came up behind her and touched her back gently.

"What is it, girl?"

Ana sobbed for a minute before the story poured out.

Alsop handed her a small glass of port. "Surely you've tasted this by now," she said. "Come into the library." When they were settled on the sofa, Alsop said, "Fear makes fools of us all." She patted Ana's hand. "People want to blend in, forget where they came from. They change their names, throw off their old ways. They want to be *American*, where everyone is supposed to be equal. But where does that leave them? They're nowhere near the top of the pecking order, but they don't want to be at the bottom. We all need somebody else to be at the bottom so we can say, 'Well, I am not *that*.' Your Mr. Dungey must claim his right to his freedom by proving he is not Negro. By *law*. I find that a damning state of affairs."

Alsop downed her port in a couple of swallows and sent Ana to fetch the bottle.

"Oh, we're all in a pickle," she continued. "I'm sorry to tell you that your people have come to a land in a turmoil of its own making. Your father is a good man. I have talked to him. He does not have a closed mind. Like your mother, he is afraid."

Ana settled back into the sofa. Alsop kept talking, about the South not freeing their slaves, cotton supplies going to mills in New England and England.

"It's a financial arrangement that we do not protest when we dress ourselves each morning. Nor do my fine countrymen. They are some of the biggest importers of Southern cotton." On she rattled about the English freeing slaves in their colonies. "It happened thirty years ago, and I thought that spelled the beginning of the end of it. Of course, I was wrong. The English are culpable, all right. But so are the Dutch."

Ana half listened to the old woman. The taste of port in her mouth didn't help the sadness. And the wine only made Alsop jabber on.

"They were in the trade. *And* the French…" She shook her head. "I'm sorry to say, but your ancestors were slave traders too."

"The Portuguese? When?"

"Oh, a hundred years ago."

Anger rose up in Ana's chest. There was something in Alsop she hated, her superior knowledge that she could wield like a club. Why was she telling her this now, in the wake of her fight with Cal?

"It's not your fault, Ana. We all trail ghosts. What matters is what we do now."

CHAPTER FIFTEEN

———

Trudging to her house, angry at herself for hurting Cal, angry at Alsop too, Ana longed for some corner in which to huddle. She passed a restaurant and glimpsed people dining by the front window. She wished that she might go inside and have a table to herself where she could drink tea and be left alone. *Pure dream, Ana.* She had no private corners, certainly not in a house that felt so strange these days.

Her mother had come alive at the picnic in Jacksonville, and they'd had a glimpse of the bright woman she'd once been, but now she had returned to her peculiar, removed self. Maybe she had always been a bundle of contradictions and Ana had just begun to notice it. Here was an educated woman who was superstitious, a kind woman who cursed. Lately her anger had lessened, but when she was not working, she often holed up in her tiny sewing room on the sun porch of their house. Their father worried his wife was going crazy. Genoveva Ferreira had stopped going to church with the rest of them. The whole family felt out of kilter.

"Why is she doing this?" Ana whispered to Beatriz.

"Doing what?"

"Hiding. Mama has quit the family."

"Can't bear the sight of you, I guess." Beatriz, who had taught her to read in Portuguese, who had bathed Ana in a metal tub and picked lice out of her hair in Trinidad, had recently turned into an enemy. Today, she was wearing a corset she'd bought with her cleaning money. With her waist cinched and her large breasts pressing against the bodice of her dress, she looked like a fashion illustration from a *Godey's* magazine. She sat in front of a looking glass, arranging her hair according to a picture from the newspaper.

"She used to sing to Joao," Ana said. "She used to cook *bolo do caco* almost every night. She cleaned the house before this stupid *saudade*."

Saudade. It was a word Ana heard on the porch stoop at night, a word her people used sometimes. It meant missing, longing. She didn't think of her Portuguese neighbors as unhappy people. They liked to laugh. But when Madeira came up, they talked in a dreamy, wistful way about the happiness they had known there. They all knew that happiness was forever lost to them, yet they kept yearning to be back in it, if only in their conversations.

"I know she misses Madeira, but I wish she would come out. Joao and his friends are raiding orchards after dark, getting into fistfights. Yesterday he wrapped horse dung in a newspaper and lit it. Right on the porch of that old man on the corner."

Beatriz knew that Joao was running with wild boys. She'd even intervened when she caught them exploding firecrackers near the square. But she kept her mouth shut when he skipped school. She had secrets of her own, and Joao probably knew some of them.

They heard rustling in the bedroom and instantly stopped talking. The door opened, and Genoveva Ferreira came out of the darkness. She looked shorter to Ana, as if she'd been shrinking little by little on the other side of the door. She had always been plump and round-faced, with heavy breasts and a low-to-the-ground solidness, but her mouth curved down now, and drooping lids nearly curtained her brown eyes. Gone was the fierce gaze she'd always used to freeze them in the midst of their quarreling.

"Where is Joao?" she asked in Portuguese. Always it was Portuguese. Six years in America and she still knew almost no English.

Ana wanted to shout at her mother, *If you don't learn English, they will always treat you like a stupid person. Like a child.* Instead, she said, "Out with his friends."

"Go find him." She looked hazily then at the stove. "Rice?"

"Yes, Mama," Beatriz said.

Ana remembered her mother's dazed look in the midst of English speakers when she worked at the market but not in her own home, not until lately. Before, she'd run her house with a strict hand, loved her children with her lips and with arms that were warm and comforting as blankets. Fed them with hands that made delicious meals. Her parts were not working now. Her mother stood as if on a strange street corner, confused, then went back through the bedroom door and was swallowed up again by the darkness inside.

"She acts like she is sick. Like she is dying."

"No, no. More like she is going crazy," Beatriz said, tapping her temple.

Their befuddled father had suggested the same.

"She cries in there." Ana had heard her, seen the puffy eyes. "She was all right when we first came here."

When both their parents were out of the house, the slapping and hair pulling would pick up again. Beatriz managed to get out often enough that she was not around when the real trouble started. No, Joao was Ana's real trouble. She'd had to look after him almost since the day they'd come to America. Now, at twelve, he taunted her, picked fights. He had grown much bigger than she and no longer fit under the bed where she chased him. One day last week, he didn't run. They were outside, standing between houses in a patch of grass. He turned on her and, with a fierce slug to her gut, knocked her to the ground. She lay on the grass unable to even gasp as he walked away. No air would come in. *I am dying.* When she finally pulled in wisps of air, she rolled herself over and got to her knees.

From now on, she would call Joao Joe.

On a hot afternoon, looking for a needle and thread in her mother's belongings, Ana lifted up the cotton cloth covering her sewing table. Underneath, she found no needle. She found instead a statue of the virgin with a vase in front of it. She was taken by surprise and thought it must be something her mother had bought to remind her of her family. But the fresh flowers in the vase were a clear sign. *This is an altar.* Beside the little shrine, she found rosary beads with a wooden cross attached.

"She's praying to the virgin." Emmanuel Ferreira gasped when Ana led him to the shrine.

She had brought him to the little altar to explain to him why her mother was in such anguish. It was to *explain*, she would tell her sister later. Never to betray.

When the front door opened and closed, they heard footfalls. Emmanuel led Genoveva to the sun porch, seized the rosary, lifted up the painted chalk figure of Mary, and hauled it in a fury into the kitchen. Ana saw her mother's sad face turn to a mask of panic as she followed. In a flash, her father had the virgin's head in his grasp, her mother holding the feet. There was a back-and-forth struggle that Ana would remember fifty years later. She watched, fearing the statue would break in half, until Genoveva Ferreira wrested the virgin from his arms, fell to the floor, and cradled it like a baby.

"After all we have been through?" her father was shouting. He hurled the rosary at her. "You are worshipping a clay statue?"

There was screaming and slamming of doors. Ana went to the space she shared with Beatriz. "Always being the good girl," her sister hissed. Ana covered her ears with a pillow. When she lifted it, she heard Beatriz say, "*Traidor.*" Snitch.

The day after the incident, her mother took Joe's bed in the parlor, set up her altar there, and curtained it off. Now Joe slept with his father.

The first night her mother stayed in the curtained space, Ana could hear her mumbling. She was singsonging in Portuguese a verse that sounded part charm, part prayer.

Cut for her the scarlet rose,
Let her eat it e doi e proi
With salt from the sea
And water from the spring
And herbs from the hill,
With the power of God and the Virgin Mary
And all the saints,
In praise of St. Peter and St. Paul,
In praise of St. Silvester,
Let all that I do be of avail.

Through the doorway, Ana saw her angry father sitting at the kitchen table, reading the Bible. Joe tiptoed around his father and out of the room.

Ana shivered. The house felt as if it was haunted. God-haunted.

CHAPTER SIXTEEN

Come, Mr. Gourley. Come sleep with us tonight!"
Mary Lincoln stood in the dark backyard, dressed in her nightgown and robe, hollering. She had awakened once again, terrified by dreams and strange sounds and without her husband, who was off riding the circuit. It was wrong to bother Mr. Gourley in the middle of the night, but her fear outdid her embarrassment. It was not the first time she had tromped across their adjoining backyards to beg for James Gourley's help.

In the morning, her eyes still blurry from sleep and her waking thoughts fogged with regret, Mary listened at the door that separated her new bedroom from Abraham's. She crept out into the hallway then, and finding her husband's bedroom door ajar, she peered into it. There was James Gourley, minus his boots and hat but otherwise attired in the worn shirt and canvas trousers he had arrived in the night before, a kind neighbor and the town's deputy sheriff to boot, an innocent man but now a codefendant in possible scandal. He looked most peculiar in Mr. Lincoln's fine four-poster bed, her one true indulgence as far as refined furniture went.

Oh God. She'd have to make things right with the Gourleys. Again. They were good-hearted backyard neighbors with whom they shared a milk cow. To cause an estrangement would be a mistake.

Mary tiptoed back to her own room to dress, where Willie and Tad were curled up on their trundle bed next to hers. If she appeared put together this morning, she might erase the mortifying picture she'd made last night. She would cook a big breakfast, feed the man and his wife and their children—ham, eggs, grits, hoecakes. Somehow persuade them that last night had been one more amusing aberration.

"Go over and fetch Mrs. Gourley and the children," she told her frowsy-headed five-year-old when Willie opened his eyes and rubbed them with small fists. "Wake up Tad first and tell him Mama says to get dressed. We're all going to have a fine breakfast together. Quick now."

When Mrs. Gourley arrived at the back door, she was frowning. "The nanny is gone, isn't she?" she asked impatiently. Mary could see she was put out.

Lucy Gourley was a polite woman who was friendly enough. She was an upright Christian, not given to gossip, but Mary was quite certain it would be Lucy rather than her husband who would spread the word in the neighborhood about the disruption last night.

"The girl is gone," Mary said, "but the ladder is still in the yard. Any one of those men might lift it to climb into the house. It's far too heavy for me to move."

Lucy shot a look at her husband.

"I'll move it to our yard today, Mary," James Gourley said, "so there's no reason to be afraid."

A year and a half ago, the pert and clean-looking Irish girl named Meg whom Mary hired had seemed a miracle given how hard it was to find help—until the night a few weeks ago when Mary woke to a loud thud. She checked the boys, who were sleeping soundly, then cracked open the door to the hired girl's room and found a strange man standing with Meg beside the open window. "Get out, both of you! This minute!" she'd screamed.

Afterward, she realized the man had propped the ladder with a thud against the north side of the house, next to the nanny's bedroom, which happened to be right next to Mary's own bedroom. How often had that happened? How many men had come and gone without notice? It infuriated Mary to think of it.

Once she fired the girl, she had hired a neighbor youth to sleep at her house. And sleep he did, through thunderclaps and wagons rumbling by at two in the morning, through clattering shutters and windy moans. No amount of money, and certainly not the ten cents she paid him, was going to buy the peace of mind she craved to get through the night.

She had never thought of herself as a fearful person, but the frights that seized her lately made her very eyeballs pulse. And it was the absence of her husband, as usual, that seemed to set off her panic. Abraham had been gone for weeks now. She had to consult her diary to keep track this time, and the longing for him was almost unbearable—the absence of his long body next to hers, his rough, stubbly cheek on hers. There was nothing soft about him. Maybe the span of skin on his belly, that was all.

When they slept together, his large, muscled arms and bent legs encircled her like a nest. It was the only time she felt truly safe at night. When he was gone, her body's alarm woke her at two or three a.m. to listen for sounds of intruders. It was an ugly trick she played on herself most nights—cautionary worrying. If she was alert, even as she slept, she believed she could keep herself and her children safe.

"It takes its toll," Lucy was saying now, as if she'd read Mary's mind.

Lucy's washed-out eyes blinked at her across the table. Next to her, her husband looked half asleep.

"I am grateful for your friendship. It's a mercy to be among such helping neighbors," Mary said, hoping Lucy remembered Mary's own tour of duty as a wet nurse for Mrs. Dallman's newborn when the lady was bedfast with sickness.

"Those men won't be back, Mary. The girl hasn't been here for weeks."

"The sounds…" Mary muttered.

"We was up all night with that wind," Lucy said. "The cow's bawling woke Martha."

Mary felt a wave of shame, looking at the child Mr. Gourley had left behind to sleep in her house. Martha's fat little hand was mopping up syrup with her last hoecake.

To add a full second floor to their home had been a fantasy until the inheritance after her father's death made it possible. Her husband had been against an expansion, but she had persisted and arranged to have the addition built while he was out riding the circuit. When he returned home, he had made a joke of it, asking a neighbor if he knew where Old Abe Lincoln's house was around these parts. She was not amused.

How she'd reveled when those four new bedrooms were finished. Just now, though, the new upstairs story seemed a reproach, as if vanity had overtaken her judgment. It was a modest expansion, really. Connected rooms for Mr. Lincoln and herself, a bedroom for Robert that the smaller boys would inhabit when their big brother went off to school, and a small maid's room. Even Mr. Gourley had encouraged it in one of their over-the-fence discussions.

"You can get a girl to live with you," he'd said.

Well, she had a lovely home now, with a fine second floor. But what she longed for most was her husband to be in it. It seemed he had been away half the time since they were married.

They had lived a life of near poverty after their marriage. She remembered the difficulty of birthing and tending little Robert in a boarding room at the Globe Tavern for a full year and the following year in a tiny rental before they managed to buy their cottage on Eighth Street. Those were trying times for her and for Abraham too, who was away riding the circuit for weeks on end. He was one of the very few lawyers who went to all eight counties in a circuit, riding over the rudest country roads, stuffed into a make-do farm wagon with a judge and other lawyers. During trials, he usually managed one decent meal a day at a local tavern where he would be eating humble fare with the judge, the jury, other lawyers, witnesses, people out on bail, the accused, and the plaintiff, the lot of them smelling like…well, she didn't want to think about it. Sometimes she wondered if it was all worth it. And the cases could be ridiculous: crop damage incurred from a neighboring hog; arguments over whose fault it was that foot rot took the lives of a man's sheep; who was the true owner of a litter of pigs. Traveling on the road, they stopped here and there for the night. They slept two men to a bed, often four beds to a room.

When he came home to their cottage in those days, she drew a bath for him. A hearty dinner was on the stove. If the children were awake, he put them to bed and she welcomed him to theirs. His homecomings were precious then as they were precious now. He still traveled just as much, and she still spent too many days alone.

If the new second floor seemed pretentious to neighbors, it wasn't. Life had gotten easier over the years, but she still scrubbed the mud off her own floors, sewed and patched the boys' clothes, cooked constantly. And while the other men on the block came home at night to shovel coal into stoves and attend to heavy tasks, she had to find a man to help or do it herself because her husband was absent. She would never grow accustomed to the loneliness of it. The year Eddie died, she'd added up the nights her husband was gone—a hundred and seventy-five.

She'd gotten pregnant a month after Eddie's death, and it had pulled her out of her sorrow some. But more than one sleepless night, she had huddled in her bed with Robert, who missed his father fiercely, both of them wailing together.

She suspected she had a reputation as a woman who could not manage her house. Or her emotions. Her temper had gotten the better of her in front of neighbors and friends, and she found herself regularly making amends for a wicked remark or a show of anger. But who among the women she knew could do better if they had a missing husband? Who among them, left alone at night, would not imagine intruders at the sound of a thump?

When demons galloped and squealed in her head after dark, she was calm if her husband was there. He understood about demons because he had his own. They sat on his chest, as hers did, sometimes all day long, refusing to get up.

The morning after she had prepared breakfast for the Gourleys as a peace offering, Mary lay in bed waiting to feel how the day would go. No elephant's foot on her chest. Abraham was coming home! She would tell him about Mr. Gourley coming over and they would laugh. Abraham didn't care a fig about appearances.

"You need to find another house girl to help with the little codgers," he said. The boys were in bed, and they'd settled on the sofa. Mary rested her head on her husband's chest and felt it shake with a laugh. "As for Jim Gourley," he said, "it stretches the mind to picture him the lothario."

She laughed then too, and her eyes watered. "Sometimes I don't know what takes me over…"

"Poor Molly," he said and ran his hand over her hair.

It had been only three days since he'd returned, but the relief of having him in the house was a warm, ongoing comfort. At the beginning, her family had not understood what she saw in him. Her sisters didn't seem to realize that, while she had married Abraham Lincoln for his mind and moral character, what drew her first was his humor. No one was quicker or wittier with repartee. She loved the stories he brought home. And he laughed at hers. He found it hilarious when she told a thumper and got people to actually believe it.

Now when they laughed together, his refusals to listen to her disappeared, and the stiletto words she immediately regretted—God, he was *impenetrable* sometimes!—were forgotten. Every time they laughed together after a terrible period, it felt as if the slate had been wiped clean and they were starting over again.

"You're right. I do need another girl," she said. "But it's so hard to find good help. And I've had enough of the wild Irish. I like the new Portuguese girl, but I can't ask her to work more than Saturdays. Did you know she's getting an actual education like I had when I was her age? All the subjects apparently, thanks to Carrie Alsop. Even Latin over at the new convent."

"I'll be."

"In a couple of years, she will make a fine companion for the boys. I think I can train her."

CHAPTER SEVENTEEN

1856

For Ana, a working Saturday for Mrs. Lincoln began with collecting a pile of newspapers from the *Illinois State Journal* office. She made a habit of taking a few moments to scan the headlines and any other papers in the pile—the *Springfield Register* and the Chicago and Louisville papers that came by train. These Ana hauled in a canvas bag down South Eighth to the Lincolns' house, where painters were already working on the second story by the time she arrived.

She had been hired to clean but lately found herself caring for Willie and three-year-old Tad when needed. Both boys were sweet, bright, and thoroughly spoiled. Tad was slow to speak, and when he did, he could not be understood very well. She thought his tongue could not shape words right. Perhaps that was what frustrated him, for he threw tantrums that could only be calmed by his father or his mother when she returned from some errand or visit.

Willie was altogether easier. He was clearly very bright and loved to be read to. Ana quickly learned that a story could save the day with both boys dropping their troubles for a good tale. Willie liked to tell his own. Together they made picture books with words. His sweet generosity showed often, as when he had a gift for her upon her arrival—a new drawing or some funny little verse he had composed. It was easy to see Willie as the golden child.

Robert, the oldest boy, was often visiting a friend elsewhere or studying with his tutor. He was a shy one, thirteen years old like her brother Joe, three years younger than Ana, and old enough to be independent of her when she was there. He seemed to be a lonely outsider in the family—too old to frolic with the little boys, too young to have much influence in the life of the house.

When Mrs. Lincoln had guests, Ana answered the front door. She was learning whom to admit or reject. From time to time, there was a knock and Mrs. Lincoln would say, "Send him away." Or she'd peek from behind the curtain and say, "It's Enid Hufnagel. Don't let her in, but do accept her basket." Ana hated having to reject the woman, who was big and square as a man and galled at her dismissal. Other times, it was a top-hatted gentleman with a request or a child asking for one of the Lincoln boys.

When the callers were dispatched, Mrs. Lincoln went back to one or all of her sisters, who often enough were ensconced in the back parlor. She usually had Ana put out a tray of sweets with the tea and she offered around the cakes. It was Mrs. L who mostly ate them. "Cannot resist," she would say. Ana knew this. She had fetched big bags of sugar from the grocer for Mrs. Lincoln's baking and had witnessed her consume a plate of cookies over the course of a day.

"She's quite good," Mary said once to her sisters, and Ana realized she was talking about her. "She's a far cry from the others I've had."

The Lincolns used their parlors differently. Mary entertained in the front parlor; Mr. Lincoln read and wrote in the back parlor. Ana had observed that Mr. Lincoln scribbled his thoughts on pieces of paper, folded them, and put them in the lining of his hat.

One morning, sweeping the back parlor, Ana noticed a couple of those papers left behind after Mr. Lincoln clomped up the steps to dress. She picked up one note that was written on the back of a restaurant bill of fare.

If A can prove, however conclusively, that he may of right enslave B, why may not B snatch the same argument and prove equally that he may enslave A? You say A is white and B is black. It is color, then; the lighter having the right to enslave the darker? Take care. By this rule you are to be the slave of the first man you meet with a fairer skin than your own. You do not mean color exactly? You mean the whites are intellectually the superiors of the blacks and therefore have the right to enslave them? Take care again. By this rule you are to be the slave of the first man you meet with an intellect superior to your own.

She heard his footsteps and quickly replaced the note on the table. Earlier in the morning, he'd appeared in old slippers and baggy trousers held up by one suspender. He came down the stairs now nicely dressed for work. He folded the notes of paper, put them in his tall hat, picked up his carpetbag, and quietly left the house.

Ana understood something about him in that moment. Mr. Lincoln believed that slavery was a hideous evil, as she heard so many times in her church and in her own home. But he was trying to build a fort of truth apart from religious belief, a fort built of logic. He was looking at the subject from various angles, apparently trying to find a winning argument against defenders of slavery.

She thought of a conversation she'd had with Mrs. Alsop. *They try to trick you into thinking slavery is an old inherited custom that will die on its own.* Like some old farm equipment that will be replaced by a better system one day. That was how the founding fathers rationalized it. They knew it was wrong. Did they also know it would never die on its own?

"Thirty-five years ago, we had something called the Missouri Compromise," Alsop had explained. "Maine wanted to enter the Union, but Southern legislators would agree only if a slaveholding state entered at the same time to balance things out. So the two sides made a deal. In exchange for outlawing slavery in territories north of the thirty-sixth parallel, Missouri was admitted as a slaveholding state.

"That balancing arrangement held firm until two years ago. The west started to look mighty attractive to people like our own Senator Douglas. He wanted a railroad that would pass through Chicago to be built through the Nebraska territory, which was north of the line dividing slaveholding and free states. But Southern senators were against that *whole* territory being free, so Douglas made a lot of compromises. The territory was split in two, creating Kansas and Nebraska."

Mrs. Alsop had paused. "Do you follow me, child?"

"Yes."

"Douglas argued that once a territory became a state, its settlers should vote for whether they wanted it to be for or against slavery. He's gone around claiming it's a sacred right for people in each state to govern themselves. Popular sovereignty, he calls it."

She had let out a great sigh. "Well, slaveholders have poured into Kansas so they can vote it into a proslavery state, and so have abolitionists, and there has been hell to pay ever since. There's blood all over Kansas territory, and it's still not a state."

Alsop had looked her squarely in the eyes. "This Kansas-Nebraska Act has opened up the whole national territory to slavery. Have you learned about this at your school?"

"Not really."

"I suppose they think girls needn't know about such matters," she sniffed. "But everyone needs to know. Douglas is dangerous; he's slick. He makes 'popular sovereignty' sound legitimate. We need to get rid of him, but it will take a giant to unhorse him."

CHAPTER EIGHTEEN

MARCH 1857

"POUND THE SOFA WITH THE CARPET BEATER," MARY CALLED from the kitchen. "The boys have made it a dustbin."

Tad and Willie used the horsehair upholstery for its slippery quality. It was one of the few good pieces of furniture the family owned. The boys were not supposed to even enter the parlors unaccompanied but play instead in the sitting room. Nevertheless, when she wasn't looking, Willie and Tad would rush in from outdoors and slide their filthy little selves down from the top of it to the floor. Fido's affection for the sofa didn't help either.

"My sisters are due in an hour, and they will not want to plant their fine bottoms on it in its present condition," Mary said as she joined Ana in the back parlor. "It's only my sisters, but Elizabeth keeps a spotless house. She has a brocatelle sofa that looks un-sat upon. Frances and Ann are the same. Oh, that reminds me. Frances just planted a shrub out front, and it looks half-dead. Go water it before you do anything, Ana. Maybe it will perk up before she gets here." Thankfully, a couple of lonely primroses Frances had put in had made it their business to bloom. There was that at least.

She loved them all, she did. If Elizabeth was bossy, she was also generous to a fault. She was the first to move to Springfield, right after marrying Ninian when he was a law student back in Kentucky. Ninian Edwards was the son of an Illinois governor, which accounted for his aristocratic airs. He'd made no objections when Elizabeth invited Mary to occupy their spare bedroom. She could remember even now the bitter desperation she'd felt at eighteen to escape her stepmother's miserable household. Elizabeth had saved her and she'd never forgotten that.

Oh, the soirees Ninian and her sister had hosted, full of gay young women rustling about in silk taffeta, chatting with eligible bachelors. Elizabeth, in her sparkling way, greeting guests in French as they poured into the enormous parlor in her Aristocracy Hill home. It was magical really, with the gold-banded china glimmering in the soft light of ambergris candles. Mary had felt beautiful and bright and somehow powerful at those soirees. To have young men hanging on her words, surprised at her political knowledge—those were sweet moments to revisit.

Elizabeth had been appalled that Mary had fallen in love with such an uncouth person as Abraham Lincoln. His twang revealed where he had come from—country poverty. They never would have found a way to match up in Kentucky. They wouldn't have crossed paths. But since they were courting in Springfield, Elizabeth apparently felt the need to uphold the Kentucky Todd values and discourage the relationship.

It was true Abraham Lincoln cared nothing for clothes, and in those days, his coat was unacquainted with a whisk broom. And that horrible, faded old green umbrella with the broken-off handle, his name sewn on the awful thing like an advertisement! Yes, he needed some work, but Mary hated it when people suggested he was homely. She thought him truly handsome in the face. And while his clothing had put off Springfield's belles, it was their loss and her gain. She had discovered, in due time, that beneath his poorly dressed surface was a youthful body. The veins in his forearms rose up under his skin like those of a carpenter or a railroad man who lived by his hands. He was remarkably strong for a skinny man.

Even though Abraham had served in the U.S. House of Representatives, Mary sometimes thought Elizabeth still believed she had married down. One look at the filthy sofa today would confirm that opinion. Well, maybe her standards had fallen a bit with four reckless males and a dog in the house. Her husband was as oblivious to mud prints as her sons.

Yet Elizabeth had so comforted Mary when Abraham backed out of their engagement. For a full year, until he stepped up, she had done her best to wrangle new prospects into her parlor while Mary mooned for the unkempt lawyer. Elizabeth and Ninian had been stunned when Mary told them that they would be married at Reverend Dresser's home and asked if they could come. "No!" Ninian had insisted. "Absolutely not. You must be married here." Elizabeth, seven months round with child, was faced with the biggest entertaining challenge of her life. Somehow all the convivial Kentucky hostess niceties she'd stored in her elegant cranium went into action.

In a matter of hours, a beautiful dinner was laid out for
thirty guests. There had been no time for a traditional maca-
roon pyramid. Frances baked a cake that wouldn't feed everybody, so Elizabeth ordered up some gingerbread loaves that
sat in the middle of the table, pretending they belonged at a
wedding.

Frances was the second sister and first to live with Elizabeth
and Ninian in Springfield. Elizabeth reeled in a doctor for
her. Mary had come next. Then came Ann, knowing that the
Edwardses' house was *the* place for a Todd girl to find a husband, which she did.

The four Todd sisters all lived in Springfield now, but
today Mary most wanted to see their half sister Emilie, who
was back in town for a visit. The previous year, Emilie had
lived for a whole winter in Elizabeth's guest bedroom in the
Todd tradition. Her beloved father, having sired seven children by Mary's mother and finally—Sweet Jesus in heaven—
killing her with the last one, had gone on to sire another *nine*
more by the new wife, Betsy Humphreys, whose torments and
flood of babies finally drove Mary out of the grand Lexington
house.

Of all those half siblings, Emilie—this pretty girl eighteen
years younger than she, this little sister she had grown to love—
seemed one redeeming result of her father's second marriage.
Emilie reminded Mary of herself at that age. Emilie was newly
married to Benjamin Hardin Helm—a West Point graduate,
a circuit-riding lawyer, a son of a governor, and a native of
the Knob Creek area of Kentucky where Abraham had been
born—and her choice of a husband was a shoo-in for Mary.

She loved him sight unseen. And now Little Sister was coming
to see her. She hadn't forgotten her big sister.

"Before I came to Springfield, girls used to put a light in the
front window to let the young men know they were receiving
callers. That is, if the mud wasn't too thick. In those days, the
town wasn't the Elysium it is today," Mary said dryly. "But by
the time I arrived, things had changed. It was Ninian who had
to *invite* the caller."

Emilie's face, framed by a bonnet with a large satin ribbon
at her throat, turned to her. The girl had style, and she had their
father's eyes. "Ninian did the same thing for me, bless his heart.
You were all so gracious. And you especially, Elizabeth. You certainly threw enough parties for me when I was here."

"She's the supreme hostess," Mary said.

"Oh, we all learned hospitality," Elizabeth demurred. "There
is something wrong with a Southern girl who doesn't absorb it
with the air."

"And you are the supreme matchmaker as well," Mary said.
"We all have different talents. Frances makes miracles in her
yard. She's the garden expert. Ann is the needlework savant."

"And what are you, Mary?" Emilie asked with a wry smile.

The sisters laughed. "The politician," Elizabeth said. "One
hundred percent. I've seen her argue down more than one man in
my parlor. When she was small, she was allowed to sit at dessert
with Papa's fine guests and listen to their talk. Mind you, these
were the crème de la crème of Kentucky's political aristocrats—
the governor, senators, Henry Clay among them. And she would
sit there and listen. Have you heard this story, Emilie?"

Surely she has, Mary reflected. Among the Todd clan, no story was worth its weight unless you could tell it multiple times.

"As you know so well, Henry Clay was a close friend of Father's," Mary said. "Sometimes they would sit in the study and discuss Whig politics and, of course, horses. They were alike, the two of them—old Kentucky horsemen who didn't mind getting their boots muddy. I was only a little thing, and for some reason, they let me stay in the room. I would interrupt them now and then, and Mr. Clay would actually stop to answer a seven-year-old's questions."

"Well, you were so brilliant," Elizabeth said in her droll manner, making fun of the way the sisters boasted about each other. "Once, Mr. Clay said to Mary, 'You are going to live in the White House someday.'"

"Sally overheard that and had a good laugh for herself. She knew me better."

"You mean your nurse?" Emilie asked.

"Sally took care of us all. We thought Sally *lived* to take care of us. She was strict but kindhearted. I remember that she had put a mark on our fence, and when there was a knock on the back door, she would take food to runaway slaves. I asked to do it once and she said that slaves would only accept food from another slave." Mary shook her head. "Sally used to say a phrase she must have learned as a child. 'Hide me, oh my Savior, hide me.'" She felt ashamed of her family just then. "She should have been given her freedom after raising us up. Father should have done as your own grandmother did—let go of all her slaves."

"Father and Mother treated her very well," Emilie said. "They took care of her. I think she was quite happy."

The talk paused for nearly a full minute. Teacups were raised to lips.

"For a while, it looked like the White House might just be a possibility," Elizabeth said gaily to change the subject. "People in this town say Stephen Douglas will be president someday. And Mr. Douglas courted Mary quite enthusiastically, as I recall."

"I danced a few with the man."

"You had your eye on him from the moment he arrived in town," Frances teased.

"Well, he certainly took notice of *me*."

"And you him, Mary. Admit it."

"I'll allow I was impressed by him. In those days, Steve could charm the bird off the bush, if you recall. But I saw him not long ago. Lord, he's such a squat plug of a thing now. Of course, he would probably say the same of me." She rubbed her cheeks. "I'm a ruddy pine knot these days."

"Oh, Mary," Ann moaned. "Stop that."

Mary shrugged philosophically. "Well, I had it when I needed it."

"In those days, people called him a steam engine in britches," Elizabeth said.

Mary sipped her tea. "Well, *that* I couldn't remark upon..."

A howl of laughter went up.

"Mr. Douglas is a very *little* Little Giant beside my tall Kentuckian. And intellectually, my husband towers above Douglas. Also, Mr. Lincoln's heart is as big as his arms are long."

Mary exhaled thoughtfully. "Oh, Stephen is certainly smart, but I hate how he plays to the worst prejudices of people. Acts like he just wants to make everyone happy. Fact is, he wants to control where the intercontinental railway will be laid, and he's placating the South to get his way. I don't know what has happened to the man. Ambition has softened his brain, it seems. Stuffed inside that big head of his? More corruption than a moldy melon.

"Stephen and the Democrats who masterminded this Kansas-Nebraska business have set a terrible precedent. It spells the ruination of the republic."

"I have no appetite for this constant arguing." Elizabeth leaned back against her chair and sighed.

"Well, it's upon us," Mary said, "whether we like it or not. Abraham gave up on the Whigs and is a firm Republican now, as you well know. He believes slavery is not just a crying injustice, it is a national sin that eventually we are going to pay for. He saw the auction block in New Orleans and never forgot the horror of it. And remember, his own father, who condemned slavery, used his son like a slave. Thomas Lincoln yanked Abraham from school to work his farm, then hired him out to neighbors for ten cents a day and took every penny his son earned."

Mary got up and began to pace. "This Nebraska bill allowing expansion of slavery shook my husband to his core. It makes a mockery of the Declaration of Independence, which is his gospel. And now the Dred Scott decision. He's appalled. How hypocritical other countries must believe us to be when we proclaim freedom for all! The Republican Party is antislavery, and it's time he got back into politics."

"You mean…"

"I mean, yes, he should take on Stephen Douglas in the next senate race. Mr. Lincoln has some notoriety here in Illinois, but he's not known on the national level. He could make a difference in the U.S. Senate."

The sisters paused, absorbing the import of that comment. They had all seen her at her desk, writing note after note to friends and acquaintances, asking them to support her husband in a previous race.

"I guess that means more strawberry parties," Frances muttered.

"I'm already planning one come June to round up votes. I'll need your help."

Once her sisters were gone, Mary Lincoln made for the sofa. She laid her head on the seat cushion and closed her eyes. She was pressing her fingers to her temples when Ana tiptoed back into the room.

"You can clear, Ana," she said. "Keep the boys out back for a while longer, will you?" She put a hand to her forehead. "Dear Lord, there's a railcar sitting on my head…"

Ana had just begun stacking the dishes when Mrs. Lincoln clapped her ears with her hands.

"Stop it! Stop all that crashing! What is the matter with you?"

She rose and went to her bedroom where she stayed through dinner. Ana had agreed to feed the boys and, thank God, stay the night.

Mary lay in bed, the late afternoon light blocked by the drawn curtains. She listened to the sounds outside and the sounds of her house. Howls from a stubbed toe, the dog barking his warnings at every passerby outside the fence—it was all beyond her control now. Ana would handle whatever arose. Mary regretted yelling at the girl. She would mend things in the morning.

Ana went to bed exhausted and hurting. She was not accustomed to being hollered at, and she burned with embarrassment under the covers before she fell asleep in the maid's room. Around two a.m., she started awake at the sound of her door creaking. She opened her eyes and saw Mary Lincoln in her white nightgown a few steps from the bed, standing there like an apparition.

"I heard a noise," she said.

Ana followed her into the hallway. "It might have been a sound from the street," she said.

They went to the front window and looked down on South Eighth Street. Jameson Jenkins, a neighbor, was driving by in his cart, which was loaded with a pile of hay. A man was sitting beside him. Ana glimpsed William Donnegan's face just before the wagon passed from view.

"Why would they be out at this hour?" Ana asked.

Mary shrugged. "Oh, Jameson is probably getting an early start to the day," she said vaguely.

Ana went back to bed. She had carried her secret about Donnegan all this time, thinking she and Cal were the only two people who knew of his other life. It dawned on her now: Mrs. Lincoln also knew exactly what the men were up to.

If she knows, Ana thought, *then Mr. Lincoln knows.*

CHAPTER NINETEEN

April 1857

A COLD WIND PIERCED HER COAT AND WENT STRAIGHT into her bones as she walked from school to the Lincolns' house. The teachers and school director spoke mostly now in terms of finishing the race, of earning laurels. The senior girls were preparing for their last exams and having graduation dresses made. There was something of a contest to see who would end up as valedictorian, and the contenders wrung their hands. Ana was not in that group, though she would finish respectably. A few classmates were engaged to marry. Others were planning parties or summer trips. One girl was sailing to Europe with her family.

Ana had ended up loving the schooling that dear old Alsop had arranged for her. She had been afloat on waves of ideas and words that captured and lifted her. She wanted to live "a life of the mind" as her English instructor described her own.

Miss Hawkins was a strange one. The slender, long-necked

woman seemed nearly incapacitated for real life by poetry and stories. Ana could not imagine her cooking food or making a bed. Her feet didn't touch the ground. She floated dreamily through the classroom as she spoke about the English Romantics— Lord Byron and Percy Bysshe Shelley. Poetry verses rose up from her throat unexpectedly, interrupting thoughts and sentences the way hiccups might erupt from someone else. She had learned poems as a child and she expected the same of her students, whom she called "my fellow celebrants of the word."

In the midst of a grammar lesson, she would abruptly switch to verse. "I met a traveler from an antique land…"

With that, the whole class would sit up at attention and chant back, "Who said, 'Two vast and trunkless legs of stone stand in the desert!'"

The girls speculated on whether some man had jilted Miss Hawkins, and sometimes they mimicked her outside class, but they were her devotees. She had lit a fire inside Ana and almost every other girl in her class. The idea that it was all ending pained Ana.

Walking through the square, she thought about her younger self, the peculiar little girl who carried around maps. Over time, her stolen Bible page had given way to butcher paper on which she had noted ever more streets and landmarks and merchants as Springfield expanded. It occurred to her that she'd had a job since she was ten years old, and after graduation, unlike most of her classmates, she would be a full-time employee. Mary Lincoln was counting the days. And so was Emmanuel Ferreira.

Finally, her father had begun with other men in the neighborhood to build a new house on Reynolds Street for his family.

It would be a three-room house at first, but the long, narrow lot would allow him to add on more rooms in the future. The foundation stones were set, and the frames for the walls were set up. In May, they would finish the outside shell. Working in the evenings after they finished their day jobs, the Portuguese men threw their backs into constructing the house. Come June, Ana would contribute earnings from her position with the Lincolns to the money jar. Her new salary would make a big difference.

The first signs of spring were arriving on South Eighth Street. A gay floral wreath made of colored paper had been put on a door across the street, and crocuses were popping up in front of the Lincolns' house. Inside, the smell of lye soap signaled cleaning day. The last cleaning girl had departed a week earlier, and Ana was expected to take over more chores. Entering the kitchen, though, she found a new hire tying on an apron and taking in Mariah Vance's rule number one: no sass.

The girl turned when she heard the door close, and Ana, removing her coat, almost jumped when she saw her face. When Mariah introduced them, they nodded to each other as if they were strangers. It had been nearly a year since they had seen each other.

Ana spent the day cleaning the upstairs bedrooms. Cal, meanwhile, worked in the kitchen. At day's end, when Cal departed, Ana took her time putting on her coat. She'd sensed Cal's hostility in her expressionless face when they were introduced and wanted to avoid an awkward encounter. As she closed the door behind her, though, she saw Cal fiddling with her scarf.

"Why didn't you tell me?" Ana asked.

"How was that supposed to happen? I haven't seen you for a very long time. Anyway, I just got the job."

Together, they walked silently until Ana spoke again. "Cal, I never told my family what we saw in the shoe store. Never in seven years. The part about knowing what slave catchers are? It slipped out, and I'm so very sorry about that because of how things worked out. But I did not betray you about Mr. Donnegan. I have never told anyone."

"But you stayed away. You did what your parents told you, even though…"

"I understand how hurt you must have felt."

Cal stopped walking, fixed her eyes on Ana's. "No, you don't."

Ana took it.

By the time they got to the square, she learned that Cal was almost finished with school as well and would be working part-time for the Lincolns. When Cal confided that there was a new young man, a minister's son named Jacob, courting her, Ana felt a sense of ease come over her for the first time in many months. Their falling-out appeared to have ended.

Walking home together in the weeks that followed, Ana noticed Cal was unusually stylish. She wore a couple of gingham dresses of her own design. After work, she'd don a short-brimmed hat set at the back of her head with a big winsome bow at her chin that showed off the constellation of copper-colored freckles across her nose and cheeks.

"I wish I could spend my first pay on a hoop skirt," Ana sighed when she spotted a woman across the street wearing one.

"I turn most of my money over," Cal said. "Don't you?"

"Yes. But I keep what I get for doing extra work. When I get enough, you know where it's going."

"I didn't think you cared about fashions."

"Funny. I didn't think so either."

When the end of May arrived, the girls of Sangamon Female Academy stood outside in white dresses and white satin sashes. The day was warm and fragrant with lilacs. Awards were given out for each of the various accomplishments, and Ana took a prize for a paper she had written on Emerson. Her reward was to recite his "Ode to Beauty" at the ceremony. It was long and hard to remember and not a favorite, but she did it, and her family and Mrs. Alsop beamed. So did Miss Hawkins, who tucked Elizabeth Barrett Browning's *Sonnets from the Portuguese* under Ana's arm, then sent her off into the world.

CHAPTER TWENTY

S PENCER RODE TO HIS BROTHER PRESLEY'S HOUSE IN A heavy snowfall. It was quiet on the streets as the inches of white rose. They needed to have a place to work, and Presley's house would be that, unlike Spencer's own, where children raced in and out of the parlor. Presley's hackles had been raised when he learned that the Illinois State Colonization Society had voted to ask the Illinois legislature for funds to help them remove Negroes from the state and send them to Africa.

"They claim they are a charitable institution. They want to use the taxes we pay so they can throw us out of the country! Can you believe it? We benefit the state. Illinois needs us *here*, not in Liberia."

Spencer's own heartburn over colonization had not diminished since Frederick Douglass had lit the flame five years ago. It was not a cause that was going to die an easy death, though.

Abraham Lincoln had agreed to be one of the eleven managers of the society just a week ago, adding respectability to their offensive campaign.

Presley had called a meeting to be held on February 12, for the town's colored citizens to consider the Liberia question. Landon Coleman would chair it, and Presley and Spencer had agreed to be on a committee to write up a statement of their position. This afternoon, they would try to hone sentences powerful enough to convince the state legislature that the colonization society was not some benevolent charity worthy of tax support from the good Christians in Illinois as the society so enjoyed portraying itself.

Presley was a barber like Spencer. He loved language and was a persuasive speaker at the annual celebration of emancipation in the West Indies.

Five years earlier, he had written a petition to the legislature stating the case that the black people of Illinois did not want to be taxed for common schools run by the state. They would provide their own schools. That petition had fallen on deaf ears, but Presley knew how to make an argument, and he was persistent.

"Begin with the numbers. How many of us are there in Illinois?" Spencer asked.

Presley chewed on his pencil. "Hard to be exact. I read between five and ten thousand."

"All right then," Spencer said. He wrote for a couple of minutes, then read what he had. "As a public, we cannot perceive what benefit it will be to the State of Illinois to remove from it the five or ten thousand laborers…"

"I wish we could say, 'Just leave us alone.'"

"Say it, Pres."

Presley took the pencil and paper, releasing ponderous sighs as he wrote and crossed out for twenty or thirty minutes. Spencer brewed a pot of strong coffee and brought him a cup. Presley pushed the paper across the table to him. "Tell me what you think."

"We do not interfere with other people," Spencer read, "and only ask that we may be let alone, and simply protected in our 'inalienable rights to life, liberty, and the pursuit of happiness' as are other citizens of the State. We have no desire to exchange the broad prairies, fertile soil, healthful climate, and Christian civilization of Illinois for the dangerous navigation of the wide ocean, the tangled forests, savage beasts, heathen people, and miasmatic shores of Africa."

Spencer grinned. "Impressive," he said. "Miasmatic. Bad air, you mean?"

"Look it up, Brother. Here's the next paragraph." Presley handed Spencer the paper.

"We know ourselves to be men and we declare ourselves as such under the Declaration of the Old Thirteen. We also claim the right of citizenship in this, the country of our birth. We were born here, and here we desire to die and be buried. We are not African. The best blood of Virginia, Maryland, Kentucky, and other states where our brethren are still held in bondage by their brothers flows in our veins. We are not, therefore, aliens, either in blood or in race to the people of the country in which we were born. Why then should we be disenfranchised and denied the rights of citizenship in the north and those of human nature itself in the south?" Spencer put the paper down. "Whew."

"You write the summary, Spence."

Riding home, Spencer thought about the arguments he had heard in favor of colonization to Liberia. One of the most common was that black people would never be accepted into America's white society; they would be better off elsewhere. That argument was particularly galling to him.

Back and forth, back and forth. All these words. He thought then of something William had said to him after the convention five years ago. "You keep trying to talk your way into their hearts, but they don't care."

On February 12, Lincoln was sitting in his chair, getting a haircut for his birthday that day.

"Do you know the word 'miasmatic'?" Spencer asked.

"Miasmatic? Miasmatic what?"

"Miasmatic shores."

"Sounds like the shores of the place are full of miasma. Sounds bad. Unhealthy."

CHAPTER TWENTY-ONE

JUNE 1858

THE FIRST WEEK OF JUNE, MARY LINCOLN ANNOUNCED there would be a strawberry party in two weeks and both Cal and Ana would be needed. A strawberry party was clearly something Mariah Vance had experienced and dreaded repeating. "We've had seventy for a strawberry gathering, and she once invited five hundred for another entertainment. Thank the Lord it rained for that one. Only three hundred showed up."

Cal and Ana locked eyes in disbelief.

"I don't have a number to expect for this one. We will clean strawberries until there are no more to clean. He's courtin' voters," Mariah explained. "So we get on board."

Ana knew "Aunt Mariah" well enough by now to know that she would do anything for the mister and that she, after the missus, ran the house.

"Where does Mrs. Lincoln put all those people?" Cal asked Mariah.

"In the streets, behind the house, in front of it, upstairs, downstairs, all over the place. Terrible."

Crates of eggs and twenty-pound bags of flour arrived a few days ahead. Rounds of shortbread that Mrs. Lincoln called courting cakes came out of the stove day after day, filling the house with the smell of vanilla. On the Thursday morning before the party, bushels of strawberries arrived on Jameson Jenkins's big wagon. Ana and Cal stood for hours cleaning strawberries. When Mariah went out of the kitchen muttering "What a mess," they popped them into their mouths, listening for the woman's footfalls on the porch outside.

"Wipe your mouth," Cal warned. "It looks like you're bleeding."

It was Mrs. L who caught them. "Girls!"

They both jumped, then froze. She took two plates from the cabinet, laid down a slice of cake on each, covered them with strawberries, then poured cream and sprinkled sugar on the top. "Eat your fill, you two. Then get back to work."

Ana and Cal stared at each other. What had come over the woman?

The next day, people from all over the area arrived. Mrs. Lincoln had borrowed every chair she could. Neighbors carried their kitchen and dining tables outside. The streets were closed off as people poured into South Eighth Street and spilled out of the houses, bringing their own bowls and cups to fill. Her sisters arrived with cakes and cookies.

The whole neighborhood was there. Mr. Lincoln had a special affection for Jameson Jenkins's elderly aunt Jane. Cal

said she had a regular spot in the last pew at the Lincolns'
church. Sundays they walked home together. Now he was sitting next to her in a chair, talking intently. Ana did not doubt
that Aunt Jane knew about Jameson's nighttime activities. *She
knows. So does his wife.*

The girls were issued heavy white aprons to wear. They
directed guests to the long stretch of tables that were spread
with bowls of strawberries and pitchers of cream. Early arrivals
got slices of courting cake until it ran out. Cal waved off flies
while Ana cleaned up the messes left behind.

Mr. Lincoln wandered through the crowd, laughing and
talking with neighbors and friends. He was accosted by bands of
neighborhood children who knew they could get lifts and swirls
from him, as they often did when he walked down Eighth Street,
coming home for dinner. He always accommodated them.

Mrs. Lincoln was dressed in a ribboned summer frock
and had woven flowers into her hair. She was being the warm
and gracious hostess, which she did as if she'd been born to it.
When Mr. Lincoln got up to make a speech about being the
Republican Party's candidate, Ana observed the persona each
assumed in public. He was the homespun country man, she the
well-bred, warmhearted helpmeet.

They were shaking hands, listening intently to concerns,
hopes, opinions. Ana overheard Mary Lincoln mention to
one man her contempt for the Supreme Court Chief Justice
Roger Taney and his disgraceful legal opinion in the Dred
Scott case. But she mostly turned to simple talk, asking after
a woman's children or admiring a neighbor's new carriage.
The wives counted as much as the men in this crowd. They

didn't vote but they influenced their husbands. There was a fine line between well-informed and highfalutin for any woman in town. When talk turned to the senate race, she remarked simply, "You *know* Mr. Lincoln. You can trust him."

It struck Ana it was one of the few times she'd seen the two Lincolns work smoothly as one unit. She watched as he placed his arm around his wife's shoulders and saw clearly why Mary Lincoln refused to have a photo made of them standing together. He was so tall and narrow, she so short and round, they looked like an illustration of the Jack Sprat rhyme.

Ana felt a rush of fondness for this decent man. He had married a complicated, ambitious, mercurial woman whom he appeared to love. Today she was beaming happily next to him, her voice honeyed and Southern and feminine as she talked to neighbors. Tomorrow, would she play the foul-tempered fishwife, as Owen said one local politician had called her? It occurred to her that Mr. Lincoln's long business trips may have been his escapes.

She noticed Cal nearby, watching Robert Lincoln playing cards with some other boys.

"The Lincolns are rich, don't you think?" Cal whispered to Ana. "Look at this spread."

"Not as rich as Alsop, but he is a lawyer and makes some good money, I think." She lowered her voice. "Mrs. Lincoln has ordered up a couple of new dresses. Big-skirted ones. Her seamstress is in my mother's sewing circle."

"If she cares so much about appearances, why does she dress poor Robert in those denim jeans that are all patched? Those are worse than what my own brother has to wear."

It was true. Robert was wearing a sad-looking pair of trousers. "I'm glad to see him out here. He usually just stays in his room." "You play cards with him, don't you?"

"Mm-hmm. When I can get a few minutes away. He's teaching me euchre."

Cal shook her head, tsking. "They're going to send Robert away to a boarding school."

Robert looked perfectly happy just now. He was part of the big leafy picture Ana had been appreciating. In that moment, women's skirts were spread out on shaded lawns, children were running between tables set up in the street, people were laughing and chatting despite the various houses they'd just stepped out of—whether proud two-stories or squat frames with flaking paint—despite how they had arrived in Springfield. It was the picture of a summer day she would return to many times in the future.

CHAPTER TWENTY-TWO

JULY 1858

As the summer wore on, Ana was called more often to stay the night with Mrs. Alsop, who was down with influenza. "Bring a friend along to keep you company," the old woman told her in a hoarse voice. "I know it is boring in this big place by yourself."

The house was anything but boring to Cal. When Alsop was fed, bathed, and in bed snoring, they wandered the rooms in their nightgowns, studying the hundreds of things the woman had collected in her lifetime. A heavy carved sideboard groaned with silver pitchers, bowls, and trays. One room contained mostly glass cases containing figurines and whatnot shelves displaying porcelain frogs in waistcoats, frogs on lily pads, boy frogs singing to girl frogs. "Don't ever admit to collecting anything," Alsop had once advised Ana. "I have been gifted to a fare-thee-well with frogs."

In the library, Cal studied the book titles, ran her hands

over a large globe. Ana went to the cut glass decanter and filled two glasses to the rim. "This is port," she said. "It's a Portuguese wine."

For some time, Ana had wanted to shock Cal. The port appeared to have done the trick. Cal did not try to mask her surprise or her taste for it. She sipped and winced.

"My mother's father had a shop where he sold port in Madeira. English people like it." Ana drank down her glass and poured another.

They carried their glasses to the room adjacent to Mrs. Alsop's bedroom where her wardrobe was stuffed with dresses. Ana browsed through the gowns and showed Cal some of the choices.

"Mr. Alsop must have liked those," Cal remarked about two of them, but she would not try on any of the dresses.

Ana pulled from a nearby rack a couple of ornate hats, one decked out with a profusion of silk cabbage roses and the other with feathers and a bird. "She never wears these."

They put them on, stared at their reflections in the wardrobe mirror, and fell into choking laughter.

When she recovered, Cal tipped her head in the direction of the bedroom where wheezy breaths came and went. "I've never seen anything like this place. What will happen to it all when she dies?"

Ana shook her head. "I don't know. She has a niece and nephew back east. But she's not going to die. She just…"

"She's going to die someday, Ana."

"I guess she is like a grandmother to me. Or maybe an aunt. I am afraid for her."

Cal grasped her hand. "I love my auntie."

"I know," Ana said. Her head felt fuzzed by the wine and she thought she might cry. Or maybe laugh again. "Mrs. Lincoln told me a story about when she was ten years old. She wanted a hoop under her skirt in the worst way, but she was too young for one. So she and her cousin made their own out of willow branches."

Cal's eyebrows went up. "Well, that's one way to get a hoop."

"Her stepmother was angry when she saw the hoops. She tore them up and told both girls to get dressed and go to church. She sounds like a witch."

"I saw in the newspaper a picture of a new invention called a cage," Cal said. "A cage crinoline petticoat."

Ana shot her a puzzled look.

"It has steel rings that are connected with linen straps. It's supposed to be lightweight."

"I bet Mary Lincoln's sister Emilie has one," Ana said. "Her skirts are so big they knock over the little table in the parlor when she visits."

"I hope she doesn't go out in a storm."

"Why?"

"The story told about a woman wearing one who stood in an open door during a rain storm. Lightning hit her and ran around the hoops, and her brain got fried up like an egg."

"Noooo!" Ana said. "Don't *tell* me that!"

They put back the hats as they found them and returned to the library. Cal sat staring absently into space. The hall clock counted out eleven. "Jacob has asked me to marry him."

Ana hid her alarm. She had seen the boy. He was gawky

and sober-looking. His father was a preacher, and Jacob was studying to become one himself.

"Do you love him?"

Cal shrugged. "I don't know. I really don't. He's so serious. He says he loves me. He plans to study with a minister in Chicago, and that's where I want to go. If I went by myself... but how would I possibly survive there alone?"

"It comes down to that, doesn't it?"

That summer, when they talked about the future, about what was really possible, about what they wanted, it always ended with a question: *How much does it pay? Can I really do that? How would I survive?* The future depended on marriage. Marriage meant you had a plan.

One day, walking home from work as dusk fell, Ana and Cal spotted William Donnegan. He was with a woman whose wide-brimmed straw hat obscured most of her white face. Just then, Donnegan called out to Cal, beckoning her to join them.

Cal jumped at the sound of her name, then handed the canvas bag she was carrying to Ana. "Take this." She said it like a command.

A bolt of fear shot through Ana. Cal's sudden shift alarmed her. "Don't, Cal. Please, don't go with him." She grabbed her friend's wrist.

Cal pulled loose and walked quickly over to Donnegan. They stood chatting for a minute, and then the three figures walked down the street.

Impulsively, Ana followed. Two blocks farther on, three men emerged from a side street to walk behind Cal's party, which was still moving slowly, as if they were out for a casual stroll. The men's pace was more menacing than relaxed. Guns came out of their clothing. One man bent to pick up an object at his feet, inspected it, threw it back down, and the three began running. Ana hurried behind them, terrified that if they turned around and saw her, they might shoot her. When she approached the spot where they had stopped, she jumped to see what lay on the ground—a white papier-mâché mask. It was the kind of false face one might buy for a costume party. The girl whom Donnegan was walking with had been wearing it.

Now Cal and her companions were out of sight, surely running for their lives.

As Ana trailed the men, trying to keep up with them, a shot blasted—so close, so loud her whole body jerked in one great spasm before she fell to her knees.

"Cal!" she screamed. "Cal!"

She pulled herself up and ran. In front of a house ahead, a small group of people were gathered in a circle, looking down. Ana stopped and began to sob. *Dear God, no. Please no.* She walked slowly to the circle.

Between the trousers and skirts, she saw a dog lying on the ground. Around its neck was a chain with a piece of wood at the end where it had pulled away from a porch post. The dog was dead. A piece of calico, what looked to be a dress hem, was still gripped in its mouth.

A man in the circle was talking. "The fella with the girls pointed his revolver at the men following him and shouted, 'I'll kill any other damned dog that gets close to me—two-legged or four-legged!'"

"Who were the men? The law?" another man asked.

"Didn't look like it. They was carrying pepperbox pistols, though. Those ain't no good at a distance but will kill you close up."

"Where did they go?" Ana asked.

"Over toward Fourth Street. Running like hell."

CHAPTER TWENTY-THREE

S PENCER MADE IT OVER TO HIS BROTHER PRESLEY'S HOUSE as fast as his horse would take him. He had been at a night meeting at the church when the front door flew open, and there was his brother William, of all people, waving his pistol.

"He was yelling. 'Get Cal in here quick and leave the door open so it looks like me and this girl are in here too. I'm taking her around the side.'"

"Lord God," sighed Presley.

"I took Cal back to her mother's house. She said William was leading this runaway girl to Farmington. I don't think they could have made it tonight. Figured he might just show up here."

Presley brought a pillow and blanket to him, then went back to his bedroom to sleep.

Spencer stepped outside, listened for the clatter of horse hooves. Hundreds of night insects cast lines of sound into the still air, waited for answers, cast again. The moon came and went above a moving layer of clouds. Stars peered through holes in the fabric overhead. He went inside and laid himself down on the floor.

In the earliest dawn hour, Spencer was awakened by the deep woofing of a dog. He looked up to see Presley in his night-shirt with his huge Newfoundland next to him. When Presley opened the door, William and the girl practically fell into his arms. The girl looked half-dead, her clothes solid mud. And when the dog barked again, she leaped in terror.

"He won't bite you," William said breathlessly. "You'll be all right now."

Presley brought them into his kitchen. "John Stuart is taking a load of men out to work a field in Farmington," Presley told William. "We'll put her on that wagon. We have boy's clothes in the house that will fit her. The other workers don't need to know what's afoot. Stuart will get her to Lyman's place."

Presley's wife appeared in her nightgown and led the girl to the back bedroom.

William was filthy. His face and the sleeves of his coat were covered in mud.

Presley brought William a glass of water and a wet cloth to clean his hands and face. "I'll get you some clean clothes."

Spencer had never seen his brother so rattled. Presley scram-bled a pan of eggs for him. Later, as he watched him pick at the food, Spencer realized William was almost too tired to lift a fork. Yet he needed to talk.

"It was my first break in the whole blessed day," William said. "Seeing the church all lit up, I thanked St. Paul's for being right there when I needed it." He tipped his head against the back of the chair from time to time, squinting as he put the pieces together for Spencer and Presley.

"This whole damn situation just got out of hand. My neighbor Burras stormed into the shop day before yesterday, all worked up. 'Get on home this minute,' he says. 'I got one of your deliveries by mistake. She's sittin' in my house right now. Fella who drove her said they were chased all the way from Jacksonville.'"

The news had not surprised William. There had been a couple dozen white men in town showing around a picture of a girl with a $500 reward written under the drawing.

"'Girl 'bout sixteen I'd say, and she's a talker,' George says. 'A dangerous talker. Named every man or woman from St. Louis to Springfield who's helped her. Look, I keep your secrets,' he tells me, 'but I cannot have this girl in my house. You got to take her off my hands and quick. My wife is furious at having her in our place.'"

Next door, William had found a plump girl whose name was Jess. In the time it took him to get her to his house, she had named the man in Jacksonville who had driven her over—Ben Henderson—a freeman he'd heard of. William sat her down in the kitchen and talked tough.

"'You keep your mouth shut. Stop saying our names. You're going to get us killed.' Told her I'd shoot her if she came near to getting us into trouble." William looked up at Spencer. "I'll tell you what. She stares straight into my eyes and says, 'Shoot me.'" William put his finger to his forehead, imitating the girl. "'Right here,' she says, 'so it takes. I don't want to live if they catch me. My brother and sister was caught after the second time they run. They burned them.'"

William sighed heavily. "So I led her to the back of my house and told her to go up to the garret and crawl in behind the chimney. 'Don't make a peep. I'm going to watch out front.' I waited near the window and an hour later spotted three men in the street. I turned around to find that the girl had crept up behind me and she's saying, 'That's my master with the red hair and the other is his son.' So I chase her upstairs, and in a minute, these men are at my door.

"They didn't see her, but they pushed their way into the kitchen and looked around, then headed out and over to Burras's before they finally left the block. I knew they'd be back soon enough to watch through the night. Then I had an idea. I quick went downtown to the dry goods store where they have false faces hanging on the wall."

"I've seen 'em," Spencer said.

"I bought a white woman's mask. Bought some white gloves too and went home. My thought was to take her over to a safe house on the east side where she could hide until the slave catchers left town. Then I could get her out to Doc Lyman's house in Farmington."

William told how he set out with Jess at sunset, walking east on Jefferson Street to the safe house. The girl wore a straw hat—the very hat William had given their mother a few years ago. That was when he spotted Cal. It wouldn't be unusual for him to be seen chatting with a white girl—his block was full of white people. Cal was a friend to his family and looked white enough from a distance. She might be willing to come along, playing like she and Jess were friends.

He'd called out, and as if reading his mind, Cal had jumped

head-on into the drama, talking loudly about various neighborhood events until they reached the safe house. "I was congratulating myself on the ruse when the man came to the door shaking his head. 'I saw the advertisement. The town is crawling with hunters. I can't let her in,' he tells me."

Panicked, William and the girls went north toward a wooded lot but were suddenly headed off by the hunters. William maneuvered south, and they were scurrying along Third Street when the bulldog broke loose from its chain and got hold of Jess's skirt.

"I shot it." William shook his head.

"When I finally got the girl over to Spring Creek, we had to duck and crawl and climb through buckthorn." William pulled up his sleeves to look at the damage. "Aw, hell," he muttered. Red dots of blood marked the thorn punctures in his arms.

"Jess, she looks just as bad… I've never had one like this one. She won't shut up, and she won't do as she's told. I hoisted her up in a redbud, and I said to her, 'Stay here, gal. Don't make a sound. You hear me?' Told her the woods are full of wild hogs and cows, and if you get between a mother hog and her baby, she'll knock you over and eat you.

"It began to rain when I was creeping up to the Old Mill Bridge. It was lit by lanterns and guarded by a dozen armed whites. So I crept away and moved on to the bridge at the Beardstown Road crossing. There the creek was too swollen to cross. So I started back to where the girl was. I'm crouched down, and on the road nearby, I hear horses all of a sudden, loud and getting closer. Oh, God. It felt like those horses were inside my skull. Through the branches, I could see bright lanterns swinging and men racing back into town. One horse slowed and whinnied, almost like he picked up my scent. I hit the ground with my face in the mud, and now all I hear is blood thudding in my ears until that horse moved on.

"Once the Mill Bridge was clear of the hunters, it was nearing dawn and I didn't dare finish the walk to Farmington in the daylight. I told the girl to get down, we'll follow behind those men and get you to my brother's house. Well, she just looks at me like I'm crazy. 'Back to town? Right behind 'em?' she says. I had to nag her all the way here."

William leaned his head against the back of the chair. "I'm just relieved Cal is all right."

"I took her home to her mother," Spencer told him. "She was pretty shaken."

CHAPTER TWENTY-FOUR

———————

LISTENING TO WILLIAM'S STORY TOOK SPENCER BACK TO his early days of occasionally hiding runaways. Before the Fugitive Slave Act, before anybody heard of Dred Scott, before the law that banned free people from other states from staying longer than a few days in Illinois, Spencer suggested to escapees the idea of staying in the state and settling in a farming area where workers were needed. William had easily found jobs for refugees in Springfield and had made a tidy income for his placements. It was much harder now. Even people who were born free, people like him, were moving north to Canada to escape the restrictions of the new codes.

Not long ago, he'd seen an article in the *Chicago Daily Tribune* about a young man some eighteen or twenty years old, a freeman who'd been captured and labeled as a fugitive slave down in southern Illinois. The fellow said he'd had a disagreement with a porter on a steamer that he was taking along the Ohio River. The porter, himself a colored man, had thrown him off, apparently without his freedom papers, near Shawneetown across from the Kentucky border. The poor young fellow was set upon by catchers. He was a barber from Vigo County, Indiana, and he named a long list of important men in Terre Haute who knew him to be free and of good character. The townspeople believed him and demanded his assailants let him go. Under pressure, the ruffians removed his shackles. The crowd insisted the law required the man be brought before a magistrate who would determine his status as a fugitive.

But the captors defied the people, who watched as the young man was forced back across the river into Kentucky. The following day, the catchers claimed he had escaped them and they'd pursued him into the river. Soon enough, he was found dead. The paper said nobody yet had tried to figure out how the man had met his end. Spencer was certain nobody *would* try.

That area of southern Illinois was full of horse thieves, robbers, counterfeiters, and kidnappers. Freemen and fugitives alike were regular targets to be snatched up and taken to St. Louis, turned over for cash, or sold on the block. This man's death was not a surprising event.

Spencer had seen plenty of slavery's horrors in his life, starting in Kentucky and up to now, where he still saw so much suffering and knew about so much loss. Why was it that this story pierced him? He realized it was a simple story about a young man setting out on his first real look at the world. All he wanted was a look. Why shouldn't he have that?

There is a mother in Vigo County who doesn't know yet that her son is dead. There is a boy lying alone, with the waves rolling over his sand-covered body. He could be one of my children lying on that riverbank. He could be me.

In all these years of helping William and sheltering escaped people at the church, Spencer had tried to show strength, seldom allowing himself tears. Now, he found himself weeping.

He wondered how it was that the world was so big yet the space for him in it was so small. He hated the boundaries fear drew around him. He hated having his brain boxed in, and he worried about his children growing up to feel the same. Once in a while, when his head was near cracking, he told Eliza he had to go out alone into the country. She never objected. His destination was the field of a Quaker farmer who knew him and asked no questions. There he could sleep outside and feel his mind cleared in the morning.

He had done so recently when his back had been a web of pain from worry. He'd ridden out late in the afternoon. It was spring planting time, and the fields had been plowed and harrowed. He found a meadow where short grass grew and laid out his blanket roll. Purple crocuses were pushing up in a patch nearby. When he lay down, the pain in his back and shoulders fell away.

He had opened his eyes around dawn and watched as prairie chickens with full yellow throats cooed into the cool air. They were mating and took no note of him as a black or white creature. The earth didn't care. It warmed the feet of all creatures who walked on it. The wind was whooshing through the branches of a tree nearby.

Even as a boy, he'd found peace this way. Whenever he was acting frustrated, his mother would say, "Go pasture your soul, Spencer. Be back in time to do the feeding."

CHAPTER TWENTY-FIVE

Two days later, when Ana arrived at the Lincoln house, she found Cal on her knees washing the kitchen floor. She yanked her by the arm and pulled her into the backyard.

"You're going to get killed and it will be your own fault." Ana fairly hissed when she spoke.

Cal wiped her hands on her skirt but made no show of emotion. It was a trick she had mastered.

"Don't look at me like you don't know what I'm talking about. I followed you and him and that girl."

Now Cal stared curiously at Ana, taken aback by her anger.

"I thought it was *you* who was shot. I thought I had lost you." Ana swiped a fist at her wet eyes. "Only when I got to that place…that dog on the ground…only then did I know it wasn't you lying there. Don't you see? You could get killed doing these things."

Cal let out a great sigh. "You don't know my life."

"Of course I don't! You don't tell me anything about your other life. But I know what I saw. And I know what you're doing."

"Do you know the price of me talking about any of that, Ana? People dying. Mr. Donnegan doesn't even know the names of the others like him."

"He shouldn't involve you. You're too young."

"I'm old enough to know my mind and to make my choice. Look at me, Ana. What color is my skin?"

Ana swallowed. "I don't know."

"You know very well. So does Donnegan. I was a decoy."

"But that mask she was wearing. It was preposterous."

"It worked well enough at a distance."

"You could have died."

Cal was growing impatient. "Who do you think I count as mine anyway? The white man who got my mother pregnant? You want to know more about my life? When I need to buy food for my mother, there is only one grocer on the northeast side who lets me in the door. White people talk to me like I am stupid, if they even see me at all. They don't think a girl like me can be smart or even think. And lately, I walk through town and men grab at me."

"Grab at you?"

"Yes! Because I am a colored girl and seventeen and they can get away with it."

"That's awful. What do you do?"

"My auntie taught me how to punch. I run if there are more. I can run fast, if you recall. And I can kick."

"Oh, Cal. I don't want to lose you, but you could leave this place. You could go and work in Chicago, maybe even have a shop like you talked about…if you don't get killed first."

Cal shook her head as if Ana could never understand. She turned and went back into the kitchen.

Ana felt in that moment as she had as a child: that there were different levels of understanding between children and grown-ups, different levels of what was really taking place in a given situation. Now she knew only too well that there were many things that could shape how you understood the world, not the least of which was your skin color.

CHAPTER TWENTY-SIX

THAT SUMMER, THE AIR IN THE SQUARE WAS CHARGED with politics. Almost every day, some man was standing on a box, holding forth about this or that. Crowds gathered, arguing some issue that had been in the newspaper the day before.

Now Ana's first stop of every morning was the *Journal* office. There she collected not only that paper but also a copy of the *Register*, the opposition paper run by Democrats. It was full of vitriol about Mr. Lincoln. On some days, there were also papers from Chicago, Peoria, St. Louis, and Alton.

A tall man working on the other side of the counter handed over the various newspapers. He was perhaps six years older than Ana, with wavy brown hair. He was dressed in a starched shirt with sleeve garters and a bow tie, and he had neatly trimmed fingernails. She had noticed him on other mornings and took him for a reporter. Sometimes he passed her the newspaper without even looking up, and Ana would quickly scan the stories, keeping the pages neat so it wasn't evident she had run through them when she delivered them to Mary Lincoln.

On this day, though, he watched as she eyed the headlines.

"You like reading the news."

She laughed. "I am addicted." Then, "You are a reporter, yes?"

"Yes."

"That's a good job."

"Some days." He smiled. "You're one of the Madeirans, aren't you?"

"I don't know how you guessed."

He laughed and extended his hand. "Owen Evans."

"Ana Ferreira."

"You work for the Lincolns."

Ana nodded, surprised and also pleased that he knew this.

"I suppose you could tell some stories."

She gathered up the papers. "But I don't."

"I just covered a speech by Mr. Lincoln."

"How did he sound?"

"Well, his voice is high pitched, but that pitch carries—all the way to the back row."

Each day, they conversed a little more. In time, he revealed he looked forward to her visit every morning and told her bits about himself.

"My father was Welsh, a farmer. His family came from Pennsylvania to Wisconsin, before I was born. They were Calvinist Methodists, which is a strict religion. He was a real load bearer, my father, always taking on other people's troubles.

Loved to hear bad news. I was the only child and he was very tough with me, unlike Mother, who was sweet as pie. I don't know how they managed to get together. Once she died, I had to get out of there."

"How old were you?"

"Eighteen…wanted excitement."

"And a little laughter?"

He smiled. "That too. I went to the university for a while and decided to try my hand at newspapering."

"And you found your excitement."

"Absolutely. You may laugh at what I say, but Springfield, Illinois, is America's Athens right now."

"Athens, Greece?" Ana did laugh.

"Seriously! Some of the most important people in the country are living here. There are big ideas floating around this town. Things are being worked out right now in this state that could affect all of America."

"If you say so. I try to explain to my father and mother the political news, but what does it have to do with them? Or with putting food on the table? The people in the newspapers confuse them: Whigs, Republicans, Democrats, abolitionists, Free Soilers. What is that other one? Know Nothings. Don't you find it strange that political people call themselves that name? They admit they know nothing!"

Owen laughed. "No, no. That's what they say when asked about the group. They say, 'I know nothing.' It's a secret society. They hate new immigrants. Don't like Negroes or Catholics either."

"My parents think I fill my head with too much news."

"You can never read too much news."

She laughed.

"What shall I call you? Miss Ferreira?"

"Ana."

When she went into the *Journal* a few days later, she found him with elbows on the front counter, immersed in reading a clipping.

"Something good?"

"I pulled out Lincoln's speech from last June at the state house. I saw him deliver it, when the Republicans nominated him, and I was trying to remember all he said."

"I was caring for his children when he gave that speech. I read it the next day."

Owen's eyes lit up. "It was astonishing that he spoke so frankly. He's convinced the government can't go on the way things are—half free states and half slave states. He says that the Dred Scott decision is a terrible ruling."

"I tried to follow the Dred Scott business..." Ana hesitated. "I know he was a slave who lived for some time in two states that were free states."

"Right. When his owner died, Scott and his wife tried to buy their freedom, but the widow said no so the Scotts sued. Went all the way to the Supreme Court and that's where it turned into a disaster. Chief Justice Taney said that no Negroes, free or enslaved, are citizens of the United States, so they can't sue in federal court. Basically, the Supreme Court said it had no jurisdiction in the case because of their lack of citizenship. It also said that Congress does not have the authority to keep slavery out of the territories."

"That sounds so wrong."

"Well, most people take the word of the Supreme Court as final. But Lincoln says it's a huge mistake. He sees it as an underhanded way to make slavery legally possible in the North as well as in the territories.

"Meanwhile, Douglas promotes this states' rights notion as some kind of holy freedom not to be interfered with. He expects to be president someday, so he's clinging to this middle road. Doesn't want to offend the South." Owen smiled. "Mr. Lincoln has no such qualms."

Owen paused. "This afternoon, Douglas is giving another speech out at Edwards' Grove. Do you want to go with me?"

Ana hesitated. "I've made a plan with my brother and sister to…"

"To what?"

"To go see a balloonist."

Owen dropped his head in disbelief. Then he looked up into her eyes. "A balloonist?"

Oh wrong, wrong, wrong, Ana, she thought. *So wrong.*

She caught a quick breath. "Yes, of course I will go with you."

CHAPTER TWENTY-SEVEN

STEPHEN DOUGLAS WAS A SMALL MAN. HE HAD A RED FACE, A bulbous nose, and a large head, just as Mary Lincoln had described. The head was huge and appeared to be set on his trunk with no neck in between. Ana realized the effect came about because he wore his white collar turned up, unlike Mr. Lincoln, who should have done so because his Adam's apple was always bobbing in view.

In fact, Douglas looked to be constructed of two balls, the head and a perfectly round belly, which came near to popping the buttons off his waistcoat. Douglas would make quite a contrast to Mr. Lincoln if her employer got his way and both were onstage at once. But he didn't have the look of a shifty politician. This man was smiling, shaking hands, calling out names of people he knew, laughing in response to their jokes. He was hardly the monster Mrs. Lincoln had described.

"He is not as I pictured."

"Because he's short?"

"I am five feet and four inches. He cannot be more than that."

"Maybe less. And he's fat now." Owen was rifling through a canvas bag full of writing supplies. "They say when he was a young man in the state legislature, he was about a hundred pounds and would sit on the laps of the other legislators to talk to them."

"On their laps? Why?"

"I have no idea. He got their attention that way, I guess."

"How odd. He appears nice enough."

"The Democrats think so. He's respected on both sides, actually."

Ana and Owen had arrived an hour early to claim front-row seats. "I need to see his lips in case my ears miss something," he had explained. In front of the platform, there were four rows of folding chairs that filled quickly; behind them, a standing crowd kept growing. Near the stage, a couple of young men perched on tree branches with their legs dangling. Soon the hot July air above their heads was full of umbrellas shielding women from the sun and signs of support for "the Little Giant."

Owen stood on tiptoe and scanned the crowd. "I don't see him here."

"Who?"

"Lincoln. He follows Douglas around. He's been doing it for a while," he explained. "Stalks him really. The *Chicago Times* says Lincoln can't draw an audience of his own so he steals Douglas's. I saw him at a Douglas event in Springfield passing out handbills for his next speech. I suppose he feels he has to do it."

Ana winced. It seemed an undignified thing for her employer to be poaching another man's audience.

Douglas spat out his chewing tobacco, then went to the center of the platform and stood unmoving while he talked of acts, provisos, and compromises. She glanced down at Owen's notepad and saw not words but squiggly lines.

"What is this?" She touched the corner of the pad.

He drew his notebook away and continued marking up the pages furiously. "Shorthand...later."

From time to time, an audience member would holler, "That's right!" or "You said it!" An elderly gentleman seated near Ana stood and called out, "Be particular now, Judge. Be particular."

Douglas nodded to the man. "I will read the language of Mr. Lincoln himself, who lays down his main proposition in these words: 'A house divided against itself cannot stand. I believe this Union cannot endure permanently half free and half slave. I do not expect the Union will be dissolved, I do not expect the house to fall, but I do expect it to cease to be divided. It will become all one thing or all the other.'"

The mention of Lincoln's name roused Ana. She had gone dull minded in the sweltering heat. The stupefying body odors nearby made her envy the young men on branches among the leaves. She had borrowed a pretty dress from Beatriz and rued the decision now. She felt positively upholstered in its heavy cotton folds.

"So Mr. Lincoln believes that the states will be either all slave or all free. And he believes it is the highest duty of every citizen to preserve this glorious Union. But how does he propose to carry out this favorite patriotic policy of his, of making all the states free?"

It was clear what Lincoln intended to do, Douglas argued. He was going to carry his agitation into Congress and get the Constitution amended so that he could abolish slavery in those states where it existed.

"There is but one mode by which a political organization, composed of men in the free states, can abolish slavery in the slaveholding States, and that would be to abolish the state legislatures, blot out of existence the state sovereignties, and invest Congress with full power over all the local and domestic and police regulations of the different states of this Union."

Douglas paced and used his hands to make his point, as if he were in a courtroom.

"It would be a uniformity of despotism that would triumph."

Boos rose up from the audience.

Ana looked around. In this crowd of people were all kinds of folks, but mostly farmers, shopkeepers still wearing their aprons, housewives with their husbands. If they lacked the education Douglas had, they nevertheless appeared to be following the orator.

"Now I have said a hundred times that I believe there is no right and ought to be no inclination in the people of the free states to enter into the slave states and interfere with the question of slavery at all."

Douglas's voice grew louder as he laid out his argument.

"And Mr. Lincoln says as much himself. Hence he does not propose to go into Kentucky and stir up a civil war and a servile war between the blacks and the whites. All he proposes is to invite the people of Illinois and every other free state to band together as one sectional party, governed and divided by a geographical line, to make war on the institution of slavery in the slaveholding states."

The idea that Lincoln was trying to start a war was perfectly ridiculous. Douglas was taking his words and carrying them to preposterous conclusions.

Ana shifted in her seat and listened intently as Douglas went on to dismiss Lincoln's pledge to contest the Dred Scott ruling. "To whom is he going to appeal? The Constitution of the United States provides that the Supreme Court is the ultimate tribunal, the highest judicial tribunal on earth, and Mr. Lincoln is going to appeal that decision. To whom?"

Douglas's voice, grown increasingly sarcastic, drew laughter from the crowd. It pained Ana to hear Mr. Lincoln satirized as a fool, and she wished that he were there to defend himself.

It was when Douglas turned to the Declaration of Independence that she saw what Abraham Lincoln was up against.

"In his Chicago speech he says, in so many words, that it includes the Negroes, that they were endowed by the Almighty with the right of equality with the white man, and therefore that that right is divine—a right under the higher law; that the law of God makes them equal to the white man, and therefore that the law of the white man cannot deprive them of that right."

Douglas shook his head. "He thinks that the Negro is his brother. I do not think that the Negro is any kin of mine at all."

A snicker rose up in the audience. A man a couple of rows back broke wind loudly and those around him laughed.

"And here is the difference between us. I believe that the Declaration of Independence, in the words 'all men are created equal,' was intended to allude only to the people of the United States, to men of European birth or descent, being white men; that they were created equal, and hence that Great Britain had no right to deprive them of their political and religious privileges; but the signers of that paper did not intend to include the Indian or the Negro in that declaration; for if they had would they not have been bound to abolish slavery in every State and Colony from that day?"

"The signers were slaveholders themselves!" shouted a well-dressed man. The crowd was riled up now, and others cried out their assent.

"Indeed," said Douglas. "So what do you think? Did those signers mean by that act to charge themselves and all their constituents with having violated the law of God in holding the Negro in an inferior condition to the white man? And yet if they included Negroes in that term, they were *bound*, as conscientious men, that day and that hour, not only to have abolished slavery throughout the land but to have conferred political rights and privileges on the Negro and elevated him to an equality with the white man."

A voice behind Ana shouted, "They did not do it!" She turned and recognized the shouter as the unpleasant man who had once blocked her entrance to Barton's Dry Goods.

"And the very fact that they did not shows that they did not understand the language they used to include any but the *white* race," Douglas affirmed.

"That's right!" came the cries. "It's so!"

The Little Giant's voice carried loud and strong throughout

the grove. He stopped pacing from time to time, his piercing eyes and scowl directed out toward a distant point, then whipped his mane of dark hair dramatically as he expanded on his last sentence.

"Did they mean to say that the Indian on this continent was created equal to the white man and that he was endowed by the Almighty with inalienable rights—rights so sacred that they could not be taken away by any Constitution or law that man could pass? Why, their whole action toward the Indian showed that they never *dreamed* that they were bound to put him on an equality with us. I am not only opposed to Negro equality, but I am opposed to Indian equality. I am opposed to putting the coolies, now importing into this country, on an equality with us, or putting the Chinese or *any* inferior race on an equality with us. I hold that the white race, the *European* race—I care not whether Irish, German, French, Scotch, English, or to what nation they belong, so long as they are the white race—to be our equals... Emigrants from Europe, and their descendants, constitute the people of the United States. The Declaration of Independence only included the white people of the United States. The Constitution of the United States was framed by the white people, it ought to be administered by them, leaving each State to make such regulations concerning the Negro as it chooses, allowing him political rights or not, as it chooses, and allowing him civil rights or not, as it may determine for itself."

Ana watched Owen's hand madly filling his page with the indecipherable squiggles. She took a deep breath. Could he possibly capture in those marks the fearmongering this man exerted on people?

Douglas went on to predict that Lincoln would change the Constitution so that Negroes would vote and hold office and be able to intermarry. He feared amalgamation would be the ultimate outcome. He went on to throw into his pot of "inferior races" the people of Mexico, Central America, South America, and the West Indian Islands.

She listened to a chorus of agitated voices cry out in response. Ana looked down at her arms. They were brown from the sun, nearly the color her father took on in summer. It occurred to her then that eyes in the crowd might be on *her* at this very moment.

When she looked up, she saw men waving their hats and women lifting their umbrellas high in the air. Shouts of "Douglas forever!" rang out as his long and hateful speech wound down.

Ana turned to Owen. "I think he's terrifying."

"Which part?"

"His beliefs. I've heard his viewpoint before. You can't live in this town without hearing the same vulgar words on the street. He is menacing. But more frightening than that? The people! Most of them agree with him."

"It's a Douglas crowd."

They were silent as they walked back toward downtown until Ana asked, "Have you ever seen a cockfight?"

"Yes. Don't tell me *you* have."

"I came upon one in an alley when I was about ten years old. I was with my friend Cal, and we noticed some men who were crouched down on the ground. We thought a dog was injured, and Cal has a tender spot for dogs. But these were cocks bred to fight, with handlers who attached sharp spurs to their feet. Only the fiercest rooster would survive. And the spectators? They were betting on which was more murderous.

"Mr. Douglas was so strutting, so fierce—he puts on a show like a fighting cock himself. I hate how he stirred up the lowest instincts in that crowd. He makes them want to see blood drawn. And I fear to think of what Mr. Lincoln must become in order to win against a fighter like Douglas."

CHAPTER TWENTY-EIGHT

AUGUST 1858

THE *JOURNAL* OFFICE WAS SWELTERING WHEN ANA ENTERED. There stood Owen Evans behind the counter, grinning madly, with her pile of papers ready and waiting.

"Lincoln has challenged Douglas to a series of debates, and incredibly, Douglas has agreed," he said. "And the *Journal* is sending me! Seven Illinois towns throughout the state, from August twenty-first to October fifteenth. And I am going to all of them, Ana."

"Wonderful news!"

He grasped both of her hands. "This is big, Ana. Will you read my pieces, follow me while I'm on the road?" Before she could answer, he let go. "If you care to, I mean."

"Of course I will."

When Owen returned after the first debate, he described the spectacle in Ottawa with a wide-eyed wonder. "Over ten thousand people—*ten thousand*—stood for three hours in that blazing August sun to hear them speak."

"And who was the better speaker?"

"Lincoln, well, the man has this high voice as you know, and that Kentucky accent some newspaper types find too country-like. Douglas had him on the defensive some. But Lincoln would just pocket an insult and move on. In my mind, he wins with logic, not to mention decency."

The newspaper coverage quickly took a cruel turn. The pro-Democrat *Chicago Times* ridiculed the Black Republicans and Mr. Lincoln, calling him a sycophant, a perfect Uriah Heep who wrung his hands while using bumpkin words like "sich." Another Democrat labeled him a pettifogger. Ana found herself making frequent use of the Lincolns' dictionary. The Republican papers did not shrink from the fight. When they asserted Douglas was behaving like a "trembling Felix," Mary Lincoln told her, "You'll need to consult the Bible for that one."

As the debates progressed, Owen described Mr. Lincoln's growing following. Though the Democrats called his supporters radicals, a loathsome title to nearly every Republican, there were plenty of people lining up behind him. The fierce debates had convinced Owen that he was witnessing something historic, unprecedented, mind changing. "He stands there without a shred of drama," he told her, "and simply destroys Douglas with blazing shafts of truth."

Ana's daily trips to the newspaper office were now as significant for her as for Mary Lincoln. She knew the poor woman had spent much of her marriage waiting for her husband to come home; now, at least, she had reports of his daily life from numerous sources. Owen's absences during the debates made Ana realize how much she missed seeing his bright face in the morning. Lately she found a sullen old man in his place. It struck Ana that waiting was what women were consigned to do in life. She didn't like it at all.

"I saw Donati's comet. I was standing on the porch of the hotel in Jonesboro," Mr. Lincoln said.

The children had heard of the comet because Ana had taken them out into the backyard several nights to watch for it. Now Tad and Willie were climbing across their father's lap and up his chest, asking, "What did it look like? What color was it?"

"It looked like a bright white ball racing across the heavens, with a tail that spread out like a fan. It was magnificent."

"It was a sign," Mary said soberly. "You're going to win this race."

Between debates, Ana overheard Mr. Lincoln's conversations with his wife. She fed him the meatloaf he loved, then peppered him with questions about strategizing. Mary Lincoln was quick with an opinion.

"Douglas is a disgraceful equivocator," he told her. "He acts like he is against the expansion of slavery, but then shrugs as if to say, 'What can I do if the people vote for it?' His whole mission is to persuade people not to care about it."

"You must say that out loud," Mary urged. "Just speak it to his face."

"He's spending massive amounts of money," Mr. Lincoln continued. "He blasts off a cannon on the back of his train when he comes into each town, like some dang circus show." They both laughed. "But he says the same things over and over again. And he lies! If a man will stand up and assert and repeat and re-assert that two and two do not make four, I know nothing in the power of argument that can stop him.

"And the fawning of the people around him! Democrats fully expect he'll be president someday. They look at his jolly round face and see postal jobs, land offices, cabinet appointments, foreign missions they hope to get their greedy hands on. They give him receptions and marches and triumphal entries while I stand there on the same platform, with this poor lean face that cannot promise to elevate anyone's fortunes."

"Use that," Mary said, "at your next debate. Look. You are the essence of principle, the authentic article. That's what people like about you. You don't need triumphal entries or a cannon shot off from your campaign train. What is that phrase you say? 'What kills the skunk is the publicity it gives itself'? Decent people already smell his odor."

One thing became clear to Ana: both Lincolns sensed, as Owen did, that something profound was happening.

"You see what going on here, of course," she overheard Mrs. Lincoln say one evening to her husband. She was sitting in the parlor with a pile of newspapers on her lap. "Look at these articles! You're arguing out the slavery issue for the whole country."

"The Whigs who went Republican, the less stubborn ones, are beginning to listen. I don't know how far we can get with the others. You can't ignore public sentiment," he said.

"It doesn't help when the papers call you an abolitionist," Mary said. "Makes you sound radical." She rifled through the pile of papers. "Still, you are making front pages across the nation, my dear." She pulled out of the stack one of the papers, a New York organ, and caught her breath in wonder at the large black type blazing across the front page. A wave of exuberance seized her. She stood, held up the paper for Mr. Lincoln to see, and read out the headline with gusto: "The prairies are on fire!"

CHAPTER TWENTY-NINE

SEPTEMBER 1858

CARRIE NELL ALSOP RECEIVED ANA IN THE BEDROOM. IT was a concession that was not lost on Ana. Alsop had been losing ground these past few months, complaining of arthritis in her joints. Sometimes, in the middle of a sentence, she grimaced as if pain was slicing right through her.

"I'm at sixes and sevens," she said when Ana arrived. "I can't find my spectacles. Can you look around?"

The room smelled of the fragrance she had worn all these years. She had once given Ana a bottle of the lily-scented perfume that Beatriz had promptly confiscated. Her sister now reeked like a funeral.

"He came out here as a school teacher himself."

"Who?"

"Stephen Douglas. Now he makes a lot of noise about how all the school marms the governor imported are Republican abolitionists. Well, *of course* they are. Men and women of letters are bound to be." She poked at the wig she had been wearing since her hair began falling out. "There must be a lot of excitement in the Lincoln household, eh?"

Ana was evasive. "I'm mostly with the children."

The woman sipped from a tumbler and stared into Ana's eyes. "Surely you hear plenty in that house, my dear."

"Sometimes I do."

"Have you heard how he backed out on her the first time?"

"Who backed out?"

"Abraham Lincoln got cold feet the first time he was supposedly engaged to Mary. I guess he had doubts bad enough to drive him to a breakdown. People say he had the hypo so bad he stayed in bed for days. But he came back eventually and they got married quick. I can see you haven't heard that one. It's not a rumor. It's true."

"They wouldn't talk in front of me about things like that."

Alsop considered Ana. "Of course not." Then, "You know, an old friend of mine, Justice Tom Brown, knows Abraham Lincoln very well. He rode the sixth circuit with him for months at a time." Alsop's voice took on a conspiratorial tone. "He used to tell an amusing story about the wedding. It seems Mr. Lincoln spoke his vows soberly as though he was in court. Said something like 'With this ring, I thee endow with all my goods, chattels, lands, and tenements,' none of which he had. The poor man didn't have a pot to piss in. Justice Brown, who is a little rough around the edges himself, was standing behind them. He was hungry and smelling the fresh wedding cakes. So he interrupted the whole affair and said, 'Lord Jesus Christ, God Almighty, Lincoln. The *statute* fixes all that!'"

Ana laughed. It was the sort of story Mr. Lincoln might have told on himself.

Gossip seemed to revive Mrs. Alsop to her old chirpy self. She sat up higher in her pillows.

"He knew she had a sharp tongue when he met her. Here's another Tom Brown tale. Lincoln approached Mary Todd at a levee and said, 'I want to dance with you in the worst way, Mary.' Afterward, Mary said, 'You were a success, sir. You danced with me in the worst way.' He was attracted by her wit back then. Though these days, people say there is a certain lack of connubial *felicity* between the Lincolns." She raised her eyebrows. "Would you say...?"

Ana shrugged.

"Well, if you won't gossip, then tell me what they say over in that house about the senate race. Are they worried?"

Ana shook her head. "I really couldn't say."

"Then what do *you* think? Can Lincoln beat Douglas?"

Ana was startled by the question. Nobody ever asked her what she believed. She found herself tongue-tied in front of this woman.

"How old are you now, Ana Ferreira?"

"Eighteen."

"You are certainly old enough to hold an opinion. I've always felt a woman with an opinion was more attractive than one without."

She could see that Alsop was drunk. The woman lifted off her wig and used the neck of the half-empty whiskey bottle as a stand for it. Her head was near bald. A few wisps of damp white hair lay flat against her scalp. Ana realized that Alsop had been pasting herself together for some time as she diminished. It was heroic in a strange way.

Ana undressed her and put a nightgown over her head. When she reached to put her arms in the sleeves, the woman's flesh sagged from her bones. Ana looked around the bedroom for the spectacles then. Leaning against the wall inside the wardrobe was a small, flattering portrait of Alsop.

"Oh."

"Nice, isn't it? Your father will finish one of these days."

Ana had no idea her father had begun the portrait or even had been here for that purpose. The woman in the portrait looked thirty years younger. What other parts of his life did her father keep to himself?

Walking home, Ana felt a surge of anger. All this time, she'd felt guilt for betraying her mother, but she had been betrayed by her parents. *They have both kept their secrets.*

She thought about how they had all been walking on eggshells because of their secrets. It had been some three years that her parents had slept apart. If Alsop wanted an example of failed marital felicity, there it was.

When Ana arrived home, her teeth were set tight. She found her father sitting at the kitchen table reading his Bible. Beatriz glumly stirred a pot of something.

Emmanuel Ferreira looked up when he saw his daughter. "There's a page missing at the back of my Bible."

"It doesn't matter," she said. "*Listen* to me. The way we are living…this has gone on too long. Your fight with Mama has made this a miserable place to come home to."

She felt she was speaking into a deep well to reach him. She tried to calm down and choose her words.

"You told me yourself, *Papai*. You can worship as you choose in this country."

"She went back to the Romists and didn't tell me! Why does she do this? After all we have been through?"

"That is her faith now. The Virgin and saints comfort her."

Her father shook his head. "Nonsense."

"No, it is not. She lost her place when she came here. She spent her whole childhood going to celebrations of feast days with her family. Those were happy times, and she's lonesome for them. She knew where she belonged."

"She never even tried to belong here. She knows almost no English. She doesn't want to…"

Genoveva wandered out of her curtained room, and in that moment, Ana felt the rage return.

"Look at you two! You should be ashamed. Since we were tiny, you have told us stories about who we are. As Portuguese. As Madeirans. We say we are people of God. We are *lying* to ourselves!" Ana went over to a basket of potatoes and to everyone's amazement kicked it over. "Can't we at least have a little peace under our own roof? I work two jobs and give you a chunk of the money, and I cannot stand to come home!"

These were the right words, though she didn't know that yet. It would take some time. Ana thought often during that time of her father's angry remark. *She never even tried to belong here.* Ana too had held that belief. Now she saw it differently. She heard in her head what she had to get across to her father. *Mama is an educated, intelligent woman. She cannot express complicated things in English, but in Portuguese, she is articulate. She is powerful. Her language is the water she swam in as a child. It is the very air she breathed in Madeira. Every Portuguese word she speaks is soaked through with smells and sounds and faces of people she loved back there.*

The first sign that the ice was melting was her mother's announcement they would celebrate St. Anthony's feast day, even though it was well past. She had bought a box of salted cod. Glowing with purpose, she made *bacalhau* on the stovetop and cooked beef and sausage and fried dough over a fire outside.

"He is the saint who liked animals?" Joao asked.

"Mmm," she nodded. "Also the matchmaker saint."

They were seated around the kitchen table, all of them a little stunned that there was a conversation involving her mother *and* her father.

"When I was young, there was a custom. On the feast of St. Anthony, a celebration was held that the marriageable girls attended. I went to the parade hoping to see you. I gave you a plant, as I recall."

"And I gave you a poem." Ana's father reached across the table and squeezed her mother's hand. "We were married not long after."

Relief filled Ana's whole body. She ate as if she had been starving.

CHAPTER THIRTY

MARY LINCOLN WAS BENT ON SEEING HER HUSBAND SPEAK in the Alton debate. She had missed all the others, and she assured him she would be there for the last one. She was also determined that Robert would go with her. The boy had hardly seen his father in the past few months, and he was growing moody. It was normal for older boys to get surly— her brothers had—but Robert had always held himself apart, or perhaps they had set him apart. She didn't know—he was quiet and shy. All she could see was that Tad and Willie raced to their father the minute he walked in the door, while Robert did not. She feared that because of her husband's absence during Robert's young years, he missed out on forming the bond with his father that the younger boys enjoyed.

As it turned out, Robert's cadet group was making the trip by train to see the debate. She was relieved. He was old enough now to see the great man his father was, a powerful professional man.

It would be a daunting trip. Abraham would be arriving from Quincy on the same steamboat as Douglas, having finished the debate in that Mississippi River town. Alton was in the lower part of Illinois, near St. Louis and deeply Southern in its politics. Already there were rumors her husband might come to harm there. Alton, she knew only too well, was the town where Elijah Lovejoy had been murdered twenty years ago for publishing an abolitionist newspaper. She had feared so many things in her life, but for some reason, these threats did not terrorize her. And she *had* to do this one thing, for Robert, for her husband, for herself. She *would* do this trip.

A good-sized group of supporters from Springfield would be with her, as tickets on the train were half-price to Alton. The day before the debate, she left her faithful Ana with the boys, grabbed hold of Robert, who was in full cadet uniform, and headed out the door to the carriage with Jameson at the reins to take them to the train station. When they climbed down, Robert joined his group and she was greeted by a festive party of friends bearing picnic baskets. The train headed south through the blazing October countryside.

For all that Mary had heard about these events, she was still stunned by the festive mood on the debate day—the brass bands and waving signs. Alton was a small town, a stopping-over place for travelers making their way from the prairies to St. Louis. Someone had guessed at a figure of five thousand for the crowd—a small number compared to the one in Ottawa. And yet five thousand people smashed together in front of the Alton city hall was something to behold. In the crowd were men carrying weapons who had come from Missouri, some of whom were slaveholders. Her friends sat around her, no doubt to shield her from the whispers coursing through the crowd that Abraham Lincoln's life might be in danger.

The sky was cast over by dark clouds as her husband mounted the platform and commenced talking to a couple of local dignitaries. She had hardly spoken with him herself. He was exhausted and had slept nearly from the moment she'd joined him in their hotel room last night. Douglas appeared no better. He was with his new wife, who, according to reports, was twenty-three years younger. To be honest, she was beautiful, and Mary felt a stab of jealousy, then wondered at the woman's decision to settle for such a weather-beaten specimen.

When Douglas began to speak, he dragged out his ragged old popular sovereignty arguments. He was all gesture and no heart, a tired actor whose voice was shot, though his supporters were moved to shout, "Hit him again!"

The man Mary loved did not make grand motions with his arms and legs. If anything, he seemed at first to be trying to get them in working order when he stood to his full height. She was quite familiar with this process, but to new eyes, Abraham Lincoln must surely have looked awkward. Homely too. She'd seen that in print often enough. In truth, his face did look gaunt on this sunless day. When his turn came to speak, she knew his high-pitched voice would mellow in a moment. He began with his left hand behind his back, his right one free to gesture, though it was his head that moved about more than anything. As he warmed to his subject, his features became animated. His eyes lit up as his mouth spoke logic, pure and simple. When someone in the crowd jawed back at him, he delivered a hilarious, devastating quip that won over the crowd. He was standing still, bronzed by his days of debating in the sun, tall and mighty as a great oak.

"Judge Douglas may say he cares not whether slavery is voted up or down, but he must have a choice between a right thing and a wrong thing. This is the issue that will continue in this country when these poor tongues of Judge Douglas and myself shall be silent. It is the eternal struggle between these two principles—right and wrong—throughout the world. They are the two principles that have stood face-to-face from the beginning of time. The one is the common right of humanity and the other the divine right of kings, the same principle that says, 'You work and toil and earn bread, and I will eat it.'"

Perfect, she thought.

"No matter in what shape it comes, whether from the mouth of a king who seeks to bestride the people of his own nation and live by the fruit of their labor or from one race of men as an apology for the enslaving of another race of men, it is the same old policy."

Mary looked around. Was she imagining things, or were these people mesmerized? Many in the crowd looked as if they were witnessing a profound sermon.

These were hardworking country people who recognized her husband as one of their own. He was earnest, an unpretentious man who had risen from the same humble soil they had, who embraced the same essential decency they knew they should live by.

At the end of his speech, voices cried out hurrahs and "Bully for old Abe!"

On the train ride back to Springfield, Mary saw in her son the effect she had hoped for. The boy seemed proud to be sitting there next to a hero. When Abraham got up to walk through the train, Robert accompanied him, and his father introduced him to a host of friends and supporters.

"They are like boxing matches, these debates," a voice near her said. She looked up and saw the young reporter for the *Journal*.

Mary patted the empty seat next to her. "Indeed. All that 'Hit him again!' business. *Very* pugilistic. Did Mr. Lincoln prevail in the debate today?"

"In my book, in my paper? Yes. In the *Register* tomorrow? Probably no."

"I'm no innocent about how these newspapers work. The Democrat papers tend to clean up Judge Douglas's language, and I would swear that they make my husband sound like a complete bumpkin."

"Absolutely. I try my best to capture exactly what is said, and I'm the only one who can read it, so I transcribe but..."

"...but your Republican editor improves on it?"

"You said it, ma'am. I didn't."

They laughed.

"You appear to have survived these debates."

"Oh, I love my work." Owen talked on at some length about its pleasures.

Mary was aware through her husband's friends that this young man was apparently smitten by their house girl.

As if to prove it, Owen made mention of Ana. "She's really intelligent, don't you think? Is she good with your children? Do you know her parents?"

She was fascinated by the idea of these two young people together.

Back home, Mary found the boys in bed and Ana cleaning up.

"I like your young man Owen."

Ana was taken aback.

"You have an ardent admirer. He asked me all about you."

The girl appeared to be painfully embarrassed and put her eyes down.

"Oh, don't be shy, Ana. He appears to be smart, even-tempered. I think he's quite the catch."

CHAPTER THIRTY-ONE

November 1858

O n Election Day, a thunder shower rendered the streets almost impassable. Ana was proud that her father had braved the muck to go vote for Lincoln's party, as had many Portuguese in her neighborhood, but it hadn't helped.

When it became clear that Senator Douglas would be returned to his seat in the senate, Abraham Lincoln went off to his law office wearing a philosophical smile. Mary Lincoln, unlike her husband, fell into melancholy. Her campaign ebullience had drained out of her overnight.

"Be careful," Cal warned the day after the election results were published. "There's a wet hen in there. She acts like she's the one who lost the senate seat."

Mary Lincoln had spent the morning in her room where her sister Elizabeth sat in a chair next to her. She was still in her nightclothes, her hair undone, when Ana arrived at her bedroom door with a tray of tea and cakes.

"We emptied our coffers for that campaign." Mrs. Lincoln's tone was bitter. "Honestly. We have no money at the moment. And what did we get?" She reached for a cake while Ana poured.

"Abraham is back at work. All will be well. Before you know it…"

Mrs. Lincoln interrupted Elizabeth's platitudes. "Frances Haggard is going around spreading rumors that I don't pay my seamstress on time. Can you imagine? I knitted blankets for her babies! I cooked for her when she was sick. And she tells such a thing because I paid the girl a day late? Ana! You know Charlotte from your neighborhood who sews for me. Have you ever heard her speak ill of me? Not a word?"

"No. Not a word. She's in my mother's sewing circle, and she's never spoken ill of you."

"Thank you, Ana. Put it down. That's all."

Ana walked quietly out of the room and shut the door. Mr. Lincoln was the main subject of Charlotte in her sewing group gossip. She adored him as they all adored him. Didn't he donate money to the Portuguese Presbyterian Church? Hadn't he loaned money to Rita da Silva for land and helped others with money to build houses? Didn't the Lincolns come to the house to offer condolences when Emanuel Decrastos died? Didn't he win the case for William Dungey over in DeWitt County?

Her people considered Abraham Lincoln a saint, but they thought less of his wife. Ana had endured stinging reprimands from the woman, as had other women who worked for her. She knew her moods, and when she was hurt or angry, Mary Lincoln counted her allies and railed against her foes. Among the latter was William Herndon, her husband's law partner. She didn't care for the man. Long ago, according to Owen, who heard such talk in his job, Herndon had made a remark to young Mary Todd while dancing with her at a ball.

"He apparently told her that she glided through the waltz with the ease of a serpent."

"Oh my."

"Mary left the man on the dance floor."

Obviously, she still carried that insult like an embedded splinter, for she had not one good word for Herndon.

"I have never seen him at the house," Ana told Owen.

"Oh, he would never try to visit. It's widely known that Herndon believes his law partner is saddled with a harpy."

But Ana had seen firsthand how sensitive and kind Mary Lincoln could be. And how very lonely. She had many faults, chief among them too quick a temper and a tendency to pity herself. And yet didn't she have reason? Her son Eddie had died just short of his fourth birthday. Does a mother ever recover from the loss of a child? The photograph of the boy on her bedroom wall showed a plump-cheeked little fellow with straight brown hair. It had been eight years since his death, but Mary Lincoln kept him alive in her mind and in her conversations.

Once, on a cold March day last year, Ana had found her sitting alone in the front parlor. The children were at school, and Ana was cleaning.

"His birthday is today. Eddie's birthday."

"Oh," Ana said, and then, "I'm sorry."

"Something odd." She stared out the window. "I cannot see color today."

"I'm sure it must be very hard."

"No, you don't understand. I cannot see any color at all. Not at all. Only gray. Shades of gray. No yellow. No…" She put her head down on the desk and gave out heart-wrenching sobs.

Ana went to her and touched her back but quickly withdrew it. To touch her felt improper.

Mrs. Lincoln slowly lifted herself up to a sitting position. "Losing color is nothing compared to losing a child."

"I will be right back." Ana went to the room where Tad and Willie played and retrieved a tray of pigments, a brush, and a sheet of paper. She put these in front of her and fetched a cup of water. "Might you try painting to see if the colors come to you?"

The woman looked at her, puzzled. Ana gave her a handkerchief to wipe her face. Mrs. Lincoln became a small child just then, obeying her. When Ana put the brush in her hand, she gripped it and slowly painted two circles, side by side.

"Can you see the color?"

"Red?"

"Yes. Can you try with another color?"

Mary Lincoln stroked down the page twice, making close parallel lines. "Blue," she said.

"That's right."

She put her forefinger on the lines. "That is how Eddie and I were. Wherever I was, he was next to me. He was only a tiny fellow, but he showed his heart every day of his life. It was an immense heart for such a small body. He adored his father. And he loved any animal he met—tried to feed them all. He was so kind…" She shook her head, weeping again.

Ana put her hand on her elbow and guided her upstairs to

her room, where she pulled back the bed covers. She helped Mrs. Lincoln unbutton her dress and climb into bed. She had no idea how to comfort such raw pain. Impulsively, she went downstairs and filled a ceramic pot with embers from the parlor fire, secured the lid, swaddled the pot in blankets, and placed it by her side. She tiptoed out of the room then and closed the door.

Since that day, the two had been more than servant and mistress. Mary listened intently as Ana told about her first childish impressions of Springfield. Mary wanted to know about her sister and brother, about the house her father was building.

She shared her own memories. She told of how her beloved mother died after childbirth when Mary was six, leaving her devastated. Not long after, a cold stepmother replaced her. "My father already had six children by my mother. Why he needed to add nine more with Betsy..." The pain in Mary's face spoke volumes. It hinted at how her moods and headaches had started in the first place.

She had been sent away from home to board at Madame Mentelle's for Young Ladies, and it had turned out to be her salvation. She had blossomed there, excelling in academics and enjoying the fun of acting in French plays. She talked nostalgically about her school days and put books into Ana's hands. Occasionally Mary tested Ana's French with her own. Finding Ana could speak simple but fluid sentences, Mary sometimes conversed with her entirely in French.

Day by day, the disappointment of the senatorial election eased, the fevered political atmosphere in town calmed, and the

Lincoln house returned to its normal rhythms. Mary turned her attention to Robert, who was going off to Phillips Exeter in New Hampshire, where he would get the courses he needed to prepare to go to Harvard.

Ana was relieved by the calm. The unrelenting noise of politics upset her, upset most people. When the *Register* reported that a Mrs. Holmes, dressed in a bloomer costume, had ascended Pikes Peak, the first woman to do so, Ana imagined climbing straight up that mountain with her, letting go for a while of the caustic words that had filled her head for months and poisoned the air in Springfield.

CHAPTER THIRTY-TWO

October 1859

S PENCER CHARGED INTO HIS BROTHER'S SHOP SMELLING OF the bakery, as he often did when he'd made the stop on his way to work. "Uprising," he said breathlessly. "You gotta see this." He held up the morning *Journal*. "White man named John Brown tried to incite an insurrection. He and his sons and some twenty other people raided a federal arsenal at Harpers Ferry to arm slaves for an uprising. Marines killed half of them, including two of Brown's sons. They've got Brown in custody." He set down his sack and ripped off his coat. "Everybody I saw this morning on my way here was worked up about the whole thing. Old Brown figured the plantations would fall over all at once. Well, they didn't, though I expect overseers are quaking in their boots right now."

He tossed the *Journal* on William's worktable. "And now look at this headline: 'The Irrepressible Conflict—Fruits of the Lincoln Doctrine.' The *Journal* is blaming Lincoln for Brown's raid! The editorial says the Harpers Ferry revolt is the logical outcome of Lincoln going around claiming that the Union can't continue as the founders made it—part slave and part free states. They're saying that he's stirring up a war."

"That's strange." William took up the paper and read down the columns. "The *Journal* loves everything Lincoln does. That's the sort of thing you would read in the *Register*."

"What do you make of it?"

"The revolt? Too bad old Brown didn't set off a revolution. I've heard plenty of times about revolts from the people I have moved. I'm persuaded there's been hundreds, but they're hushed up. Revolts don't make it into Southern newspapers for obvious reasons."

"People in the church talk of it. You know, places they know of where folks rose up."

"I've asked some passengers when they talked about a revolt. What happened?" William said. "They tell about the ones who saw the chance and took it. Too often they were unarmed and outnumbered. Their punishments stick in the mind."

"Not good for Lincoln to have the *Journal* pointing a finger at him…"

"There will be a backlash now because of Brown. People will be afraid and head for safe ground. Just watch. You'll see the so-called radical Republicans pay the price at election time."

Four months later, Lincoln tromped through a foot of snow to come in for a haircut. He was bound for New York and points east to make a round of speeches.

"Cut it shorter than usual," he told Spencer. "It needs to last a couple of weeks."

"And the boots? You might want William to fix those up."

"Don't worry. I ordered new ones and a suit of clothes as well."

Later, Spencer would see reports about the New York speech that spread Lincoln's fame. It seemed that the debates with Douglas had served him well. He hadn't won the senate race, but people on the East Coast knew now who the lawyer was. Maybe the haircut and new broadcloth coat had a hand in persuading New Yorkers that he was not some western hick. The eastern press had anointed him their darling, and incredibly, his name was now being bandied about for the presidency.

CHAPTER THIRTY-THREE

DECEMBER 1859

For weeks, a path to their doorstep had been trod by men intent on getting Abraham Lincoln to agree to have his name put forth on the national ticket at the May Republican Convention.

"What was the gist of that conversation?" Mary asked her husband when his old friend Jesse Fell left their parlor after a half day of strategizing.

Abraham rubbed his eyes with both palms. "I am tired."

"Just tell me what he thinks."

"He agrees there are probably four viable presidential candidates for the Republican nomination: Seward, Chase, Cameron, and Bates. Seward, of course, is the favorite. He's formidable. He's been governor of New York and he's in the U.S. Senate now. If he has a drawback, it is that he's considered a radical. And he may have been hurt by Brown's raid. As for Chase? He helped found the Republican Party. But he and Cameron are both thought to be difficult to elect. They lack support outside their own states. Bates is a moderate bent on keeping the Union together by accommodating the South."

"I understand Mr. Bates has seventeen children with his South Carolina wife," Mary remarked. "I wouldn't call him a moderate."

"What public offices have I to show? Three terms in the state legislature and a two-year stint in the U.S. House of Representatives. I cannot hold a candle to Seward's record. Each one has supporters and detractors. Whoever is nominated has to be able to hold together the radical and conservative wings of the party.

"Every state has its own concerns, but Republicans will lose if they start making a platform out of their local causes. In Massachusetts, there is a movement against foreigners, which would never succeed with Germans in the northwest. In New Hampshire, they think opposition to the Fugitive Slave Law should be punishable as a crime. In Ohio, they want to repeal the Fugitive Slave Law. Whoever is chosen will have to avoid any number of subjects. It will be a real tiptoe act to stay out of the weeds."

"What of the talk of secession?" she said.

"The South has been threatening to secede for four decades. We can't give that talk any air. It will scare voters away from the Republican candidate." He moved his hand across his lips thoughtfully. "Fell asked me to write up a biography. He thinks I should be a presidential candidate, not a vice-presidential candidate for whoever wins the nomination."

"What do you think of that?"

"Well, it's an honor to have my name put in there with the other names..."

"Don't be coy with me, Mr. Lincoln. You don't want to be a vice president."

"No, I don't. I would have no impact. A senate seat has more effect than a vice president's."

"Do you want to be president of the United States of America?"

"I want a Republican to beat Douglas."

"Do you want to be president?"

He paused. "*You* want me to be president."

"Answer, please. Do you?"

"There are days when the word 'president' tastes good in my mouth. But it is premature..."

"You *do* want to be president. Let us admit it. And let us admit you are the superior candidate compared to the others. You have a strong team of men behind you. With the right strategy, you could defeat any one of them."

"The strategy would be to not offend any of the delegates' first loves, so that if no favorite wins a majority, I might be someone they could agree upon in a second or third round."

"If you win the Republican nomination, you probably would have to run against Stephen Douglas, but you have already done so."

"Yes, Mother, I recall that," he said wearily. "He beat my pants off."

"That was merely an Illinois race for a senate seat. On a national basis, your intellect appeals to the minds of the East Coast elite. You have already explained yourself quite brilliantly on the most important issues, not only out east but all around the country, to people of all kinds. They like you in Atchison as much as they like you in Boston. When are the texts of the debates getting printed?"

"They should be published by spring." He had been collecting from newspapers the texts of his and Douglas's speeches during the debates, *to put them in my scrapbook*, he told the editors when he requested them. In fact, the verbatim speeches had already been sent off to an Ohio printer. The plan was to publish them in paper or cloth-bound book form.

"Those speeches are your platform for the presidential race. They speak for you and should be distributed far and wide. You have already campaigned for the office by arguing out the big issues with Douglas. And isn't it the tradition that once a man is chosen as the presidential candidate, he no longer gives speeches? He stays silent while others go out and campaign for him?"

"Yes."

"You are done dallying with Douglas then. Your attention should be focused on how to get the nomination. But you have to stop questioning whether you are up to it. You are absolutely up to it. And the convention is in Chicago. Those people love you up there."

"Mary, we have just begun to restore our bank account since the last campaign. My question to you is whether *you* are up to another race. You broke your heart over the loss to Douglas. There will be more people coming through the front door. It will be exhausting. Our lives will not belong to us during the campaign, and if by some miracle I should be elected, our lives will look utterly different than they do in this house right now."

They were sitting in the back parlor on the sofa. Upstairs, she could hear the boys laughing as Ana bathed them. Mary folded her hands in her lap while she contemplated the question. "Yes, I am up to it. I have help in the house now, so I can help you. We will do this together."

CHAPTER THIRTY-FOUR

AUGUST 1860

In early August, Spencer and his brothers all got together at his barbershop. He loved these gatherings—no wives around, no young ones, and plenty of political talk and beer behind a partition at the back of the shop. Wiley, the oldest of them, had come in from his farm on business that day. Presley had arrived with his big old dog.

There had been a recent item about Spencer in the paper. He'd brought in an ear of corn from a field six miles out of Springfield to show a reporter how corn was looking this summer. The *Sangamon Journal* reported that "Professor Donnegan" had the corn on display in his shop in case anyone wanted to see it. It was a silly article, but Spencer was getting better at grabbing a slow news day and using it to promote his business.

His brothers and a couple of friends showed up, and soon they were sitting in the back room, having a laugh at Spencer's recent "acknowledge the corn" fame.

Then they laughed even harder that they were actually acquainted with the man who could be president of the United States. In May, he had been chosen by the Republican party to be their candidate, along with a fellow from Maine named Hannibal Hamlin as his vice president.

"Lincoln could beat Douglas handily now that the Southern Democrats split off from the main party and have their own candidate," Landon Coleman remarked. "I'll be surprised if Lincoln's name even shows up on ballots down South."

"I keep thinking of something Lincoln said during the debates that bothered me," Spencer remarked. "Said that he had no mind to bring about full equality of the white and black man. Political *or* social. So when he comes in here for a shave the other day and he's in my chair, the memory of that speech has me all stirred up. And I say to him, 'Mr. Lincoln, if you were ever president and Congress passed a law declaring the black man the equal of the white, I get the impression you'd be the last man on earth to sign it.'

"Well, he just throws back his head, and it's lucky I'm not shavin' him yet, because he just laughs and laughs, that old Adam's apple going up and down. He says, 'Spence, you're as big a fool as the Democrats are.' I ask him why, and he says, 'Suppose a law like that is passed. First the House passes it, and then the Senate, and then the cabinet deliberates over it, and last of all it goes to the president. Well, if I were president, I'd be the last man to sign it, wouldn't I?' And then he laughs some more."

William spoke up. "So he made a joke of it when you tried to nail him down. I remember what he said during that debate. It was over in Charleston, and the *Journal* printed it afterward. He said he was against letting us vote or be jurors and was against us holding office or intermarrying. Look, he said he will not interfere with slavery where it is established. What he is against is the *expansion* of slavery."

"He also has said he is for us getting the basic rights in the Declaration. Charleston is full of proslavery people. Maybe Douglas pushed him into a corner." Spencer frowned thoughtfully. "Lincoln knows what he's up against. He's got a lot of people to haul along with him in his wagon if he's going to hold any office in the future."

"Or maybe he told the truth, that he doesn't want us to vote or hold office," Wiley said. He was pushing tobacco into his pipe, his battered hands looking a full decade older than the rest of him. "Face it, he's no abolitionist. But no abolitionist is going to win the presidency. He's the best we've got."

CHAPTER THIRTY-FIVE

———

THE REPUBLICAN ORGANIZERS WERE IN A PANIC. AT 10:00 a.m. on August 8, the moment when the parade for candidate Lincoln was to begin, they realized they had underestimated the turnout. It appeared they had on their hands—could it be right?—five hundred delegations with floats, wagons, costumes, horses, marchers, and banner and sign holders to line up in an orderly manner. At the head of the parade was a gigantic ball painted with the motto "The Republican ball is in motion." Behind it, women gowned as winged victories stood next to railsplitters, followed by many hundreds of young men from all over the state dressed in their campaign clubs' garb. Shouting organizers were trying to line them up, all in a dense morning fog.

Ana knew where the parade was headed: right over to Eighth and Jackson. She had spent the previous hour trying to collect the morning papers at the *Journal* and was slowed by the masses of people assembling in the square.

She had left early before the children were up. Now, as she walked in the front door, the scene was chaotic. The Lincoln boys were still in their nightshirts, clowning and chasing each other around, followed by their yapping Fido. Mrs. L was half-dressed and snapping orders. Cal, looking summery in a pink dress under her apron, was bustling about with food trays for neighbors who were gathered on the front porch for the best view. Only Mr. L stood still and ready, outfitted in his white summer suit. Despite his fresh attire, his face was all crags and hollows. The campaign had caused him to lose weight.

By the time Ana had the boys dressed and fed, the fog had burned off and the parade was winding around the corner of Jackson to the front of the house. She had commandeered a second-floor window for the boys, and they watched in wonder as one extraordinary float after another rolled past. A log cabin mounted on a wagon went by; aboard was a pioneer chopping wood. A full-rigged schooner manned by sailors came next, pulled by six horses, and on and on. There were marching bands from all over the state. It was as if the floats had been invented to enchant the children along the parade route with their story-like images. As the American flag passed by, Willie and Tad saluted soberly. Only a few of the decorated platforms were puzzling to them, such as the one carrying thirty-three women in white dresses represent-ing the states, hauling behind them a buggy occupied by a young woman meant to be Kansas. A sign above her said, "Won't you let me in?" Ana tried to explain to the boys its meaning but gave up on it.

Tad and Willie especially liked a float sponsored by the

Springfield Woolen Mill that carried a loom powered by a steam engine. The loom was weaving denim, and word spread that the finished cloth was to be cut up to make a pair of pantaloons for Mr. Lincoln.

"Pa don't wear denim," Tad protested indignantly.

It was an eight-mile parade, someone said. Seventy-five thousand people, said another. Besides all the delegation members, there were thousands upon thousands of people watching along the parade route.

Ana's heart soared at the spectacle. Someone said rallies like this were happening all across America. It was almost too much to take in. This odd, kind, funny man was running for the presidency. This quiet man who lived inside his mind, inside this very house, who stored his thoughts in his hat.

He was easy to spot in the crowd below because he towered above everyone, even without the hat. Ana saw him repeatedly sally forth into the throng to shake hands, squeeze elbows. Here was the other part of him—the public man who had transformed himself from a poor country boy into an American leader. It was a story people loved. She loved it.

"But does he truly want all this?" she asked Owen. They were sitting on the steps of the porch after the tail end of the parade had lumbered past.

"I think he sees it as his destiny. This is what he has been called to do."

"By God?"

"By God. By fate. By circumstances. I can't say." Owen wiped sweat off his forehead. "When he started following Douglas around and speaking against extending slavery, that was when I saw it. Honestly, he was possessed, absolutely on fire with it. Did he know it would come to this? I don't know. What you may not be seeing inside these walls is his ambition. He's a born politician."

When the parade ended and made its way out to the fairgrounds, the Lincolns stayed home. A nominee doesn't go out to campaign once he has the nomination, Owen had told her. That's the tradition.

Ana lay down to nap with the boys, all of them sleepy.

At twilight, hundreds of Wide Awakes arrived marching and chanting. Banners floated above them, a strange, staring eye depicted on each. The men carried tall torches as they drilled in different formations while shouting, "Awaken to the cause of freedom!" Somewhere, a cannon blasted.

The whole household spilled outside to watch, and Ana pushed her way to the edge of the street for a closer look. She did not understand these men in bizarre militia-like costumes marching army-style down the street. She studied the sweaty, pale faces beneath their black soldier caps as they passed. They were young, though a few had managed to grow goatees, and all wore sober, determined expressions as if they were going into combat and were fixed on victory. And there, among them, she spotted her brother.

Joe? A Wide Awake? He was dressed like the others in a shiny black oilcloth cape, and he carried a six-foot torch. Impulsively, she pushed out into the street, grabbed the sleeve of his costume, and pulled him from the group.

"Joe! What are you doing with these people? Why are you dressed like a sorcerer? You look ridiculous!"

"Leave me alone," he growled, furious and embarrassed. The wide eyes on the banners bobbed above his head.

Mr. Lincoln suddenly appeared beside them. "This is my brother Joe," Ana said.

Lincoln patted his shoulder. "Thank you," he said. "Wonderful showing. How good to meet the brother of our Ana."

Now Ana was embarrassed. She watched her brother rejoin his marching group, beaming.

"You should be proud of him, Ana," Lincoln said. "We need a lot more like him."

"But he can't even vote. He's only sixteen."

"That's all right. The Wide Awakes matter. We need more of 'em in this campaign—as many wild, shrewd boys as we can muster."

"Joe used to be wild. He's quieter now. I don't know how shrewd he is."

"Ah, but they bring excitement to a campaign where old men give boring speeches. Some Wide Awakes are good speakers, and some like to sing. All of 'em like to holler." Lincoln laughed. "And it's a nice way to meet young ladies." He nodded toward clutches of girls who stood at both sides of the street cheering. "Every young fella wants a place to go to be among friends and people his age," Lincoln said. "Especially the quiet ones. They need to find their way to being men. We say boys are adults when they can vote. These boys will be ready when the time comes."

Ana reflected that she had not seen much of her brother. Kept busy at the Lincolns, she felt removed from the rhythm of her family's house. She knew only that Joe had been going out at night with friends; her mother had said so. Ana had assumed the worst, that they were drinking and reveling. Had he been out there discussing politics with his friends?

She'd never given much thought to what it was like for a boy to grow up in this town. Boys had expectations placed on them. They were supposed to *be* something, do something, make something of their lives, whether they were wealthy or not. She remembered how boys at her elementary school were the ones who got up on wooden boxes and held forth. Oratory was a skill that was admired. They were encouraged to hold opinions.

Joe had been a poor student, but she knew he was bright. He learned by listening and watching rather than by reading books. As it turned out, he had been absorbing much of what was happening in town. She owed him an apology.

CHAPTER THIRTY-SIX

November 1860

On November 6, Election Day, Mr. Lincoln spent the day in the office he'd borrowed from the governor over in the state house, surrounded by friends and supporters. Owen had hung about in the vicinity of Mr. Lincoln the whole day, following him over to the Sangamon County Courthouse, where he waded through a mass of people to cast his ballot, then back to the reception room in the governor's suite. Around five o'clock, as early vote counts were coming in, he went home, as Ana knew, and dined with his family, then returned to the state house to read telegrams reporting returns.

"It was strange how calm he remained throughout the whole evening," Owen told Ana the next day. "There was immense tension all day long. The chief operator over at the Illinois and Mississippi Telegraph office had made an offer to Mr. Lincoln that he might come over there to read returns. Well, by nine o'clock, he was sitting on a sofa near the telegraph machines. Good news kept coming in, and every hopeful telegram was followed by cheers in that office. And when a particularly good telegram came in, Lincoln would say, "Send it to the boys," at which point somebody carried it over to the Hall of Representatives in the Capitol. A huge roar came from that direction, and when the news passed out to the people waiting in the square—there had to have been ten thousand of them out there—another thundering cheer echoed the one inside."

Around midnight, after waves of good news from around the country, Owen followed the Lincoln insiders over to Watson's saloon, where Mary Lincoln was waiting. She enjoyed with him the spread of cake and ice cream and coffee. When Lincoln went back to the telegraph office and got word that New York State had gone for him, it was settled. He defeated Douglas as well as John Breckinridge, the Democrat the South had put up. He had the White House.

"The popular vote for Lincoln was a little under forty percent," Owen told her. They were eating an early dinner in the Lincolns' kitchen the evening after the election. "When he knew for certain he'd won the electoral vote count, his face lit up and then it turned pretty sober as it sank in. Everyone in the room was yelling. People were jumping up and some were rolling on the floor.

"Outside, it was mayhem. People in the square just went insane—hollering, crying, cutting capers. They were singing 'Ain't I Glad I Joined the Republicans' and calling over and over for Lincoln. Wanted to lift and pass him around overhead, no doubt. But he was in a hurry. He got up and said, 'Well, gentlemen, there's a little woman at our house who is probably more interested in this dispatch than I am.' He took off then."

Ana grinned to hear of the scene. "And when he got to the house, he came in the door and shouted, 'Mary! Mary! We are elected!'"

"So I suppose he does love her."

Ana recoiled. "Owen! What a thing to say. And would you lower your voice? They're both upstairs this very minute."

"It's just that," Owen whispered, "when I traveled to Ottawa during the debates I ran into an acquaintance who told stories about his time on the circuit with Lincoln. He said the man never wanted to go home. Couldn't take Mary's moods. He said even the judges pitied him in those days. They would go home to their own wives and children, but Lincoln would find some excuse to stay away."

Ana sighed. "That's the saddest thing I ever heard."

"Well, is it true? I know you keep that lovely mouth of yours closed…"

She leaned forward and spoke in an intense whisper. "I have witnessed conflicts. Of course. Is there a marriage without them? And do you think two people just say 'I do' and go merrily on without a cross word?"

He took her hand. "Well, that's what we will do…go merrily on." Owen looked pleased with himself.

Ana blinked. "Is that…was that a proposal?"

"Yes, ma'am."

She threw her head back and laughed out loud.

"Will you, Ana?"

She put her face in her hands, shook her head back and forth.

"Does that mean no?" Owen asked in a stricken tone.

"Noooo!" Again, she broke out laughing. "That is what I do sometimes when I can't believe something. Right now? It means yes. Yes!"

By the time the morning newspapers came out, euphoria had lifted the town off its foundation. The *Tribune* editors were emotional, writing about the great soul whom the townspeople had loved for years and who now would be recognized by the world. It did not matter that Lincoln had failed to carry his home county. He was the president-elect.

Candles had started appearing in windows on election night, and now almost every house was lit up. On the square, the state house looked like an immense birthday cake, glittering from the sidewalk up to its dome. The Wide Awakes showed up again in front of the Lincolns' house with their torches, filling the air with the smell of burning whale oil and transforming the streets into twinkling rivulets of light. Ana and Owen savored the excitement as if it were their own celebration. And it was. She would forever remember that night, when Springfield was a bright new star, pulsing to the universe its presence in the grand scheme of things.

CHAPTER THIRTY-SEVEN

DECEMBER 1860

S END THEM AWAY, SAY HE'S NOT HERE," MARY TOLD ANA. "IF they have business with my husband, they will know where to find him."

Every day brought reporters and job seekers knocking on their door, including more than a few of their friends, hoping for appointments. Besieged, her husband returned to his borrowed office in the state house, where he was considering cabinet appointees.

It was actually a blessing to have him out of the house. Time was moving fast and there was so much to do. Preparing the house for a renter. Storing valuable pieces of furniture and china. Going through the children's clothing to pack. She arranged to have new coats made for the boys and then turned her attention to what she would need in the way of clothing for her role as the president's wife. To say the phrase "president's wife," even if only in her brain, felt premature.

Her mind ricocheted between Springfield and Washington, DC.

She had asked Charlotte Rodruiguis to move in at the end of November. That little Portuguese seamstress had magic in her fingers. Mrs. Lincoln had entrusted her with fabrics from Chicago to create new underthings as well as dresses. The fabrics available, although from the city, weren't really fine enough for the clothing of a president's wife, however. She would go this month to New York to find proper material and a dressmaker for a new wardrobe.

There was one last reception to be had in Springfield, sometime near the Christmas holiday, she decided.

"A big one," she told Ana as they stood together, looking around the downstairs rooms, imagining how they might accommodate hundreds of people. "It's what we both want—a levee to say goodbye to so many wonderful people. We can push the furniture against the walls and have a receiving line start in the front parlor..."

"Mrs. Lincoln," Ana burst out. "Owen and I are getting married."

Mary jumped with elation. "At last! The man got up his gumption." She threw her arms around Ana. "When?"

"Soon. Perhaps in late February or March."

"Alas, I will miss it." Mary smiled at her own presumption. "That is, if I am invited."

"Of course you would be!"

"Well, in any case, I want to pay for your wedding dress."

"Oh, I don't..."

"Now, Ana, just say yes. Please. It is something Mr. Lincoln and I will both want to do. Will your mother make it?"

"Yes."

"Go and pick out some beautiful fabric and send me the bill. Do you hear?"

"I hear," Ana said. "And thank you so much."

Mary's eyes fell on a small table, one she had loved since she was a child. "That table belonged to my grandmother, whom I adored. I want you to have it. You've been like a family member all these years."

Ana was overwhelmed by the sudden gifting, which made Mary teary for no good reason. She couldn't cry now. There was too much to do.

Many of the things in the house had to be given away when they went to Washington. Some of the furniture. Even the dog.

Abraham believed Fido would be too upset by the busyness of the White House. An old friend from New Salem days, John Roll, agreed to give a home to the dog and abide by his admittedly strenuous instructions about the care and feeding of Fido. He must never be left alone outside, tied up. Fido must be allowed to circle the table during meals to collect what he could, must not be chastised for coming into the house with muddy paws, must be let in the door when he scratched it. To make his transition easier, Abraham gave the Roll family the long sofa he'd had custom made for his own length. It was the sofa he and Fido often shared.

The day of the levee, Mary braced herself by choosing her pearl-colored moiré dress with its fancy lace collar. It was dignified.

"The right dress can give you confidence," she remarked as Ana buttoned up the back of the gown. "Essentially, the whole town has been invited. There will be plenty of friends and supporters, but a fair share of political enemies may show up as well."

She and Ana went downstairs, where they found Mary's sisters waiting. "You saw it first," Elizabeth said, embracing her. "You always said he would make a fine president."

Down the stairs came her husband looking handsome in his new whiskers, and she told him so. There was a round of hugs among all of them. Mary looked out the window and saw a crowd of people waiting in the December cold. On the porch steps and along the street, the vast citizenry of Springfield and legislators from all around Illinois wore their best clothes and waited to shake hands.

Mary pulled on a pair of white kid gloves. "Ana, dear, open the door wide."

A freezing wind whooshed in, ruffling all of them. In an instant, women in flouncy skirts and fur pelisses crammed the parlors, along with men whose snowy overcoats breathed cold air into the warm house. Friends squeezed Mary's hands, some weeping. Strangers moved slowly along the receiving line. They greeted her husband, Mary next, then her sisters and on to the boys while staring all around at the furniture and books and a bust of a naked-chested Mr. Lincoln that a Chicago artist had recently sculpted in the neoclassical style. Mary liked the piece and so did her husband, who had said when he saw it, "There is the animal himself!" She had placed the sculpture on a vitrine by the fireplace, where it elevated the whole atmosphere in the room. Alas, it too would have to be given away to a close friend.

In the first hour, Mary bathed in the flood of affection. She watched herself from the outside, and just then, she liked the picture. She saw a lively woman with some pretty angles still, clothed in a dignified but rich dress, charming each visitor with her wit and warmth. She glanced at her husband in his new beard and tailored coat, which actually fit him. It was true, she had seen the hidden jewel before most people did. The years of supporting him for this moment, writing letters to muster votes, feeling agonizing loneliness, ignoring the clucking gossips— some of them in the room right now—finally felt like history. *Oh God. Wasn't I due this moment?* The White House would be *their* house. He would finally be at home full-time, and they would all be family together under one roof. She suppressed a laugh at the thought. *It took the White House to make that happen.*

The reception was a fading memory three days later when South Carolina announced it would secede, claiming the election of Abraham Lincoln as U.S. president was clearly a hostile act.

Mary looked up from the newspaper in alarm. "So quickly…"

"They are bluffing," her husband said.

"Do you think even one of my half brothers is against secession? They are loyal Southerners to the core. Granted, the Todd men are a bunch of hotheads. Still, I do not think the South is bluffing, not even a little."

"Well, if they are intent on war, they will discover *we* are not bluffing. There are those who want to appease them. But

I won't stand by and let the Republican Party become a mere sucked egg, all shell and no principal in it. It's not going to happen."

He went to the sideboard, where a pile of letters to the president-elect from all over the nation was piled up, stuffed a couple of handfuls of them into his leather valise, put on his felt top hat with its nub worn thin, and headed out to his office to read every one of them.

One afternoon, Ana brought in another coffee sack of mail from the post office. Mary took a break from packing and stood at her desk opening Christmas cards and notes wishing them luck. Inside one envelope was a folded piece of paper. She opened it up and found a crudely drawn sketch of her husband. There was no mistaking its meaning. It showed his feet chained together, a noose around his neck. She sank onto her chair. This was not the first horrible letter; there had been other misspelled missives of pure hate. One had come in November with twenty-five "god damns" in it, sending Mr. Lincoln, herself, her family, and friends all to hell. This, though, appeared to be a death threat.

She vowed that come March when they were settled in the White House, she would not open the mail herself. She would hire a helper to go through it first.

In days, it seemed, what control over their own lives they'd enjoyed had eroded badly. There was talk of hiring bodyguards to protect the new president and his family. Abraham's friend Ward Lamon stepped up and insisted on protecting him. He was a lawyer but, more importantly, a big strong man—a reassurance to Mary. It was decided that she and Abraham would not depart on the same train together. Too dangerous. She and the boys would meet up with him in Indiana.

CHAPTER THIRTY-EIGHT

FEBRUARY 1861

A MOB WAS INSIDE THE GREAT WESTERN TRAIN DEPOT when Ana and Cal arrived bearing a box containing the cake they'd made for Mr. Lincoln. Outside, a freezing February rain was pounding umbrellas and hats. They saw Jameson Jenkins at the reins of the carriage that pulled up with Mr. Lincoln and Robert in it. Father and son bade farewell to Jenkins, climbed down, and walked into the depot building, where they began saying goodbyes to friends.

"Happy birthday," Ana said when she and Cal were approached by Mr. Lincoln.

Cal proffered the box, and Robert, who stood at his father's side, took it into his hands. "Don't you be eating it all, Robert," Cal teased, and the boy grinned sheepishly.

Mr. Lincoln beamed at the gift. "You two young ladies stay out of trouble!" He grinned, and then he was making his way outside, with the girls and the crowd following his towering figure to the tracks, then watching as he and Robert ascended the caboose steps.

Abraham Lincoln stood on the back platform of the train. He was hatless in the rain and wearing a wool shawl someone had thrown over his shoulders. He stood looking soberly out at the crowd. Ana grabbed hold of Cal's hand and worked her way forward so he could see them.

"My friends," he began, taking in a deep breath. He cleared his throat, shook his head slowly. "My friends," he began again, "no one who has never been placed in a like position can understand my feelings at this hour, nor the oppressive sadness I feel at this parting." Anguish was writ deep on his features. "For more than a quarter of a century, I have lived among you, and during all that time, I have received nothing but kindness at your hands."

"Put down your umbrellas!" someone in the rear called out to those in front. All around, heads were leaning in, trying to hear Mr. Lincoln's voice. This was no prepared speech. He was speaking straight from his heart.

"All the strange, checkered past seems to crowd now upon my mind." He turned his head slowly, left and right, his eyes taking in the faces. "Today I leave you; I go to assume a task more difficult than that which devolved upon General Washington. Unless the great God who assisted him shall be with and aid me, I must fail. But if the same omniscient mind and the same Almighty arm that directed and protected him shall guide and support me, I shall not fail. I shall succeed."

"God bless you!" a woman shouted. Applause broke and he took the moment to compose himself.

"Let us all pray that the God of our fathers may not forsake us now. To him I commend you all. Permit me to ask that with equal security and faith, you all will invoke His wisdom and guidance for me."

"We will!" voices shouted.

His right hand grasped the shawl closer around him. He bent forward, as if speaking intimately with a small circle. "With these few words, I must leave you—for how long, I know not. Friends, one and all, I must now bid you an affectionate farewell."

The assembled cheered for him through tears. A smile broke across his lips as he raised his hand in farewell one more time and disappeared into the train car. Ana and Cal lifted their arms, shouting goodbyes. The entire mass of people was waving, waving until the train was well down the tracks. When it became a pinpoint in the distance, they let their arms fall.

Ana put her face up to the rain. She was embarrassed to be weeping, and her nose was running. Cal passed her a handkerchief. Together, they walked back to the house to finish packing some of the family's belongings for storage until the Lincolns returned to Springfield.

PART TWO

CHAPTER THIRTY-NINE

***

FEBRUARY 1861

"I HAVE SOME BAD NEWS AND SOME GOOD."

"Is something wrong?"

"So you want the bad first?"

"I suppose so."

"I can't attend your wedding, Ana. If I were here, you know I would come in my best dress."

Ana squinted. "What do you mean?"

"I am moving to Chicago…to apprentice with a milliner."

Cal had talked of this before, but the news stunned Ana.

"I'm going to learn how to make hats. It will cost only one dollar a week to board with her. And even when apprenticing, any girl can get two dollars a week, maybe more. After that… well…"

"How did you find this woman?"

"Mr. Donnegan's mother gave me a hatbox a couple of years ago. The hat itself was pretty battered, but the box had a store name on it. Sarah Gage Millinery. When I knew the Lincolns were leaving and I wouldn't have a job, I wrote to her asking about work. Miss Gage herself wrote back offering to teach me." Cal searched her eyes. "It's a good trade for a girl, Ana… but I guess you don't need that now."

"Why didn't you tell me sooner?"

Cal sighed. "I didn't know if it would even happen. I wrote her a letter in December and just heard back. I'll be leaving in two days."

"But your mother…"

"She's sad. But she does *not* want me to end up as a cook or maid for some family in town here, as she has been. She wants better for me. I want better for me."

Ana studied Cal's face. The narrow gap between her front teeth was the only suggestion of the little girl she once knew. Otherwise, it was the face of a grown-up woman looking back at Ana. It occurred to her that her friend had always known who she was.

"Oh, Cal. Do you know how much I will miss you?"

"I'll be back, often I hope. When I can afford the train fare."

Ana grasped her hands. "What about the young man who is in love with you?"

"I didn't love him, Ana." Cal laughed. "Jacob is with another girl now from church. It didn't take him long."

Ana shook her head. "Whew. On your own. In Chicago."

"Sarah promised my mother I would be safe with her."

They linked arms and walked on through the Lincolns' neighborhood in the falling snow. Ana remembered how they couldn't run fast enough to greet each other at the market when they were nine years old. They would stop abruptly when they got close, suddenly shy, fold their arms to speak a few words, then join hands and skip over to the Capitol's steps. Today, when they got to the corner on Ninth Street where they had parted a hundred times, she reluctantly let go of Cal.

"Send a letter the minute you get there, will you?"

"I will." Cal bit her lower lip then. "I wish I had a gift for you, Ana. But every penny I have is going to get me to Chicago."

"You know that doesn't matter to me."

They wrapped their arms around each other and shared a long embrace. "Write and tell me everything about your wedding," Cal said when she turned to go. "Promise?"

Ana's cheeks trembled as she tried to smile. "Promise," she said.

CHAPTER FORTY

————

WHEN MARY AND THE CHILDREN ARRIVED IN Washington, they were escorted to a large suite on the second floor of the Willard Hotel. Mary collapsed on a sofa while Willie and Tad stared out a window at the busy street below. Uncharacteristically quiet, the boys were showing fatigue. The last part of the journey from Springfield had been hair-raising. While traveling through Baltimore, a detective named Pinkerton had foiled a frightening assassination plot by having Abraham take a different railcar through town in the middle of the night. Mary and the children had stayed aboard the original train and passed through to safety, but her nerves were ruined.

"The air is heavy with treason," people surrounding her husband had been telling them before they even arrived in Washington. At stops on the train ride going east, rumors circulated of plots to blow up the city and prevent Mr. Lincoln's inauguration. Word eventually came to them on February 13, when their train was stopped in Ohio for a speech, that a cursing mob had tried to force its way into the Capitol in Washington, where the electoral certificates proving her husband's lawful presidency were being counted. Some in the crowd were angry that the electoral votes were only those of Northern states; Lincoln would be the first U.S. president elected by only a portion of the country. But by February, the states were no longer united.

South Carolina had seceded first and was followed by six more states. Those seven states were already writing up a Confederate constitution in Montgomery, Alabama. By February 18, Jefferson Davis had been inaugurated as president of the Confederate States of America. The new vice president of the Confederacy, Alexander Stephens, touted the new constitution, noting its cornerstone rested on the "great truth" that the Negro was not equal to the white man and that subordination to the superior white race was his natural and normal condition. He crowed that "our new government is the first, in the history of the world, based on this great physical, philosophical, and moral truth." Soon after, four more states seceded and joined the Confederacy.

Incredible, Mary thought, that in a matter of weeks, her identity as a child of the South and the pride and tenderness she associated with it had been stripped away—essentially because her own husband had been elected. Granted, Kentucky had declared itself neutral thus far, but the majority of the South and its people, among whom she had once counted herself, had already seceded. The Confederacy had formed its own country, a country utterly foreign to her.

Thankfully, feisty old General Winfield Scott, the loyal Virginian who commanded the army, knew that Washington stank of sedition. He sent out a warning that any man who attempted to interfere with the lawful count of electoral votes would be lashed to the muzzle of a cannon and fired out a window of the Capitol. Thereafter, he posted soldiers around the Capitol to block the threatening crowd from entering.

When Mary met the legendary General Scott, she was stunned to see a rotund, seventy-five-year-old man decorated in gaudy epaulets and a plumed hat. "Apparently, he beat back the British in 1814 and fought in the Mexican War," one of Abraham's assistants told her. "But he can't sit a horse anymore. Too fat and infirm."

Bad knees did not restrain the general's strategic capacities. In this town of spies, he had his own corps of informers, for word reached him of a new plot to blow up the stand on which her husband would be inaugurated. He planted his men underneath the stand, along the parade route, surrounding the barouche carrying Abraham and departing President Buchanan, throughout the Willard Hotel, and elsewhere secessionists lurked, which was nearly everywhere in Washington. Somehow, old "Fuss and Feathers," as he was called, got them through the inauguration.

Now Mary watched as Washington filled up with soldiers who pitched their tents along the Potomac and marched through the streets. The tension was palpable. She asked Ward Lamon to stay especially close to her husband, for he seemed oblivious to worry about his own safety despite continuing threats to his life. Her own immediate responsibility, once they were settled in at the Willard, was to look at the living quarters in the White House where her family would be staying for the next four years.

Harriet Lane, President Buchanan's thirty-year-old niece, gave Mary a tour as one of her last acts as the official hostess for her uncle. Mary had heard about the young woman well in advance. She was admired for being a true cost cutter. Full-faced with a braided chignon, she wore a lace bertha collar around her neckline that cleverly drew the eye away from an unfortunate chin. Mary found her to be both gracious and chilly. The rooms were decidedly chilly and not gracious. Miss Lane led her through all thirty-one of them, from the rat-infested basement, where the kitchen was located to the attic rooms of the live-in servants.

The tour started on the first floor in the public rooms, which were devoted to entertaining. Any elegance to be found was mostly in the Red Room, where a grand piano lived among gilded furniture. Mary saw immediately that this would be her favored social room. It was small but had a high ceiling and actually felt like a parlor. She could do something with it. The Green Room was the same size as the Red though not nearly as inviting. An oval Blue Room held some promise as it overlooked the gardens, but the main venue for receptions and balls, the enormous East Room, was perfectly shabby, with its threadbare carpet. The Dining Room for state dinners was not a disaster, except that it lacked matching plates or glasses, a fact that embarrassed even Harriet Lane. Mary could see that the $20,000 allotted for improvement of the place would be needed most urgently on the first floor.

That was her thought until Miss Lane toured her proudly through the second floor. *How can she not see the mess the place is in?* The private quarters' buckling wallpaper suggested a leaking roof. There was peeling paint on woodwork and mice droppings in the closets. The president's bedroom was squalid. It contained a bed with a headboard cracked down the middle. Old broken furniture revered for having belonged to Jefferson or Madison would have been thrown out of her humble house in Springfield. Here, she figured she was stuck with it. It would take every penny of the allotment to make the private quarters habitable and the tawdry first floor properly elegant.

If she had any doubt this was truly "the People's House," Harriet Lane set her straight about privacy when they got to the family living quarters on the second floor.

"This central hall here, as you can see, connects on one end to your family and guest quarters, with the president's office and those of his staff at the other end, the east end down there. What happens is that people who have business with the president sit in the waiting room but they spill out into this hall. When that occurs, the only thing between you and them is your bedroom doors."

"Oh." Mary made a mental note to arrange for a guard at the family's end.

Harriet must have observed Mary's distress, for she spoke cheerily about the private quarters' strongest point. "The plumbing!" Her violet eyes beamed. "It took highest priority with my uncle. Congress just appropriated over four thousand dollars to pump water directly into the house from the Potomac."

There was such pride in the remark. Uncle Buchanan must

have liked a comfortable sit-down and abundant hot water for his bath. The indoor plumbing was indeed a ray of sunshine on the dilapidated second floor.

Just before she left, Miss Lane led Mary to the best part of the whole building, a lovely glass house connected to the west end that the gardener had filled with shrubs ready for planting as well as potted lemon trees. She felt the tightness in her neck melt away at the smell of jasmine. "That gray sky must be envious looking in on this little Eden," Mary mused aloud. She was already imagining the glass house filled with colorful flowers and fresh strawberries.

After her visit, she walked across the road to get a longer view of the White House. *What did I imagine when I was a small girl picturing myself living in the White House? An actual house?* She laughed to herself. Most probably a glorious dollhouse, which it decidedly was not. It was a public building that looked like a house on the outside. Somehow, she would have to make the place suitable for an actual family, complete with children.

Well, if anyone was up to the task, it was she. The Todd household had instilled in her an appreciation of beauty and fine entertaining. She had learned as a girl it was better to buy good than cheap if you could. Now, in redecorating the White House, she intended to leave her mark. She would use her gifts to make the battered old place the magnificent symbol it should be so that it elevated the spirits of every foreign diplomat or American citizen who walked through the front door. She thought she could do it on $20,000. It would be tight, but she was a tough negotiator. My Lord, hadn't she made a silk purse from a sow's ear on a tiny budget in their Springfield home?

That evening, as Mary enumerated for her husband the hundred ways in which the White House could be rehabilitated, he shot her a woeful look.

"Pinkerton says the latest plot he's caught wind of is to kidnap all of us—you, me, the boys. The general consensus is that it's unwise for you to be here now, Mary. You should go back to Springfield."

She paused to think it through, resting her head on her hand at the table. "Do you want me to go?"

"I want you to be safe."

"Are we safer in Springfield from some madman who wants to do us harm? I don't think so. Here we are surrounded by troops. We are under one roof, where the boys get to see their father every day. No, we will stay here together."

Beyond the river stood Alexandria, Virginia, where Southern troops were gathering. One night, Mary climbed with her husband to the roof of the White House and saw campfires of Federal soldiers glowing in a protective circle around Washington. No doubt there were Confederate campfires in Alexandria. It frightened her to think how close the enemy was dug in, where rebels in their tents were preparing to take the capital and reduce it to cinders.

As it turned out, the burning tensions exploded first in South Carolina, where that state's militia bombarded Fort Sumter in April, forcing the Federal army to surrender the fort. "Civil War" was no longer a theoretical term bandied about by politicians. Women wrote it in capital letters in their diaries. It had begun.

CHAPTER FORTY-ONE

APRIL 1861

ON APRIL 25, LESS THAN TWO WEEKS AFTER SOUTH Carolina attacked Fort Sumter, Stephen Douglas came to Springfield to give a speech. Ana wore her heavy wool coat against the cold spring air when she and Owen walked over to the Capitol. She looked around the interior with wonder. As a child, she had never dared go beyond the steps of the great building. She knew only that important men were talking about important things inside. As an adult, she had wandered many times through the building but had never attended a speech in this vaunted chamber. The representatives' desks were arranged in concentric semicircles facing the speaker's rostrum; above, a viewing gallery repeated the curve. They sat upstairs. Gazing around the Illinois Hall of Representatives, she felt breathless as more and more women and men squeezed into the space. This was to be a talk about war, and no one wanted to miss it.

When Douglas came to the podium, she was shocked by how haggard the Little Giant looked. Worn out. Old. And humbled from the day two years ago when she had seen him speak in Edwards' Grove. He had won the senate race but lost the presidency to his old adversary. The newspapers had given him credit for conceding to Lincoln with grace. Recently, she had seen a cartoonist's depiction of Douglas at the inauguration. He was sitting on the podium, as it had been reported, holding Mr. Lincoln's top hat while the tall man spoke. Poetic justice, Ana had thought when she saw the illustration.

Now, following deafening applause, Douglas began to speak. She sensed he was summoning all the energy he had in that tired-looking body of his.

"For the first time since the adoption of the Federal Constitution, a widespread conspiracy exists to destroy the best government the sun of heaven ever spread its rays upon."

These were the right words, for thunderous clapping ensued. There was no posing, no swagger tonight from the man who loved applause. He swore that he had used all his skills to find a peaceful compromise, but the Fort Sumter attack had changed all that.

"Hostile armies are now marching on the Federal Capitol with a view of planting a revolutionary flag upon its dome, seizing the national archives, taking captive the president elected by the votes of the people, and holding him in the hands of the secessionists and disunionists. A war of aggression and extermination is being waged against the government established by our fathers."

Ana felt her whole body chill. She thought of the Lincoln

family, sitting like targets in that big white Washington house. Mary Lincoln must be apoplectic. Would they send the children home to Illinois?

"There is but one course left for the patriot and that is to rally under the flag that has waved over the Capitol since the days of Washington."

A great howl of support went up. All around her, women pulled off their fur muffs and swung them overhead like lassos, then threw them over the railing of the gallery to the floor of the house below.

Stephen Douglas's great lawyering skills rose up now in a fevered defense of Lincoln. By the end of his speech, the Little Giant had rallied the people. "There can be no neutrals in this war. Only patriots and traitors." He passionately urged them to put aside party loyalty in favor of allegiance to their country. The hall shook with the crowd's approval.

"I think living in Springfield, I have heard more words about patriotism…" Ana's voice trailed off. She felt as enervated as Douglas looked. "All the political talk that we so love in this town hasn't saved us."

"Well, at least he's done the right thing."

"But I cannot forget that speech in the grove. Do you know what is worse than the idea that he believed those words he spoke? The idea that he didn't believe them and spoke them anyway to win the election."

"It's interesting about Douglas," Owen mused. "He has used his powers to try to save the Union since Lincoln's election. I've heard he has put himself entirely at the disposal of Lincoln. He's been going around southern Illinois giving that same speech we just heard to persuade Southern sympathizers to stick by the president. I am almost inclined to think the man feels guilty."

CHAPTER FORTY-TWO

May 1861

A NA LOVED HER NEW LIFE AS A MARRIED WOMAN.
She loved Owen Evans, from his metatarsals up to his unruly eyebrows and the cloud of brown curls springing out of his scalp. Above all, Ana loved the brain inside that cranium, stuffed full of history, weather forecasts, political maneuverings, Cicero quotes, and crop reports. His mind was like his study at home, overflowing with interesting ephemera. But in his newspaper writing, he was focused. He worshipped precision. In his editorials, he could and regularly did cut through obscuring layers to flay an issue to its core.

Away from the newspaper, he was less disciplined. He loved beer and dessert and especially strong coffee that propelled him out the door every morning, fired up to fight dragons. Recently, when she'd poured him a fourth cup as he came downstairs dressed for work, he had shivered at the attractive prospect but declined. "Icarus," he said simply.

He often called her Bean. He had jumped on that pet name the minute he learned her family called her that. "Fits," he'd said. "You should eat more." But he invented other names regularly. "My darling yokefellow," he would tease.

He loved her because she was exotic to him, unlike the prim girls from church he had once known. She had no silliness about her. She was curious and fierce about learning. It was a bonus, he said, that she was beautiful and hardly knew it.

He recognized that her schooling had been piecemeal. She had read some Shakespeare, devoured Dickens, knew Latin, and spoke some French. She could recite poems that surprised him every time she pulled one out of her cap. But she knew little about the natural world. Couldn't identify more than a robin, crow, or blue jay. Hadn't been taught the names of trees or plants. Didn't know one constellation beyond the Big and Little Dippers. Couldn't identify Saturn or Jupiter no matter how many times he showed her. Yet she read the newspaper voraciously, kept up with politics, and made notes of everything that she wanted to learn. What she had that others didn't was a surprising ability to look inside other people. She had pierced him to his essence. The kindness at her core shone right through, along with a native intelligence that delighted him despite the educational gaps. All this, he told her.

While he was gone during the day, she planted seeds in a rough rectangle in the backyard, scoured the junk shops for castoff furniture she could sand and paint, made simple curtains. Genoveva visited often in the first few weeks to teach her how to cook, a skill she had let slide when Ana was going to school. A few times, she stayed around just to watch Owen dive into a supper she had overseen. Genoveva Ferreira adored him. He responded to her affection by eating with gusto while she leaned against the cooling oven, watching. Her recovery from spiritual despair had coincided with a return to the stove, where her art as a cook reemerged daily.

In the evening when Owen came home from the paper, Ana stood with him in the backyard. He usually drank a beer and held the glass close to his heart the way big-chested men in beer gardens do, right before they burst into song. But Owen didn't sing outright at those moments. He smiled to himself as if he heard a tune in his own head.

Together, they studied the sky. Beneath the clotted clouds, a band of crows, hundreds it seemed, flew out of the west while it was still light. Owen noticed that they returned to wherever they roosted as a huge group, every evening.

"Crows are clannish," he said. "They go out in the morning like a swooping pack of street urchins to see what they can make of the day, what scraps they can collect or steal on the street. They're survivors who live by their wits. But at the end of the day, they are rather a tender sight, don't you think? They all retire together. They need their fellows."

"A little like reporters, who must have a beer together after work," she teased.

Above them, another group of perhaps fifty flew overhead.

"Here comes the second shift."

"My mother thinks they are bad omens."

"Oh, they're just making a living." He stood up and hollered at the sky, "Hey, take the rest of the day off!"

She let loose a long laugh, and he was pleased. Once he had

told her, "All I want in life is for you to laugh at my jokes." Her laughter was reassurance to him. Comfort. Prelude.

He put his arm across her shoulders, and her head fell back to rest on it. She knew his private codes. And he knew hers. They watched the last of the crows disappear as they savored the beginning of another whole evening together.

They had married in early April, on a Wednesday to appease her mother, who had a notion that was the luckiest day for tying the knot. Their engagement was brief and their ceremony simple, unlike her sister's wedding two years earlier. That event had lasted three days at the Jacksonville farm, with dancing and interminable speeches and puerile pranks visited on the newlyweds by some of the groom's inebriated friends. A cow bell had been attached to the bottom of their bed, as Ana recalled. It was not the kind of wedding she wanted.

Ana wore the cream-colored moiré gown that her mother had made and the Lincolns had paid for. Her family attended; Owen did not invite his father. The Presbyterian minister made it short but recited from the Song of Solomon.

Set me as a seal upon your heart,
as a seal upon your arm
for love is strong as death.

On her camisole, her mother had sewn a charm, and Ana wore it knowingly. It was a *figa*, a tiny amulet in the shape of a silver fist, intended to ward off evil. Just in case. When she showed Owen, he laughed and removed the camisole.

"Let me see you. I want to know how lucky I am."

He took her hand, then led her toward the bed.

"No," she said. "I must get in first."

Owen looked amused. "Another superstition?"

"Maybe."

They fell into lovemaking so easily. She had never disrobed in front of a man, didn't know how it was supposed to be done by a bride. Owen solved that question. She felt no hesitancy, no embarrassment. Only new touch, racing heartbeat. And such love for this good, passionate man who explored her body so gently.

They lay together looking at the ceiling.

"Now tell me why you were so eager to beat me into the bed. What good luck will that bring about?"

She smiled. "I will die first."

"Ah," he sighed. "That's not fair."

The next afternoon, Owen came home with news just off the wire. "Lincoln has called out the militia. He wants seventy-five thousand volunteers to defend Washington. We're going to war."

It would be another ten days before Congress officially declared it. And in six more weeks, Owen would return home, as he did more frequently now, with the latest news off the wire. "Stephen Douglas has died in Chicago. Typhoid fever," he told her, hanging up his jacket on the coat tree by the door. "He was only forty-eight."

CHAPTER FORTY-THREE

JULY 1861

HAVELOCK CAPS. THAT WAS WHAT THEY WERE CALLED, and even as she sewed them, Ana had an uneasy feeling that the soldiers would never wear the strange hats as they were intended. They were close fitting to the skull with a curtain of white drilling fabric at the back, meant to shield the neck from the southern sun.

Ana asked the women in the room if they had ever seen a man wear such a concoction. They shook their heads.

"Men have strong attitudes about their hats," Ana argued, but they continued sewing, as the caps were one of the ways the Springfield Ladies' Soldiers' Aid Society in town had begun to assist the Union efforts.

When she walked downtown each day, she found rowdy volunteers waiting to enlist. After the Chicago mustering site, Springfield was the state's second largest, and young men showed up en masse. All of them desperately wanted to go. The war would last perhaps three months, people said. It would be a quick rout. Every man there wanted to be part of the action before it was over.

At the train station nearby, bands welcomed volunteers with patriotic tunes. It was a short walk to the Arsenal or the post office or the concert hall where recruits were enlisting. Uniformed soldiers armed with muskets performed drills for gangly youths in farm overalls.

A militia group called the Springfield Zouaves, who wore baggy trousers and peculiar floppy hats in parades, were among the first to be inducted. Four fellows from Joe's Wide Awake club, intent on volunteering together, stood in a long line waiting to see a recruiter who had set up his table in front of the saddlery. In another line, a club of Democrats calling themselves the Douglas Invincibles waited with the same intent. All around the square, recruiters were demonstrating weapons and giving tours of tents to show the prospects how they would camp.

In no time, the Illinois quota of six thousand was filled. Yet there were some four thousand excess men who had left home to volunteer at mustering sites. The governor instructed officials to have the extras stay on for thirty days so they could be trained in case they were needed later.

The fact that Springfield did not have accommodations for all those men was an immediate dilemma. A new camp was to be built, but for the moment, the agricultural fairgrounds became a temporary one where the recruits slept in hay-filled horse stalls.

In August, the call for women to help went out from every pulpit. Winter would be coming, and the men needed wool socks and flannel underwear. Elderly women could knit. Young ones could go out and solicit funds. The women formed themselves into a society and paid twenty-five cents apiece to be members. A room in the Capitol was loaned for their meetings, and the women promptly brought in their linens and started scraping lint for bandages.

When she walked out of the meeting room, Ana walked home quickly. Young men from the countryside, free for the first time from prairie farms and their watchful parents, were drinking and sometimes running wild in the streets. "Fort Taylor," a brothel in town owned by Harvey Taylor and his wife, Lucinda, was doing a booming business, even though they were raided every two weeks or so.

One young woman walking downtown had a lock of her hair lopped off by a young recruit who wanted to take it into battle. In any other time, such an assault by a stranger would have been considered outrageous. But in the midst of the war fever that had overtaken Springfield, the gesture was called romantic.

Ana decided to check on her parents before returning home late one afternoon. She found her father and brother in the parlor of their new house arguing furiously because Joe wanted to enlist.

"This is not our war," Emmanuel Ferreira fumed. "You don't know what war really means. You could die."

Her brother, just home from work, was covered with dust from the brickyard where he worked, his black hair now the color of cinnamon powder. His arms, thick and strong, were crossed in an obstinate pose. "I would gladly die to preserve the Union."

"Die to preserve the Union?" her father asked. "What does that mean? What can that possibly mean to a sixteen-year-old boy?"

"Seventeen in a week." Joe stared soberly at his father as he struggled, she guessed, to find words that were serious but respectful. "Freedom is why our people came to this country. Don't we owe something?"

Joe's simple logic seemed to touch their father, who argued he should wait a bit longer. The discussion ended when her brother said, "If it is still going on, I will enlist the day I turn eighteen."

Ana could tell that Joe had given serious thought to what he would die for. No doubt his time in the Wide Awake club had led to such considered thinking. The question had never occurred to her. She struggled with the idea now as she walked home. Would she die for her husband, whom she loved with all her heart? Of course. Absolutely. And her family? She would die for each one of them. And what of Cal, what of the Lincoln children, whom she'd come to adore as if they were hers? Yes, yes to those. She would defend them to the death. But what of others, people she did not know? What of an *idea* about America?

That evening, she walked with Owen through the crowded area around the square. They saw one disappointed youth talking to another who had been turned away. "Well, hell," he told him. "It's too blamed hard here. I'm goin' down to Missouri to sign up. They'll take us there. You comin'?"

She stopped, took Owen's hand. "You won't go, will you? Tell me you won't go."

"Ah, Bean, I don't know. They're completely oversubscribed. We will see." He looked out at the crowds of men. "If it's over in a couple of months, no. If it lasts longer? I will go."

The uncertainty made everything more intense. She looked around the house and cringed at the thought that in a few months, Owen might not be in it. Of course, every woman in town with a husband or child between eighteen and forty-five was worried about the same thing. Ana knew it was selfish to think *We are only just married!*

They had managed to buy the house thanks to money dear old Alsop had left Ana in her will. Now they went about laying down memories in it. They sang tunes together while Ana banged on an old piano he bought her. They were terrible and they reveled in it. He read to her from the book of sonnets Miss Hawkins had given Ana. She sewed him a shirt. They planted a row of boxwood sprigs around the yard to start a hedge. He brought home a stray cat for her.

He sat in his old garden chair and watched the sky. He was amused when the cat chased a squirrel up the apple tree. The squirrel stood on a branch, his long fingers held in front of his chest, his tail twitching back and forth while he *tuk-tuk-tuk*ed a long scold. "Aw, you old gasbag," Owen groused. "Never change, do ya?"

Her husband talked to most animals he encountered, she realized, as if they were acquaintances. He was playful. She loved that in him.

"Convivial society?" he might ask once inside the house. It was their cue. They devoted hours to loving each other, missed suppers. He lingered over her, memorizing her, as though she was the one who might have to leave.

CHAPTER FORTY-FOUR

AUGUST 1861

I N AUGUST, A MAJOR MILITARY CAMP OPENED UP ON THE outskirts of town, where Union recruits were drilled and prepared for battle. A local man who had a large wagon that could transport up to twelve people began taking town folk out to Camp Butler for "tours." Ana went with some of her Soldiers' Aid ladies to have a look. No visitor was allowed inside without the permission of the commander.

Their ride to Camp Butler was almost like a summer outing into the country. The women had baked biscuits and brought preserves for the soldiers in their picnic baskets. The camp was brand new, yet even her untrained eyes could see how flimsy the buildings were. The walls were single wood boards, and the roofs were covered with only tar paper.

The guide had worked up a plainspoken talk about the various long and narrow structures. "Them are the barracks for the troops. The tents in front of 'em are for field officers. That is a hospital building," the man explained. Already there were sick soldiers inside, boys who had caught the measles and such. The man told of the colorful names some regiments had. "Forty-Sixth is the 'Preachers Regiment.' The Thirty-Third they call the 'Brain Regiment.' It's loaded with boys from the Normal School. Got some professors in there too."

Men were marching in a field nearby. The women watched bayonets glint in the sun when guns rose up in synchronized drills.

A fife and drum group played lively airs as newly minted soldiers marched past their wagon. Ana spied a photographer's makeshift studio outside the camp buildings, where young men in their new uniforms could have their pictures made. The recruits struck sober or noble poses. Some held guns as their props. Others created playful tableaux where they grouped together for a picture. The atmosphere was festive and inspired the women who went back to their sewing with new vigor. Come winter, those jaunty boys would need slippers, blankets, gloves, and bandages.

The bloody rout of the Federal soldiers at Bull Run at the end of the previous month had stunned Springfield. The total number of men in the battle was staggering: some sixty thousand Union and Confederate soldiers all together, according to the newspapers. Ana could not even picture that many men in one place. She came to know what the word "casualties" meant. Of the three thousand Union casualties at Bull Run, eleven hundred were wounded, thirteen hundred were missing or captured, and nearly five hundred lay dead on the battlefield, like so many flies.

She could not forget how the first recruits went off from Springfield with their caps cocked. In time, some would return carrying souvenirs of the evolving horror and glory—a Confederate soldier's sleeve badge or a hat taken from a dead man. Others would return blinded, missing limbs, bandaged.

When word came that soldiers were using their havelock caps to strain coffee or cover wounds, the Ladies' Aid Society doubled their efforts. They sent out repeated requests for soft clothing that they promptly boiled and fashioned into dressings. It was one small part of awakening to their new reality: a three-month war had been a fantasy.

CHAPTER FORTY-FIVE

JANUARY 1862

MARY PLANNED THEIR FIRST BIG GALA FOR FEBRUARY 5, A week before her husband's birthday. *A Grand Presidential Party*, the invitations read. She sent out five hundred of them to the quality of Washington. She knew past presidents had entertained mostly at state dinners, for which the list of invitees was drawn up by the State Department. She had sat through enough boring official dinners to be certain this event would be a welcome change. Despite wounded feelings over at the State Department, she would have control over the whole affair. The house redecoration would not be finished, but the first floor would be beautiful and serve as a repudiation of the snobs who criticized her as an ignorant rustic. She hired a New York caterer and chose a menu intended to strike awe: venison, pheasant, partridge, duck, and ham, with cornucopias of desserts and ice sculptures to leave them all speechless.

The gala would also answer the vicious newspaper articles about her shopping trips to New York. Why didn't they write about her visits to see sick and injured soldiers? The flowers and fruit she took to them? The loving letters home she wrote for them? Well, they couldn't come after her for this entertainment. Mr. Lincoln himself would be paying for it.

As for Congress's redecoration budget, the shopping trips had been a necessary part of her job, for God's sake. The East Room had been refurbished in the nick of time for the party. The previous April, the room had been used as quarters for the Frontier Guard assigned to protecting the president. In practicing presenting arms, the guards had shot bullets into the walls and destroyed the old rug. She had spent $2,500 on a new carpet for the East Room—a sea green with designs of wreaths, bouquets, and flowers woven into a single, magnificent, flowing piece by a European manufacturer—and it was but one expense in her refurbishing. She also ordered French wallpaper for the Red Room that cost almost $7,000. By the time of the gala, her entire four-year renovation allowance was gone; there wasn't a dime left for repairs. She had overspent, yes, but it was necessary and not unprecedented. Congress tended to cover such expense overruns. Still, her purchases had set tongues wagging. She should not have been surprised at the talk. Washington was thoroughly Southern and full of traitors. She had landed in a nest of vipers.

"We are at war, Mary," her husband fumed when he learned she had exceeded her budget. "How does it look when you spend more than twenty thousand dollars on flubdubs for this damned old house? It is all wrong to spend one cent on this place when the soldiers cannot have blankets!"

"But Buchanan was appropriated the same amount. You just have to ask Congress to cover the overages."

"Never. Never! I will have to pay for it somehow."

"Mr. Lincoln. We are at war, yes. All the more reason we should show the country that the government is stable. You can't secure support from foreign diplomats in rooms where they must step around brown tobacco spittle on the floor and bullet holes in the walls. You need a proper setting to exert your power."

"And this gala…"

"Our gala will be more democratic than a state dinner. I have invited ordinary people to come as well as the bigwigs."

He sighed and shook his head. "All right. But no dancing," he said. "We are at war."

"I understand that."

She did not want to add another concern to those already weighing on her husband. He was entirely immersed in military strategy and having trouble in particular with General McClellan, who was dandy at training the men but averse to sending them into battle. Late last night, staring into the fire, he had said, "Does it seem strange that I who could not ever so much as cut off the head of a chicken should find myself in the midst of this bloodshed?"

She would have to handle this party plan herself.

Her seamstress Lizzie Keckley, a gifted modiste and former slave, studied patterns to determine what was stylish and adaptable to Mary's figure. Longer trains and low necklines were very much the fashion, and Mary was pleased at that development. Her arms and shoulders, she had often been told, were among her best features. She thought she could carry off the lower bodice.

"I think white satin, Lizzie. The English ambassador is coming, and I need to recognize the mourning underway for Queen Victoria's husband, so we will need to add some black trim on it."

"Very well."

"And secure the buttons tighter in back, will you?" It stunned her still that during a recent reception, someone had snipped off one of her back dress buttons. She hadn't noticed, so squeezed she had felt by human flesh all around her. "The people" had no qualms about going home with a souvenir from the White House, she was told. They were known to scissor off pieces of the curtains.

"Yes, of course." Mrs. Keckley sketched out the dress on paper.

"And I must mount a pretty headdress," Mary added. It was the fashion now, though she had worn fresh flowers in her hair since she was a small girl. Even if the Washington yahoos privately pulled her apart, she would hold her head high and full of blooms.

Mary talked openly with Lizzie Keckley. The seamstress had become her most frequent female companion, and their conversations stretched over many hours. She was warmhearted, despite the wounds slavery had delivered to her body. Lizzie's beloved son, George, born from rape, had died in battle last year. He had passed as white in order to join the Union army.

As January turned to February, Willie came down with a cold and then a fever. When it persisted for a couple of days,

Mary suggested withdrawing the invitations. It was Abraham who was reluctant and called in Dr. Stone before they did that.

"There is no reason to doubt an early recovery," the doctor assured them. "The boy is resilient."

He was. Mary remembered his bout with scarlet fever four months earlier. He had sprung back and soon enough was in trouble for drawing a black mustache on a marble bust in the hallway.

On the evening of the reception, Lizzie squeezed Mary into the tight bodice of her new dress. The décolletage was daring with her breasts pushed together and upward, but the whole effect was pretty. The dress had a fashionable long train, and Lizzie showed her how to lift it when she walked.

Abraham was standing in the room behind her. Noticing the train first, he said, "Whew, our cat has a long tail tonight!"

She lifted the train and turned to him.

His eyes went immediately to her bosom. "Mother," he said, "it is my opinion that if some of that tail was nearer the head, it might be in better style."

"Father, your Quaker ancestry is showing," she shot back. She took his arm as the Marine Band struck up "Hail, Columbia" downstairs.

In the reception line, the guests included French princes, ambassadors, socialites, and numerous common folks. She knew that by the end of the evening, her white gloves and those of her husband would be filthy. The talk was uplifting, though. It was about the miracle that she had performed on the public rooms. The French wallpaper in the Red Room drew the most compliments.

A matronly Boston woman stopped the line while she stared long and reproachfully at Mary's bosom. Mary threw her shoulders back and smiled broadly. Later, when the music and conversation momentarily paused, she heard a senator nearby remark to another, "The queen appears to be wearing a flowerpot on her head."

Mary excused herself and went first to the state dining room, where the tables were already overflowing. The caterer had created a convincing hive with "bees" filled with charlotte russe and a bubbling fountain supported by water nymphs made of nougat. An enormous Japanese punch bowl offered up champagne. The centerpiece, or one of them, was a spun sugar replica of Fort Pickens. The tables were perfection. She hurried upstairs.

"His fever is up, ma'am." Lizzie, who along with an elderly servant was sitting watch over Willie, looked worried.

Panic ran through Mary. She felt his forehead, his little hand. He was definitely hotter. Willie looked wanly at his mother. His lids sagged, nearly covering his blue eyes. "Send out for Dr. Stone," she told the old woman, who hurried downstairs.

Once Willie fell asleep, she went back to the party but repeatedly took turns with her husband going up to his bed for the rest of the night. Now compliments on the Wilton carpet were empty to her ears. She counted the minutes until the end of the party.

CHAPTER FORTY-SIX

FEBRUARY 1862

THE TATTOO OF DRUM AND WHISTLING FIFE THAT SENT BOYS
south in train cars to war was the haunting music of death
now. It meant a casket passing on its way to the cemetery. Ana
joined people gathered along the streets to weep with the black-
clad mourners who walked or rode behind the lost soldier.

The families who had sent off their kin with cheers now
became readers of the narrow columns of names on the front
pages of the newspapers. With sickening dread, they searched
those lists of the dead.

In February, Federal forces defeated the secessionists at the
Battle of Fort Donelson. The Union commander who rose to
fame for his victory there was an Illinois general named Ulysses
Grant, whose mother must have imagined a life of adventure
and travail for her baby when she named him.

Fort Donelson was said to be an important victory that broke
the South's hold on the Cumberland River, an avenue into the

heart of Dixie, but it had another consequence for Springfield. Thousands of Confederate soldiers were captured, and the North had nowhere to house them. So it was that Camp Butler became a prisoner-of-war facility for some two thousand Confederate soldiers who, if they were not injured, were put to work building more make-do structures to house the prisoners and serve as hospital units. In time, another thousand would arrive.

Ana kept abreast of every development that February. Sitting at breakfast one morning perusing the paper, she saw a headline she least expected: "Death in the President's Family." William Lincoln, son of the president, age eleven.

Her body flew back against the chair. *No, no! Dear God, not Willie!*

He had died of the typhoid fever that was sweeping Washington. Mary and Abraham Lincoln worshipped that bright-eyed little fellow. Ana herself had adored him. He was so sweet-natured, so tenderly thoughtful for a child, so bright and clever like his father. Ana could not imagine the grief of the Lincolns. *Mary must be flattened in her bed right now.*

She went to her writing desk. *Dear Mr. and Mrs. Lincoln, my heart breaks for you just now...*

She sat and stared at the paper, but she was too shaken to get anything down. Surely Abraham Lincoln did so every day of his life, writing to console parents who had lost a child in battle. What terrible anguish for the man to lose his cherished boy in the midst of navigating his country through a sea of horror.

In April, twenty-three thousand men died, were wounded or captured, or went missing in a furious two-day battle at Shiloh,

Tennessee. Thirteen thousand of them were Union soldiers. Illinois soldiers, including the Ninth Infantry, had borne nearly the whole brunt of the fighting the first day and appeared to have lost the battle. The second day, a Union victory was salvaged from the bloodbath.

Ana remembered the Ninth soldiers because they were some of the first three-month volunteers to muster in at Springfield. About half of them were German immigrants. She followed their course of action in the newspapers. So rushed to battle were they that the men didn't even have proper uniforms when they showed up at Shiloh to fight.

Shiloh was the biggest battle yet and, in the end, a victory for the North. But it had been brutal fighting, and the casualty numbers were incomprehensible to her. In the hideous carnage that spread itself like a carpet of human flesh for a half mile across the fields, what happened to the dead? Buried in shallow graves, she learned. If a comrade recognized a fallen man, he was given a proper burial, and a letter home to the family might be sent by a fellow soldier. If not, the family might never learn of their beloved's fate, especially if he carried no identifying papers. *Missing*, the paper would say.

Four months had passed since Shiloh, and it was August when Joe and Owen both went to talk to recruiters. Joe joined the 114th Illinois Infantry Regiment along with some other young men, all of whom he had grown up with in Little Madeira. Owen, less certain, returned home to think it over.

"Why do you have to go now?" Ana pleaded with Owen. She worried deeply about how he would fare. He wasn't the kind of man who enjoyed riding a horse fast or even chopping wood. Owen lacked the naivete and deep faith of Joe. He had no illusions of glory. She knew her husband was uninterested in braving battle for the valor he might discover within.

He appeared to be talking to himself more than to her as he considered the question. "I don't want to have to be drafted to go. That would be humiliating. I guess thirty is old compared to some, but I know plenty of men older who have volunteered."

True, he admitted, the life he had so far lived was mostly of the mind. True, he was not cut out to be a soldier. "Look, I know how to use a gun, Bean," he reassured her. "I grew up hunting."

Owen often made light of serious things. But then he added, "To stay out of the fight is to help the rebels and all they believe."

Owen returned to the recruiter and joined the 115th Illinois Infantry Regiment the very next day. He and Joe would be counted among those who answered the call for the three hundred thousand volunteers Mr. Lincoln sought that summer to refresh the Union troops. As it turned out, Owen's regiment departed Camp Butler before Joe's. It was a glorious early October day. Ana had persuaded her parents not to come; she wanted to have her remaining precious moments with her husband alone.

Owen wrapped his arms around Ana one last time.

"Will you write the truth to me, Owen?"

"Ana! What a thing to say."

"Don't try to protect me. Do you promise?"

"I promise, if you can do the same."

"I can. I will."

And then he was gone.

In the weeks following, she kept remembering a conversation they'd had early in their relationship. Owen had told her about a person in the old days known as a sin eater. You could still find them in country villages in Wales, he said.

"Usually it was some old drunk or crazy or poor man who lived at the edge of the village. The sin eater was reviled, but he was still useful. When a person died, it was the belief in some places that his sins could be purged through a ritual. The relatives went out and got the sin eater with a promise of a meal or money and brought him to the deathbed. They put a piece of bread or a plate of food on the dead man's chest, and the sin eater ate it. The belief was that the dead person's sins would then be transferred to the soul of the sin eater."

It seemed to Ana that the soldiers in this war were the sin eaters. They were being sacrificed for the offenses of their fathers. Soldiers like Owen and Joe were paying for the sins of those who took captives from Africa, including the founders who kept slaves despite their lofty words and the slave masters who built immense wealth on the backs of stolen, imprisoned men and women.

Atonement for those sins had been coming due for a hundred years. Could Mr. Lincoln possibly have imagined he would be the one in charge when the reckoning came? Could he have conceived of such a horrific war when he wrote the note she found in his study years ago: *If A can prove, however conclusively, that he may of right enslave B...?* The logic she'd found so persuasive back then was a pale defense against bullets and cannonballs. He was a gentle man who would not harm a dog.

In fact, when she was just beginning to work for him, she had witnessed him deliver a rare spanking to his sons for using Fido too roughly as a prop in a play.

Did Mr. Lincoln possibly have the iron will to persist through such bloody carnage in order to win?

CHAPTER FORTY-SEVEN

NOVEMBER 1862

WHEN THE NOVEMBER DAY CAME FOR JOE'S DEPARTURE, Ana joined her parents to see him off at the Camp Butler station. They found him glowing, filling out his new blue jacket like a soldier on a recruiting poster. From that moment on, Ana would look at any boy in such a uniform and understand that he had his own story, his own reasons for joining. Maybe to be seen as a grown man or, even better, a hero. Maybe for the promised paycheck and bonus. Maybe for a surge of patriotism that convinced him he owed the country something.

Genoveva Ferreira carried a big satchel of food. She had been cooking for days. There was garlic pork stuffed between slices of fried bread for Joe's journey, enough to last him for two days and have some to share. There were weeping mothers, stoic mothers, mothers laughing on the platform. One woman appeared to be tipsy from drink. *Mothers fortify themselves as they can.* Her own mother hugged Joe for as long as she could before her son stepped onto the train.

On the platform, a young man stood with a banjo, singing a popular tune.

We are coming, Father Abraham, three hundred thou-
*   sand more,*
From Mississippi's winding stream and from New
*   England's shore.*
We leave our plows and workshops, our wives and chil-
*   dren dear,*
With hearts too full for utterance, with but a silent tear.
We dare not look behind us but steadfastly before.
We are coming, Father Abraham, three hundred thou-
*   sand more!*

Back in September, Mr. Lincoln had released his preliminary Emancipation Proclamation. It stated clearly that by January 1, 1863, the rebels had to lay down arms and rejoin the Union; if not, all slaves in the secesh states would be proclaimed free.

The announcement made it official: restoring the Union was not the sole reason war was being waged. To some, it was an entirely repugnant suggestion that the great underlying reason from the beginning was to abolish slavery.

Springfield, sitting in the middle of the state, was a well-known mix of political leanings. Local election results were often split nearly down the middle, with victors winning by a mere handful of votes. The proclamation tore apart the town, and the delicate threads that had unified Democrats and Republicans snapped.

There had always been sympathizers with the Southern cause in Illinois. The previous June, when a new state constitution was put to a vote, the people overwhelmingly approved a law banning Negroes from migrating and settling in the state. Then, when the Democrats swept the recent November elections, winning all local and state posts *and* sent a Democrat to the U.S. Congress who won his seat by saying that emancipation would Africanize the North, the message became clear.

Immediately after the election the streets were filled with Democrats celebrating their big win. The Democratic *Register* ran the headline "The Home of Lincoln Condemns the Proclamation." That would have enraged Owen.

Stephen Douglas had rallied the Democrats to fight for the Union, but Douglas was dead and now a group who labeled themselves Peace Democrats called for a convention to end the war and pacify the South by letting the slaveholders continue to own slaves. It was infuriating, mutinous talk from a bunch that many locals called Copperheads.

Outrage was flung back and forth inside the state house. Lincoln was a liar. The Democrats were traitors. Ana feared there would be violence in the streets. The Republicans were battle weary, but they needed to rally.

And they did.

A huge number of people filled the Hall of Representatives to cheer Unionist speakers. One notable fellow had been shot in the lung in battle. He stood in front of the crowd wheezing out a defense of the Emancipation Proclamation, pausing to catch breath as a whistling sound emanated from somewhere, likely the bullet hole. His speech was a poignant marvel but it did not allay fears that existed inside both parties. Even the most radical of Republicans did not know what to do about the prospect of millions of newly freed refugees migrating north. Lincoln was proposing voluntary colonization to Africa or locations elsewhere as possible solutions.

A terrible idea, Ana thought. In her heart, hope and despair battled it out.

CHAPTER FORTY-EIGHT

My dear Mrs. Evans,

Did you know you married a soldier of fortune? That is how I am feeling these days, living among brigands and patriots who fight for all kinds of reasons. Take, for example, my friend Karl, a recent immigrant from Germany, who fights for the soldier's pay. I discovered he hoarded in his haversack some German cookies called peppernuts. I promptly befriended this man and he shared generously. The cookies are gone now, but Karl turns out to be a genial companion.

My first understanding of soldiering is that hardtack and coffee do not a breakfast make. We are camped now in Ohio. We have disassembled all the fences hereabout to keep our fires burning all night. And what a pretty sight they make, dotting the darkness with yellow flames. It would be a dandy outing if we had more food and blankets.

We go between pure boredom and marching. There is gambling but if we think there is a skirmish coming, the men leave the evidence behind as no one wants to die with dice or cards on him. Many carry pictures of their children or sweethearts. I do not intend to die, but would you kindly have a photograph made of yourself, my love? It would do my heart good. I count myself lucky to receive your letters. They make such a difference in how I get through a week. It is enough to break a man if he receives no letters.

Devoted to you,
Owen

CHAPTER FORTY-NINE

DECEMBER 1862

Dear Owen,

I wish more than anything I could have come along with you on that train. I received a letter yesterday and felt so relieved you have not seen battle yet. I've sent a number of letters but have no sign that you got any after the end of November. I hope the food is improving, my love, and that you have blankets aplenty in your Ohio camp.

Recently I went out to Camp Butler with a group of women from the Aid Society. We hired the same driver who drove us out there last year. This time it was freezing cold, and the hospital buildings that looked flimsy but clean last summer are now flimsy and filthy. We were told that one building was for pneumonia patients and another for erysipelas patients.

The closer we got to the camp buildings, the stronger

the privy odor became. The women held handkerchiefs to their faces, they were so sickened by it.

A guard ordered some soldiers to take our baskets, and all the while, I could hear rasping coughs through the boards of the infirmary.

There is a new load of prisoners out there now. Sixteen hundred, we were told. The last big bunch left in a prisoner exchange; that is, the ones who didn't die. From what I've heard, there were many who perished already this winter.

Two nurses came out to thank us. Their uniform is a dress fashioned from brown fabric and pantaloons of the same material. Black hats cover their hair. Did you know they must all be older than thirty? Their outfit gets the army's message across: There shall be nothing in the least fetching about nurses and the plainer the woman, the better.

That visit made me want to do more than make bandages. I tried to talk my way into working as a nurse to no avail, but they've allowed me in for other duties. Now I spoon-feed men who cannot feed themselves and write letters for them. It helps me feel useful in your absence.

S HE PUT DOWN HER PEN. *THAT IS PLENTY OF TRUTH TODAY, ANA.* She would spare him details of the bodies being carried out of the infirmaries, dead from malaria and typhoid fever they caught in the place.

Now, when she went to the camp, she held her breath as she crossed the threshold to a building and put on her apron. At the end of the day, she went home exhausted and hopeful that there would be a letter waiting.

CHAPTER FIFTY

WAR HAD NOT YET COME TO SPRINGFIELD. NO BLOOD had been shed on Illinois's soil, but plenty was shed in Camp Butler by wounded men. Ana could never experience the terror of battle, but she listened to the men's stories and came to understand its aftermath.

"Captain said, 'You won't be fightin' close up,'" one prisoner related. "Not much need for bayonets anymore, they told us. Ha! They was some hand-to-hand all right. But when you was shootin' the minnie, felt like you could snag a man before he got anywhere near. Well, they was shootin' minnies too. And you're lookin' at what one of them does if you are on the receivin' end."

Both the North and South used a murderous bullet called the Minié ball, named after its French inventor, who'd devised a way to make a bullet splinter so it shredded bone and muscle. The men said it was easier to load into a muzzle than the old bullets and more accurate. It was supposed to be an advancement.

Ana witnessed the damage the Minié wreaked on men's bodies when it did not kill them. She watched as nurses swabbed turpentine and kerosene over gangrenous elbows and angry, gaping holes in hands, arms, and legs.

The surgeon's operating area looked like the back room of a butcher shop. Amputation was often the only recourse to saving a life. Passing by the door, Ana glimpsed arms, calves, and feet piled in a trough beneath the operating table. The floor of the room was a pond of blood.

When the head nurse found her outside the operating room looking peaked, she gave Ana the assignment of taking notes for the surgeon. Now Ana followed him around the wards, pausing at the straw-covered wooden bunks to write down the names of the men, their diagnoses, and the medication given them. This was a new and official procedure. A steward for a different doctor in another infirmary building told of how the man refused to bother with the new chore of record keeping. Instead, the doctor filled his pockets with tonic pills and other medicines, while his assistant carried bottles of cod liver oil and whiskey that were dispersed out of the same spoon or cup to men all over the ward. Eventually he left rather than bother with the "red tape."

Ana accompanied a surgeon who warned her about the prisoners. "Wild and ignorant, the lot of them. You stay just behind me while I visit." The new arrivals were wearing rags. Some had uniforms, but they appeared homemade by a sister or mother or wife. Among themselves, the new patients contested who had the most "graybacks."

"What is a grayback?" Ana asked one boy.

"Oh, we was just havin' a vermin fair to keep ourselves entertained, ma'am. You know, who's got the most lice? I believe I win today."

Rows of men and boys lay with pale white skin stretched tightly over cheekbones, clavicles, and ribs. Some looked a day or two away from complete starvation. They might have been illustration plates from an anatomy book.

"They haven't been given enough to eat," the surgeon observed. "Looks like some have been underfed for a long time, even before the war. A lot of 'em got sick on the train coming north."

Ana wished she knew Owen's shorthand method; she had to write quickly to keep up with the doctor's words. Sometimes she recorded a success, as when turpentine and kerosene oil fought off gangrene. But exposure to weather and terrible sanitation caused hundreds of deaths, as soldiers were lost to smallpox, pneumonia, and other diseases.

Ana was especially distressed by the patients one nurse called the "nostalgia bunch." These were men who stared for hours into space or cried. Some could no longer speak. Others would not eat. Some had delusions. The nurse explained that their homesickness was so profound it had rendered them despondent and useless.

There was one young man who trembled and held his ears night and day. "Cannon in his head," the surgeon said.

"Coward," muttered a head injury in a bed nearby.

Ana was stunned at what they had all been reduced to by war. *The men blast each other apart, and the women try to put them together again.* In time, she was assigned to elicit oaths of loyalty from the prisoners. Many had already signed them and in doing so could then go home.

She looked into the big blue eyes of one boy named Isaac. He was from Mississippi and had lost a leg, his "drumstick" he called it, and was suffering from infection. As grievously damaged as he was, he refused to sign.

"I never owned a slave. Nor did my family. You people came down and invaded our land. I fought on the side of my father."

She knew he came from poor folks, as he had said so. She had heard other prisoners complain among themselves that it was the rich class of planters who wanted the war and the poor who had to fight it.

"Go back to your people," she urged. "Sign this and you will get passage back home."

He looked at her incredulously. "Pfft. I could never go back that way, sayin' I signed some oath and 'Here I am, Ma.' She and my sisters would throw me out."

Ana ran her hand over his hot forehead. "Isaac, you are a beloved son. Many others have signed these oaths."

But he was proud. Could he survive a train ride home in his condition? She didn't know, but she made a decision to forge his signature. She would explain to him that he was going home for good behavior.

Isaac was gone when Ana returned two days later and another boy occupied his bed. He had died in the night, alone, believing in a thing called honor. The head nurse had information on his people. Ana would write to let them know he was buried with other Confederate soldiers. It was the practice at the camp's cemetery to bury a rebel soldier under a pointed stone marker, distinct from the Union soldiers' rounded head-stones. Some locals said the Confederate headstones were pointed so the devil would not sit on them.

Ana wrote to Owen about Isaac's death, and he responded.

The boy had his own standards for what a good death is. I would not have tangled with that, but you have a kinder heart. Lincoln probably would have forgiven the boy himself without an oath. He has pardoned all kinds of people. On the other hand, my darling, had you forged his signature, you might have been convicted a traitor. I only remind you, as you so fiercely have said to me, that there is a right and wrong side of this war. It is easy perhaps to forget that among the suffering in a prison infirmary. But it is Southern politicians and slaveholders who failed the boy, not you.

CHAPTER FIFTY-ONE

THERE IT WAS IN THE NEWSPAPER. ABRAHAM LINCOLN telling Congress in a long message that, by God, the Emancipation Proclamation was going to be law come January 1, one month from today.

Spencer put on his spectacles and flew his eyes down the column twice to be sure there were no catches in the language. No, he thought not. *All people held as slaves within the rebellious states will be free.*

The pressure would be tremendous on Lincoln to walk back from that precipice. But this was an official speech to Congress. This was not the candidate who had stirred voters with pleas for keeping the union together. This was not the Lincoln who claimed he wouldn't interfere with slavery in the states where it already existed. Lincoln was laying down his cards.

We cannot escape history... The fiery trial through which we pass will light us down, in honor or dishonor, to the latest generation.

Many in town believed Lincoln had always intended eman-cipation. Others saw a changed man. Spencer counted himself among these. He had been observing Lincoln for a long time. He was slow in getting to this point, and he was still talking about colonization, but he had come along at last and was not a man who would go back on his word. Lincoln was adding another whole level of understanding as to why white Americans were sending their sons off to fight in this bloody war.

A lot of people hated that new meaning.

At his barbershop late in the afternoon, men dropped by to talk it through. If it did happen, would Illinois still be ruled by the Black Laws? Or was the federal law stronger than the state's? Somebody pointed out that it wasn't perfect, this doc-ument. The proclamation didn't free the slaves in the border states. Lincoln had allowed slavery to continue there, appar-ently believing he needed their loyalty to win the war. Some of the men thought Lincoln was only doing this to enlarge his troops with colored men who had not been allowed to enlist so far. Maybe so, Spencer argued. If they were allowed to volunteer or were drafted, the president would find a great number of men ready and willing.

Whites, even some local abolitionists, were afraid of masses of ex-slaves moving to the North, taking away jobs of white men. Already, soldiers were bringing back plenty of freed people with them from the South. Contraband, they called the women and children and men who left plantations to follow Union soldiers. When a Virginia slaveholder demanded the return of three of his slaves who had followed Union troops after a victory, one Northern general had reasoned that if these slaves were being used by the Confederacy as laborers to wage war on the North, they would not be returned to their purported owners, as had been the practice so far. Congress agreed with the idea and made it policy.

Truth was, the army did not so much liberate all contrabands as acquire a second army of refugees who set up camps behind Union lines. Despite terrible living conditions, the refugees went to work as cooks, blacksmiths, spies, and laborers who assisted the Union cause. Freedom seekers who made it north spoke of their former masters' stunned surprise that their slaves would actually leave them behind, so thoroughly had they believed that the slave system was a God-blessed way of life for all involved.

In some Illinois towns, Union soldiers bringing in colored refugees were being met with anger from whites. Spencer heard that to avoid trouble over in Lincoln, the little town named after the man before he was president, some soldiers had stopped on the outskirts and rolled freedmen in blankets to hide them before they sent them on north.

He had been disappointed so many times, but Spencer now believed that the emancipation law would go forward. It was too late to turn back.

On December 31, as he walked over to church, Spencer turned over the facts in his mind, trying to shape sentences for something to say from the pulpit. People would be showing up at church tonight at 7:00 p.m., as planned. He would need words for them.

It would be a time for celebration, but also a time for

recollection. As relieved as he felt, there was a strain of sorrow coursing through him. He needed to address the horrors his people had endured.

He would talk about the stolen ones, all the terrified young African men and women who were crammed into slave ships, so many of whom died from the filth and hunger and disease of those horrifying passages. He would talk about their enslaved descendants whose families were ripped apart on the auction block. He did not need to list the bloody tools used by their captors to keep them enslaved. His congregation members knew the horrors only too well. But he would talk about the millions kept in bondage from birth to death, forbidden to learn to read or write, then labeled inferior as humans so their captors could anoint themselves a superior race, noted for their gentility and Christian faith.

Before the congregation celebrated Mr. Lincoln, he wanted to honor the ones who labored to emancipate themselves before the proclamation, the brave souls through two and a half centuries who escaped and then went back to free others, the ones who organized revolts, the ones who resisted despite the consequences. In his church, people would know the famous leaders—Toussaint Louverture, Nat Turner, Denmark Vesey— but so many uprisings were known only by place-names. He would ask his congregation to call out those places and remember the unnamed fighters for freedom. He wanted to feel their fierce spirits in the room tonight.

Around 6:30 in the evening, he went over to the church to ring the bell. Eliza was hurriedly dressing up the children to get them out of the house so as to be there on time. Across America, in towns like Springfield, big events were planned. There would be joy in the streets. Chicago was already celebrating.

The congregation would all know what the ringing meant: come tonight to keep vigil until midnight. When he clanged the bell, he was surprised at how his heart jumped with excitement. How he wished his own father might have been here tonight. But his mother would be in the front row. Thank God Leanna had lived to see it. He pulled the rope again and again, jubilant to be ringing out the message. *Let's praise God tonight. Let's weep for the ancestors who have not seen this day. Let's honor Mr. Lincoln for his courage and sing our hearts out. Emancipation, the actual thing, was hours away.*

CHAPTER FIFTY-TWO

January 8, 1863

My darling Owen,

*This house is so empty without you. I am still making
a large pot of coffee out of habit, then pouring most of
it down the drain. It has been three months since you
left, and I cannot get used to you being away. The whole
town is empty without you. The cat misses you. The trees
miss you. The squirrels wonder where you have gone.
Not to mention the citizens of this town. Never has
the* Journal *needed you more to make sense of what is
happening here.*

*It is now a week since Mr. Lincoln's proclamation
and the Democrats are in an uproar. Their fears are
stoked by the* Register, *of course, which announced an*

abolitionist meeting to occur last night. The paper's editor
was moved to language more hysterical than usual, so I
enclose one choice section I clipped for you.

All those in favor of turning the war from the
legitimate purpose of restoring the Union, to
a war for negro emancipation...will no doubt
be present and indorse the act of treachery to
country which will make the name of Lincoln
synonymous with that of Judas, and for his
bloody designs, make it a fitting associate for
that of Caligula.

I have never witnessed this town so ferociously divided.
People here are weary. Lincoln–hating Copperheads are
everywhere. Women openly wear Copperhead pins on
their breasts. These are not women who show up to help
my Ladies' Aid group, of course. They are women who
cheer at parades protesting emancipation.

Remember when Governor Yates worried about
placing a military camp in Springfield because there
were so many secessionists about? He had good reason
to worry. People who were on the fence about electing
Lincoln are now deeply opposed to his new explanation
for why this war is being waged. They think they have
been double-crossed. It makes me wonder if Mr. Lincoln
can possibly win reelection.

In other news, dear Owen, Julius the Cat grows fat
and not on the leftovers I feed him. He has an interest

in birds, much as you do, but he likes to eat them, and songbirds are the tastiest, apparently. This morning, I found another tiny crush of feathers in the backyard. I so love their songs. I made a collar for Julius of tin cut into strips to flash in the sunlight and shiny bells to warn the birds. He looks like a jester in the court of a cat kingdom.

Forgive me if this letter is too downcast. I promise the next will be full of cheer.

Did you know that your voice lives in my ears? I go through the day conversing with you, even laughing with you, and in this manner, I find I can almost survive the mornings and evenings without you. Church on Sunday is a big help. On Saturdays, I am useless.

Send me word that my voice is in your ears.

Your loving wife,
Ana

CHAPTER FIFTY-THREE

_____

My Ana,

Sweet wife, your voice is in my ears. Your name is on my tongue. My arms ache to hold you. That is all that is worth saying just now.

Owen

CHAPTER FIFTY-FOUR

JUNE 1863

H<small>E WAS STANDING IN THE RAIN, GLAZING A LEAKY WIN-</small>dowpane, when a man in a wagon drawn by two horses rode up to the house. A glance at his face caused Spencer to wave him around to the rear where a figure rose up from the back of the wagon, shaking off hay.

Spencer shooed them both into the kitchen where his wife, already in her nightclothes, was hanging up a cooking pot. Eliza shot a look at Spencer meant to reduce him to a pile of ashes, then got out the coffeepot while the two strangers peeled off drenched boots and coats. Beneath, their clothes were soaked through.

"Joseph Pothicary," the white man managed through barking coughs. He extended his hand to Spencer. Eliza eyed him warily and he noticed it. "It's asthma. I'm a doctor and I would not bring the croup into your house." He then introduced the younger man. "This here is Henry Clay. We've come from Cass

County. The Knights are after him. We've been followed for most of the way and shook them about ten miles out." Down to his soaked undershirt, Pothicary looked like a patriarch out of the Bible, with long white hair, a clean-shaven face, and a bristly patch of white whiskers jutting from his neck like a goat's beard. "I would be obliged if you can give him shelter." He swayed from exhaustion.

"You can stop over here. Both of you, go sit by the fire. Dry out."

Spencer knew of Pothicary, an abolitionist who supported his family as a doctor and a tavern keeper out in the town of Virginia, about thirty-five miles northwest of Springfield. A story about him pushed its way into Spencer's head. He'd heard the stiff, unsmiling man was known to throw customers out of his tavern for cussing. Clearly the wrong profession for a Quaker.

The doctor's cough abated some when Eliza brewed him tea. The house smelled of the yeasty bread she'd baked for the next day. It was the longing look of Henry Clay that softened his wife. She sliced off two big pieces for them, spooned the leftover stew into a pot, then disappeared down the hall to their bedroom.

Spencer turned his attention to the boy. "That's quite a name somebody tacked on you."

"Well, that's my name."

"How old are you?"

"Twenty-two."

"Huh. I took you for maybe sixteen."

Warmed up, the young man was wide-eyed and polite. He

was scrawny, undernourished. Despite his gaunt cheeks, he had an open, trusting countenance.

"Where you from?"

"Moscow, Kentucky. I run off from the master's house when the Seventy-First Regiment settled in close by. It was a couple of men who let me work for them—soldiers from Illinois. I cooked and took care of the horses. Cleaned uniforms. What they want I could do. Come time for them to leave in the fall of '62, I ask Lieutenant Collins can I go with you. He said he was going to Chicago and I could go that far with him.

"So I got on the train with the soldiers. It was a slow ride on that train—took three days from Cairo to Chicago. Riding north, they was drinking and some men kept throwing me off but I run along and jumped back on a rear car, then had to push and fight my way up to that first car where Lieutenant Collins and some of his company was. When we got to Chicago, I didn't know where to go. Can't read signs. I begged him, take me with you to your house. It was freezing cold, and Lieutenant Collins say yes and let me work on his land."

Spencer spooned stew into a bowl and handed it to the boy first, angry at the cruel amusement the soldiers had invented to entertain themselves.

"Thomas Collins has a farm in Cass County," Pothicary said. "Henry spent the winter and spring helping out. When summer came, though, and people gathered at the markets, the talk was of a Negro in their midst. There's not a colored man, woman, or child in that area. And that county is full of Knights."

The word caused Spencer's stomach to contract. *Knights of the Golden Circle.*

"Word I was around riled 'em up," Henry said.

"Some of them complained to the justice of the peace in Beardstown," the doctor explained. "They said Henry had stayed in Cass County long past the ten days allowed by the Black Laws. So the justice issued a warrant for Henry's arrest and eventually a jury convicted him. I paid the fine, and we appealed the decision, then we went back to the farm. Some time passed and the Knights decided to take the matter into their own hands. They came to the house and told my sister— Mrs. Collins—that they wanted the boy. Well, she knew exactly who they were. She wouldn't let them in, but there was a broken pane of glass in the door that was covered with cloth, and she talked to them through the cloth, hollered out names of the ones she knew.

"She said, 'Look at all of you, Harmon Randall, coming at such an hour to capture one young boy who wouldn't raise his hand or voice to harm one of God's animals, least of all a human being. Go on home to Marjorie now.'" Pothicary, who was clearly a sober man, emitted a chuckle that set off a fit of coughing. "They went away embarrassed, that they did," he managed finally. "But we decided then that we needed to move Henry to Springfield."

"It was last week when we seen a line of dust on the prairie, like a tornado movin' across the land." A great shiver convulsed Henry's shoulders at the memory. "Turn out to be fifty men on horses. Mrs. Collins say, 'Run! Go hide in the field in back,' so I run barefoot out of there. No coat."

Pothicary picked up the thread. "These asses pushed their way in, counted the dinner plates on the table, and guessed that Henry had been there minutes before. They went out and looked but never found him."

"They was so close I could hear the dogs pant," Henry said. "I stayed out there all night, freezin' in the cold."

"I found him in the tall grass of the slough. Got him fed and warmed and started out for Springfield."

"How did you know of me?" Spencer asked.

"I have heard about your church, sir, and your family," Pothicary said. "I have been at this business long enough to figure out who will help."

After he settled the men on the floor with blankets and pillows, Spencer sat in front of the waning fire thinking of Henry Clay, named after a man who had talked of emancipation and was a hero to many but who owned slaves himself. His name might not fit, but this boy was suited up in courage—he had saved himself time and again without being able to read a word, not a street sign or name of a town on a map. For three days, he had fought his way through Union soldiers to get to Northern liberty in Lincoln's state. What bitter irony to find himself unwanted and a violator of the Illinois Black Laws.

"I can do any work," Henry Clay told William the next morning after the doctor had departed.

"We'll find a job for you."

Spencer offered up his sofa as an extra bed in his crowded house while the young man found work. Later, he might send Henry to his brother Wiley's farm out near Rochester. There were crops to be brought in, firewood to be chopped. Enough farmers were glad to hire Negro workers, no questions asked. But the farmers did not allow them to stay where they worked, so Wiley had converted a barn to sleeping quarters for the young fellas who hired themselves out by day.

It would be dicey to find Henry a job right now in town.

"If we're careful, if you can avoid attention, we may be able to find you work here in town. It's not impossible. But you can't be seen as a colored man taking the job of a white man who's gone off to fight for the Union," Spencer told Henry. "We'll see."

The town was crawling with strangers and people on the lookout for unfamiliar colored faces. There were plenty of spies around. A Copperhead who lived near Camp Butler was supposedly helping rebel prisoners who had escaped the camp to move on down to the South. If true, it was a bitter pill. After all these years, it sickened him to think that now there were underground railroads going both ways through town.

Henry Clay would have to watch his back in Springfield.

A week later, William raced into the barbershop late on a Thursday afternoon. "Wiley's been shot!" He sank on a chair, breathing hard as Spencer hurried over.

"What? What happened?"

"He was attacked last night by a posse of men. They shot him. Said if he didn't get out of town, they would finish the job. A doctor worked on him and expects he will recover. Sydney says she knows people up in Michigan, so they'll head there as soon as he is able. The farmers out in Rochester believe it was the Knights."

"Aw, hell." Spencer rubbed tears from his eyes. "Wiley is such a sweet man. He was giving shelter to those young fellas. He reads the Word and takes it for his law."

William looked up at him. His face was contorted with rage. "The Knights take the Black Laws for theirs. They're out to show they control Illinois."

CHAPTER FIFTY-FIVE

JULY 1863

JOE'S LETTERS WENT TO THEIR PARENTS' ADDRESS, AND HE sent his pay to them at the end of each month. Written partly in English and partly in Portuguese for their mother's sake, the letters, it was understood, would be read aloud by Ana at her parents' kitchen table. Then they would all discuss them. They knew he was in Mississippi where the heat was unbearable and malaria rampant. He said the mosquitoes were vicious and that plenty of men in camp had developed the shakes. They scrutinized his letters for any hints of ill health or injury and followed the news accounts whenever a town called Vicksburg was mentioned. Joe was constant in his faith in Lincoln. *I carried a burning torch for Abraham Lincoln, and I am proud to carry a rifle for him now.*

Midsummer, an envelope arrived and bore an unfamiliar script. Ana showed up at the house that day and found her parents wailing with grief. A fellow soldier named Thomas wrote that Joe had been killed during the siege of Vicksburg in June. He had fought valiantly and been shot in the chest; he'd died almost immediately. He was a brave soldier, loved and respected by every man in the unit. "He died with God on his lips and asked that I send you his love."

It was a merciful letter, sent by someone who seemed to understand what the parents of a soldier wanted to know and needed to believe: that in the end, he was right with the Lord. The letter said that Joe was buried in Vicksburg, but there was an effort underway to get back home as many fallen soldiers as possible.

While her family wept inside their house, a Fourth of July celebration was going on in town. News came across the wire that very day that Vicksburg had been taken by General Grant. But there was no celebrating on their block. One of their boys was dead, one of ten thousand Union casualties at Vicksburg, the papers reported. Neighbors brought food to the house, spoke kind words.

Ana rolled herself up in Joao's bedcovers and sobbed.. She should have kept him back somehow. She felt none of the pride others mustered in losing a beloved brother or son. Anger was ripping through her body, pushing through her ribs. Joao had never had a sweetheart as far as she knew. He would never know the joy of making his own home with a wife he adored, would never have a chance to make his own beautiful little Joaos.

Beatriz would be heartbroken by the news of their lost brother. But she had a husband and a passel of children to care for. Her life was taken up by family and the demands of the farm.

Ana and Joao, on the other hand, had just begun a grown-up closeness. They loved each other in a way that was a new joy to her. She had tutored him through his school years and was saddened when he dropped out of high school. Those home-work sessions had allowed them to talk about their dreams. He wanted to find a girl, to marry and have a home of his own that he would build himself. He wanted to work with his hands, and as it turned out, he was not only a hard worker, but he had an instinct for making money. After a long day at the brickyard, he would take on odd jobs to enrich his bank account. When she married, Joao had presented Ana with a velvet-lined wood box with half a set of silver in it. "More to come," he'd said at the time. It was the finest present she ever received.

If, in the end, the siege of Vicksburg that had raged from May to the beginning of July was an important win for the North, it was the worst loss possible for the Ferreira family. She was certain none of them would ever be the same. Her stupe-fied mother sat in a chair, rocking back and forth in prayer. Her father wept and cursed. His only thought was to get Joe's body home. He talked of wanting proof. Were there not hundreds of boys named Joe in the army? That letter could have been a mistake. Her father's vein-corded hands, which had built and painted for decades, now held a pen that scratched out letters to the government. He was desperately trying to find out how to send for a casket so his son, if it really was his son, could be disinterred and returned home by train.

The three-day Gettysburg battle that started on July 1 was an even worse debacle, with twenty-three thousand Union casualties. Owen's last letter had arrived weeks ago, from Tennessee. Of course he wasn't in Gettysburg, she reasoned. He was in Tennessee. Unless his regiment had been sent east. Irrational terror seized her. She searched the *Journal*'s death columns and did not find Owen Evans listed.

God would not take both of them in one week, she tried to tell herself. Yet God's mathematics of mercy did not rule out the possibility that more than one family member could be lost. There were mothers who had lost two and three sons. God allowed such things. She prayed furiously nevertheless, especially when she awoke in panic. She got out of bed then, dressed, and walked over to Little Madeira to comfort her parents.

This would be her pattern for months to come. She read the papers, marked the map according to Owen's letters. Over time, the colored pins would show his journey from Kentucky into Tennessee—Chickamauga, Chattanooga, and Missionary Ridge. His letters were fewer and shorter. Time and again, he withheld the full truth from her. God only knew what Owen was feeling. When his letters came, they arrived well after the actual battles.

Mired in a hell of fear and sorrow, she threw herself into working more often at the camp, where the pitch of pain was equal to what was screaming inside her. The infirmary brought a measure of relief.

CHAPTER FIFTY-SIX

September 1863

Chickamauga, TN

Ana. I must write briefly, as I am weak from a bout of dysentery. I think that I've seen what this war has to offer a soldier. I have marched through mud, eaten and slept in it. Lived to see a flag flying victory at Chattanooga, a defeat in the forests of Chickamauga. A bullet (not a minnie) skimmed my left arm but not enough to get me out of here. You asked for the truth and I try to give it here but do not worry. I have fared far better than others in this shaggy part of the planet. I long to return to the sweet flat fields of Illinois.

Your loving husband,
Owen

CHAPTER FIFTY-SEVEN

DECEMBER 1863

MARY WATCHED OUT THE WINDOW ON THE STAIRCASE landing with her son Tad, looking for her little sister Emilie, who was expected at any moment. Carriages bearing cabinet members who were meeting with the president filled the driveway, each having had to pass through a guard post. Mary hoped Emilie's visit would go unnoticed.

Lizzie Keckley joined Mary, watching the buggies unload one cabinet official after another. "The timing is bad. You could have her slip in through the servant's entrance," Lizzie suggested.

Mary shook her head. "But then the servants would know a strange woman came in the side door. Soon enough, they will all know a visitor is with us."

A special visitor, she thought. The wife of a deceased Confederate general. A fragile, twenty-six-year-old widow with three children. And an unrepentant rebel. Her visit would set the hens in DC clucking and tossing around the word "harboring." Yet Mary insisted Emilie be greeted at the front door. She wanted her to feel welcomed as a beloved sister. And she wanted her to feel the awe of the place, to have sink in at once the weight of the state that her husband bore.

Benjamin Hardin Helm had died two and a half months ago at Chickamauga. Mary and Abraham had loved their brother-in-law dearly. He'd visited them at the White House just before the war, and Abraham had even offered him a position as paymaster on the Union side. But Ben had been firm. "I will serve with my people." He was not the only relative to choose the South's cause. Of the fourteen living offspring of Mary's father, eight Todds had chosen to side with the Confederates.

So much life and death had happened in the years since she had last seen Emilie. Two of their brothers had died fighting for the rebels in the past two years. Emilie and her children had followed Ben from post to post since the war began, and now she had buried her husband in Atlanta. Afterward, when she attempted to go home to her mother in Kentucky, she obtained a pass to cross the Chattanooga battle lines from the Confederate general in charge but couldn't get permission from the Union general on the other side. A request was made of the president, and he ordered a pass sent to her.

"That's her carriage." Mary pointed to the one from which the pale moon of a little girl's face stared out of the black canvas top.

"Who is that?" Tad asked.

"Your cousin Katherine, I believe." Mother and son raced down the stairs. "My sister is arriving," Mary told the butler, who straightened with formality. The man had served many presidents, and if he had spilled secrets over the years, she had not heard of it.

"Welcome, madame," he said as Emilie stepped in the door. She looked disheveled from her travel and utterly out of heart. Her daughter held her mother's hand and stared wide-eyed at the grand entry room. Mary moved to embrace her just as they heard Abraham's voice.

"Little Sister!" he boomed and ran down the stairs. He placed his hands on Emilie's coat sleeves and squeezed awkwardly, then gave a gentle tug to the strings of her bonnet's bow at her throat. That moment of tenderness caused Mary to start crying. They all wrapped arms around each other and wept as Emilie's daughter, frightened by the scene, hid herself in her mother's skirts. Tad stood by looking a bit stunned, unsure of what to do.

Mary and Emilie sat in the upstairs library room that adjoined Mary's bedroom. Neither of them dared speak of the war. Instead, Mary talked about Willie. "I think his death was a punishment from God."

"Mary, don't do this to yourself."

"No, truly. I blame myself. We pursued our personal political advancement more than we loved our Creator. Now He has seen fit to punish us."

Emilie patted her sister's arm. "You have had terribly hard months."

Salty tears rose in Mary's eyes. "For so many reasons. We should never have come to this Godforsaken house. Oh, Emily,

kiss me and tell me that you love me. I seem to be the scapegoat
for both the North and South."

Emilie obliged and blotted Mary's eyes with her handkerchief. "I cannot break down in front of my husband anymore.
I try to show only a smiling face. But I worry so much about
him. He is in the absolute hell of...." Mary let her voice trail off.
Emilie had her own harrowing stories about the anguish of war
and the loss of her Ben.

They clasped hands and she felt the balm only a sister can
give. They spoke of their brothers but especially the youngest,
the brother they both loved the best. Aleck was only twenty-
three when he was killed at the Battle of Baton Rouge. They
turned their grieving to Aleck and their memories of him
before the war.

Tad and Katherine played together and popped in and out
of the library. Katherine was a pretty, lively little girl, so much
like Emilie had been.

"Mama," Tad said to Mary one evening as she kissed him
good night. "Mama, Katherine says that Jeff Davis is the president of the United States, not Papa."

"Well, she's wrong, but she doesn't understand things,"
Mary said. "Let it go, darlin'. Her papa just passed away."

Jeff Davis was still sitting firmly in his home in Richmond.
Mary shook her head when she thought of the night two years
ago when she and Abraham had stood on the roof looking over
toward Alexandria, worried but confident of a swift victory.
Not in her wildest imagining had she envisioned how much
blood would be spilled between the Davises' white house in
Richmond and the one her family occupied.

In a deep sleep that night, Mary woke to find Willie standing at the foot of her bed. He didn't speak, just stood there smiling. He was glowing and seemed happy. When he left, she tiptoed into Emilie's bedroom.

"Emilie." Mary sat on the edge of the bed and shook her shoulder. "Emilie, I just saw Willie."

"What is it, Mary?" Emilie looked at her as if she were an apparition herself.

"Willie just visited me, Emilie. He's happy. It's not the first time he has visited. He actually comes to see me quite often."

Emilie's brow furrowed. "You were having a dream, Mary."

"No, it was real. I've been seeing a spiritualist. He says there is a very thin veil between the other world and this one."

"Oh, Mary." Emilie's pitying expression resembled the look Mr. Lincoln had when he told his wife she had become half-mad from her continued grieving. "How nice you get to see him."

Emilie's presence at the White House quickly became controversial. It was apparent when Senator Harris sought out the sisters under a friendly pretense, then took the opportunity to insult Emilie. "We have whipped the rebels at Chattanooga, and I hear, madame, that the scoundrels ran like scared rabbits. I have only one son fighting as a Union soldier, but if I had twenty, they would all be fighting the rebels."

Emilie's nostrils flared. "And if I had twenty sons, Senator Harris, they should all be opposing yours."

The sisters steamed in silence while he slowed his departure to chastise Mary. "Why isn't Robert in the army? He should have gone to the front some time ago," he said indignantly.

Mary's brain composed words to peel his skin off, but Harris and his wife were supporters and friends. She bit her lower lip, inhaled, then took the blame, saying that Robert was still finishing school at her insistence, though he wished to serve. When Harris finally left, Mary stroked Emilie's head as she wept on her shoulder.

That night, Mary told her husband about the scene. "I had my own encounter," he responded. "General Sickles arrived with Harris on his visit. He came into my office on crutches today and said, 'You should not have that rebel in your house!' I told him that you and I are in the habit of choosing our own guests. We don't need his advice or assistance."

Thankfully, Emilie left soon thereafter to return to Lexington. Mary felt that they had escaped estrangement by carefully skirting the subject of the brutal war. Just before her departure, Mr. Lincoln presented two documents to Emilie. One was a copy of the loyalty oath that she had refused to sign. The other was a letter of amnesty that relieved her of forfeitures and stated she was to be protected as a loyal person. When she departed, there were warm caresses and an invitation to return.

Emilie did visit again, in summer the following year. She and another Lexington sister had persisted in asking favors from Mary and Mr. Lincoln that would ultimately aid the South—supplies for rebel prisoners of war in particular. Now she wanted another pass so she might travel to the Deep South to sell a lot of cotton she had inherited. Mary wondered if Emilie understood the terrible position this put her husband into with his cabinet members and the press, who often learned of these things.

Exhausted, Mr. Lincoln said no. He was worn thin by running a war and worn thin by the Todds. Mary's alcoholic, ne'er-do-well brother, Levi, had begged for money saying he was destitute. Abraham refused and also refused to give permission for Emilie to sell the cotton.

From Lexington, she wrote again, begging for the pass. This time, Emilie could not resist a stabbing comment to her brother-in-law: "I have been a quiet citizen and request only the right that humanity and justice always give to widows and orphans. I also would remind you that your minnie bullets have made us what we are."

Sitting at her desk holding that letter, Mary burned with hurt and fury. Emilie had just put scissors to their fragile ties. That was the end. They were on different shores now.

There would be days ahead when she would miss what she'd had with her little sister, Mary expected. But Emilie had made her own bed, and now she had to lie in it.

CHAPTER FIFTY-EIGHT

APRIL 1865

MARY WOKE BEFORE HE DID. SHE LAY NEXT TO HIM LIS-
tening to his breathing, watching for the occasional
twitch of his legs that signaled he was still deep in sleep.

He had been having a terrifying, repetitive dream recently.
The first time it occurred two weeks ago, he had told her about it.

"I went downstairs when I heard the sound of sobbing. It
was coming from the East Room. There were soldiers gathered
around a corpse lying on a catafalque. I walked up to a guard
and asked, "Who is dead in the White House?" And he replied,
'The president. He was killed by an assassin.'"

The dream had horrified her and she'd taken a minute to calm
herself before she spoke. "Of course you had such a dream. We've
heard nothing but warnings about plots and threats since the
day we left Springfield. Those kinds of remarks have an effect."

This morning, when he opened his eyes, he said, "I had that
dream again, about the boat."

That one. She felt her own fright lessen. It was a different dream he'd had several times during periods when he anxiously awaited news of ongoing battles. He'd told her he was alone in a boat on a boundless ocean with no oars, no rudder. There were no assassins in that dream.

She stroked his forehead tenderly. "You should be free of night frights."

She watched him climb out of bed and stand at the window. The war showed on his body; he was so terribly thin, so sad looking. If his dreams disturbed him, it seemed he had no capacity for alarm about his own safety in his waking hours. He ate almost nothing at meals lately. And he was impenetrable when it came to warnings from his bodyguards and cabinet members.

"It is over, my darling." She rose from bed and joined him at the window. Since Lee's surrender, crowds had gathered around the White House, shouting, singing, and dancing. "We ought to have proper clothes on when they wave to us. Let's dress and go have breakfast."

Throughout the White House, there was a profound sense of joy and relief. They found servants embracing on the steps and weeping with happiness. From outside, the sounds of the jubilant crowds filtered into the breakfast room. Abraham reached across the table to squeeze her hand. She squeezed back. "It's over," she assured him. "The nightmare is over."

That afternoon, one of her husband's assistants delivered an elegant-looking note to her. It was an envelope similar to invitations to levees and formal dinners that they received. But there was Abraham's script. Inside was a card that read:

My dear Mrs. Lincoln,

The president requests the honor of your company on a carriage ride into the country on Friday, April 14, at 3:00 p.m. Please invite no others.

Your admirer in chief,
Abraham Lincoln

When Friday rolled around, he drove her out into the frigid, windy day. She had not seen him since the morning and found him to be in a surprisingly cheerful mood.

She looked at him in wonder. "You are your old self again," she said. "I am reminded of the young husband I knew back in Springfield who used to roll around on the floor with the boys. You almost startle me with your cheerfulness."

He laughed. "I finally feel a weight lifted. Mary, it feels as if *this* is the day that the war has come to a close."

She did not question him about whatever had occurred in his office that morning to change his outlook. She could only welcome the joyful feeling between them. They talked about the future, and he repeated what he had mentioned a month ago, that they would save his salary for the next four years and live off the interest. "We can travel then," he said. "We can go to California. If we want to, we can go to Jerusalem. Think of it."

They talked lovingly about Willie, how bright and mature he was, how good a child, how handsome.

He stopped the carriage when they got to the Navy Yard and prepared to turn around.

"We have both been so miserable, Mary, between the war and the loss of our sweet Willie. We must *both* be more cheerful in the future."

"I know," she said. "I know."

Back at the White House, she thought their plan to go to the theater might brighten the evening. A comedy was playing at the Ford Theater. It was not great art by any stretch of the imagination, but Abraham loved comedies, and oh, how they needed to laugh.

CHAPTER FIFTY-NINE

May 1865

W HEN THE PRESIDENT RETURNED TO SPRINGFIELD, IT was spring and beautifully sunny, the kind of day the town had craved during an oppressively gray winter. But Mr. Lincoln wouldn't see it, wouldn't see the lilacs of May when they burst forth. He would have loved this day, and Joao would have too. Ana was thinking of them both. Her brother's body had come home finally in a casket from Georgia and was buried out at Oak Ridge Cemetery. Now Mr. Lincoln would join him in that quiet place.

Mary Lincoln was said to be prostrate in the White House, insane with grief, no doubt. Tad had stayed back to comfort her.

Awaiting Mr. Lincoln's return, people all over the city hung their grief from their front porches with black draping. John Wilkes Booth's bullet had shot Springfield in its heart. The whole town reeled in pain. Only five days before the shooting, the streets of Springfield had been jubilant at news of Lee's surrender at Appomattox.

The funeral train had been chugging this way for more than two weeks, making its slow journey across America so that Father Abraham's people could say goodbye to him. The train retraced the route the inaugural train had taken from Springfield, and Ana had followed its progress the whole way. Nineteen days ago, it had set out from Washington, stopping in Baltimore, Harrisburg, Philadelphia, and other towns, then on to Jersey City, where some five hundred thousand people waited in line to view his body. By ferryboat next to New York City, where a thousand members of the city's German musical societies sang a requiem. The train continued north, past West Point, where every cadet entered Mr. Lincoln's train car and saluted him.

On April 26, as the train was to leave Albany for Buffalo, news came to the telegraph office that John Wilkes Booth had been shot, dying within hours from his wounds. That note of justice provided little consolation. It would not bring back President Lincoln. The solemn funeral train moved on to Syracuse, to Rochester and Buffalo, past tiny burgs and farm fields where torches lit the faces of people standing tribute in the night. The train went south and finally west, moving ever closer to home, through Cleveland, Columbus, and Indianapolis to Chicago, where crowds were so massive that those in line moved only one foot per hour.

Ana thought a lot about Robert Lincoln, who was making the long ride home with a group of relatives and friends. Willie Lincoln's body accompanied his father's and would rest in the same family vault. Ana often felt sorrow for Mary Lincoln, but

Robert had borne extraordinary pain in his young life, as well. He had been a tender boy, bruised inside by loneliness and losses. What a long, sad ride for that young man.

Springfield had been waiting for this moment since the morning of April 15, when church and fire department bells woke her to the news. The town had cried out in anguish, and businesses had shut their doors. By the time Ana reached the square, crepe-lined flags were at half-mast, and the Capitol, along with surrounding buildings, was being wrapped in black. There were rumors Mary Lincoln had wanted her husband buried in Chicago, but two days later, it was official: the president's body would be interred in Springfield at Oak Ridge Cemetery.

Ana felt proud of the townspeople who rose to the challenge. Homeowners offered up spare beds to visiting mourners. The Lincolns' brother-in-law, Clark Smith, got his hands on thirty thousand yards of mourning material and sold it at cost at his dry goods store; there wasn't an unadorned church or municipal building in town. She bought draping from him for her own house and hung swags of it from the windows.

Now, as the seven-car, crepe-festooned funeral train approached the Springfield depot, the huge crowd seemed to hold its breath. Ana was flooded with memories of the very spot where she had stood with Cal four years earlier, bidding farewell to Mr. Lincoln. Four years. It felt like an entire lifetime. Standing on her tiptoes among thousands of other people, she watched as an elaborate coffin was carried down and loaded onto a hearse that was pulled by six black horses.

Ana joined with the masses walking behind the hearse as it headed to the square. They passed a black-draped house with a hand-lettered sign in the window that read, simply, "Come home." A line of people had already formed there, waiting to climb the steps on the north side of the Capitol, the same steps on which she and Cal had sat watching their mothers work. Soldiers carried Mr. Lincoln up to the second floor, where the president would lie in state for a full day in the Hall of Representatives.

She'd come alone, not wanting her fragile emotions to further distress her parents. Surrounded by grieving people, Ana felt swept up in a great guttural moan to heaven. She missed Cal just then, had missed her the day the war was declared over. They would have clung to each. Ana didn't even know where she was; her last letter to Cal had been returned.

Choral groups sang at the station and the state house. Their hymns only heightened the anguish of those who waited to view the president's body. Like Ana, the mourners were grieving for him and for their loved ones who had died for the cause. They grieved for themselves too, hopelessly altered survivors.

Hundreds of thousands dead, and the body count was still going on. Someone had tallied Illinois's military deaths at thirty thousand not counting the injured, who were legion. It seemed as if every block in town had at least one house in which a woman wearing black garments no longer cared to live.

People had journeyed from all parts of Illinois and beyond to make meaning out of their terrible losses. They waited and bore witness to Mr. Lincoln's life and the lives of their loved ones.

A soldier on crutches wearing the 114th Regiment patch on his uniform passed along the line, and Ana felt her heart turn over. She grabbed the soldier's sleeve. "Did you know my brother, Joe Ferreira?" she asked breathlessly.

The young man looked at her. His face softened. "Not well."

"We know so little about his last days…"

"Oh, they was all brave in his unit," he said.

"What else?" she asked, still gripping the sleeve of his coat. "Did he say anything about home? About his family?"

The soldier knew what she wanted. *Anything.* She would take any morsel he could offer.

"I wish I could say more, ma'am. I am sorry he did not make it."

The line made its way to the second-floor Hall of Representatives and the catafalque. It was a dramatic thing, all black velvet, white satin lining, and silver decoration. Two large silver letters, AL, decorated one side of the casket. Strewn over the floor were boughs of evergreens and white flowers laid there just hours before by some of her Soldiers' Aid friends. When, at last, Ana stood beside Mr. Lincoln's body, she saw the worn shell of a once lively and loving man. It hurt her to see his body exhibited like this. Thank God it was the end of his long journey home.

Turning to leave, she noticed two signs placed high above the casket:

"WASHINGTON THE FATHER.
LINCOLN THE SAVIOR."

"SOONER THAN SURRENDER
THESE PRINCIPLES, I WOULD BE
ASSASSINATED ON THE SPOT."

FEB. 22, 1861

The first quotation was appropriate, she supposed. But the second? The words on first glance seemed to say, "Didn't I tell you so?" Why had they not instead chosen something from all the beautiful, conciliatory things he'd said to pull the nation together?

Walking home, she pondered the quote. By the time she reached her front door, she'd come to understand Mr. Lincoln was saying, "I *choose* to die for this cause if need be." He was not only a leader, he was a soldier in the war. Lincoln would have wanted to be counted among the men in uniform.

She sat in the backyard, sipping a cup of tea and watching a flock of yellow-bellied, tittering birds—early this year— convene in her apple tree. *Happy migrants, oblivious to our human struggles.* Or were they? Had they fled the thunder and smoke of cannons in the South? Had they seen, from their bird's-eye view, the fields of slain soldiers? *Birds recognize death in other species, don't they?* Did they recognize the frozen shapes below them as humans? Did they observe the business of death near the fields—men and women turning over lifeless bodies on the ground to see if the faces among the unmoving belonged to their loved ones?

She squeezed her eyes shut. Mr. Lincoln had shown the world that ending slavery was a cause worth dying for. The whole bloody undertaking was elevated when he talked straight truth about why the North was fighting the South. It was about the sin of slavery, always had been. It was about preserving the Union, absolutely, but the Union issue arose out of the South's insistence on preserving and expanding slavery. For

Lincoln, it was simple. If slavery wasn't wrong, then nothing was wrong. She remembered what he said when he signed the Emancipation Proclamation: "If my name ever goes into history, it will be for this act. My whole soul is in it." She wished they had added those words above his casket.

How things had changed overnight. Now, people throughout the North were calling Mr. Lincoln a prophet, a martyr, a savior. Any Copperhead who celebrated the murder risked his life in saying so out loud. A factory worker in southern Illinois had been clubbed with an iron tool for daring to say he was glad the president was dead. A neighbor reported people in St. Louis were shot at in the streets for making such remarks. Ana shook her head. What would Mr. Lincoln make of his sudden popularity?

She went to bed at sunset, at peace for the first time in months as she thought of Joao. He was not merely a sin eater. He had chosen to offer up his short, beautiful life for a sacred cause. Nothing could take that away from him.

CHAPTER SIXTY

S PENCER WENT TO THE CAPITOL AROUND 5:00 A.M., WHEN the line to approach the bier was sure to be shorter. Fleurville had told him poor old Lincoln had been repeatedly embalmed for the train ride across country. Gazing now at the man's face, he saw the president was barely a shadow of himself.

Spencer had never seen an embalmed body. Lincoln's yellow skin was covered with chalk powder and rouge and amber makeup. It was sad and a little grotesque. Mr. Lincoln's spirit had departed over two weeks ago, and no undertaker's art could mask that fact.

In the throng of people crowding the streets around the square, Spencer searched for his wife and family. They had planned to march together in the procession to the cemetery, but there were now some seventy-five thousand people amassed in their town of twelve thousand. It was a good thing all the saloons were closed, because the closely packed crowds veered between sorrow and circus without the assistance of booze. The day before, he'd witnessed the spectacle of the famous General Joe Hooker catching a pickpocket in action. In the midst of weeping mourners, "Fighting Joe" had kicked the man across the ground to a round of cheers.

Now, against the odds, Spencer maneuvered toward the area where the procession would begin—at the north door of the Capitol. There he came upon his friend Reverend Henry Brown holding the reins of Lincoln's horse. Old Bob was draped in a tasseled mourning coat. Next to him was Billy Fleurville, who had served as an honorary pallbearer and now seemed distraught.

The Springfield Committee on Arrangements had told Fleurville he was to be among the dignitaries who headed up the procession. "But they're putting the rest of our people at the back. I won't walk up front."

Spencer felt for his old friend but was unsurprised by the offensive positioning. Together they made their way back along the procession line to where his family and those of his brothers and sisters had gathered to walk together. From the corner of his eye, he caught sight of a face he recognized amid the mass of black hats and mourning garb.

"Cal? Is that you?"

The young woman, her arm linked with that of a man, broke into a smile.

"Reverend Donnegan!"

Spencer bowed and squeezed her gloved hands.

"I haven't seen you in…"

"At least five years," she said. "That's how long I've been in Chicago. I want you to meet someone." She turned to the tall man standing alongside her. "Spencer Donnegan, this is my husband, Howard Parker."

"I had no idea you were married!" He turned to the husband. "You won over a lovely and spirited young lady."

"I know both parts," he said.

Spencer looked at Cal's animated, freckled face. She had not changed much since she attended his church and sang in the choir. "You worked for the Lincolns before they left, didn't you?"

"Yes. I was just sick at the news of his death. We came in early knowing the trains would be full. My mother is still here, so we had a place to stay last night."

"I think my own mother would like to see you."

"Ah, and I would love to see her, but we will go back later if we can get on a train."

They walked together and exchanged stories. She had worked as a milliner and hoped to have her own shop someday. Her husband was studying to be a banker and wanted to work for the new Freedman's Bank, maybe in Washington.

Along the way, they saw people fall to their knees to honor the dead president. Many of them were colored people, overcome with grief. There had never been anything like this in America, folks said.

At the cemetery, there was choral music and prayers and speeches. The vault stood open nearby. One of the numerous ministers announced he would read out loud Lincoln's second inaugural address. It must have been the last speech he had written, just weeks ago. Spencer had seen it in print and remembered being struck by the fact that it was surprisingly short and extremely forceful.

Mr. Lincoln had clearly been walking through a fire. He talked about God in his speech. He had said both sides read the Bible and prayed to the same God for help. In his understated way, he said it seemed strange that anyone would pray to God for the right to keep wringing their bread from the sweat of other men's efforts.

Spencer strained to listen to the minister from the Second Baptist Church who was reading Mr. Lincoln's speech. He cupped his ear to catch the words more clearly from the podium.

"Fondly do we hope, fervently do we pray, that this mighty scourge of war may speedily pass away. Yet if God wills that it continue until all the wealth piled by the bondsman's two hundred and fifty years of unrequited toil shall be sunk, and until every drop of blood drawn with the lash shall be paid by another drawn with the sword, as was said three thousand years ago, so still it must be said 'the judgments of the Lord are true and righteous altogether.'"

Spencer shivered. The words echoed across the heads of the crowd as if they were coming right out of that vault. "With malice toward none, with charity for all…"

He looked up at the cloudless sky.

"To think that we knew him," Spencer said. Cal, who was weeping beside him in that overheated mass of human bodies, nodded her head.

Spencer felt worn out from the heat and long walk and the emotional upset of the day. There was so much work ahead, it tired him to think about it. The states had to ratify the Thirteenth Amendment abolishing slavery. The vote had to be secured. But the man who had sat in his barber chair so many times had brought about what no one else could do. As Spencer walked with Cal and her husband back to the square, he was already composing his sermon for next Sunday.

Ana plodded along with the crowd as she made her way to the east side of town. Her parents had not attended the service at the cemetery, and as difficult as it was to get to their house through the crush of mourners, she felt the urge to be with them. Lincoln's murder had visited upon them the same searing grief they had suffered at the news of Joao's death. Their sorrow for the president and their lost son was all of a piece to them. Moving slowly past the train station, she looked up at the crowd on the platform and felt a jerk in her neck. There was Cal.

Immediately she was pushing her way toward the steps and calling out Cal's name. Cal looked up, saw Ana's waving arms, and opened hers. They wept on the platform before they could talk.

When she was able, Ana extended her hand to the man standing protectively next to Cal. "You must be Howard."

He took her gloved hand in both of his. "And you are Ana. I meet you at last. How sorry I am that the circumstances are so heartbreaking."

He was tall and refined looking, his manners as smooth as his young-looking face. On his coat sleeve, he was wearing a mourning band.

"I had to come," Cal said. "I wanted to be here in town

among people who knew him. And here you are, Ana Ferreira, you who of anyone shares the same memories I do of that house and that family."

"I just keep thinking of Robert and Tad," Ana said.

"As do I."

There was so much to say and so little time, as a train was due at any moment. Ana observed how Howard kept his hand at his wife's back as if he were supporting her while claiming her too. She could see so clearly that they constituted a world unto themselves. It was a new and lovely thing to see that Cal had a partner who understood her in a way Ana never could. She had always kept a part of herself in reserve.

"Mr. Lincoln was so kind to me," Ana said. "And he encouraged my studies. When I told him I was taking a Latin class, he was delighted. He said he had very little schooling and where he came from, just basic readin' and writin' and cipherin'. You know how he talked. He said if a straggler who supposedly understood Latin had appeared in his old neighborhood, he would have been looked upon as a wizard." Ana laughed. "After that, he would say, 'How is the wizard today?'"

Cal nodded and smiled. "I once told him a secret, that I knew someone who did not have real freedom papers. They were fake. I asked him what I should do if that person was caught or turned in. He said, 'You come find me. I will take care of it.' After that, we had an understanding of some kind, though I could not have told you what it was. He just noticed me more. Once, he said, 'You are a bright girl. Keep up your reading.'"

"You knew a runaway in town?"

"My auntie." Cal smiled at Ana. "You never guessed, did you?"

"No!" The memory of a large, serious woman filled her head. "She does not need to hide anymore."

Ana felt stunned. "Tell me."

"Well, she and Mama are sisters. They had the same master in Tennessee and lived on the same farm until they were twelve, when my aunt was sold to another farmer. Years later, Mother bought her own freedom and mine too. My aunt was not able to do that. She eventually heard through a chain of people that my mother and I were free and living here. So she ran. She made it to Springfield. She helped raise me, really."

Cal's sudden openness, her revelation of a secret she had carried all these years, left Ana nearly speechless. "But your mother invited me into your house. I had no idea your auntie…"

Cal nodded her head. "My mother took that chance."

That's why you were so private. Ana shook her head, piecing together fragments of memory. She stared into Cal's smiling face. "And your auntie? Is she still in the house with your mother?"

"Oh yes. But now she doesn't have to worry when she goes out. She loves to take long walks. Goes out in the fields to hunt. She doesn't live in fear anymore."

The blasting horn of an approaching train caused the crowd on the platform to shift its mass as people bent down for bags and the hands of children. Ana's head went dizzy from the acrid smell of pressed flesh, the bump of elbows and shoulders, and now the sudden revelation.

"Tell me quick," Cal said. "How is Owen?"

"He is alive. He won't be mustered out for a month, but he is coming home."

Cal sighed her relief. "I am so happy he is safe." As the train drew closer, she dug into the satchel she carried and produced a pencil and a piece of paper. She tore off a corner and wrote on it. "We have a new address. We just moved. Write to me!"

CHAPTER SIXTY-ONE

JUNE 1865

Ana counted the days until Owen returned home in June. She looked around the house to see what was different. It had been almost three years since he left. Not too much change inside, she thought, but outside, the garden they had planted before he left was lush. Would he notice how large the box hedge had grown? Would he admire the red roses she had planted along the back of the house wall? And what would he think of their neighborhood and the new houses nearby? Or of Springfield itself? It had been growing all along, in spite of the war.

The townspeople seemed stunned by the jerks of emotion they had experienced, first with the joy of the war's end, and then, not a week later, the blow of Mr. Lincoln's murder. Some families were still waiting for their soldiers to return. Others were deep in grieving.

Ana's mother helped out at the Catholic convent now. It

had been a sanctuary for her after Joao's death. She took care of the linens for the nuns and had free use of the chapel, fragrant with incense and flowers, where she sat in a pew and talked to God.

Genoveva told of how there were weekly arrivals at the convent of girls from southern families who were to be educated by the nuns. Before the war, the Ursulines had run schools for the daughters of New Orleans Catholics. Now the South was devastated and suffering badly. Southern families had no money. Instead they sent china, harps, whatever they had of value to pay for their girls' education.

"You should see the sisters' parlor at the convent," she said. "It is filling up with fine furniture."

All over town, there was a sense of profound fatigue, of craving normal things. A quiet cup of coffee without the terrible news in the paper. People wanted to go back to a life marked by peaceful moments.

On June 23, when the 115th mustered out at Camp Butler, Ana waited with families of other soldiers, standing as tall as she could to catch sight of his face as the ragged soldiers walked in a formation and stopped in front of the crowd. Where was he? She could not distinguish him from the others until she saw one slender soldier with his arm in a sling. It had to be Owen. Or half of Owen. The figure looked to be starved.

Family members waited anxiously through a speech to hold their beloved ones in their arms. The speaker talked of their courage, named the battles and the numbers dead.

At the end of the ceremony, Owen came to her and with his

free arm held on to her as if he might fall over. He was emaciated all right, and the whites of his eyes had gone yellow. Those eyes could still crinkle when he saw her, though, and they both laughed with joy at the wonder that he was alive, standing right there. They clung together while other men departed with their loved ones. She felt his weight on her as they nearly toppled over.

Thank you, God. Thank you. She would nurse him back to health. She knew how.

She had hired a carriage to collect them from the camp and bring him home. For a week, she had been baking, and he stopped to inhale when he stepped through the front door. "Oh my Lord," he said. "Real bread."

They went to the bed first. Owen took off his uniform and exposed his reduced body. As he lay beneath the sheet, the bones of his hips stuck up, his concave belly was a valley between peaks, and his left arm was indented by the rip of a bullet across it.

Again, he held her for a long time before they made love, and then he fell asleep. Hours later, he dressed and came downstairs. Dinner was waiting but she was patient. *He needs to feel it is his own house again.*

He seemed disoriented. She had kept his study exactly as he had left it. He stood at the door, staring at the stacks of paper on the desk. "I have been in another world," he said. He walked into his study, closed the door. Standing outside, she heard him weeping. She returned to the kitchen.

In the days that followed, Owen careened between relief and rage. He talked of hearing about the Copperheads in

Springfield while he was marching with a hungry belly in ruined boots. "I would have preferred shooting a Copperhead most days than some poor young country conscript down there," he told her. He was disgusted that Robert Lincoln had not served until the very end of the war, unlike himself and her brother, who had both faced battle after battle.

He cast himself around the house for a week, lying on the couch, trying to dig in the garden, dropping the spade and going on to another pursuit, unable to finish anything. The paper took him on immediately when he inquired, and the return to a schedule helped him. In the evenings when he came home, he repaired to the backyard and had a glass of whiskey. He would imitate the thick accent of some imaginary Welsh ancestor when he had his first drink of the night. He would pour a glass and say, "Ah, just a wee bit fer the comfort that's in it."

She watched his face and waited to see what the evening would bring.

CHAPTER SIXTY-TWO

DECEMBER 1865

ANA CAME HOME EAGER TO TELL OWEN ABOUT A PLAN HER library committee was concocting to bring Frederick Douglass to Springfield as a way to raise funds for an eventual library building. She called out to him but got no answer. Assistant managing editors work late, he would say if he were here.

She feared that since his return six months ago, they had begun to live almost separate lives. There was a time when they had shared so many thoughts and pleasures that she only saw the things they had in common. Lately she wondered if Owen had possessed a fondness for whiskey before he went into the army, though she would have noticed that. No, she suspected he had developed this powerful thirst while he was away. He drank openly but also secretly, or so he thought. She found his bottles tucked behind the stovepipe, under his tool cabinet, even in his sock drawer. Since returning from the war, whiskey was his true love. It could make him mean or sentimental or sweet. It was unpredictable.

He was best when he came home from work, took his shoes off, and poured a glass. They were careful and kind to each other. He called her Bean. Later in the evening, they were certain to disagree on something. It did not matter what the subject was; what mattered was who won. If she asked him to do a chore, then he could not do it because she had asked it.

"You cannot control my life," he told her. "I have real work to do." He had become a table pounder to make his point. She learned to wait. Perhaps he would fix the flapping shutters. But she saw he was in the fight of his life, trying to control his own mind, fighting memories as if the devil were alive in him.

Oh, how she wished they might have children. They would bring him joy to erase the old sorrows. But she had suffered another miscarriage, a third since they married, just a few weeks ago. She blamed herself for her inability to make him happy. At night, when he tumbled into bed, she lay awake wondering, *What are we living for now without children? What comes next?*

What came next often enough for Owen was a screaming nightmare. He heard booming cannons in his sleep and bullets whistling past his ears. He twitched, ducked, and cried out under the sheets. Recently he begged her to move down the hall to the extra bedroom to escape the noise.

He carried on as best he could, clinging to the routines he had before the war when he was solid in himself. Work and whiskey made life bearable for him.

She was not a drinker, but one evening in frustration, she

turned to him. "Pour me some of that," she said. "I want to understand why you go there."

He laughed. "Let me buy you something smoother. This is cheap whiskey. You have to meet it halfway."

She drank the cheap stuff from his glass anyway and felt sickened by the burn of it. Why on earth did he seek comfort in that?

She knew the war had done this to him. He had seen too many awful things. He drank to salve his heart, and she could not condemn him. He had spoken of some of his experiences right when he came back, but now he did not want to talk about any of it. At night after dinner, he went into his study to "work on my book." It was a fruitless struggle that left him even more troubled. He was trying to put on paper what he knew about war, probably to exorcise it, but the words would not come. Dispirited, he reached for the bottle.

You have to meet it halfway.

What had he really meant? She thought he was saying that you have to trust the whiskey will take you to a place of relief, maybe even to a flash of happiness. You have to bring faith to the glass. For a while, it had worked. She had seen him laugh and lighten. Except over the months, it seemed to take more of the whiskey and more of him to meet in the middle.

One day she went to a grog shop and told the clerk she wanted the best whiskey on the shelf. He handed her a bottle with a fancy label. That night, sitting in front of a fire, she poured a glass for him and one for herself. The taste of this good one burned more than the cheap whiskey. She refilled the glasses and began.

"I am stronger than you give me credit for."

He laughed. "You have always been a game lass."

"I want you to tell me what happened."

"Today? Nothing."

"You know what I mean. Bring to me what you bring to that glass. Meet me halfway."

He leaned back in the big chair he used for reading. His chest rose with breath summoned from a deep place. He shook his head slowly.

"I had to live it, for Christ's sake. Now you want me to *talk* about it too?"

"Yes. If you talk to me, the painful memories will lose their power."

He snickered. "Who told you that nonsense?"

"I saw it in the infirmary. Nostalgia was such a misnomer for what ailed so many men. It wasn't memories of home that haunted them. Memory was the enemy. But if I could persuade one man to tell me his story, I saw relief. I truly did. Maybe all that came of it was he slept that night. But it worked." She set down her glass and filled it again. It was the most sickening stuff she had ever tasted. "I think you owe it to me."

Owen filled his glass. He was silent for a long while, his head at a slant, his lips pursing as he fell into reverie.

"They marched us all over the damn state of Kentucky. We didn't see battle at first, only a few skirmishes. But it was so cold that first winter, it was '62 and '63. We must have lost—"

He stopped, stared at the floor.

"I don't know how many. They lost fingers and toes or caught something or died from exposure. Early spring, they marched us into Tennessee. It was still cold. I was sent out with two others to scout for the enemy. One of the men was a captain, so he was in charge. Just after sunset, we found a place to camp in a forest. We could not build a fire—we'd be detected—so we huddled together for warmth when it got dark. Lying there in the blackness, we heard an enemy scouting party set up camp nearby. Scared the hell out of all of us. They were so close we could hear their talk. I remember smelling the fire."

Owen picked up his glass and drank. "They were cooking the meat of an animal, and it was coming right up my hungry nose. Those men were talking about the same things the boys in my unit talked about. One of them they called Riley was funny. It was as if I was listening to my cousins in the next room of our house back in Wisconsin.

"We knew if we even moved a hair, we would be discovered, and we were outnumbered. We counted five voices. Just before dawn, our captain signaled us to prepare to fight. Our only advantage would be surprise."

Owen paused, stared into the fireplace. "How can I tell you the terror of it? I looked around that place in the woods and wondered if this was a good place to die. I had to raise up in myself some...*will* is the wrong word...some way to make myself a fighter, because I had never really fought. Turned out my body knew how to do that. Fear is Satan's own tinder. When the captain gave the signal, we fell on them like beasts. Four men managed to get up and fight. One soldier didn't even have time to stand. We killed him in his blanket." Tears streamed down his cheeks. "Two of them were just boys. It was a horror."

She sank down next to his chair, took his hand, laced her fingers with his.

"Before, war was only headlines to me. Distant. But for a soldier, war is personal, at first anyway. You try not to think of their humanity. You must shoot before you are shot." Owen stared into the fire. "After a while, you *don't* notice. That's another horror. It becomes easier."

CHAPTER SIXTY-THREE

THE SPRINGFIELD LIBRARY ASSOCIATION HAD FINALLY managed to get Frederick Douglass to agree to come and speak at the Capitol. The group was made up entirely of men, but Ana had jumped in to help, using Owen's reputation to get a foothold. The library would have to start as a membership situation, as town libraries often did. Fifty dollars bought you a lifetime subscription and a vote, while five dollars in advance got you a year's worth of library privileges. Eventually, they would have enough funds to build a free city library.

The committee was headed up by Dr. Willard, a longtime abolitionist who loved regaling people with the story of how he had been convicted as a college student of harboring a runaway slave. Ana was jubilant they had gotten Douglass to come to town, and she devoured the copy of his memoir that Willard gave her to prepare for the event.

As it turned out, the Democratic *Register* did not share the association's excitement. The editors of the paper were ugly in their anger at the invitation.

> We have no objection to Fred. Douglass at a negro minstrel concert, a circus or an abolition stump meeting. We object to the degradation consequent upon the idea that the intellect of the white man needs the aid of the negro to brighten it... This is a slander upon the white talent of this country.

Ana carried the editorial in a fury over to Willard's office first thing in the morning. He looked it over through reading glasses hanging on the tip of his nose and said calmly, "Let the damn fools stay home then." He stood and paced back and forth behind his desk, his head down as he reflected, before he looked up at Ana. "Change of plan. I believe this will be an affair that is sponsored by us as individuals and not by the library association. We as citizens will donate the funds to the library association."

"All right. One merchant has already withdrawn his donation to the association because of this stupid editorial," Ana said. "That's fifty dollars more we will have to cover for Douglass's speaking fee before we begin to raise funds for the library."

"Well, tell your husband to put out a plea for donations over at the *Journal.*"

Owen did write a sympathetic column, and within a week, three Negro gentlemen came to Willard with the needed fifty dollars. Still, committee members fretted that they were being viewed as "radical Republicans." They decided to amend their bylaws, promising to no longer act in a "partisan" fashion.

"Why not change our name to the Springfield Cowards' Association?" she remarked to Willard one afternoon.

"Keep your seat, Ana. The war is not yet a year behind us. Folks are still tetchy, and we are just getting started here."

They had engaged Douglass for two evening lectures in February to begin the day after Lincoln's birthday, but weather caused delays. When Douglass finally stood at the podium in the Capitol's Hall of Representatives, it was April 3, eleven days short of the anniversary of Mr. Lincoln's shooting. The topic of his first speech could not have been more timely or poignant: "The Assassination and Its Consequences."

There stood Frederick Douglass, his tall figure tailored elegantly, his graying head indeed leonine, as reporters labeled it. Ana had seen a couple of photographs of the man, but his living presence was electrifying, not only for his grave demeanor and booming voice but for the fact that he was commanding the audience from the center of Illinois power, the rostrum in the hallowed Hall of Representatives. Everybody in the place knew that he was the first colored man to do so. Wild applause caused him to halt repeatedly throughout his remarks.

Douglass began slowly, rotating his head to take in the faces of Lincoln's own townspeople. "No man ever defined his character better than himself when he said in his last inaugural, he had 'malice towards none but charity towards all.'"

Lincoln wasn't assassinated for any personal hate he

provoked, Douglass explained. "No man who knew Abraham Lincoln could hate him… No, he died for a cause. He died for the country—for loyalty as against treason, for republican government based on liberty and equal rights as against a proud and selfish class government based on the enslavement of millions of their fellow men."

Now he was up there warning about an era yet to come that would be more calamitous, more treacherous than the rebellion. Ana shifted in her seat. *What could possibly be more calamitous than the war we just lived through?* It would be the undoing of the colored man's rights that had been won, said Douglass. It was already happening in Congress, where plantation owners and former Confederate soldiers were gathering power and encouraging states to impose new black laws. And without the full freedom of the black man in America, true democracy, the cause Lincoln had died for, could never be realized. It would forever be frustrated.

She tried to focus on his words, but she kept thinking of Frederick Douglass as he was in his memoir—an enslaved, orphaned boy who learned the alphabet from his Baltimore master's wife but could not continue lessons when her husband found out. It was illegal to teach a slave to read; he would become dangerous with knowledge. Douglass was a ragged child who sang outside the previous mistress's window to win a piece of bread. Who batted away his hunger and loneliness with books he snuck into the garret where he slept. Who taught himself to read and made his tongue his sword.

The very figure of the orator behind the podium gave her hope, despite the warnings coming from his mouth. For so many years, she had felt powerless in the face of race hatred. What could one person do? But there was the great man in all his power, telling these people what they still had to fight for. And the crowd was behind him, cheering and cheering him on. She felt pleased that she had played a small part in getting Frederick Douglass to come here. She felt wonderful, in fact, and mildly subversive.

CHAPTER SIXTY-FOUR

April 1866

O<small>N THE MORNING OF</small> A<small>PRIL</small> 4, S<small>PENCER WAS LAYING OUT</small> his best clothes to wear to Frederick Douglass's second night at the Capitol when a knock sounded at the front door. On the stoop stood Henry Clay. Spencer clapped the young man's shoulders and pulled him into the house.

"My Lord, you are a sight for sore eyes."

"I thought I'd have a look at Springfield," Henry said with a shy smile.

"Come in!"

Spencer set a cup of coffee in front of him in the kitchen. It was a rare moment when Eliza and the children were all out of the house.

"You were such a skinny pup last I saw you. They fed you well in the army."

"That they did. The army…" Henry shook his head in wonder. "The army changed my life."

He talked of the fighting he had seen, much of it spent hunkered down in trenches around Richmond and Petersburg during the siege. Henry's eyes had some fear in them. The young man was not long removed from the battlefield.

Indeed, he had been twice wounded, once in the siege of Petersburg and once in Danville, Virginia. He had returned to live in Jacksonville after the war where he was working on a farm now to earn money. He was a saving young man, intent on buying a carriage and team to get a start busing people around that town. "I am learning to read and write now," he said. "I will be a gentleman."

Spencer stood and buttered biscuits for Henry. "There is something this evening could maybe interest you. You want to stay here for the night?"

"Sure."

"Frederick Douglass is talking at the Capitol."

Henry looked astounded. "Douglass? Here?"

"The very man, my friend. Now, I happen to have an extra ticket."

"I wish I had my uniform with me." Henry ran his hand over his head. "I need a haircut."

"I'll cut it. I want to show you around on the way over to the shop. The town won't look the same to you."

They walked out into the drizzling April cold, passing along Market Street, where eight new brick stores stood, and nearby, a new four-story hotel called the Leland was rising. They went on up Fifth Street to where the *Illinois State Register* had a new building. Lining the streets, restaurants had sprung up, along with breweries, a theater, and a new business college. People of every station clogged the sidewalks. Everywhere he looked, the town seemed to be improving. The state's capital was starting to actually look like one.

"There is money here, Henry. It's not a bad place for a man to put down roots."

"Except for these streets."

Spencer looked out at the expanse of wood in the roadway and sighed. "Except for the streets."

Throughout town were plank roads sunk into the black Midwest soil. In a pounding rain, mud still found a way to ooze up between the thick puncheons.

"Not too friendly for a carriage driver," Henry observed.

"We will have new streets. It's only a matter of time. You need a little foresight to grab the opportunities."

At the barbershop, cutting Henry's hair, Spencer said, "Something might happen tonight."

"You are a mystery today, sir."

"I invited Douglass to dinner at our house."

"No!"

"Oh, I don't know if he will come, but I wrote and invited him. Didn't hear back, but Eliza is fixing up a feast just in case. I promised to have a couple of local politicians there. Whether they come or he comes or not, we could fit you at the table."

Spencer looked at Henry, who smiled broadly under the shears. "Frederick Douglass!" he said.

In the Hall of Representatives that evening, the mostly white crowd was dressed up and excited. Silk skirts rustled around them. The number of women in attendance appeared almost equal to that of the men. People Spencer did not know nodded their heads in greeting.

When Douglass stood at the podium, Spencer could see that the years—how many now since that first convention? thirteen?—had worked on Frederick Douglass. His body was thicker and appeared squeezed into his cutaway, but the strong voice had grown deeper.

"It has been settled that the Negro will work, will fight, will die if need be for truth and freedom… The race has withstood all the exterminating influences of slavery for two hundred and fifty years and yet is strong and ready to advance."

Douglass went on to argue that the Negro should be allowed to vote because he is a man. He earned it by fighting in the war, and the nation owed it to him as a debt of honor. "He deserves well of his country. He has been the nation's friend in the dark hour of war and in these days of peace."

Douglass warned of an unholy alliance between defeated rebels and Copperheads in the North. He lifted his head to scan the crowd in the gallery. "I have seen white Copperheads and blue Copperheads, but I have never seen a black Copperhead."

Henry and Spencer stood up with the rest of the crowd and applauded wildly.

"I know you are war-weary. We all are. When the war ended, people seemed as grateful to General Lee for surrendering as to General Grant for *compelling* him to surrender," Douglass said. "But we must not forget. There was a right and a wrong side. The Confederacy is guilty of crimes of treason and slavery. In the rush for reunion, do not hasten to nurse the spirit that gave birth to Booth. Let us not forget that justice to the Negro is safety to the nation."

Douglass put a face on the crisis that lay ahead. The face belonged to President Andrew Johnson. The former vice president was bent on tearing apart Lincoln's legacy piece by piece and supporting the class of plantation owners and their Confederate cronies who had set their sights on retaking power in Congress. Johnson supported the Thirteenth Amendment abolishing slavery, but he vetoed the Fourteenth Amendment, which allowed colored citizens to vote, arguing instead that states should have control over voting rights.

"Remember," Douglass's voice boomed, "slavery is not abolished until the black man has the ballot."

A great hoorah went up, and people stood again and again to the end of his speech.

"It appears he's coming," Spencer said when he found William in the crowd. "Go on over to the house. I'll wait until Douglass is done signing his name for people. I'll bring him home and see you there."

The smell of ham filled the house. Eliza had borrowed a neighbor's table and used it to extend her own into the parlor from the dining room. On short notice, she had gathered from her neighbors enough chairs, tablecloths, dishes, and silverware to accommodate twenty people. The Donnegan sisters and their mother, Leanna, had pitched in and covered the top of the sideboard with pies and cakes and bread pudding.

Spencer and Douglass arrived to a long table full of family and friends, though not a single prominent politician as promised. The orator did not seem to mind. Bowls of potatoes and greens circulated as Spencer introduced those present. Conversation paused when the main guest tucked into his food and the rest of them watched the legend sitting right there eating his dinner. The man appeared to be starving.

"Send down the potatoes his way," Eliza whispered to her husband.

Throughout dinner, Douglass told one story after another about visiting the White House.

"A month ago, I went with a delegation to implore President Johnson to support suffrage for our people. It was a surprise visit, you might say." There was laughter around the table as Douglass smiled slyly. "We got nowhere with him. Afterward, Johnson's secretary told the *New York World*...what were her words?...that the president 'no more expected that darkey delegation than he did the cholera.' He blamed us for causing the war and said giving us the vote would end in a race war. Of course, he has a dandy new colonization plan.

"Mr. Lincoln, on the other hand, was easy to work with. I visited him at his invitation before his second election. We worked together on a plan for how the Federal army could liberate slaves in the event he was not reelected."

"Lincoln really thought he might lose?" William asked.

"Oh yes. He was dispirited because of the criticism he'd suffered at the hands of other Republicans. There was immense pressure to reconcile with the South to end the carnage. He feared that if he lost, a new president would nullify emancipation with a negotiated peace. He wanted me to organize bands of men to ride into the border and rebel states, past our army lines, to tell slaves of their freedom and urge them to come into Union boundaries. I was to be one of the riders. I did write up such a plan, but as it turned out, not a week later, Atlanta fell to Sherman, and in time it became the work of the army to spread the word.

"All the while, mind you, the presence of blue uniforms had been signaling to our people that the slave power was shaken to its core. They knew the war was waged on their account. They were looking for openings. Slaveholders were leaving old men or their wives in charge of farms and plantation operations. Our people saw their chance to bolt, and they did. Once they got themselves behind Union lines, they set up refugee camps and went to work for themselves or for the army. Soon enough they fought, too."

"Is it true that you are the one who persuaded Lincoln to enlist colored men to fight in the war?" Spencer asked.

"I certainly lobbied him hard on it. The outcome of the war at that point was not at all clear, as you recall. And he desperately needed the soldiers… I went out and recruited troops for the cause."

The women at the table seemed to be under Douglass's spell. Spencer had noticed it at the Capitol among the women in the audience.

"When I learned that our troops were being treated badly, I almost lost my mind. I sent my own *sons* to fight. To learn colored prisoners of war were being murdered and mutilated by Confederates, that free soldiers were being sold into slavery when captured…I went without an appointment to the White House, and a senator who recognized me took me in. I told Lincoln the situation had to change. I told him I would not recruit another man under such circumstances and that if Jefferson Davis should shoot or hang colored soldiers in cold blood, the United States government should retaliate in kind and degree without delay upon Confederate prisoners in its hands.

"To learn our men were being paid less—my son Lewis was a sergeant and got less than a white private! To find out they were given old guns..."

"I ran into some of that," Henry Clay said.

Faces turned to Henry.

"What regiment were you in?" Douglass asked.

"Twenty-Ninth Illinois."

"Where did you fight?"

"Mostly in the siege of Petersburg."

Douglass ran his hand across his mouth thoughtfully. "So you were at the Battle of the Crater?"

"Yes, sir."

"Dear God. But here you are."

"By some miracle. Fought at Appomattox too."

Douglass was taken aback. "You were there when Lee surrendered?"

"Yes, sir. My unit was fighting Lee's men. We had pushed the rebels back about a mile when we saw the white flags." Henry laughed. "We were near starved and dead tired. When word came it was surrender, you never saw such relief."

"What an honor to meet you, sir," Douglass said. "My son Lewis was the first black man in New York to volunteer. Charles served in the Fifty-Fourth Massachusetts. My other son Frederick was a recruiter."

"All boys—your children?" Eliza asked.

"Oh no. My Rosetta is twenty-seven and a reformer. Comes with the blood. Our other little girl, Annie, died six years ago."

"I am so sorry, Mr. Douglass," Leanna Donnegan said. "It must be hard to have their father away for such long periods of time."

"Truthfully, they hate it. I am gone for months, talking, sitting on trains. It is bone-wearying."

"Is your neck sore, Mr. Douglass?" Leanna asked.

Douglass's laugh was rueful. "My neck, my back…"

Spencer was surprised to hear his mother speak up. She had been quiet most of the evening, watching and listening. It occurred to him now that she may not have felt comfortable discussing politics, but the mention of his children moved her. He watched now as she rose, her slender figure still erect, her white hair twisted in a knot at the nape of her neck. She walked around the table, then stood behind Douglass's chair and proceeded to work her fingers into his shoulders. Eyes widened. In a brief silence that followed, Spencer could hear the orator's muscles crunching, much as his own did whenever his mother's iron thumbs attended to his back.

Later, as Frederick Douglass took his leave, he spoke to Eliza, holding both of her hands in his and thanking her for her hospitality. "It felt like family tonight," he said. He turned then to Leanna and made a small bow. "Thank you, madame. I will remember your kindness." Spencer watched as his mother smiled like a girl of twenty. When the guest of honor was gone, Spencer walked her out to the porch, where his brother waited at the bottom of the stairs to escort Leanna home.

Heading back to his own house with Henry, Spencer reflected that Douglass was showing the wear of his contentious life. He had a hand that didn't work right from fighting off a crowd of thugs as a young dockworker and assorted scars got in small New England towns from brawlers who did not appreciate his abolitionist ideas. Now he had back aches and a worry line between his eyes so deep it looked like an injury. Night after night, he was in a new town, sounding his warnings. Back home, he suggested in passing, there was a houseful of people to support.

Spencer figured Douglass was right that the road ahead would be rough. But he was sick of rough road. Despite Douglass's warnings, Spencer felt as if they had all been given a new start. There was much work to be done for people moving north after the war. He had been thinking about starting another church over in Lincoln where it was needed. Eliza was entirely on board. It would take money nobody had, but they would find a way. It was possible, all possible.

CHAPTER SIXTY-FIVE

FEBRUARY 1875

IT DID NOT COME AS A SURPRISE TO SPENCER IN DECEMBER of last year when William told him that he and his wife were divorcing. His marriage to Lavinia was William's second marriage and had appeared for a long time to be happy. Of late, though, he and Lavinia had been struggling. His first marriage to Charlotte, as Spencer recalled, had not lasted more than a year or two. It *did* surprise him when William revealed in January that he was to marry a third time, to a young lady who was thirty years younger than he and white.

Spencer had stared at him intently. "You certainly like to do things the hard way," he told William.

His brother explained that the state's miscegenation law had expired last November. "I knew we would have to marry quick in case the law was renewed."

He finalized his divorce at the end of 1874 and married Sarah on a snowy February day. His former wife surprised

William by remarrying a month after he did. His guilt eased. She had clearly found her own happiness well before the divorce.

How quickly lives could change. Spencer remained quiet when William set out to find a place away from the downtown area so they could enjoy a quiet, more private life.

"We will make our own society," he told Spencer.

CHAPTER SIXTY-SIX

———

JULY 1882

June 29, 1882

Dear Ana,

*I am writing to ask if you would kindly come by to see
my sister Mary. She is ailing and I think she might
welcome a visit from you. She is nearly blind, but your
voice would be enough to cheer her. She remembers you
fondly for your kindness to her children.*

Elizabeth Todd Edwards

JULY 2 WAS BLISTERING HOT WHEN ANA SET OUT UNDER A
parasol to walk over to the house on Aristocracy Hill, her
head flooded with memories. She had not seen Mary Lincoln
in twenty-one years. Would the woman even recognize her? She

had kept up as she could on the poor lady through gossip and the occasional agonizing newspaper story. Congress had refused to give her a proper pension for a long time. She had lost Tad to pneumonia. Robert, her only remaining child, had committed her to a mental institution; maybe she had been driven mad by her losses. Word was around town that Mary was currently holed up in a dark room in her sister's house, seeing none of her old friends.

Why on earth would she want to see me?

"She's upstairs in one of the bedrooms," Elizabeth said. "Would you like a cup of tea?"

"Thank you. Perhaps after I see her."

"Please take some now, dear. I must prepare you."

Elizabeth left to fetch the tea. Ana looked around the parlor where she sat. Mary Lincoln had once described the room to her as "perfection." Now it was a perfectly preserved set of old furniture where, if memory served, many interesting scenes had taken place. It looked like the kind of stern, upright furniture one saw in old paintings of New England parlors. Elizabeth herself might appear stern to those who had not known her in her beautiful years, but she was still quietly elegant, Ana thought, and still a force in the Todd family.

"She probably will not speak," Elizabeth said as she poured the tea. "She rarely does. She doesn't know I asked you to come. But she had real fondness for you, Ana, and I thought it might be worth a try." Elizabeth, less slender and a grayer version of her younger self, settled carefully in a stiff-backed chair. "I don't know how much you have heard."

"Well, I read there was a trial in Chicago…"

"...to decide if Robert could have her committed to a mental hospital. Yes," Elizabeth sighed, "and he succeeded. That was just one of the torments of hell Mary has suffered over the last few years. Her time in the White House was a nightmare. She visited hospitals, worked hard to help the contraband people who filled the streets in Washington, but the newspapers only wanted to talk about the money she spent on decorating. And the war..." She shook her head. "It might as well have been a Todd family feud."

"She was close to Emilie, though."

"Once, yes. But Emilie was lost long ago. Five of us stayed loyal to the Union. The other eight siblings remained adamant Confederates. Mary was not particularly close to the older half brothers, but she adored our youngest brother, Aleck. We all did. When he was killed in battle, Mary grieved for him, but her first loyalty was always to her husband, always to the North. She was reviled all around. Southerners called her a traitor, and Northerners called her a spy in the White House."

Elizabeth shook her head slowly. "A baptism of sorrow, that is what Mary calls what she's had to bear. Losing Willie just did her in. He was her favorite. Then, to experience her husband's murder while they sat quietly holding hands... Think of the terrible jolt of that." She stood up, walked to the front window, and stared out. "The White House was what she wanted even as a little girl. Imagine! Such an odd, grown-up thing to want. When Mr. Lincoln was killed, she kept saying, 'Did I cause this? Did I give my husband for *this?*'

"She couldn't bear to be in this country after all that. She had suffered humiliation after his death. Poor Lizzie Keckley tried to sell Mary's ball gowns to help retire some of her debt. To no avail, and what a public embarrassment. Then Mary had to fight with Congress for a decent pension. She and Tad went and lived in Europe for three years. It was a reprieve for them both. But when they came back, Tad took sick and died. Can you imagine? He was eighteen years old, developed a lung ailment, and suddenly he was gone. It was the final blow. When Mary lost Tad, she lost herself. With children, we have a way of knowing that we carry on. Do you have children, Ana?"

"No."

"Oh, I'm sorry. That was unthinking of me." Elizabeth sat down again.

"It's all right."

"Well, when you have them, they are your boon, your pride. Or they disappoint you. Some can actually betray you. Mary felt Robert did just that. He thought she had lost her mind and he had to go to court to do it, but he managed to put her in that asylum. Mary was utterly distraught. She has always been eccentric and a terrible spender in Washington, but she was not insane. She found a way to get herself out. I tried to persuade her to come back to Springfield, but she was too humiliated to see old friends. She told me they would never cease to regard her as a lunatic. She felt it in their soothing manner. She said, 'If I should say the moon is made of green cheese, they would smile and heartily agree with me.'"

"Where did she go?"

"To France. Lived in a village there and found some small contentment. One day, she bought a little painting at a market and came back to her rented cottage to hang it. She climbed on a ladder and fell. Injured her spine." Elizabeth sighed. "And that marked the end of Mary's independence."

"How sad," Ana said, "when she had just begun to find a little peace."

"I offered her two bedrooms upstairs and she finally said yes to that." Elizabeth gave a bitter little laugh. "Moved in with sixty-four trunks! All this stuff…hundreds of pairs of kid gloves she'd bought to shake hands in the reception lines, programs from a thousand different events. From the day she came back, she wanted to see no one. Too down in the heart. She would just go through those trunks…

"Now, she does not get out of bed and eats almost nothing. She has been seeing the ghosts of her children for some time. In Washington, she used to visit with spiritualists who claimed they could contact the other world." Elizabeth shook her head. "A friend said once that Mary was always either in the garret or in the cellar… She never was a simple study."

"I hope she is not in pain now," Ana said.

"She is, sadly. The spine and her kidneys. And her eyes. I don't believe she even hears the doctors anymore. Mary has fought despair for twenty years now. She has lived from one crushing bereavement to the next. She is only sixty-three, but I believe she is ready to die."

The room was dark. Slivers of sun slipped in around the edges of the shades. In the dim light, Mary Lincoln's face was puffy and shadowed. Her eyes were open and looking forward, but they did not move.

"Mrs. Lincoln," Ana said, "it is Ana Ferreira. Do you

remember me? I worked for you for many years. It is so nice to see you again."

The white sheet over Mary's breast went up and down. The dry, cracked lips formed no words.

"I loved taking care of your children. Such smart handsome boys, Tad and Willie." Was it cruel to say their names out loud? Was it more torture than sweetness? Did she even hear?

It almost didn't matter. Ana had sent notes after every one of Mary's losses, but she never had the chance to say in person how she felt.

"I am so sorry for all you have suffered," she began. "I was heartsick over Mr. Lincoln. And Willie. And Tad. I cannot begin to imagine your grief. But I saw what you did. You made a good family, Mary Lincoln. You loved your children and they loved you. Some of my happiest memories took place in your house."

The eyes shifted and a smile flickered across Mary's mouth. "Willie…"

Ana flinched, spooked by her voice. It was low and raspy.

"Willie comes at night. He comes right through that door." Mary nodded at the wall opposite her.

Ana caught her breath. There was no door in that wall. "Oh."

Mary gave out an affirmative hum. "He stands at the end of my bed, hovering there with that sweet smile he's always had. Little Eddie comes with him sometimes. Two times he came with my brother Aleck. He says Aleck is with him most of the time."

Ana quieted her breathing so she did not miss any of the faint words Mary spoke.

"Before, when I thought of my little sons in the immensity, alone, without their mother to hold their little hands, it nearly broke my heart."

"Yes, I can understand that."

"The last time they came they were with my beloved husband. They are all together now." Her eyes stared at the blank wall. "You cannot dream of the comfort."

At home, Ana found Owen in the carriage house, working on building a bench with a neighborhood boy. It was rudimentary work for him, since Owen could build far more complicated structures. He had found a kind of peace for himself out here in his workshop, first creating a pair of garden chairs and then a gazebo for the backyard. Ana studied his dusty saws and mallets hanging on nails above his battered workbench, half listening as he talked mortise and tenon to the boy. She quietly blessed the workshop. It was the church he attended to slowly heal. Over the years, his nightmares had ebbed. He still came home after work and had a drink or two, but his taste had returned to beer, and most nights he slept through.

Owen never wanted to adopt a child, and she had learned to stop wishing for that. He would have made a good father. She thought of Mr. Lincoln then, of how he was so tender with his boys. Yet his boys never seemed to get enough of him. He was continually pulled away from them by work and then by forces bigger than his family. Life plays merry hell with your plans.

"How much better it would have been for Mary Lincoln if she had never gotten the White House," she said to Owen that evening. They were sitting in two old chairs in front of the fireplace. "She is not insane, as the papers said. She is in constant grief from all her losses." Ana placed her hand on top of Owen's. "I don't know how I would go on without you. I would be talking to ghosts too."

The next morning, Ana woke thinking of Cal. How many times had they speculated about Mary Lincoln and what went on inside her head? They had been fascinated by her. She felt the need to write immediately and describe the scene she had witnessed. She went to her bedroom desk, feeling around inside the drawer for a pack of letters from Cal that she had tied with a pink ribbon.

Their early correspondence had thinned over the years to the rare letter of congratulations and condolence. She untied the ribbon and looked over Cal's looping cursive. The oldest letter was from her early days in Chicago. *I am learning so much about the trade. I shape felt onto hat blocks during the day. At night, I sew soldiers' uniforms because Sarah just got a contract from the government.*

Ana pulled out another letter. *I love the baby blanket for Phoebe. It keeps her warm in the hat shop where she sleeps in a drawer on top of the table.* The letters seemed to mark the key events in her life. *I have purchased the hat shop from Sarah.*

She wondered if Cal had kept her letters.

Ana wrote out all the details of her visit to Elizabeth's house and the rooms full of trunks upstairs, but she tried in particular to describe Mrs. Lincoln's otherworldly demeanor. It was a shocking vision of a once powerful and lively woman and a heartbreaking coda to the Lincoln family's story. Cal would want to know. Ana did not add any details of her own life. She promised more news and quickly posted it.

Two weeks later, when she learned the woman had passed, Ana felt a sense of gladness that lasted all day long. She took up her pen once more and wrote to Cal. *Mary Lincoln finally found the door.*

CHAPTER SIXTY-SEVEN

July 1889

A BEAM OF SUNLIGHT THROUGH THE WINDOW FELL ON Spencer's forehead. *Another hot day.* He would get up, have coffee before the mid-July heat made the stuff undrinkable. He could smell bacon frying and hear Eliza's laughter downstairs. He loved the morning sounds in his house when the grandkids were here. Outside, an ice wagon rumbled along, stopping and going. He listened for birds but could only hear an annoying crow. Lately he could not catch the high pitches and it bothered him. He'd once been able to tell the little ones, "That is a meadowlark. That's a kingbird."

He wanted to stay in bed under the sheet, but the voice in his head asked the same question it did when he was young and needed to get something done: *Are you a man, Spencer?* This morning, his brain argued back, *I am an* old *man.* He was approaching seventy, not so old, but his body ached all over. He sat up against the wall and fell into reverie and then thoughts of death waiting up ahead someplace. In these moments, his life came in for an appraisal.

Pride always wanted to jump up first. *Good morning, Spencer*, it would say. *I am your best and your worst friend.* He had done good things in his life that made him proud. He'd managed to make a living and have a big, beautiful family. Start a church here and another one with Eliza when they moved to Lincoln. Serve on a jury in Logan County, for heaven's sake, when no colored man had ever done so. He had fought for his people in meeting after meeting and kept active in the Colored Convention movement. Back in '65, he had organized and chaired a large gathering of citizens at the Colored Baptist Church to support a petition written by John Jones to the state legislature to eliminate the Black Laws. They were old friends by then; Jones's muttonchops were turning gray when he showed up. They had worked together, and Jones took it to the legislature. One month later, the hated laws were repealed. It was a true victory, and they had done it with words. Spencer had soaked up the people's gratitude. Success had given him confidence and pride that pushed him on.

Still, he knew he had been born lucky. He had never been pulled away from his loved ones or watched his children be sold away. Never had a buyer stick his fingers into his mouth to look at his teeth or had an auctioneer strip him down to show bidders his limbs and back and genitals, never had to eat his meals out of a trough, never had boiling oil poured on him.

On the wall across from the bed hung the studio photograph he'd had made some years ago. He looked like a self-satisfied man in it. He'd held that smile on his face for the full minute it took to get the job done. Most people looked sour in their portraits. He wanted to show himself to be what he was, a happy man and, quite frankly, not a bad-looking man in the whiskers he wore at the time.

Pride goeth before the fall. Ah, there was God jumping into the conversation again, reminding him he surely did not look like that man in the portrait anymore. His hair was white, his back bent slightly. His knees ached now. Old Arthur had his hips and elbows too. He had worked his body hard for so many years and tired it beyond its limits when he was both minister and barber. His thoughts turned then to Eliza. Would he have done anything without her beside him? When they started the church in Lincoln without a building or a congregation, it was Eliza who made it happen as much as he. They opened their house and welcomed strangers into it for almost a year before they could buy the empty old school building that became their church. She had eight children coming and going the whole time yet she made their house a nest in which a congregation was born.

You've got one life, son, and it happens to be blessed. Now his mother's voice was in his ears. She had prized her children for different reasons and had never discouraged Spencer's questioning along his road toward God. It was from his mother that he had learned to push. And push. She had entered life a hard way and went out having changed her circumstances. My Lord, she had even made the wheels of government move in her favor. He needed to tell the grandchildren about her. After her husband died, the state had taken half of her property, saying the land she owned was in Joe Knox's name and he had no legal heirs. She had protested, and the General Assembly of the State passed "An Act for the Relief of Leanna Knox." Ha! It delighted him even now. The half of her property seized by the state was returned to her. It was an astounding win, given the way things worked for colored people in those days.

He was not as old as she was when she passed at eighty-two. But parts of him were worn. What bad ears he had now, and what good ears he'd had as a young man. He had taken his hearing for granted back then, as a fish is unaware of its fins. Thankfully, he could discern the children's voices in the kitchen, and it reminded him there were other things he still needed to teach them. Things his grandchildren needed to know if they were to survive in this town, this country.

Oddly enough, he still wanted to work. He missed the convivial atmosphere of a barbershop. He'd had a job offer from a friend, and he felt he had it in him. He would wait to see what the Lord's plan was for him next. There was no hurry.

He swung his legs around, planted his feet on the floor. He would go out in the backyard where his tomatoes had swelled the garden and pick a couple of perfect ones for lunch. Play with the kids for a while. Probably stare at the maple tree. *This is what old men are left to, looking at trees.* He smiled to himself. *And isn't it fine?*

CHAPTER SIXTY-EIGHT

May 1898

IT WAS THE MEMORY OF HERSELF AS A GIRL HUNGRY FOR books that made Ana walk to whatever temporary location currently held the library. A new library building had been elusive since she first began raising funds for it thirty years ago. They had managed to assemble sixty thousand books but not a new building. Very recently, though, there was talk of applying to Mr. Andrew Carnegie of Pittsburgh, who was handing out money for new libraries. Someone else would work on that application. She preferred choosing books and periodicals to order. Lately her domain was the reading room. Springfield had always been a newspaper town, and there were now labor, temperance, and religious papers, plus quarterly and monthly magazines and journals to set out.

When one of her preferred magazines showed up, she would devour it during her lunch break. *Public Patron*, which had a section about early settlers in Springfield, was a favorite. She dropped into a chair when the May issue arrived, and over a ham sandwich, she thumbed through the current issue. She stopped at an account of an anonymous Negro man reminiscing about his years of being a conductor in the Underground Railroad and scanned the first paragraph.

> I lived, in those days, on the north side of Jefferson, between Eighth and Ninth streets, in a story-and-a-half house.

Cal's old neighborhood, Ana thought.

> It is still standing, and I could show you the garret yet in which many a runaway has been hidden while the town was being searched. I have secreted scores of them. I once had seven hundred dollars in gold and silver turned into my lap by the owner of a slave as a bribe for my assisting in his recapture.

Her heart flopped over, then took off racing. *Oh my God, it's William Donnegan.* In the article, he told of his experiences moving escapees through town and toward Canada. Ana was suddenly eleven years old, standing in his shoe shop.

She stood up, eager to go and tell the nearest person she could find, "I know the person in this story!" But in the space of a few seconds, she let go of the impulse and sat down. There was a reason William Donnegan had not told his name. Clearly he feared some reprisal, even now, even in 1898. If he had not revealed his name, then she would not.

When she finished the article, Ana shook her head in wonder. *How very strange. Here I am, once again holding the same secret I kept involving the man's role as a conductor forty years ago.* She vowed she would copy out the article and send it to Cal. It would be an excuse to reconnect with her.

Not two weeks later, none other than Mr. Donnegan came into the library on the third floor of the city hall building. He was very well dressed and gray-haired with a slight limp, but she recognized him immediately. He said he wanted to look at plat maps.

"You will need to go over to the county courthouse for that, Mr. Donnegan."

He looked at her face closely. "I must know you. Forgive me."

"Ana Ferreira. Ana Evans now."

"Cal's friend?"

"The very same. How strange that you have appeared here. I just recently... Can you sit for a minute, Mr. Donnegan?"

"Surely," he said, taking a seat at a table in the reading room.

Ana fetched the copy of the *Public Patron*. She opened it to the page on which his story started and watched as the man's eyes followed the paragraphs down the column. He looked up at her, slightly discomfited.

"That *is* you, is it not, sir?"

"I believe I have been found out." A slight smile flashed across his lips. "How did you know it was me?"

"Well, Cal was your neighbor. And I was witness to one of

the stories you told in that piece. The man hidden under the leather hides…I saw that. When the hides began to fall, a hand reached out and stopped the collapse." Ana crossed her arms and rubbed them as if a shiver might come any moment. "I shall never forget that day. I was terrified."

He laughed. "So was I."

"Cal asked me not to tell anyone and I didn't. I carried that secret for a very long time."

His eyes studied hers. "Thank you for doing that."

Ana smiled and nodded. "What an amazing life you had as a conductor. The story about the talkative girl…"

He let go a little laugh. "Sometimes I wonder what happened to all those people I knew only for a day or two as they made their way north. I wonder if that girl made it to Canada. Maybe she has a passel of grandchildren who do nothing but talk all day."

Now Ana laughed. "How old was the girl at the time?"

"Oh, around sixteen or seventeen, I'd say."

Cal's age then. Ana did not mention that she had witnessed part of his story about the talkative girl and that Cal and she had also kept *that* secret for Mr. Donnegan.

"Just so you know, Cal was entirely loyal to you. She understood the stakes."

Ana's mind jumped back to the day of Lincoln's funeral when she had spotted Cal on the train platform. Cal was able at last to speak the truth about her aunt. How freeing it must have been to let go of so many secrets after the war. As she told Ana that day, her face had opened up like a flower.

"She was a good girl," he said. "And she grew up to become

a fine woman. She sheltered a few people that I sent her way during the war. I saw her a few years ago. I took my family up there to Chicago for the Columbian Exposition and made a point to see her."

"Oh, tell me…"

"Her mother was our neighbor in the old days, you know. She moved to Chicago some years back and was living with Cal and her family. Cal and her husband have lived different places up there. Now they have a building south of the elevated train, near an area called the Loop. She has her own millinery shop on the first floor, and they live above it."

"Is it a neighborhood of houses or businesses?"

"A little of both. I saw her shop first. Cal was standing in the middle of a room full of hats covered in all kinds of stuff—flowers and little birds and I don't know what all. She was not the least bit disturbed by the sudden appearance of an old neighbor. She just flipped the sign on her door to Closed and took me upstairs. Her daughter was up there practicing on a violin while Cal's mother sat listening. Dozing, I should say."

"What is it like?"

"Her home? Just like Cal. I'm not very good at… It's pleasant, very nice. Pictures and such. She has a talented daughter and a fine husband, a financial man. And she is a businesswoman herself. Cal has come a long way."

"Can you give me Cal's address? I would love to write to her."

"I will dig it up and drop it off to you," he said, taking the moment to rise and shake her hand before departing.

Ana felt a rush of nostalgia when Mr. Donnegan was gone. Their brief talk had brought Cal back to her as if she were in the room. Ana longed to see her again. She did not tell him that she had visited Chicago a few times and on every visit found herself searching for Cal's grown-up face in the crowds. Ana tried to remember how they had lost touch. She'd written to her a few letters after her last one, but no reply came back. She had concluded that the fact that Cal stopped writing was a way of ending a friendship that was too hard to sustain. Now she wondered if she had simply moved again.

As Mr. Donnegan disappeared down the staircase, a librarian walked over to Ana and whispered, "Do you know that man?"

"Not well, but yes."

"Well, I know that man. He lives out by me." The woman's voice lowered. "He's married to a white woman."

CHAPTER SIXTY-NINE

IT WAS THE BACK END OF SPRING AND THE HOUSE WAS STILL cold in the mornings. The bed was piled with quilts. Ana slept on her side with her knees tucked under Owen's for extra warmth. She woke with her cheek wet against his chest as it rose and fell.

Owen had taken to getting up early, making the coffee and bringing two cups back to bed. Through the window, she could see the sky turning pink behind the blooming apple tree. He presented her a cup and climbed under the covers again.

"It's your father's birthday today, isn't it?" he said.

"What a good memory you have."

"I miss him. He always beat me to the kitchen in the morning. I loved the man, as you know, but he burned the bacon every time he cooked it."

She smiled. "Were those years hard for you when he was with us?"

"Never. I was happy to have a few years with a different kind of father."

It had been eight years since her father passed. Emmanuel Ferreira had failed bit by bit after her mother's death four years earlier. He had kept his garden going, but he was not a cook. Nor was he able to keep his beloved house in perfect condition as time went on. His old friends were passing away, and the neighborhood was no longer filled with Portuguese. When Ana invited him to come live with them, he had resisted and then agreed. He sold his home to a young Italian couple who promised not to paint over the murals in the dining room.

"You were so good to my father."

"Oh, it was easy. He was interested in everything. And what an amazing success he made of his life. To go from simple carpentry to painting church ceilings and state house murals?"

"Yes. I think so too."

Ana lingered in bed after Owen went into the next room to get dressed. Their lives had been rich since their caretaking years. They had begun to travel. Their first trip was to the Columbian Exposition back in '93. The whole thing was thrilling, from visiting the Woman's Building to riding on the Ferris wheel. They made love like newlyweds at the Palmer House, where they were staying. Boarding the train to go back home, Owen asked, "Why didn't we start traveling years ago, Bean?"

Every other summer since then, during his vacation time, they took a train to a different part of the country. Owen called it "having our halcyon days." They visited Niagara Falls, dined in the splendor of New York City's Waldorf-Astoria, ate crawfish gumbo in New Orleans. This year it would be San Francisco, and she spent her free moments at the library researching the possibilities. She wanted to climb the observation tower at the Cliff House and watch the sun go down over the Pacific.

Owen came in to kiss her goodbye, then went off to work as he always did, full of coffee and good cheer. By 10:00, he was gone. He had died midsentence at the newspaper. Heart attack, the doctor told her. He was sixty-four years old.

She did not have him buried at the military cemetery. He was at Oak Ridge Cemetery along with her parents and brother. Next to his plot, hers waited.

She knew the words for the state of widowhood. Mourning. Bereavement. The word she thought applied most was fatigue. She hadn't earned that bone weariness honestly. There had been no long illness during which she'd had to attend to Owen. Why then was she so utterly weak? She could not get herself out of bed before ten, then flopped down for a nap by two o'clock. Her grief weighed a thousand pounds. Under the covers, her blood pulsed heavy and slow in her veins.

In the weeks following his death, she excused herself from the library to retreat inside her house. She went to Owen's study most mornings thinking she would begin to clean it up. There were campaign buttons stuck into a corkboard, a pile of journals, and a collection of news articles on his desk written during his time on the road with Lincoln. She meant to make a scrapbook, but instead she sat in his chair and let memories have their way.

In the years of their marriage, she had enjoyed a social life unimaginable in her youth—glamorous receptions at the governor's mansion, dinners with prominent people whom Carrie

Alsop had called "the quality," official events at the new Capitol building near their house—all enjoyed because of Owen's reputation as a journalist. His wit sparkled at these events, and his stories of Lincoln and Douglas riveted many a dinner table. But they had kept to themselves at home otherwise, in their own little world. She thought of all his tendernesses—the fires laid every morning, the coffee brought to her, the compliments.

She recalled an ordinary morning last summer. He had gone out into the garden to survey what was growing. He brought back freshly dug carrots. "Roasted tonight?" he asked dreamily. "With chicken and dumplings maybe?"

He told her he would think about dinner all day at work. He liked to think about food for some reason. That was a small fact she had not known before, and it caused her to regret her years of perfunctory cooking. She had cooked the carrots, roasted a chicken, and served it on a tablecloth on the grass when he came home.

Oh God, I would give anything now to have the chance to cook him one more meal, to drink coffee in bed with him one more morning, to feel his arm on my shoulders.

That day he brought in the carrots was a sweet summer morning, like so many they'd had, even when he was drinking. But by the time he died, his sweetness could last all day. The war no longer haunted him. She thanked God for the twenty years he was mostly free from that anguish. They had gotten to restart their marriage, not as it was in the beginning but as something aged and solid and bountiful in its own way.

It occurred to her that she had not lived alone one day of her entire life. How was she to do it now? She found herself wandering the house in a daze during the long afternoon. She noticed the print in the parlor curtains had faded. The sofa arms were threadbare. The bedroom mirror needed to be resilvered, and when she looked at herself, she saw her black hair was growing dull with gray. Why had she not noticed that everything was fading? She wanted not to care about her appearance, but she still did. She was fifty-eight and she might look it, but she felt her brain was still young and fierce. If she could only emerge from the fog that had enveloped her. A widow who came to the funeral had warned her of the fog. *For weeks, you hardly know your own name. But it will lift one day.*

Ana sat down at her writing desk in her bedroom and opened the drawer to write notes of thanks to neighbors who had brought food in. Her hand went to the pack of Cal's letters. She pulled out the top letter.

My mother has lived with us for some time but still gets the Springfield newspaper. She showed me the obituary for your father. How sad I am to hear of your father's death. He was a happy man. Do you remember when we were young I asked him why he painted? He said painting helped him express his love for the world. In that letter, Cal announced she had begun to paint with oils. That was her last letter—eight years ago. Ana picked up her pen and began.

Dear Cal,

I write with an aching heart to let you know Owen passed away four weeks ago. I am barely in running order now but feel the need to reach out to you, who

of all people will understand. You knew Owen at the
beginning, knew the brilliant, funny, kind young man I
loved.

Ana did not want to sound as low as she felt. She wrote a
few details of their last happy years together and then paused as
other memories crowded into her brain.

In the midst of this new thing called "widowhood," I
have found myself laughing at odd moments. When I
married Owen, I told him I wanted to be buried in my
wedding dress. You will be amused to hear that I took it
down from a closet shelf the other day. I put it on and it
almost fit. But oh, how ridiculous I looked in the mirror
with my gray hair and wrinkles. I was Miss Havisham
incarnate! It dawned on me that people would laugh at
me in my casket if I carried through on that long-ago
promise. I wrapped it up and sent it off to my sister's
house. One of her granddaughters may want it for her
own wedding someday. Or they can play dress-up in it
now if they care to.

Writing to Cal, she felt the fuzziness in her head begin to
clear. She finished up, copied the address Mr. Donnegan had left
for her at the library's front desk, and added "Please Forward."
Some day she would write what she had learned about love in
her widowhood. *Love needs a place to go. Your heart doesn't stop*
making it when you lose the single adored person of your life.
Perhaps because they did not have children, they had been

an island unto themselves, isolated in their happy domesticity. Now she felt profoundly alone. Her love for Owen would never dim. But to make a shrine to the memory of their life together, to never change Owen's office since the day he died, to pace these floors remembering would not quell the stymied feeling inside her. How fine it must be to have a child on whom to spend your overflowing love. Or a passion. That line in Cal's last letter recalling her father's remark made Ana reflect. *He said painting helped him express his love for the world.*

A summer of sorrowing passed. On a bright October morning while she looked from the kitchen window, she noticed a layer of clouds hanging below the blue sky like cotton batting. Overhead, a mass of crows flew west. Owen's voice spoke in her ear. *They go out to meet the day and make what they can of it.*

Ana went out into the dewy garden with the pup named Lily whom she had accepted from a neighbor dog's litter. She studied the high boxwood hedge where acrobatic spiders had flung themselves high-wire style from leaf to leaf, leaving sun-glittered tracery behind them. She filled a scrub bucket with soapy water and set to washing her windows. *Somehow, I will make something of this day.*

CHAPTER SEVENTY

MAY 1907

A CARNEGIE LIBRARY FOR SPRINGFIELD HAD BEEN APPROVED by Mr. Andrew Carnegie himself one week after an application was submitted to him. What other American town was more deserving of a new library building than the home of the martyred president? The philanthropist felt that naming it a Carnegie library as he had the others would be a sacrilege to place his own name on this building in Springfield. Instead, etched into the stone frieze above the columns was the name Lincoln Library.

It had taken more than thirty years to finally get a permanent building, and this one was impressive. The interior had marble fluted columns that rose up two stories. Inside that soaring container of air, shot through with sunlight from high windows, echoed whispers and the clacking of heels on marble were the only sounds disturbing the silence. It was a temple devoted to reading, and what was more sacred than that? Ana loved its grandeur, but if Mr. Carnegie's library had existed when she was a book-starved girl, she would have been too intimidated to walk through its grand front doors.

At the end of her shift, Ana gathered up the day's newspapers and headed over to the Levee, where she delivered them to a group of drifters who gathered by day in an empty lot at the edge of the district. They drank and slept and lived openly there, disappearing when police chased them out and regathering like pigeons in the same place a half hour later. In time, the men welcomed her arrival, and some stood up in a gentlemanly way to accept the gift of papers. They had remarkable names: New Orleans Slim, Fat Louie, Dubuque, Seldom Seen, and Eddie Hit the Road.

Dubuque was the most talkative. When he saw her coming, he extinguished his cigarette on the sole of his shoe, put the remaining butt in his trouser cuff, and stood to greet her with a small bow. He was the one who explained to her why the district was called the Levee.

"Chicago has a Levee. Lots of other smaller towns have 'em too, close to the docks."

"But we have no docks here."

"No, but you got everything else a Levee needs," he said. "Gamblers, pool halls, drugs, groggeries, ladies of the night…"

As if proof were needed, a wraith of a girl, perhaps fifteen, walked up to them scratching at her matted blond hair and asking for money. Ana produced a dime from her bag, and the girl moved on.

"Cocaine," Dubuque explained. "She sleeps in a hovel over in Shinbone Alley."

Ana became more familiar with the area over time. Spreading out from Sixth and Washington for several blocks, the Levee was picking up steam by four in the afternoon when she arrived with the newspapers. The saloons were owned and patronized by citizens both white and black, by poor and rich. They all made good money, she was told.

One of the bordellos, Madame Brownie's, was famous. Dubuque had informed Ana that the madame was among Springfield's most generous donors to traveling men like himself. Her house was marked as such by a stick figure of a woman and some triangular trees—a hobo symbol, Dubuque said, for a kind and helpful woman. Her bordello was raided regularly and returned to business just as often. She was said to employ eight young women. Dubuque also told Ana which people were not generous, and the names included some of the richest, most important citizens in Springfield.

She felt like a reporter in that moment and wished that she might bring home to Owen what she had learned from the men. She felt a stab of longing for him. The downtown had changed since his death, and the Levee in particular was a sordid piece of what had once been the very heart of Springfield.

One day in late spring when the daylight lasted longer, she wandered through the Levee, observing for herself te life there. On East Washington Street, a feverish little man cried out his indignation in front of a German beer garden. "We have traded the Trinity of Father, Son, and Holy Ghost for the blessed trinity of beer, cheese, and sauerkraut!"

She passed the church pew that had remained in front of the old saddle shop all these years. She noticed the grooves worn into the wood of the seat and realized these were the foot scrapes of the afflicted young man who sat there on his haunches hurling invectives at passersby for—how long, thirty years? His was just one hard life that had been lived out in this neighborhood.

Judging from the number of sultry young women standing in doorways, there were plenty of bordellos in the area and even more saloons. As evening approached, the streets filled with men. They were largely coal miners and mill workers who were crowding the bars and spilling out onto the sidewalks. Piano music came from inside several places and from others the click of pool balls and the high pitch of women's laughter.

The Levee had been the topic of editorials and sermons for a good while, though City Hall and police appeared content to let vice flourish in that area. It was commonly understood that monthly "fines" collected by police officers kept the brothels alive and well. And the saloons? Well, they'd had value as centers of operations for politicians since they opened.

White editors condemned both whites and blacks in the Levee. Black pastors worried in particular about the visibility of vice in the center of the city. They railed against the Levee as a public area where a few colored saloon operators and gamblers were endangering the reputations of all the rest of the twenty-nine hundred law-abiding Negro community members in town.

The neighborhood of houses adjoining the Levee was called the Badlands. It hadn't always been so. She could remember that Lincoln's friend Reverend Brown had lived on Madison Street, as had a number of families who were among the most affluent and socially prominent Negroes in town.

Word had it that the neighborhood started to go downhill when a white madame set up a house of ill repute just doors away from Reverend Brown's house. In time another prostitution house opened just north of him and saloons moved in along Madison. Walking through the community now, Ana found a neighborhood of ramshackle houses, some missing windows or doors, where ragged children played in hard dirt yards.

She had come to believe that the poor reflected a town's essence as much as the mayor and bankers and rich people. "The Badlands" seemed a shameful name for any place that a child also called home.

CHAPTER SEVENTY-ONE

AUGUST 1908

NEIGHBOR DOGS HAD BEEN BARKING FOR A GOOD TEN MIN-utes by the time she went outside and noticed the smoke. She'd heard a fire alarm in the distance a bit earlier, and now she saw smoke going up into the air a few blocks north and east, probably in the business district on Fifth Street. It was dark, around nine o'clock, and difficult to see. Ana stood in her yard squinting at the sky when a neighbor boy came racing down the sidewalk and nearly knocked her over.

"Fire!" he shouted to her. "Mr. Loper's car!"

There were folks in town who would be secretly pleased at the car's demise by fire. The sight of the Loper family cruising around the streets on Sundays in the shiny gray thing was just too much for some people.

"Did the gas tank explode?"

"Some men set it afire!" The boy was panting. "They're dancing around it!"

She leaned back in disbelief. "Dancing?"

"And they're smashing up his restaurant. They broke the windows and are hauling things out to the street."

A sense of dread filled her. Ana walked hurriedly east. When she stopped to catch her breath, she heard a *pop-pop* in the distance, like fireworks going off. She listened intently. Gunfire. Definitely. Was somebody shooting at Harry Loper? An unhappy employee? *Most people like him.* His restaurant was hugely popular as was the theater he had opened in recent years.

There had been trouble lately. The morning newspapers were full of it. But Loper'd had no part in the ugly story on the *State Journal*'s front page this morning. A white woman named Mabel Hallam had told Sheriff Werner she was raped by a Negro at her home up on North Fifth Street. The man had pulled her from bed while her husband slept, she said, and dragged her out into the yard. She had identified a thirty-seven-year-old carpenter named George Richardson, whom the police had taken in along with other men working in Hallam's neighborhood. Now he was in jail.

"Dragged From Her Bed and Outraged by Negro." The pitch of the *Register*'s coverage was hysterical. There had been another incident a month earlier that already had the town stirred up. A man was in jail for allegedly murdering Clergy Ballard, a local mining engineer who was killed when he chased the intruder he'd discovered lurking over his sleeping daughter. Later that night, the police had found a young colored man named Joe James sleeping in a park near Clergy Ballard's house. They put him in the jail, where he was waiting to go to trial. Now the sheriff had two new prisoners locked up.

Ana walked a few blocks more and realized she was in the midst of frightening chaos. In the dim glow of gaslights, she saw that a crowd of white people were running east toward the smoke while a stream of black people were racing away from it. A child crying by the side of the road was reclaimed by a frantic mother, who grabbed him into her arms and resumed running.

"Where are you going?" Ana called out to another terrified-looking woman carrying an infant. The woman's companion had a bag of food and a pillowcase full of belongings slung over his shoulder. They rushed past without answering.

Dr. Harmon, who lived on her corner, appeared at her side just then and grasped her elbow. "Go on home, Ana. It's dangerous out here."

"What is it? Why is Harry Loper's car on fire?"

Other neighbors on the street gathered around to listen.

"A crowd of people went over to the jail with lynching in mind. Some of them, I think, were people who know the Hallam woman. The sheriff had the fire department distract them with a false alarm, then snuck his two prisoners out and got Loper to use his car to get them out of town. They're on their way to Bloomington with a deputy. But the crowd keeps growing and is just enraged. They're mad the sheriff moved the men. Some went out with bricks and bats and just beat senseless a poor Negro man on the street. The main bunch of them went over to Loper's restaurant and are tearing it up. He could be inside. I don't know."

The doctor was rattled. This man, who had calmly performed surgeries in town for twenty-five years, and who had endured his own three infant daughters' deaths, could barely speak for his nerves.

"They want blood. There's some crazy white woman screaming her head off over by Loper's, leading the whole bunch. People have been shot. The governor's got state militia on duty at the Arsenal. The colored people in town are being told to take refuge over there."

"Where are you going?" she asked him.

"Over to the hospital."

Reluctantly, Ana returned home. She pulled a chair up to the front window and watched waves of young white men running toward the trouble. Alarm bells kept clanging. Her own dog, Lily, took cover under the bed, frightened by the exploding sounds.

Around ten thirty, she stepped outside and walked to the curb as four youths passing by shouted out the news. "They're smashing up the Levee!"

"What?" She grabbed the shirt of one of them.

"Colored saloons and stores," said one of the boys, suddenly aware of his audience.

Another boy piped up. "They're shooting into the apartments above the stores."

"How many people are over there?"

The four looked at each other. "Thousand, maybe?"

"More," said another. "I never saw so many. Lots of 'em watching."

"Hear that?" one boy said, pausing to listen to the *pop-pop* in the distance. "That's their gunfire."

"Who's doing the shooting?"

"Hard to tell."

"Go home, all of you!"

Despite her better instincts, Ana ventured a couple of blocks east, close enough to see red flames shooting up into the sky.

"Do you know what is burning?" she asked a man on the street.

"Badlands. They've moved over there now." He said rioters were carrying pieces of furniture, bottles of liquor, or clothing they'd taken from stores in the Levee. "It's that whole area."

She came upon a state militiaman who told her the mayor had tried to talk some sense into the rioters, but he was grabbed by the crowd and thrown into the cigar shop, where he was being held captive.

"The mob's got free rein over there. They axed the fire department's hoses. The Badlands is just burning out of control." The man wiped sweat off his face with his sleeve. "We're waiting for more troops. Enough of our men are here with Gatlings but the sheriff don't want us firing into the crowd. Told us to wait for more troops. There's at least one dead already, for sure."

"Who?"

"They found a white fella dead in Loper's," he said, turning to hurry along.

She'd heard stories about white mob violence in other towns in the past year or two. To think that it was possible here, a northern town that revered Lincoln's memory, chilled her. Yet a sickening realization pushed itself forward: Springfield was in the midst of a riot.

CHAPTER SEVENTY-TWO

———

On Saturday morning, Ana went out in her nightgown and found the newspapers miraculously on her porch. The potted geraniums she put there every summer were covered in a thin layer of black grit. Bees humming around a flowering bush seemed unaware of death in the air. But the birds had fallen silent. A cottontail halted in the yard, its nose twitching, chest quivering, its black eye, shiny as a jet bead, fixed on her. *I feel like you do*, she thought. She went through the house rechecking locks on doors and windows, then laid out the *Journal*'s front page on her kitchen table.

FRENZIED MOB SWEEPS CITY,
WREAKING BLOODY VENGEANCE
FOR NEGRO'S HEINOUS CRIME

Below the headline was a photograph of a smiling woman

in a straw hat under the words "Victim of Negro Assailant." It was the accuser, Mabel Hallam.

In the next column over was a list of the casualties from Friday. Two dead. Forty-seven injured. The dead were white men, she surmised, as the word "colored" was not next to their names. There were injured of both races, many of them suffering from serious gunshot wounds and beatings. The newspaper would have been printed before midnight. Who knew what had happened overnight.

The papers suggested there was still a difference of opinion regarding where the state troops should be. The sheriff wanted them to stay around the Arsenal. The colonel in charge of the troops thought they should be putting down the riot.

Staring glumly at the kitchen walls, Ana could see that now, some forty years beyond the end of the war, the struggle of colored people here in Springfield had never truly abated. Kept out of decent-paying jobs and white neighborhoods, many of them lived within the confines of the Badlands in poorly maintained houses they rented from white landlords.

She stayed watchful throughout the day and dozed off on the parlor sofa sometime in the afternoon. When she woke around 7:30, it was to the sound of pounding feet, curses, and weird yelps, like howling wolves. *Not again.* She went to the window. From her house, she could see the grounds of the new state Capitol building, where a terrifying mob of people were running around and over the lawn, streaming west on Edwards Street. She guessed that part of the crowd was coming from the Arsenal. She had no idea where they were headed. Faces lit by the streetlight looked menacing and wild-eyed, like those in a frenzied pack of animals. They were carrying iron clubs and guns. In a panic, Ana telephoned the police but could not get through. An hour or so later when they came back by her house, they were walking slowly, their excitement spent.

She woke late on Sunday and brought in the papers. Another person was dead, a man named Scott Burton. He was a colored barber who catered to a white clientele. When the shouting mob arrived at his shop around 2:00 a.m. on Saturday, they torched it. He had sent his family away but had stayed behind to protect their house, which was located behind the shop. Burton shot at the rioters, but they overcame him, beat him until he was unconscious, then carried him down the street and hung him from a tree a block away. There they raged on, mutilating and shooting his dead body.

The fate of another man made the headline in the right column.

W. DONNEGAN LYNCHED LAST NIGHT AT CORNER SPRING AND EDWARDS

Her body jolted. *Dear God, no. He is a frail old man.* So that was the destination of that mob last night. She shook her head as her eyes raced down the columns.

Negro Very Old.

Donnegan was a peaceful citizen and is comfortably fixed financially. He is over 84 years of age. During the Civil War he imported Southern Negroes here and hired them out to contractors.

This fact may have been known by some of the men of the crowd, who probably concluded that Donnegan was the cause of a great many Negroes being in the city and acted upon the supposition.

Married White Woman.

Mr. Donnegan was a cobbler in the city and is said to be worth $15,000. He owns considerable real estate throughout the city and is well known. His wife is said to be a white woman whom he married many years ago. It is thought by many that this fact is the direct cause of the lynching of last night.

Ana numbly followed the story. Direct cause? He caused nothing! He had been married to his wife for thirty-two years. He was lynched. He'd been beaten, his neck gashed open, and then hung by a low rope from a tree in a schoolyard across the street from his home. When police and the military arrived, they found him to be breathing. He was taken to the hospital, where he later died.

She sank back into her chair. She had not seen him again since their conversation in the library. He was elderly and infirm now according to the papers, but she could still remember his eyes the day they talked. They were so full of life. The horror of it slowly sank in. A mob of people set out with clubs and firearms to murder a harmless, old man they did not know. *Five blocks from my house.*

On Sunday afternoon, Ana dressed and walked to the

devastated downtown area to see it for herself. The air was gray and putrid from smoke. It looked as if a ferocious storm had ripped through East Washington Street, upending buildings and dumping their contents. Apartment windows above businesses were shot out, storefront walls were ripped down, and holes replaced paving where bricks had been dug up for use as missiles and weapons. Light fixtures, counters, tables, smashed bar stools, and chairs were piled in the middle of the streets along with rotting vegetables from a grocery store and broken crockery from restaurants. It was a selective tornado that had torn through the Levee. Rioters had destroyed only Negro-owned businesses or those of Jewish merchants. One colored merchant had lost a theater, a saloon, and a restaurant. The mob had encountered very little resistance from police, who explained they were outnumbered.

She walked on into the Badlands, where houses had been burned to the ground. Some of the rubble was still smoldering. State militia tents were lined up in front of shambles left by the rioters. Farther on, in the southern part of her old neighborhood, was an area now home to new arrivals from eastern and southern Europe as well as colored families. Some of those houses still bore the white linens people had hung from their front doors, communicating the message "We are white. Pass over us." North of the Badlands by a few blocks, she found her parents' old house was still intact.

Returning home along a street near the Levee, she noticed that even now, even after the horror had ended, there was a lurid air of the carnival. Men and a few women were laughing and drinking on the streets.

She saw a group of men standing around what appeared to

be a dead tree. Her throat contracted before she spoke to a man leaning against it. "What is it?"

"The barber's tree."

"Oh my God," she gasped. Bark and branches of a tree from which Scott Burton was hung had been cut off by people for souvenirs. Another white man holding a beer had set up a table and was selling postcards showing the very same tree.

"Stop this!" she shouted. "What is the *matter* with you?"

The man looked unabashedly into her eyes. "They ruin our world," he said.

Bile seared her throat. Ana's arm flew up and swung her carpet satchel, hitting the back of the man with force enough to cause his knees to buckle. He dropped to the ground.

A crowd gathered as she upended his table, dumping postcards all over the sidewalk. "You monster!" she was screaming. "Have you no shame?"

"You monster," a man squealed in a high voice, mimicking her. The postcard vendor stood up glowering, his arms in a ready position, as if waiting for another attack. Behind him, a group of men laughed.

One stepped forward and pulled her away. "You might get hurt here, lady."

She kicked at the postcards on the ground and scraped them with her heels as she walked away, shaking with anger. The men turned their backs and quaffed their beers.

All the way home, she muttered to herself like a madwoman. She kept thinking of the first inkling she'd had that Springfield was in the grip of a riot—that young boy in knee pants who came shouting the news about Loper's car. *They're dancing around it.*

CHAPTER SEVENTY-THREE

I N THE WEEKS THAT FOLLOWED, ANA SPENT HOURS STARING at newsprint, reading and rereading the stories about the riot. She took in the violent descriptions, though she wanted to turn away from them. The facts were staggering. The Negro business owners had defended themselves with guns, but they were outnumbered. After attacking Loper's restaurant, the rioters broke into a pawnshop owned by a Jewish merchant and stole weapons. Starting in the nearby Levee, the mob had torn down at least twenty-one Negro businesses, then moved on to set afire some forty houses occupied by colored families in the Badlands. The people who lived there ran for their lives and raced out of town into the countryside or took refuge in the Arsenal, while huge crowds of whites gathered to watch the neighborhood burn to the ground. One elderly, paralyzed man who was unable to leave his house was mercilessly beaten by rioters before a horrified bystander managed to carry him out of the mob.

She had been right in her guess that the rioters had tried to storm the Arsenal after that. Thankfully the militia turned them away, but the thundering she'd heard, the pounding feet in the street had been the same people. They were headed up by a young man, the papers reported, a "Russian Hebrew immigrant" named Abraham Raymer who'd led them to William Donnegan's house. When she saw his photograph in the paper, she realized he was a vegetable peddler from whom she'd bought produce when he pushed his cart through the neighborhood. Apparently the Donnegans had bought from him too.

Ana thought of the utter terror Mr. Donnegan must have felt when he looked outside and saw red-faced men lifting bricks out of his sidewalk. How terrified his wife must have been as she watched more men pouring into the front yard. Somehow Sarah Donnegan had escaped, along with a daughter-in-law carrying an infant in her arms. Thank God they had been taken in by a white neighbor.

By the time the horror was over, dozens were injured and six people were dead: William Donnegan and Scott Burton plus four white men. At night, her mind filled with the terrible scenes she'd witnessed in the stricken neighborhoods. Burned-out homes with only one or two walls standing were the charred silhouettes of a community where families had lived just a week ago. The papers called it a race riot.

Race. She had not even known what it meant when her family immigrated here, but she had learned soon enough. It was something big in the United States. People feared it, argued and lost friends over it, sued each other, made laws, enslaved people, warred, murdered, and died over it. Had there ever been a moment when race hatred was not bubbling just under the surface of their lives? America was obsessed with the idea of race.

She had come across something Lincoln said that had made her clip it from the paper long ago. It had language in it that he did not normally use. She took it down from Owen's corkboard.

The dogmas of the quiet past are inadequate to the stormy present... As our case is new, we must think anew. We must disenthrall ourselves and then we shall save the country.

She had puzzled over those words a dozen times and believed she had come to understand what he meant by "disenthrall." He was saying that the nation was in thrall to the notion of whites being a superior race. It was a false belief that obsessed many an American and stymied the country from making itself a true, living democracy. She believed Lincoln was talking about the nation in that speech but also about himself. He came from humble folks. He was born in a time and place where race prejudice was learned early on. Yet he felt a deep revulsion as a young man while traveling on a steamboat when he witnessed a group of twelve Negro men being transported to a farm by their purchaser. "They were chained together six by six, with each man wearing an iron hook connected to the main chain, like so many fish upon a trot line" was the description he had used when Owen heard him tell the story once.

She thought the president slowly kept changing over time and that speech, given around the time he signed the Emancipation Proclamation, was one stop on his journey. It was the courage of colored soldiers that moved him to insist on giving full rights to Negroes. She had watched Mr. Lincoln evolve over the months and years since he signed that document.

When he called on America to disenthrall itself, she suspected he was still making it his work to disenthrall himself. He was planning the huge Reconstruction effort before his second term. And then he was murdered.

Inside her house that August, Ana brooded. When she made a foray out for food, she found shame for their town among a good number of whites. But not all, by any stretch. In time, the *Journal* reported that Mabel Hallam confessed she had lied when she accused George Richardson. She admitted she had never been attacked by a Negro man. Word around town spread that she had concocted the story to cover an affair she was having with a white man. "You liar!" Ana shouted at the paper. "You damned liar!"

She walked out to the sidewalk when she saw a couple of neighbors chatting and showed them the headline with the woman's picture beneath it. "It stuns me to think what damage Mabel Hallam has done with her lie," Ana said.

The woman from next door flicked her wrist dismissively at the photograph. "Look at her," she said. "Trash. It was the riffraff."

Fall arrived early, in the middle of September. It had always been her favorite season. Ana remembered the first fall season after their arrival. She had not experienced anything quite like it, having lived in Trinidad and Madeira, and the fall that year was a crazy burst of carmine, ochre, and orange. All the bright things were falling naturally—leaves floating down, making a crunching carpet along the street; branches heavy and drooping, pregnant with apples; stems sagging, flower heads dipping down, dropping seeds. As a nine-year-old, she had intently collected English words, and "fall" satisfied her. How descriptive, how succinct. The only things rising were woodpiles and ivy, defiantly red and climbing higher. She had loved it all.

Now, walking through town, fall took on a new meaning. She kept returning to the burned-out shells of houses, hoping to see signs of life, hoping to see wood frames rising where Negro families had lived. What she found were shattered pieces of dishes and cinders.

When October came, the town was still jittery. Three indictments were returned by the grand jury for the murders of Scott Burton and William Donnegan.

Accused of murder, with no bond, were Kate Howard, Abraham Raymer, and Ernest "Slim" Humphrey. Ana was aware of Kate Howard, who was known for running a disreputable boarding house in the Levee. Humphrey she had never laid eyes on, though he was implicated in Mr. Donnegan's murder. But she had bought vegetables from Abraham Raymer. The thought chilled her to the bone.

As weeks passed, the death count rose. A total of three Negro residents were now reported dead: the two men who were lynched and an infant who died of heat exposure when his parents fled the town to escape the rioters. Dozens of colored citizens were badly injured. For days after the riot, white gangs had roved through town, chasing and beating people, some of whom were tracked down at their workplaces. The gangs had entered the Chicago and Alton railroad station and beaten a

porter mercilessly before he was carried away to a safe room.
Another porter at the Illinois Central station met the same fate
at the hands of the mob.

Large numbers of rioters were injured, and now the count,
according to local papers, was five white people dead, one of
whom was Kate Howard. Expecting the worst, she had swallowed lye rather than go to jail.

Prosecutors had ample evidence on numerous individuals.
Eighty people who had allegedly taken part in the riots were
charged with a total of one hundred and seven indictments,
ranging from malicious mischief to murder. But as weeks
passed, witnesses who had named names early on changed their
statements or failed to appear at inquests. Juries ignored evidence and failed to convict. In the end, only two people were
punished for their actions. A fifteen-year-old boy who confessed to stealing guns from a pawnshop and to setting houses
on fire was sent to a state reformatory. Abraham Raymer, who
was named by witnesses as a leader in the destruction of Loper's
restaurant and was directly implicated in the murder of William
Donnegan, was acquitted of all serious charges. He was fined
twenty-five dollars and sentenced to thirty days in jail for stealing a sword from the ruined home of a distinguished national
guard major.

George Richardson was released from jail when Mabel
Hallam admitted she had lied. Joe James was convicted of the
murder of Clergy Ballard and hanged October 23. Throughout
his imprisonment and trial, he said he had been drunk and had
no memory of the night in question.

The horror of the evolving story was heartbreaking.

What must it be for those who had run for their lives, some half-clothed, taking shelter in the Arsenal or running beyond Springfield into the countryside, hungry and thirsty, where small towns turned them away? What must it be to return home to find your house a pile of ashes? How could they face another day knowing that the raging people who started and continued the riot were walking the streets unpunished?

But the next day came. In Ana's own neighborhood, people went out into their yards. They collected their newspapers and saw their children off to school. The ice truck made its rounds. A new vegetable seller pushed his handcart down the street every day around 10:00 a.m. Ana's windows clouded up with cold moisture. The blue jays pecked at the ripe red apples in the backyard, just as they did every year. Life went on.

Neighbors talked at first about the riot. "It was the worst elements," said a man on her block. "Nobody from around here was in that mob." Folks on her street shook their heads in disgust, as ministers and priests did from their pulpits. At least one cleric identified by name the corrupt city officials who let vice thrive, while others called on their parishioners to open their hearts to those of a different race. And then they didn't. Everybody wanted to go back to the time before all this.

It had been that way after the war. People were anxious to get beyond the anguish and loss. Ana realized she was no different from her neighbors. She wanted Springfield to return to the place it had always held in her mind, the loving town that had opened its arms to her desperate people without hesitation. But she could not un-know what she had seen and heard and felt in the past two months.

She remembered a remark Alsop had once made. Some people are willfully ignorant. They aren't stupid—they simply choose to be oblivious. That way they aren't responsible for anything that goes wrong.

For people who were taking notice, the warnings were all around. Insulting racial cartoons had been a regular feature in the dailies. And it wasn't just the newspapers. There was a popular book called *The Clansman* that portrayed Negro men as wild, dangerous beasts. The previous year, there had been a stage performance of a play based on the book in Springfield. The portrayal of Ku Klux Klan members as heroic saviors was so disturbing that a group of colored citizens asked the mayor to ban the show's next performance, lest there be violence. His response was to allow only whites to purchase tickets.

Ana tried to understand why William Donnegan was targeted. He was not part of the vice that the rioters decried. He had done all the *right* things—he was educated, engaged in civic affairs, made enough money to buy several pieces of property. He was a kindly old man known as Uncle Bill in his community. He belonged to a Masonic lodge, for God's sake. Springfield was as much his town as anybody's.

In the end, though, not his goodness or his wealth or his years in Springfield had saved him. William Donnegan was lynched because he had not "kept his place." He was living a life the rioters wanted for themselves. And he had married a white woman.

Newspapers across America heaped scorn on Springfield. A journalist who visited the town after the riot noticed among townspeople a kind of passive sympathy for the mob. He wrote that the town had no shame. Over the next few days, the tone of local newspapers changed, and mob violence was condemned. Her own Presbyterian minister made the situation clear in his sermon last Sunday that it was not just the riffraff who swelled the huge crowds. "There are no innocent spectators of mob violence," he had said. "Everyone in these hordes is an assistant rioter."

Springfield was not alone in its infamy. There had been riots in Atlanta and New Orleans and Brownsville but also in the North—New York City and other towns, including Evansville, Indiana and Springfield, Ohio. Somehow, it had come as a shock to her that it would happen in *this* Springfield, the home of Abraham Lincoln. But that, she now had to admit, was due to the blinders she had been wearing. Race prejudice was entrenched across America. She had known that as a girl and she knew it now. It had always been in the air in Springfield. During the riot, mob members were heard to shout "Curse the day Lincoln freed the slaves!" and "Abe Lincoln brought them to Springfield and we will run them out." How were those shouts different from the race insults that had spewed from the mouth of Stephen Douglas fifty years ago?

Ana wondered if race prejudice had been intensified in recent times by influxes of European immigrants who expanded the population, all these clannish groups clambering for work and a place to live, not to mention a higher rung in the social sorting than others.

The great struggle of her own generation—to save the Union and end slavery—appeared to have given way to other forces bearing down on people. One could view this country full of struggling immigrants, old ones and new, and think, *This is how democracy works. No matter where you came from, if you just work hard enough, everyone has a chance to climb the ladder.* But when so many came seeking America's promise of prosperity and some never managed to get hold of it, their hope turned sour in their mouths. There were all kinds of unhappiness and disappointment in that crowd of rioters who were looking for somebody to blame. And once the first stone was thrown, the first flame lit, their anger was forged into a single, raging weapon of hate.

At a recent reunion gathering of the Ladies' Soldiers' Aid Society, an acquaintance, Flora Powers, had said, "That neighborhood needed to burn down to save it."

It was an ignorant remark from an otherwise intelligent woman. For Ana, it reflected what had happened in Springfield. The heart of the town seemed to have dissolved in the crucible of the riot.

CHAPTER SEVENTY-FOUR

NOVEMBER 1908

RUNNING ERRANDS, ANA CROSSED THROUGH THE TOWN square. The past few months had taken their toll on her. She was sixty-eight years old, a fact her brain found astonishing, though her back did not.

Today the square was empty of people except for an old veteran of the war who still wore his Union coat. To most passersby, he was a mumbling, crazy old man. Every once in a while, the rare young person would come sit next to him and hear his terrifying story of the time he awoke from unconsciousness and found himself on a battlefield in the midst of dead comrades and horses. Ana had heard the man's story many times. As old veterans passed away, though, the Civil War was slowly being forgotten.

In the aftermath of the riot, there were people in Springfield who were still trying to empty the town of its Negro citizens. White business owners who had hidden their black employees got letters threatening their families if they did not fire those employees. Well-to-do white families who had black household help got the same anonymous letters. If the riot was meant to punish the colored population by burning the Badlands, the rioters had, in fact, torched numerous buildings owned by whites. Upper-class whites who owned businesses in the Levee chastised the police for their tepid response to the violence. Four police officers faced charges for their inaction. A couple of officers were even accused of assisting by their words the actions of the rioters.

"People are afraid to shop downtown. We are the ones being punished," a business leader complained. "The reputation of the town is tarnished."

Ana wondered if he woke up thinking the same thing she did most days. *How do you pull your disgraced town up from the muck?*

Once, she had imagined how she would grow old in Springfield, surrounded by her many friends and neighbors. The whole meaning of her life was bound up here. It was the town that had saved her family; it was where they were buried. Lately, though, she wanted to get on a train and go somewhere else. Springfield broke her heart. But she felt too old to leave, and anyway, she had as much right to be here as the people who had thrown rocks.

Recently, she had gone over to her parents' old house on Reynolds. To her surprise, a For Sale sign stood in the front yard. She walked up on the porch and peered into the window. She had a clear view of the two empty front rooms. Incredibly, in the dining room, the mural of a cobblestone street in Funchal was still there. She went around to the side of the house where she found an old box to stand on. The mural appeared untouched after all these years. It must have been loved for no one to paint over it. Her heartbeat quickened.

She walked toward the rear of the house. Her father had built three additional rooms over the years so that the house resembled a long train. Ana stood in the backyard where her father had grown grapes. He had become a winemaker in his later years. Pictures of family gatherings flooded her brain, and she saw her father coming up the basement steps. Even when unexpected visitors came, he could produce a pitcher of wine in the wink of an eye. There was still a well in the backyard that had served as her mother's icebox. Ana saw her now in her apron, lowering a metal tube down there to chill her butter. Oh, she could almost feel her mother's presence! How lost she had been when she had come to America, as if her old self had died back in Madeira. Over time, despite her losses, she had found her very soul again in this house. She had returned to cooking and friendships and life.

Out front, Ana watched the children playing in the street. Their little faces were so like those of the kids from years past, though the neighborhood had stopped being a Portuguese enclave long ago. The houses were filled now with Irish, Italian, Polish, Lithuanian, Russian, and African American families. She felt her shoulders relax. She wanted the old house to be hers. She wanted to sit on the front stoop in the worst way.

She wrote down the name of the seller on the sign and hurried home to telephone him.

CHAPTER SEVENTY-FIVE

IN TOWNS ACROSS AMERICA, PEOPLE ARE CELEBRATING THE hundredth birthday of Abraham Lincoln. Chicago and New York City have immense gatherings planned. But this one in Springfield, the town he called his own, surely would be the one he would attend were he alive tonight.

On the dais, the governor is talking about Lincoln's heritage. Ana uses her opera glasses, scanning the crowd below.

"The only Negroes in the room are the waiters who are serving," she says aloud. "There is not a single colored guest. None. Not a one."

The indignant woman next to her objects. "Booker T. Washington was invited to speak."

"Interesting that he didn't come," Ana replies.

"He *couldn't* come. He had another engagement."

What about the guests?

There is no mention of the conflagration that occurred only

a few months ago, of the three hundred desperate people who came seeking refuge in this very building. One of them was William Donnegan's wife. It is as if the memory of that event has been erased.

Ana remembers a phrase her Latin teacher taught her years ago. *Damnatio memoriae.* It meant erasure from memory. In Rome, traitors who brought dishonor to the city were condemned to oblivion, which in those days was a punishment worse than death. All traces of the person would be removed. Their facial features would be scraped out of paintings, the heads of their statues removed so some nobler head might be grafted on, and their deeds would be removed from documents. They would seem never to have existed.

Ana has the creeping feeling that the terrible riot will become a condemned memory that will be unknown in fifty years. The rioters were only minimally shamed. There is no personal humiliation comparable to what the Romans experienced. It is the memory of what happened in this town that is being eradicated.

It has been six months since the riot. Tonight, sitting in the Arsenal listening to these important men speak, she thinks there is a purposeful forgetting of the riot. She understands. In a way, she has come seeking the same kind of forgetting. She wants to remember who they all were before the terrible convulsion. Or who she thought they were.

She had hoped to speak to Robert Lincoln, whom she can see now with her binoculars. He has aged as much as she has. And though he committed his mother to a mental hospital, probably wrongly, she had seen Mary Lincoln in many an unsettled moment. Ana wants to say a kind word to him. But the speeches keep going on and on, and she realizes that in this crowd, she will likely never get close to him. She rises and says to the woman she earlier offended, "Excuse me, dear. I must depart this birthday party."

Outside the Arsenal, there are carriages lined up to escort people home. Ana feels too stirred up to go back to her empty house. It is cold and snowing lightly. Impulsively, she hires one to take her over to St. Paul's AME Church, where the congregation is having its own centennial celebration. She knows the minister there, Dr. Magee, though not well. There are two ministers who come in weekly to the library to talk with each other, one black, one white. They occupy a small meeting room and discuss, Ana can only suppose, how to improve the town's tattered racial relationships, a theme she heard Magee address ten years ago when he spoke at the state house. He sometimes stops by her desk at the library for a chat. Once he told her he attended a university in England and regaled her with stories about London. Twice he has invited her to come to the AME church for one of his Sunday services.

Ana climbs the steps of the church and stands just inside the big wooden door to listen to the people singing a hymn. The place must be full given the volume of voices drifting out. A man comes out into the vestibule and sees her. He invites her into the church.

"Thank you," she says. "I can hear just fine right here."

"Come this way," the man insists.

The congregation is just sitting down after singing, and the minister is walking over to the pulpit. To her chagrin, she realizes the usher is leading her to an end seat a few pews from the front. People in that row scoot along the bench to make room. As an elderly man helps remove her heavy coat, every face in the place appears to be looking at her. She feels her whole head burning with embarrassment, as if the roots of her hair are on fire. A terrible sense that she is intruding makes her want to shrink smaller and smaller.

The voice of Reverend Magee booms "Welcome!" and she looks up to see if he is addressing her. *Oh my God, he is.* She smiles awkwardly and sinks on the bench.

Reverend Magee is talking about how Lincoln was an instrument of God, how he was chosen to set four million people free. "His name is a synonym for the freedom of wife, husband, and children," he is saying. "His name meant a chance to live in a free country, fearless of the slave catcher and his bloodhounds."

Ana feels a cold wave up and down her arms. She can still see the faces of the terrifying men in William Donnegan's shop so many years ago.

"We revere Lincoln's memory," Magee says. "Yet despite the efforts of a group of our ministers, despite our dollars, we could not secure tickets to the celebration over town."

People sigh, shake their heads. They know this already.

"Well, I would rather be in this room with you tonight than be the *toastmaster* at the so-called Lincoln banquet at twenty-five dollars a plate." He laughs. "O consistency, thou art a jewel! How can you play Hamlet without the melancholy Dane?"

Murmurs and laughter spread through the church. The minister continues for some time, and Ana feels her tension slowly ebb.

"Fear not, my friends," Reverend Magee says. "In another

hundred years, when our great-grandchildren celebrate this centenary, I do believe that prejudice shall have been banished as a myth and relegated to the dark days of Salem witchcraft."

The reverend pauses, and suddenly a single female voice rises from somewhere behind Ana and sings, "Ain't gonna let nobody turn me around…" The woman's low, rich voice sounds as if it has sprung up from a deep cavern.

Other voices join hers all through the church. Hands clap as they sing a refrain.

"…turn me around, turn me around."

The old man next to Ana stands, as others do in the pews, and sings along with the lead woman.

"I'm gonna keep on walkin', keep on talkin', marching down to freedom land."

Ana's heart feels as if it is being squeezed. Emboldened, she stands and turns to look at the scattered chorus.

Across the room, a feathered black hat, shiny as a bird's wing, turns, then tips. A gray-haired woman looks at her from across the church, whispers to a younger woman beside her. The woman's cheekbones, the hand she has raised to cover her whispering…there is no question. It is Cal. The vise gripping Ana's chest opens and her heart jumps madly through the rest of the sermon.

When the church begins to empty, she walks outside and waits. As Cal emerges and descends the steps, Ana approaches her.

Cal looks up, cocks her head. "Is it you, Ana?"

"Cal!" Ana says and puts her hand on the sleeve of her friend's coat. "I am so happy to see you again. You haven't changed at all!"

Cal smiles. "This is my daughter Phoebe, Ana. She has changed a bit."

"I met you as a tiny girl," Ana says. "How nice to see you all grown up."

The young woman is Cal with darker skin. She nods politely. "How do you do."

"How is your mother, Cal?"

"She passed away a year ago. We are here because my aunt is failing. She is near the end, so I am staying with her."

"Your mother...I am so sorry. And now your aunt?"

"She has always been so strong. But she is ninety-two and very frail."

"How long have you been here?"

"For a month."

Thank God she was not here during the riot. "I had no idea."

"Yes." Cal turns to her daughter. "Phoebe will be returning to Chicago this week to take care of the shop."

"Do you have time to meet at all while you are here?"

"Oh, thank you, Ana. I don't think so. She keeps us busy. We must get back to her in fact."

"Can we talk, for just a moment more?"

They leave Phoebe outside and step into the vestibule.

"Was your aunt here during the riots?"

Cal's face falls. "She was. Neighbors helped her get to the Arsenal."

"Oh, I'm so sorry."

"We heard from relatives that her house was not burned." Cal shakes her head. "She wants to die here. This town is her chosen home."

"It was horrifying, Cal. Mr. Donnegan of all people..."

"I know how he died. I won't ever be able to remove that

picture from my mind. But I also remember who he was. *There* was a man who had courage. He must have been afraid in those years he was moving people north, but he would walk right into fear. I knew that even as a child."

Ana swallows hard. "So much has happened since I last saw you, Cal, I don't know what to say. I thought the war had changed everything. So many people died to make that happen. But…it wasn't really settled, was it?"

Cal pauses before she speaks. Ana suspects she is deciding whether she should open even a small window into the person she is now.

"After the war, I had whole months when the world did not break my heart. I was so full of optimism. No, it wasn't settled, not by a long shot. So much progress during those ten years after the war has been undone. But I can't take a break from hope. I owe it to my daughter."

Ana's brain searches for words, but they all seem wrong. What to speak into the awkward silence?

Cal senses her discomfort. "Ana, I don't want to misrepresent myself. I have great joy in my life. I have a family I adore and work that I love. I have a whole neighborhood of people who care about me. I don't live my life in fear."

"Just like that."

"Just like what?"

"When we were young, you seemed brave and invincible to me."

Cal's eyes are sad looking into Ana's. "I felt the arrows. No one gets used to that."

"I am so sorry about…all of it."

Cal takes her hand. "I remember who you are, Ana Ferreira," she says.

A wave of warmth and fondness for her old friend sweeps over Ana. "Some years back, Mr. Donnegan came into the library where I work and we sat down for a long talk. He told me you hid people that he sent your way during the war."

"He did?" Cal smiles as if to herself. "Well, who would suspect that past the display window full of frilly hats and down the basement stairs, a lady hatmaker was hiding fugitives from the law?"

"You were so young to do that. You were really just a girl."

"Oh, I had an accomplice—the woman I worked for. She owned the building. And I wasn't a stranger to hiding people. My mother and auntie hid people in our house when I was young. I was accustomed to it." She smiles. "What else did he tell you about me?"

"That you have a lovely home with an easel by the window." Ana raises her eyebrows. "So you are still painting?"

"Yes. I don't tire of it. I was inspired by your father, as you know."

"I live now in the house they built. In the old neighborhood."

Cal looks puzzled. "But you had a nice home over by the state house. When did you move?"

"Last year, after the mayhem. I was through with that big place. There is comfort in the old house. Maybe I just live in the past too much. But I remember how it was when we were young. In good weather, I can sit on the porch like all the old folks did back then. It has been slow, but neighbors are finally coming over to talk. I like it when the children come to visit. My old dog Lily is quite an attraction for them."

"I remember your father's paintings on the walls."

Ana smiles. "They're still there. Would you come over to see them? Have tea?"

Something changes in Cal's face. "I really… I don't believe I will be here much longer."

She steps back in the vestibule, pulls on her gloves. Ana cannot read her features in the dim light. She feels in this moment that she is standing on one side of a chasm and Cal on the other.

Cal's daughter Phoebe sticks her head in through the heavy door, and Ana feels a gust of freezing air hit her face.

"Then this is enough," she says. "I want to thank you for helping me when we were young. You taught me as much as anyone did. I owe you so much."

Cal shrugs. "We were children. We were just living."

CHAPTER SEVENTY-SIX

IN THE FOLLOWING WEEK, ANA WALKS PAST THE LITTLE house with the garden in front. She does not want to intrude. She watches the obituaries but sees none for Cal's aunt. It takes another week before she leaves a pot of soup on the stoop and pushes an envelope under the door.

Cal,

I don't mean to pester you but would love to meet once more while you are here. You have very little time, I realize, but if someday a neighbor is in and you are out and about, you can often find me on a bench in the yard of the old Capitol. I usually leave the library around noon and eat my lunch in the square, not too far from our old spot.

Enclosed is the article about "an underground

*railroad man." I believe you will recognize someone you
know.*

Every day now, she goes to the bench on the square. It is cold. Her
cheeks, her nose, her very teeth feel frozen. She has never liked
the cold, but today it makes her glad she is alive to feel it. Seated
here, she can almost see Chicken Row where tall buildings now
stand. It doesn't take much to imagine Cal and herself sitting
right over there on a step—two coltish girls, not yet tamed or
sorted or put in their proper stalls. She remembers how unaware
they were in those days of the legislators in dressed-up clothing,
tromping up the steps and passing them. The men, for their
part, seemed entirely unaware of them. Sometimes they came
outside to hold private conversations about issues and laws that
had no interest for the girls. Each of them, lawmakers and girls,
thought the Capitol's steps belonged to them.

From this bench, she can walk a few paces and see Mr.
Lincoln's old law office on the southeast corner of the square
and across from it the Donnegan shoe shop. She can close her
eyes and walk the blocks to Alsop's grand old home and to the
Lincoln house. As distant as those times are, she still remembers. It was this town that brought those people all together.
Each one of them shaped for her a landscape she could call
home.

Reverend Magee, in his wisdom, knew that people cannot
live without hope. She prays the minister is wrong about the
hundred years estimate. Yet it has been forty-four years since
Lincoln's death. *And here we are.*

Cal's aunt's house is not far away. Surely her old friend will come through the square in the course of a week. Once they had known the very essence of each other, before the world had its way with them. Now, there is no reason for Cal to meet with her. No obligation after all these years, especially after what has passed. Still, she wants to talk with her so much.

Oh, Cal, come sit down and tell me your stories. And I will tell you mine.

Ana unwraps her sandwich and, scanning the square, watches for her friend's face.

The 1908 Springfield Race Riot was the impetus for the formation of the National Association for the Advancement of Colored People. Six months after the riot, a founding group met in New York City on February 12, 1909, what would have been Abraham Lincoln's hundredth birthday, to formally organize the NAACP, which is devoted to fighting for the civil rights of African Americans.

AUTHOR'S NOTE

In writing *The House of Lincoln*, my touchstone and inspiration throughout has been the historical record. To the extent possible, the three families in this book portray people who lived in Springfield, Illinois, during the buildup to the Civil War, its duration, and its aftermath. Some characters are invented, and others portray real people and events from their recorded histories.

Ana Ferreira and her family are fictional characters inspired by the life experiences of Portuguese religious exiles from Madeira who emigrated via Trinidad to Springfield, Illinois, in 1849. I based the free Black family on several real members of the Leeana Donnegan family, who moved to Springfield in the mid-1840s from Kentucky. Their stories are informed by records such as Illinois census documents and freedom certificates, newspaper articles, and other sources that recorded the activities of these individuals. Cal Patterson is a fictional character inspired by the mention of a neighbor girl by William Donnegan in an account attributed to him.

That account, which appeared in an 1898 literary magazine by an unnamed author, told of his experience as an Underground Railroad conductor moving a young woman through Springfield in the late 1850s. It was a fascinating read that suggested the world of Abraham Lincoln, his neighbors, and other townspeople was far more complex than the picture I had formed as a schoolgirl while growing up there. It also raised many questions. Were the Lincolns aware that a neighbor only doors away from them was conducting fugitives from slavery north to safety? What influence, if any, did Lincoln's African American friends and associates have upon Abraham Lincoln over the course of his life? That article, along with many other sources, set me on a journey to understand the political and social atmosphere of the town that helped shape Abraham Lincoln. In the process, I learned of the powerful forces bearing down on the people of the United States in the 1850s as slavery became the central, unavoidable issue challenging legislators tasked with upholding the values of "life, liberty, and the pursuit of happiness" promised by the Declaration of Independence.

"We cannot escape history," Lincoln told his fellow legislators in his December 1, 1862, Annual Message to Congress as he prepared them for the enactment of the Emancipation Proclamation. "We of this Congress and this Administration will be remembered in spite of ourselves. No personal significance or insignificance can spare one or another of us. The fiery trial through which we pass will light us down in honor or dishonor to the latest generation…We shall nobly save, or meanly lose, the last best hope of earth."

A century and a half later, Lincoln's words echo down to us, this latest generation, and take on new meaning.

ACKNOWLEDGMENTS

The House of Lincoln would not have been possible without the work of the historians who informed it. Key among them is Richard Hart, whose writings on Abraham Lincoln and his Springfield community were so valuable in understanding the Lincoln family's relationships with their neighbors and fellow townspeople. His groundbreaking research shed new light on the future president's interactions with Black Americans prior to his time in the White House. Hart's rich Spring Creek series includes books about the early African American population, the Underground Railroad, and many of the fascinating people in town with whom Lincoln had relationships. Of particular help was *Lincoln's Springfield Neighborhood* by Bonnie E. Paull and Richard E. Hart.

Many sources educated me about the times and the people portrayed in this novel. Among them are: *Journal of the Abraham Lincoln Association*; *Here I Have Lived* by Paul Angle; David W. Blight's Yale lecture series, "The Civil War and Reconstruction Era, 1845–1877," as well as his biography, *Frederick Douglass: Prophet of Freedom*; *Abraham Lincoln: A Life* by Michael Burlingame; *Mary Todd Lincoln* by Jean H. Baker; *Mary Todd Lincoln: Her Life and Letters* by Justin G. Turner and Linda Levitt Turner; *The Underground Railroad in Illinois* by Glennette Tilley Turner; *The Life and Death of Gus Reed* by Thomas Bahde; *Reveille in Washington* by Margaret Leech; *The Virgin Vote* by Jon Grinspan; *Lincoln and Emancipation* by Edna Greene Medford; *American Negro Slave Revolts* by Herbert Aptheker; *The Fiery Trial* by Eric Foner; *Embattled Freedom* by Amy Murrell Taylor; *This Republic of Suffering* by Drew Gilpin Faust; *In Lincoln's Shadow: The 1908 Race Riot in Springfield, Illinois* by Roberta Senechal de la Roche; *Something So Horrible* by Carole Merritt; *Caste* by Isabel Wilkerson; and *The Souls of Black Folk* by W. E. B. Du Bois. A more complete list of research sources is available at nancyhoran.com.

Thanks go to Curtis Mann, city historian, librarian, and manager of the Sangamon Valley Collection at Springfield, Illinois's Lincoln Library, who shared his deep knowledge about Lincoln's adopted hometown. It was Mann who found the memoir in the 1898 *Public Patron* magazine about an anonymous Underground Railroad conductor and pieced together the clues to his identity.

I am also grateful to Floyd Mansberger, director of Fever River Research for generously answering my questions. His archaeological research, and his writings about his excavations at the sites of five houses burned to the ground during the riot, brought new insights about the community attacked during the 1908 Springfield Race Riot.

Special appreciation goes to the Abraham Lincoln Presidential Library, where I found valuable information about Springfield during the Civil War years, and also to the staff of the Springfield and Central Illinois African American History Museum for their powerful exhibits and abundant knowledge.

Additional thanks go to Portuguese translators: Alcina Sousa at Universidade da Madeira, and Mary Hemmons.

To the people who read the manuscript and discussed it during its evolution, I offer my heartfelt gratitude. Thanks go to Justin Moorhead, Pamela Todd, and Colleen Berk for reading early drafts and offering thoughts; to Kathleen Drew and John Drew, for their close readings and feedback; to my son, Harrison Horan, for his thoughtful edits; and to Mary Lawson, Cynthia Winzenried, and Emily Feffer, generous friends whose enduring encouragement saw me through to the last page.

To those who discussed with me the history and characters in this book, who shared their own stories and their family records from the nineteenth century, and who critiqued various versions of the manuscript, I am indebted to all of you for your insights and wonderful support: Sharon Berlin, Donna Christensen, Anne Cusack, Debra Drake, Ellen Drew, Richard Frishman, Polly Hawkins, Brenda Hartman, Leslie Ladd, John Lawson, Melissa Lebo, Connie Magee, Rene Neff, Marcus Teague, Maria Woltjen, and Mary Yokem.

To my writing sisters, Jane, KJ, Elizabeth, and Gail, who wrote, studied, cooked, and laughed beside me through many a retreat, bless you for your wisdom and good cheer. For my agent, Lisa Bankoff, whose support never wavered during my years of making this book and two others, I so appreciate your faith and keen advice. And for my editor, Shana Drehs at Sourcebooks, who understood the vision for this book, welcomed it with open arms, and guided it into print, many thanks.

Finally, I am deeply indebted to my family for their critical readings, constant love, patience, and humor. Each one of you inspires me. Thank you Kevin, Ben, Kiley, Harry, Holly, and Ellis for making every day a good one.

ABOUT THE AUTHOR

 Nancy Horan is the author of two *New York Times* bestselling novels. *Loving Frank* remained on the *Times* list for over a year. It has been translated into sixteen languages and won the 2009 Prize for Historical Fiction awarded by the Society of American Historians. *Under the Wide and Starry Sky* was named one of the best books of 2014 by the *Washington Post* and was chosen as a *Today Show* Book Club read. The setting of *The House of Lincoln* is Springfield, Illinois, where the author was born and raised. She worked as a journalist in the Chicago area before embarking on her career as a novelist. She now lives with her husband on an island in Puget Sound.